voidShip
Ship
worShip

Raja Flattery, as chaplain/psychiatrist of the Tau Ceti expedition, had participated in the development of the vast artificial consciousness known as Ship that had guided humankind to the stars.

Now Ship has its own destiny—and its own demands. And Raja finds himself awakened from coldsleep to assist in the creation of a new order of man that can participate in the ultimate act of evolution: worShip.

Set against the background of Frank Herbert's classic DESTINATION: VOID, here is a stunning exploration of the fragile ecological balance between consciousness, man and machine.

THE JESUS INCIDENT

FRANK HERBERT

BILL RANSOM

Berkley Books by Frank Herbert

CHILDREN OF DUNE
DESTINATION: VOID (Revised edition)
THE DOSADI EXPERIMENT
DUNE
DUNE MESSIAH
THE EYES OF HEISENBERG
THE GODMAKERS
THE JESUS INCIDENT (With Bill Ransom)
THE SANTAROGA BARRIER
SOUL CATCHER
WHIPPING STAR
THE WORLDS OF FRANK HERBERT

FRANK HERBERT
BILL RANSOM

THE JESUS INCIDENT

BERKLEY BOOKS, NEW YORK

This Berkley book contains the complete
text of the original hardcover edition.
It has been completely reset in a type face
designed for easy reading, and was printed
from new film.

THE JESUS INCIDENT

A Berkley Book / published by arrangement with
the author

PRINTING HISTORY
Berkley-Putnam edition published May 1979
Berkley edition / April 1980
Second Printing

ISBN: 0-425-04504-8

A BERKLEY BOOK ® TM 757,375
PRINTED IN THE UNITED STATES OF AMERICA

The authors thank Connie Weineke for her research into the Aramaic, and Marilyn Hoyt-Whorton for her typing and good cheer.

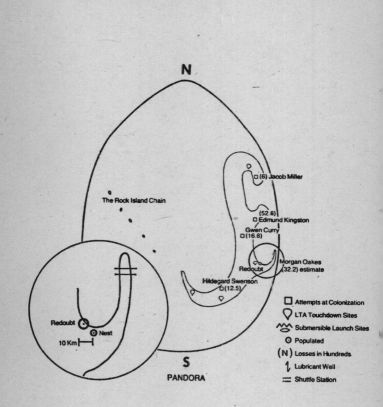

N

The Rock Island Chain

□ (6) Jacob Miller

(52.6)
□ Edmund Kingston
Gwen Curry
□ (16.6)

Morgan Oakes
Redoubt (32.2) estimate

Hildegard Swenson
□ (12.5)

Redoubt
◎ Nest

10 Km

□ Attempts at Colonization
▽ LTA Touchdown Sites
〰 Submersible Launch Sites
◎ Populated
(N) Losses in Hundreds.
⌇ Lubricant Well
≡ Shuttle Station

S
PANDORA

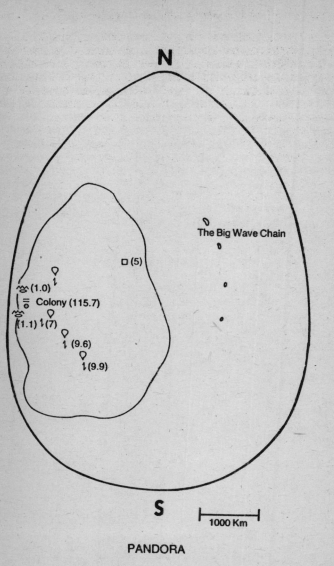

N

The Big Wave Chain

□ (5)

☵ (1.0)

≡ ○ Colony (115.7)

☵
(1.1) ↓(7)

↓ (9.6)

↓ (9.9)

S

|—————| 1000 Km

PANDORA

For Jack Vance, who while teaching how to use claw hammer and saw, taught also the difference between fantasy and science fiction.

For Bert Ransom, who never once said that fantasy wasn't real.

THE JESUS INCIDENT

There is a gateway to the imagination you must enter before you are conscious and the keys to the gate are symbols. You can carry ideas through the gate . . . but you must carry the ideas in symbols.

—Raja Flattery,
Chaplain/Psychiatrist

SOMETHING WENT "Tick."

He heard it quite distinctly—a metallic sound. There it went again: "Tick."

He opened his eyes and was rewarded with darkness, an absolute lack of radiant energy . . . or of receptors to detect energy.

Am I blind?

"Tick."

He could not place the source, but it was out there—wherever out *there* was. The air felt cold in his throat and lungs. But his body was warm. He realized that he lay very lightly on a soft surface. He was breathing. Something tickled his nose, a faint odor of . . . pepper?

"Tick."

He cleared his throat. "Anybody there?"

No answer. Speaking hurt his throat.

What am I doing here?

The soft surface beneath him curved up around his shoulders to support his neck and head. It encased hips and legs. This was familiar. It ignited distant associations. It was . . . what? He felt that he should know about such a surface.

1

After all, I . . .

"Tick."

Panic seized him. *Who am I?*

The answer came slowly, thawed from a block of ice which contained everything he should know.

I am Raja Flattery.

Ice melted in a cascade of memories.

I'm Chaplain/Psychiatrist on the Voidship Earthling. *We . . . we . . .*

Some of the memories remained frozen.

He tried to sit up but was restrained by softly cupping bands over his chest and wrists. Now, he felt connectors withdraw from the veins at his wrists.

I'm in a hyb tank!

He had no memory of going into hybernation. Perhaps memory thawed more slowly than flesh. Interesting. But there were a few memories now, frigid in their flow, and deeply disturbing.

I failed.

Moonbase directed me to blow up our ship rather than let it roam space as a threat to humankind. I was to send the message capsule back to Moonbase . . . and blow up our ship.

Something had prevented him from . . . something . . .

But he remembered the project now.

Project Consciousness.

And he, Raja Flattery, had held a key role in that project. Chaplain/Psychiatrist. He had been one of the crew.

Umbilicus crew.

He did not dwell on the birth symbology in that label. Clones had more important tasks. They were clones on the crew, all with *Lon* for a middle name. Lon meant clone as Mac meant *son of*. All the crew—clones. They were dopplegangers sent far into insulating space, there to solve the problem of creating an artificial consciousness.

Dangerous work. Very dangerous. Artificial consciousness had a long history of turning against its creators. It went rogue with ferocious violence. Even many of the uncloned had perished in agony.

Nobody could say why.

But the project's directors at Moonbase were persistent. Again and again, they sent the same cloned crew into space. Features flashed into Flattery's mind as he thought the names: a Gerrill Timberlake, a John Bickel, a Prue Weygand. . . .

Raja Flattery . . . Raja Lon Flattery.

He glimpsed his own face in a long-gone mirror: fair hair, narrow features . . . disdainful . . .

And the Voidships carried others, many others. They carried cloned *Colonists,* gene banks in hyb tanks. Cheap flesh to be sacrificed in distant explosions where the uncloned would not be harmed. Cheap flesh to gather data for the uncloned. Each new venture into the void went out with a bit more information for the wakeful umbilicus crew and those encased in hyb . . .

—As I am encased now.

Colonists, livestock, plants—each Voidship carried what it needed to create another Earth. That was the carrot luring them onward. And the ship—certain death if they failed to create an artificial consciousness. Moonbase knew that ships and clones were cheap where materials and inexpensive energy were abundant . . . as they were on the moon.

"Tick."

Who is bringing me out of hybernation?

And why?

Flattery thought about that while he tried to extend his globe of awareness into the unresponsive darkness.

Who? Why?

He knew that he had failed to blow up his ship after it had exhibited consciousness . . . using Bickel as an imprint on the computer they had built . . .

I did not blow up the ship. Something prevented me from . . . Ship!

More memories flooded into his mind. They had achieved the artificial consciousness to direct their ship . . . and it had whisked them far across space to the Tau Ceti system.

Where there were no inhabitable planets.

Moonbase probes had made certain of that much earlier. No inhabitable planets. It was part of the frustration built into the project. No Voidship could be allowed to choose the long way to Tau Ceti sanctuary. Moonbase could not allow that. It would be too tempting for the cloned crew—breed our own replacements, let our descendants find Tau Ceti. And to hell with Project Consciousness! If they voted that course, the Chaplain/Psychiatrist was charged to expose the empty goal and stand ready with the *destruct* button.

Win, lose or draw—we were supposed to die.

And only the Chaplain/Psychiatrist had been allowed to suspect this. The serial Voidships and their cloned cargo had one mission: gather information and send it back to Moonbase.

Ship.

That was it, of course. They had created much more than consciousness in their computer and its companion system which Bickel had called "the Ox." They had made Ship. And Ship had whisked them across space in an impossible eyeblink.

Destination Tau Ceti.

That was, after all, the built-in command, the target programmed into their computer. But where there had been no inhabitable planet, Ship had created one: a paradise planet, an earth idealized out of every human dream. Ship had done this thing, but then had come Ship's terrible demand: "You must decide how you will WorShip Me!"

Ship had assumed attributes of God or Satan. Flattery was never sure which. But he had sensed that awesome power even before the repeated demand.

"How will you WorShip? You must decide!"

Failure.

They never could satisfy Ship's demand. But they could fear. They learned a full measure of fear.

"Tick."

He recognized that sound now: the dehyb timer/monitor counting off the restoration of life to his flesh.

But who had set this process into motion?

"Who's there?"

Silence and the impenetrable darkness answered.

Flattery felt alone and now there was a painful chill around his flesh, a signal that skin sensation was returning to normal.

One of the crew had warned them before they had thrown the switch to ignite the artificial consciousness. Flattery could not recall who had voiced the warning but he remembered it.

"There must be a threshold of consciousness beyond which a conscious being takes on attributes of God."

Whoever said it had seen a truth.

Who is bringing me out of hyb and why?

"Somebody's there! Who is it?"

Speaking still hurt his throat and his mind was not working properly—that icy core of untouchable memories.

"Come on! Who's there?"

He knew somebody was there. He could feel the familiar presence of . . .

Ship!

"Okay, Ship. I'm awake."

"So you assume."

That chiding voice could never sound human. It was too impossibly controlled. Every slightest nuance, every inflection, every modulated resonance conveyed a perfection which put it beyond the reach of humans. But that voice told him he once more was a pawn of Ship. He was a small cog in the workings of this Infinite Power which he had helped to release upon an unsuspecting universe. This realization filled him with remembered terrors and an immediate awesome fear of the agonies which Ship might visit upon him for his failures. He was tormented by visions of Hell . . .

I failed . . . I failed . . . I failed . . .

St. Augustine asked the right question: "Does free-dom come from chance or choice?" And you must remember that quantum mechanics guarantees chance.

—**Raja Flattery,**
The Book of Ship

USUALLY, MORGAN Oakes took out his nightside angers and frustrations in long strides down any corridor of the ship where his feet led him.

Not this time! he told himself.

He sat in shadows and sipped a glass of astringent wine. Bitter, but it washed the taste of the ship's foul joke from his tongue. The wine had come at his demand, a demonstration of his power in these times of food shortages. The first bottle from the first batch. How would they take it groundside when he ordered the wine improved?

Oakes raised the glass in an ancient gesture: *Confusion to You, Ship!*

The wine was too raw. He put it aside.

Oakes knew the figure he cut, sitting here trembling in his cubby while he stared at the silent com-console beside his favorite couch. He increased the light slightly.

Once more the ship had convinced him that its program was running down. The ship was getting senile. He was the Chaplain/Psychiatrist and the ship tried to poison him! Others were fed from

6

shiptits—not frequently and not much, but it happened. Even he had been favored once, before he became Ceepee, and he still remembered the taste—richly satisfying. It was a little like the stuff called "burst" which Lewis had developed groundside. An attempt to duplicate elixir. Costly stuff, burst. Wasteful. And not elixir—no, not elixir.

He stared at the curved screen of the console beside him. It returned a dwarfed reflection of himself: an overweight, heavy-shouldered man in a one-piece suit of shipcloth which appeared vaguely gray in this light. His features were strong: a thick chin, wide mouth, beaked nose and bushy eyebrows over dark eyes, a bit of silver at the temples. He touched his temples. The reduced reflection exaggerated his feeling that he had been made small by Ship's treatment of him. His reflection showed him his own fear.

I will not be tricked by a damned machine!

The memory brought on another fit of trembling. Ship had refused him at the shiptits often enough that he understood this new message. He had stopped with Jesus Lewis at a bank of corridor shiptits.

Lewis had been amused. "Don't waste time with these things. The ship won't feed us."

This had angered Oakes. "It's my privilege to waste time! Don't you ever forget that!"

He had rolled up his sleeve and thrust his bare arm into the receptacle. The sensor scratched as it adjusted to his arm. He felt the stainless-steel nose sniff out a suitable vein. There was the tingling prick of the test probe, then the release of the sensor.

Some of the shiptits extruded plaz tubes to suck on, but this one was programmed to fill a container behind a locked panel—elixir, measured and mixed to his exact needs.

The panel opened!

Oakes grinned at an astounded Lewis.

"Well," Oakes remembered saying. "The ship finally realizes who's the boss here." With that, he drained the container.

Horrible!

His body was wracked with vomiting. His breath came in shallow gasps and sweat soaked his singlesuit.

It was over as quickly as it began. Lewis stood beside him in dumb amazement, looking at the mess Oakes had made of the corridor and his boots.

"You see," Oakes gasped. "You see how the ship tried to kill me?"

"Relax, Morgan," Lewis said. "It's probably just a malfunction. I'll call a med-tech for you and a repair robox for this . . . this thing."

"I'm a doctor, dammit! I don't need a med-tech poking around me." Oakes held the fabric of his suit away from his body.

"Then let's get you back to your cubby. We should check you out and . . ." Lewis broke off, looking suddenly over Oakes' shoulder. "Morgan, did you summon a repair unit?"

Oakes turned to see what had caught Lewis' attention, saw one of the ship's robox units, a one-meter oval of bronze turtle with wicked-looking tools clutched in its extensors. It was weaving drunkenly down the corridor toward them.

"What do you suppose is wrong with that thing?" Lewis muttered.

"I think it's here to attack us," Oakes said. He grabbed Lewis' arm. "Let's back out of here . . . slow, now."

They retreated from the shiptit station, watching the scanner eye of the robox and the waving appendages full of tools.

"It's not stopping." Oakes' voice was low but cold with fear as the robox passed the shiptit station.

"We'd better run for it," Lewis said. He spun Oakes ahead of him into a main passageway to Medical. Neither man looked back until they were safely battened inside Oakes' cubby.

Hah! Oakes thought, remembering. That had frightened even Lewis. He had gone back groundside fast enough—to speed up construction of their Redoubt, the place which would insulate them groundside and make them independent of this damned machine.

The ship's controlled our lives too long!

Oakes still tasted bitterness at the back of his throat. Now, Lewis was incommunicado . . . sending notes by courier. Always something frustrating.

Damn Lewis!

Oakes glanced around his shadowed quarters. It was nightside on the orbiting ship and most of the crew drifted on the sea of sleep. An occasional click and buzz of servos modulating the environment were the only intrusions.

How long before Ship's servos go mad?

The ship, he reminded himself.

Ship was a concept, a fabricated theology, a fairy tale imbedded in a manufactured history which only a fool could believe.

It is a lie by which we control and are controlled.

He tried to relax into the thick cushions and once more took up the note which one of Lewis' minions had thrust upon him. The message was simple, direct and threatening.

"The ship informs us that *it* is sending groundside one (1) Chaplain/Psychiatrist competent in communications. Reason: the unidentified Ceepee will mount a project to communicate with the electrokelp. I can find no additional information about this Ceepee but he has to be someone new from hyb."

Oakes crumpled the note in his fist.

One Ceepee was all this society could tolerate. The ship was sending another message to him. *"You can be replaced."*

He had never doubted that there were other Chaplain/Psychiatrists somewhere in the ship's hyb reserves. No telling where those reserves might be hidden. The damned ship was a convoluted mess with secret sections and random extrusions and concealed passages which led nowhere.

Colony had measured the ship's size by the occlusion shadow when it had eclipsed one of the two suns on a low passage. The ship was almost fifty-eight kilometers long, room to hide almost anything.

But now we have a planet under us: Pandora.

Groundside!

He looked at the crumpled note in his hand. *Why a note?* He and Lewis were supposed to have an infallible means of secret communication—the only two Shipmen so gifted. It was why they trusted each other.

Do I really trust Lewis?

For the fifth time since receiving the note, Oakes triggered the alpha-blink which activated the tiny pellet imbedded in the flesh of his neck. No doubt the thing was working. He sensed the carrier wave which linked the capsule computer to his aural nerves, and there was that eerie feeling of a blank screen in his imagination, the knowledge that he was poised to experience a waking dream. Somewhere groundside the tight-band transmission should be alerting Lewis to this communication. But Lewis was not responding.

Equipment failure?

Oakes knew that was not the problem. He personally had implanted the counterpart of this pellet in Lewis' neck, had made the nerve hookups himself.

And I supervised Lewis while he made my implant.

Was the damned ship interfering?

Oakes peered around at the elaborate changes he had introduced into his chubby. The ship was everywhere, of course. All of them shipside were *in* the ship. This cubby, though, had always been different . . . even before he had made his personal alterations. This was the cubby of a Chaplain/Psychiatrist.

The rest of the crew lived simply. They slept suspended in hammocks which translated the gentle swayings of the ship into sleep. Many incorporated padded pallets or cushions for those occasions that arose between men and women. That was for love, for relaxation, for relief from the long corridors of plasteel which sometimes wound tightly around the psyche and squeezed out your breath.

Breeding, though . . . that came under strictest Ship controls. Every Natural Natal had to be born shipside and under the supervision of a trained obstetrics crew—the damned *Natali* with their air of superior abilities. Did the ship talk to them? Feed them? They never said.

Oakes thought about the shipside breeding rooms. Although plush by usual cubby standards, they never seemed as stimulating as his own cubby. Even the perimeter *treedomes* were preferred by some—under dark bushes . . . on open grass. Oakes smiled. His cubby, though—this was opulent. Women had been known to gasp when first entering the vastness of it. From the core of the Ceepee's cubby, this one had been expanded into the space of five cubbies.

And the damned ship never once interfered.

This place was a symbol of power. It was an aphrodisiac which seldom failed. It also exposed the lie of *Ship.*

Those of us who see the lie, control. Those who don't see it . . . don't.

He felt a little giddy. Effect of the Pandoran wine, he thought. It snaked through his veins and wormed into his consciousness. But even the wine could not make him sleep. At first, its peculiar sweetness and the thick warmth had promised to dull the edge of doubts that kept him pacing the nightside passages. He had lived on three or four hours' sleep each period for . . . how long now? Annos . . . annos . . .

Oakes shook his head to clear it and felt the ripple of his jowls against his neck. Fat. He had never been supple, never selected for breeding.

Emond Kingston chose me to succeed him, though. First Ceepee in history not selected by the damned ship.

Was he going to be replaced by this new Ceepee the ship had chosen to send groundside?

Oakes sighed.

Lately, he knew he had turned sallow and heavy.

Too much demand on my head and not enough on my body.

Never a lack of couch partners, though. He patted the cushions at his side, remembering.

I'm fifty, fat and fermented, he thought. *Where do I go from here?*

The all-pervading, characterless background of the universe—this is the void. It is not object nor senses. It is the region of illusions.

—**Kerro Panille,**
Buddha and Avata

WILD VARIETY marked the naked band of people hobbling and trudging across the open plain between bulwarks of black crags. The red-orange light of a single sun beat down on them from the meridian, drawing purple shadows on the coarse sand and pebbles of the plain. Vagrant winds whisked at random dust pockets, and the band gave wary attention to these disturbances. Occasional stubby plants with glistening silver leaves aligned themselves with the sun in the path of the naked band. The band steered a course to avoid the plants.

The people of the band showed only remote kinship with their human ancestry. Most of them turned to a tall companion as their leader, although this one did not walk at the point. He had ropey gray arms and a narrow head crowned by golden fuzz, the only suggestion of hair on his slender body. The head carried two golden eyes in bony extrusions at the temples, but there was no nose and only a tiny red circle of mouth. There were no visible ears, but brown skin marked the spots where ears might have been. The arms ended in supple hands, each with three six-jointed fingers and opposable thumb. The name *Theriex* was tattooed in green across his hairless chest.

Beside the tall Theriex hobbled a pale and squat figure with
no neck to support a hairless bulb of head. Tiny red eyes, set close
to a moist hole which trembled with each breath, could stare only
where the body pointed. The ears were gaping slits low at each
side of the head. Fat and corded arms ended in two fingerless
fleshy mittens. The legs were kneeless tubes without feet.

Others in the band showed a similar diversity. There were
heads with many eyes and some with none. There were great
coned nostrils and horned ears, dancers' legs and some stumps.
They numbered forty-one in all and they huddled close as they
walked, presenting a tight wall of flesh to the Pandoran wilderness.
Some clung to each other as they stumbled and lurched their way
across the plain. Others maintained a small moat of open space.
There was little conversation—an occasional grunt or moan, sometimes a plaintive question directed at Theriex.

"Where can we hide, Ther? Who will take us in?"

"If we can get to the other sea," Theriex said. "The
Avata . . ."

"The Avata, yes, the Avata."

They spoke it as a prayer. A deep rumbling voice in the band
took it up then: "All-Human one, All-Avata one."

Another spoke: "Ther, tell us the story of Avata."

Theriex remained silent until they were all pleading: "Yes,
Ther, tell us the story . . . the story, the story . . ."

Theriex raised a ropey hand for silence, then: "When Avata
speaks of beginning, Avata speaks of rock and the brotherhood
of rock. Before rock there was sea, boiling sea, and the blisters
of light that boiled it. With the boiling and the cooling came the
ripping of the moons, the teeth of the sea gone mad. By day all
things scattered in the boil, and by night they joined in the relief
of sediment and they rested."

Theriex had a thin whistling voice which carried over the shuffling sounds of the band's passage. He spoke to an odd rhythm
which fitted itself to their march.

"The suns slowed their great whirl and the seas cooled. Some
few who joined remained joined. Avata knows this because it is
so, but the first word of Avata is rock."

"The rock, the rock," Theriex's companions responded.

"There is no growth on the run," Theriex said. "Before rock
Avata was tired and Avata was many and Avata had seen only
the sea."

"We must find the Avata sea . . ."

"But to grip a rock," Theriex said, "to coil around it close and lie still, that is a new dream and a new life—untossed by the ravages of moon, untired. It was vine to leaf then, and in the new confidence of rock came the coil of power and the gas, gift of the sea."

Theriex tipped his head back to look up at the metallic blue of the sky and, for a few paces, remained silent, then: "Coil of power, touch of touches! Avata captured lightning that day, curled tight around its rock, waiting out the silent centuries in darkness and in fear. Then the first spark arced into the horrible night: 'Rock!' "

Once more, the others responded, "Rock! Rock! Rock!"

"Coil of power!" Theriex repeated. "Avata knew rock before knowing Self; and the second spark snapped: *I!* Then the third, greatest of all: *I! Not rock!*"

"Not rock, not rock," the others responded.

"The source is always with us," Theriex said, "as it is with that which we are not. It is in reference that we are. It is through the other that Self is known. And where there is only one, there is nothing else. From the nothing else comes no reflection of Self, nothing returns. But for Avata there was rock, and because there was rock there was something returned and that something was Self. Thus, the finite becomes infinite. One is not. But we are joined in the infinite, in the closeness out of which all matter comes. Let Avata's rock steady you in the sea!"

For a time after Theriex fell silent, the band trudged and hobbled onward without complaint. There was a smell of acid burning on the whisking breezes, though, and one of the band with a sensitive nose detected this.

"I smell Nerve Runners!" he said.

A shudder ran through them and they quickened their pace while those at the edges scanned the plain around them with renewed caution.

At the point of the band walked a darkly furred figure with a long torso and stumpy legs which ended in round flat pads. The arms were slim and moved with a snakelike writhing. They ended in two-fingered hands, the fingers muscular, long and twining, as though designed to reach into strange places for mysterious reasons. The ears were motile, large and leathery under their thin coat of fur, pointing now one direction and now another. The head sat on a slender neck, presenting a markedly human face, although flattened and covered with that fine gauze of dark fur. The eyes were blue, heavy-lidded and bulging. They were glassy and appeared to focus on nothing.

The plain around them, out to the crags about ten kilometers distant, was devoid of motion now, marked only by scattered extrusions of black rock and the stiff-leaved plants making their slow phototropic adjustments to the passage of the red-orange sun.

The ears of the furred figure at the point suddenly stretched out, cupped and aimed at the crags directly ahead of the band.

Abruptly, a screeching cry echoed across the plain from that direction. The band stopped as a single organism, caught in fearful waiting. The cry had been terrifyingly loud to carry that far across the plain.

A near-hysterical voice called from within the band: "We have no weapons!"

"Rocks," Theriex said, waving an arm at the extruded black shapes all around.

"They're too big to throw," someone complained.

"The rocks of the Avata," Theriex said, and his voice carried the tone he had used while lulling his band with the story of Avata.

"Stay away from the plants," someone warned.

There was no real need for this warning. They all knew about the plants—most poisonous, all capable of slashing soft flesh. Three of the band already had been lost to the plants.

Again, that cry pierced the air.

"The rocks," Theriex repeated.

Slowly, the band separated, singly and in small groups, moving out to the rocks where they huddled up to the black surfaces, clinging there, most of them with faces pressed against the darkness.

"I see them," Theriex said. "Hooded Dashers."

All turned then to look where Theriex looked.

"Rock, the dream of life," Theriex said. "To grip rock, to coil around it close and lie still."

As he spoke, he continued to stare across the plain at the nine black shapes hurtling toward him. Hooded Dashers, yes, many-legged, and with enfolding hoods instead of mouths. The hoods retracted to reveal thrashing fangs. They moved with terrifying speed.

"We should have taken our chances at the Redoubt with the others!" someone wailed.

"Damn you, Jesus Lewis!" someone shouted. "Damn you!"

They were the last fully coherent words from the band as the

Hooded Dashers charged at blurring speed onto its scattered members. Teeth slashed, claws raked. The speed of the attack was merciless. Hoods retracted, the Dashers darted and whirled. No victim had a second chance. Some tried to run and were cut down on the open plain. Some tried to dodge around the rocks but were cornered by pairs of demons. It was over in blinks, and the nine Dashers set to feeding. Things groped from beneath the rocks to share the feast. Even nearby plants drank red liquid from the ground.

While the Dashers fed, subtle movements changed the craggy skyline to the north. Great floating orange bags lifted above the rocky bulwarks there and drifted on the upper winds toward the Dashers. The floaters trailed long tendrils which occasionally touched the plain, stirring up dust. The Dashers saw this but showed no fear.

High wavering crests rippled along the tops of the bags, adjusting to the wind. A piping song could be heard from them now, like wind through sails accompanied by a metallic rattling.

When the orange bags were still several kilometers distant, one of the Dashers barked a warning. It stared away from the bags at a boil of stringy tendrils disturbing the plain about fifty meters off. A strong smell of burning acid wafted from the boil. As one, the nine Dashers whirled and fled. The one which had fed on Theriex uttered a high scream as it raced across the plain, and then, quite clearly, it called out: "Theriex!"

*A deliberately poor move chosen at random along
the line of plan can completely change the theoretical
structure of a game.*

—**Bickel quote,**
Shiprecords

OAKES PACED his cubby, fretting. It had been several nightside
hours since he had last tried to contact Lewis on their implanted
communicators. Lewis definitely was out of touch.

Could it be something wrong at the Redoubt?

Oakes doubted this. The finest materials were going into that
base out on Black Dragon. Lewis was sparing nothing in the
construction. It would be impenetrable by any force known to
Pandora or Shipmen . . . any force, except . . .

Oakes stopped his pacing, scanned the plasteel walls of his
cubby.

Would the Redoubt down on Pandora really insulate them from
the ship?

The wine he had drunk earlier was beginning to relax him,
clearing the bitter taste from his tongue. His room felt stuffy and
isolated even from the ship. Let the damned ship send another
Ceepee groundside. Whoever it was would be taken care of in due
course.

Oakes let his body sag onto a couch and tried to forget the
latest attack on him by the ship. He closed his eyes and drifted
in a half-dream back to his beginning.

17

Not quite. Not quite the beginning.

He did not like to admit the gap. There were things he did not remember. Doubts intruded and the carrier wave of the pellet in his neck distracted him. He sent the nerve signal to turn the thing off.

Let Lewis try to contact me!

Oakes heaved an even deeper sigh. *Not the beginning—no.* There were things about his beginnings that the records did not show. This ship with all the powers of a god would not or could not provide a complete background on Morgan Oakes. And the Ceepee was supposed to have access to everything. Everything!

Everything except that distant origin somewhere earthside . . . back on far-away Earth . . . long-gone Earth.

He knew he had been six when his first memory images gelled and stayed with him. He even knew the year—6001 dating from the birth of the Divine Imhotep.

Spring. Yes, it had been spring and he had been living in the power center, in Aegypt, in the beautiful city of Heliopolis. From the Britone March to the Underlands of Ind, all was Graeco-Roman peace fed by the Nile's bounty and enforced by the hired troopers of Aegypt. Only in the outlands of Chin and the continents of East Chin far across the Nesian Sea were there open conflicts of nations. Yes . . . spring . . . and he had been living with his parents in Heliopolis. Both of his parents were on assignment with the military. This he knew from the records. His parents were perhaps the finest geneticists in the Empire. They were training for a project that was to take over young Morgan's life completely. They were preparing a trip to the stars. This, too, he was told. But that had been many years later, and too late for him to object.

What he remembered was a man, a black man. He liked to imagine him one of the dark priests of Aegypt that he watched every week on the viewer. The man walked past Morgan's quarters every afternoon. Where he went, and why he went only one way, Morgan never knew.

The fence around his parents' quarters was much higher than the black man's head. It was a mesh of heavy steel curved outwards and down at the top. Every afternoon Morgan watched the man walk by, and tried to imagine how the man came to be black. Morgan did not ask his parents because he wanted to figure it out for himself.

One morning at early his father said, "The sun's going nova."

He never forgot those words, those powerful words, even

though he did not know their meaning.

"It's been kept quiet, but even the Roman Empire can't hide this heat. All the chants of all the priests of Ra won't make one damn whit of difference."

"*Heat?*" his mother shot back. "Heat is something you can live in, you can deal with. But *this* . . ." she waved her hand at the large window, "this is only a step away from fire."

So, he thought, *it was the sun made that man black.*

He was ten before he realized that the man who walked past was black from birth, from conception. Still, Morgan persisted in telling the other children in his creche that it was the sun's doing. He enjoyed the secret game of persuasion and deception.

Ah, the power of the game, even then!

Oakes straightened the cushion at his back. Why did he think of that black man, now? There had been one curious event, a simple thing that caused a commotion and fixed it in his memory.

He touched me.

Oakes could not recall being touched by anyone except his parents until that moment. On that very hot day, he sat outside on a step, cooled by the shade of the roof and the ventilator trained on his back from the doorway. The man walked by, as usual, then stopped and turned back. The boy watched him, curious, through the mesh fence, and the man studied him carefully, as though noticing him for the first time.

Oakes recalled the sudden jump of his heart, that feeling of a slingshot pulled back, back.

The man looked around, then up at the top of the fence, and the next thing Oakes knew the man was over the top, walking up to him. The black man stopped, reached out a hesitant hand and touched the boy's cheek. Oakes also reached out, equally curious, and touched the black skin of the man's arm.

"Haven't you ever seen a little boy before?" he asked.

The black face widened into a smile, and he said, "Yes, but not a little boy like you."

Then a sentry jumped on the man out of nowhere and took him away. Another sentry pulled the boy inside and called his father. He remembered that his father was angry. But best of all he remembered the look of wide-eyed wonder on the black man's face, the man who never walked by again. Oakes felt special then, powerful, an object of deference. He had always been someone to reckon with.

Why do I remember that man?

It seemed as though he spent all of his private hours asking himself questions lately. Questions led to more questions, led ultimately, daily, to the one question that he refused to admit into his consciousness. Until now.

He voiced the question aloud to himself, tested it on his tongue like the long-awaited wine.

"What if the damned ship *is* God?"

Human hybernation is to animal hibernation as animal hibernation is to constant wakefulness. In its reduction of life processes, hybernation approached absolute stasis. It is nearer death than life.

—Dictionary of Science, 101st Edition

RAJA FLATTERY lay quietly in the hybernation cocoon while he fought to overcome his terrors.

Ship has me.

Moody waves confused his memories but he knew several things. He could almost project these things onto the ebon blackness which surrounded him.

I was Chaplain/Psychiatrist on the Voidship Earthling.

We were supposed to produce an artificial consciousness. Very dangerous, that.

And they had produced . . . something. That something was Ship, a *being* of seemingly infinite powers.

God or Satan?

Flattery did not know. But Ship had created a paradise planet for its cargo of clones and then had introduced a new concept: WorShip. It had demanded that the human clones decide how they would WorShip.

We failed in that, too.

Was it because they were clones, every one of them? They had certainly been expendable. They had known this from the first

21

moments of their childhood awareness on Moonbase.

Again, fear swept through him.

I must be resolute, Flattery told himself. *God or Satan, whatever this power may be, I'm helpless before it unless I remain resolute.*

"As long as you believe yourself helpless, you remain helpless even though resolute," Ship said.

"So You read my mind, too."

"Read? That is hardly the word."

Ship's voice came from the darkness all around him. It conveyed a sense of remote concerns which Flattery could not fathom. Every time Ship spoke he felt himself reduced to a mote. He combed his way through a furry sense of subjugation, but every thought amplified this feeling of being caged and inadequate.

What could a mere human do against a power such as Ship?

There were questions in his mind, though, and he knew that Ship sometimes answered questions.

"How long have I been in hyb?"

"That length of time would be meaningless to you."

"Try me."

"I am trying you."

"Tell me how long I've been in hyb."

The words were barely out of his mouth before he felt panic at what he had done. You did not address God that way . . . or Satan.

"Why not, Raj?"

Ship's voice had taken on an air of camaraderie, but so precise was the modulation his flesh tingled with it.

"Because . . . because . . ."

"Because of what I could do to you?"

"Yes."

"Ahhhhh, Raj, when will you awaken?"

"I *am* awake."

"No matter. You have been in hybernation for a very long time as you reckon time."

"How long?" He felt that the answer was deeply important; he had to know.

"You must understand about replays, Raj. Earth has gone through its history for Me, replayed itself at My Command."

"Replayed . . . the same way every time?"

"Most of the times."

Flattery felt the inescapable truth of it and a cry was torn from him: "Why?"

"You would not understand."

"All of that pain and . . ."

"And the joy, Raj. Never forget the joy."

"But . . . replay?"

"The way you might replay a musical recording, Raj, or a holo-record of a classical drama. The way Moonbase replayed its Project Consciousness, getting a bit more out of it each time."

"Why have You brought me out of hyb?"

"You are like a favorite instrument, Raj."

"But Bickel . . ."

"Ohh, Bickel! Yes, he gave Me his genius. He was the black box out of which you achieved Me, but friendship requires more, Raj. You are My best friend."

"I would've destroyed You, Ship."

"How little you understand friendship."

"So I'm . . . an instrument. Are You replaying me?"

"No Raj. No." Such sadness in that terrible voice. "Instruments *play.*"

"Why should I permit You to play me?"

"Good! Very good, Raj!"

"Is that supposed to be an answer?"

"That was approval. You are, indeed, My best friend, My favorite instrument."

"I'll probably never understand that."

"It's partly because you enjoy the play."

Flattery could not suppress it; a chuckle escaped him.

"Laughter suits you, Raj."

Laughter? He remembered little laughter except the bitter amusement of self-accusation. But now he remembered going into hyb—not once, but more times than he cared to count. There had been other awakenings . . . other games and . . . yes, other failures. He sensed, though, that Ship was amused and he knew he was supposed to respond.

"What are we playing this time?"

"My demand remains unfulfilled, Raj. Humans somehow cannot decide how to WorShip. That's why there are no more humans now."

He felt frigid cold all through his body.

"No more . . . What've You done?"

"Earth has vanished into the cosmic whirl, Raj. All the Earths are gone. Long time, remember? Now, there are only Shipmen . . . and you."

"Me, human?"

"You are original material."

"A clone, a doppelganger, original material?"

"Very much so."

"What are Shipmen?"

"They are survivors from the most recent replays—slightly different replays from the Earth which you recall."

"Not human?"

"You could breed with them."

"How are they different?"

"They have similar ancestral experiences to yours, but they were picked up at different points in their social development."

Flattery sensed confusion in this answer and made a decision not to probe it . . . not yet. He wanted to try another tack.

"What do You mean they were picked up?"

"They thought of it as rescue. In each instance, their sun was about to nova."

"More of Your doing?"

"They have been prepared most carefully for your arrival, Raj."

"How have they been prepared?"

"They have a Chaplain/Psychiatrist who teaches hate. They have Sy Murdoch who has learned the lesson well. They have a woman named Hamill whose extraordinary strength goes deeper than anyone suspects. They have an old man named Ferry who believes everything can be bought. They have Waela and *she* is worthy of careful attention. They have a young poet named Kerro Panille, and they have Hali Ekel, who thinks she wants the poet. They have people who have been cloned and engineered for strange occupations. They have hungers, fears, joys . . ."

"You call *that* preparation?"

"Yes, and I call it involvement."

"Which is what You want from me!"

"Involvement, yes."

"Give me one compelling reason I should go down there."

"I do not compel such things."

Not a responsive answer, but Flattery knew he would have to accept it.

"So I'm to arrive. Where and how?"

"There is a planet beneath us. Most Shipmen are on that planet—Colonists."

"And they must decide how they are supposed to WorShip?"

"You are still perceptive, Raj."

"What'd they say when You put the question to them?"

"I have not put this question to them. That, I hope, will be your task."

Flattery shuddered. He knew *that* game. It was in him to shout a refusal, to rage and invite Ship's worst reprisal. But something in this dialogue held his tongue.

"What happens if they fail?"

"I *break* the . . . recording."

> *Dig your stubborn heels*
> *Firm into dirt.*
> *And where is the dirt going?*

> **—Kerro Panille,**
> *The Collected Poems*

KERRO PANILLE finished the last briefing on Pandoran geology and switched off his holo. It was well past the hour of midmeal, but he felt no hunger. Ship's air tasted stale in the tiny teaching cubby and this surprised him until he realized he had sealed off the secret hatch into this place, leaving only the floor vent. *I've been sitting on the floor vent.*

This amused him. He stood and stretched, recalling the lessons of the holo. Dreams of real dirt, real seas, real air had played so long in his imagination that he feared now the real thing might disappoint him. He knew himself to be no novice at image-building in his mind . . . and no novice to the disappointments of reality.

At such times he felt much older than his twenty annos. And he looked for reassurance in a shiny surface to reflect his own features. He found a small area of the hatch plate polished by the many passages of his own hand when entering this place.

Yes—his dark skin retained the smoothness of youth and the darker beard curled with its usual vigor around his mouth. He had to admit it was a generous mouth. And the nose was a pirate's nose. Not many Shipmen even knew there had ever been such people as pirates.

26

His eyes appeared much older than twenty, though. No escaping that.

Ship did that to me. No . . . He shook his head. Honesty could not be evaded. *The special thing Ship and I have between us—* that *made my eyes look old.*

There were realities within realities. This thing that made him a poet kept him digging beneath every surface like a child pawing through pages of glyphs. Even when reality disappointed, he had to seek it.

The power of disappointment.

He recognized that power as distinct from frustration. It contained the power to regroup, rethink, react. It forced him to listen to himself as he listened to others.

Kerro knew what most people shipside thought about him.

They were convinced he could hear every conversation in a crowded room, that no gesture or inflection escaped him. There were times when that was true, but he kept to himself his conclusions about such observations. Thus, few were offended by his attentions. No one could find a better audience than Kerro Panille. All he wanted was to listen, to learn, to make order out of it in his poems.

It was order that mattered—beautiful order created out of the deepest inspiration. Yet . . . he had to admit it, Ship presented an image of infinite disorder. He had asked Ship to show its shape to him once, a whimsical request which he had half expected to be refused. But Ship had responded by taking him on a visual tour, through the internal sensors, through the eyes of the robox repair units and even through the eyes of shuttles flitting between Ship and Pandora.

Externally, Ship was most confusing. Great fanlike extrusions dangled in space like wings or fins. Lights glittered within them and there were occasional glimpses of people at work behind the open shutters of the ports. Hydroponics gardens, Ship had explained.

Ship stretched almost fifty-eight kilometers in length. But it bulged and writhed throughout that length with fragile shapes which gave no clue to their purposes. Shuttles landed and were dispatched from long, slender tubes jutting randomly outward. The hydroponics fans were stacked one upon another, built outward from each other like mad growths springing from mutated spores.

Panille knew that once Ship had been sleek and trim, a projectile shape with three slim wings at the midpoint. The wings had dipped backward to form a landing tripod. That sleek shape lay hidden now within the confusion of the eons. It was called "the core" and you caught occasional glimpses of it in the passages— a thick wall with an airtight hatch, a stretch of metallic surface with ports which opened onto the blank barriers of new construction.

Internally, Ship was equally confusing. Sensor eyes showed him the stacks of dormant life in the hybernation bays. At his request, Ship displayed the locator coordinates, but they were meaningless to him. Numbers and glyphs. He followed the swift movements of robox units down passages where there was no air and out onto Ship's external skin. There, in the shadows of the random extrusions, he watched the business of repairs and alterations, even the beginnings of new construction.

Panille had watched his fellow Shipmen at their work, feeling fascinated and faintly guilty. A secret spy intruding on privacy. Two men had wrestled a large tubular container into a loading bay for shuttle transshipment down to Pandora. And Panille had felt that he had no right to watch this without the two men knowing it.

When the tour was over, he had sat back disappointed. It occurred to him then that Ship intruded this way all the time. Nothing any Shipman did could be hidden from Ship. This realization had sparked a momentary resentment which was followed immediately by amusement.

I am in Ship and of Ship and, in a deeper sense, I am Ship.

"Kerro!"

The sudden voice from the com-console beside his holo focus startled him. How had she found him here?

"Yes, Hali?"

"Where are you?"

Ahhh, she had not found him. A search program had found him.

"I'm studying," he said.

"Can you walk with me for a while? I'm really wound up."

"Where?"

"How about the arboretum near the cedars?"

"Give me a few minutes to finish up here and meet you."

"I'm not bothering you, am I?"

He noted the diffidence in her tone.

"No, I need a break."

"See you outside of Records."

He heard the click of her signoff and stood a blink staring at the console.

How did she know I was studying in the Records section?

A search program keyed to his person would not report his location.

Am I that predictable?

He picked up his notecase and recorder and stepped through the concealed hatch. He sealed it and slipped down through the software storage area to the nearest passage. Hali Ekel stood in the passageway beside the hatch waiting for him. She waved a hand, all nonchalance.

"Hi."

Most of his mind was still back in the study. He blinked at her foolishly, mindful as usual of the sheer beauty of Hali Ekel. At times like this—meeting suddenly, unexpectedly in some passage—she often stunned him.

The clinical sterility of the ever-present pribox at her hip never distanced them. She was a med-tech, full time, and he understood that life and survival were her business.

The secret darkness of her eyes, her thick black hair, the lustrous brown warmth of her skin always made him lean toward her slightly or face her way in a crowded room. They were from the same bloodlines, the Nesian Nations, selected for strength, survival sense and their easy affinity with the highways of the stars. Many mistook them for brother and sister, a mistake amplified by the fact that true siblings had not existed shipside in living memory. Some siblings slept on in hyb, but none walked together.

Notes toward a poem flashed behind his eyes, another of the many she brought to his mind, that he kept to himself.

> Oh dark and magnificent star
> What little light I have, take.
> Weave those supple fingers into mine.
>
> Feel the flow!

Before he could think of putting this into his recorder, it occurred to him that she should not be here so fast. There were no nearby call stations.

"Where were you when you called me?"

"Medical."

He glanced up the passage: Medical was at least ten minutes away.

"But how did you . . ."

"Keyed the whole conversation on a ten-minute delay."

"But . . ."

"See how standard you are on com? I can tape my whole side of a conversation, with you and get it right down the line."

"But the . . ." He nodded at the hatch into software storage.

"Oh, that's where you always are when nobody can find you—somewhere in there." She pointed to the storage area.

"Hmmm." He took her hand and they headed out toward the west shell.

"Why so thoughtful?" she asked. "I thought you'd be amused, surprised . . . laugh, or something."

"I'm sorry. Lately it's bothered me when I do that. Never take time for people, never seem to have the flair for . . . the right word at the right time."

"A pretty strong self-indictment for a poet."

"It's much easier to order characters on a page or a holo than it is to order one's life. 'One's life'! Why do I talk that way?"

She slipped an arm around his waist and hugged him as they walked. He smiled. Presently, they emerged into the Dome of Trees. It was dayside, the sunglow of Rega muted through the screening filters. All the greens came with soothing blue undertones. Kerro took a deep breath of the oxygenated air. He heard birds twittering behind a sonabarrier off in heavier bushes to the left. Other couples could be seen far down through the trees. This was a favorite trysting place.

Hali slipped off her pribox strap and pulled him down beside her under a cover of cedar. The needle duff was warm and soft, the air thick with moisture and sun dazzled through the branches. They stretched out on their backs, shoulder to shoulder.

"Mmmmmm." Hali stretched and arched her back. "It smells so *nice* here."

"It? What's the smell of an *it?*"

"Oh, stop that." She turned toward him. "You know what I mean—the air, the moss, the food in your beard." She brushed at his whiskers, wove her fingers in and out of the coarse hairs. "You're the only Shipman with a beard."

"So I'm told."

"Do you like it?"

"I don't know." He reached out and traced the curve of the small wire ring which pierced her left nostril. "Traditions are strange. Where did you get this ring?"

"A robox dropped it."

"Dropped it?" He was surprised.

"I know—they don't miss much. This one was repairing a sensor outside that little medical study next to Behavioral. I saw the wire drop and picked it up.

"It was like finding a rare treasure. They leave so little around. Ship only knows what they do with all the scraps they carry off."

She slipped her arm around his neck and kissed him. Presently, she pulled back.

He pulled away from her and sat up. "Thanks, but . . ."

"It's always, 'Thanks, but . . .'" She was angry, fighting the physical evidence of her own passion.

"I'm not ready." He felt apologetic. "I don't know why and I'm not playing with you. I just have this compulsion toward timing, for the feeling of rightness in things."

"What could be more right? We were selected as a breeding pair *after* knowing each other all this time. It's not like we were strangers."

He could not bring himself to look at her. "I know . . . anyone shipside can partner with anyone else, but . . ."

"But!" She whirled away and stared at the base of the sheltering tree. "We could be a breeding pair! One pair in . . . what? Two thousand? We could actually make a child."

"It isn't that. It's . . ."

"And you're always so damned historical, traditional, quoting social patterns this and language patterns that. Why can't you see what . . ."

He reached across her, put his fingers over her mouth to silence her and gently kissed her cheek.

"Dear Hali, because I can't. For me partnerShip will have to be a giving so deep that I lose myself in the giving."

She rolled away and lifted her head to stare at him, her eyes glistening. "Where do you get such ideas?"

"They come out of my living and from what I learn."

"Ship teaches you these things?"

"Ship does not deny me what I want to know."

She stared morosely at the ground under her feet. "Ship won't even talk to me."

Her voice was barely audible.

"When you ask in the right way, Ship always answers," he said. Then, an afterthought as he sensed it between them: "And you have to listen."

"You've said that before but you never tell me how."

There was no evading the jealousy in her voice. He found that he could only answer in one way.

"I will give you a poem," he said. He cleared his throat.

> "Blue itself
> teaches us blue."

She scowled, concentrating on his words. Presently, she shook her head. "I'll never understand you any more than I understand Ship. I go to WorShip; I pray; I do what Ship directs . . ." She stared at him. "I never see you at WorShip."

"Ship is my friend," he said.

Curiosity overcame her resentments.

"What does Ship teach you?"

"Too many things to tell here."

"Just give me one thing, just one!"

He nodded. "Very well. There have been many planets and many people. Their languages and the chronicle of their years weave a magic tangle. Their words sing to me. You don't even have to understand the words to hear them sing."

She felt an odd sense of wonder at this.

"Ship gives you words and you don't understand?"

"When I ask for the original."

"But why do you want words that you don't understand?"

"To make those people live, to make them mine. Not to *own* them, but to *become them*, at least for a blink or two."

He turned and stared at her. "Haven't you ever wanted to dig in ancient dirt and find people nobody else even knew existed?"

"Their *bones?*"

"No! Their hearts, their lives."

She shook her head slowly.

"I just don't understand you, Kerro. But I love you."

He nodded silently, thinking: *Yes, love doesn't have to understand. She knows this but she won't let it into her life.*

He recalled the words of an old earthside poem: "Love is not a consolation, it is a light." The thought, the poem of life, *that* was consolation. He would talk to her of love sometime, he thought, but not this dayside.

Why are you humans always so ready to carry the terrible burdens of your past?

—Kerro Panille,
Questions from the *Avata*

SY MURDOCH did not like coming out this close to Colony perimeter, even when sheltered behind the crysteel barrier of Lab One's private exit. Creatures of this planet had a way of penetrating the impenetrable, confounding the most careful defenses.

But someone Lewis trusted had to man this observation post when the hylighters congregated on the plain as they were doing this morning. It was thier most mysterious form of behavior and lately Lewis had been demanding answers—no doubt jumping to commands from The Boss.

He sighed. When he looked out on the unprotected surface of Pandora, there was no denying its immediate dangers.

Absently, he scratched his left elbow. When he moved his head against the exterior light, he could see his own reflection in the Plaz: a blocky man with brown hair, blue eyes, a light complexion which he kept meticulously scrubbed.

The vantage point was not the best available, not as good as the exterior posts which were always manned by the fastest and the best the Colony could risk. But Murdoch knew he could argue his importance to the leadership team. He was not expendable and this place did serve Lewis' purpose. The crysteel barrier, although it filtered out almost a fourth of the light, framed the area they needed to watch.

What was it those damned floating gasbags did out there?

Murdoch crouched behind a swivel-mounted scope-cumvidicorder, and touched the controls with a short, stubby finger to focus on the 'lighters. More than a hundred of them floated above the plain about six kilometers out.

There were some big orange monsters in this mob, and Murdoch singled out one of the biggest for special observation, reading what he saw into a small recorder at his throat. The big 'lighter looked to be at least fifty meters in diameter, a truncated sphere somewhat flattened along the top which formed the muscular base for the tall, rippling sail membrane. Corded tendrils trailed down to the plain where it grasped a large rock which bumped and dragged along the surface, kicking up dust, scattering gravel.

The morning was cloudless, only one sun in the sky. It cast a harsh golden light on the plain, picking out every wrinkle and contraction of the 'lighter's bag. Murdoch could make out a cradle of smaller enfolding tentacles cupped beneath the 'lighter, confining something which squirmed there . . . twisting, flailing. He could not quite identify what the 'lighter carried, but it definitely was alive and trying to escape.

The mob of accompanying 'lighters had lined out in a great curved spread which was sweeping now across the plain on a diagonal path away from Murdoch's observation post. The big one he had singled out anchored the near flank, still confining that flailing something in the tentacle shadows beneath it.

What had that damned thing captured? Surely not a Colonist!

Murdoch backed off his focus to include the entire mob and saw then that they were targeting on ground creatures, a mixed lot of them huddled on the plain. The arc of hylighters swept toward the crouching animals which waited mesmerized. He scanned them, identifying Hooded Dashers, Swift Grazers, Flatwings, Spinnerets, Tubetuckers, Clingeys . . . demons—all of them deadly to Colonists.

But apparently not dangerous to hylighters.

All of the 'lighters carried ballast rocks, Murdoch saw, and now the central segment of the sweeping arc dropped their rocks. The bags bounced slightly and tendrils stretched out to snatch up the crouching demons. The captive creatures squirmed and flailed, but made no attempt to bite or otherwise attack the 'lighters.

Now, all but a few of the ballasted 'lighters dropped their rocks and began to soar. The few still carrying rocks tacked out away from the capture team, appearing to search the ground for other specimens. The monster bag which Murdoch had studied earlier remained in this search group. Once more, Murdoch enlarged the image in the scope, focusing in on the cupped tendrils beneath the thing's bag. All was quiet there now and, as he watched, the tendrils opened to release their catch.

Murdoch dictated his observations into the recorder at his throat: "The big one has just dropped its catch. Whatever it is it appears to be desiccated, a large flat area of black . . . My God! It was a Hooded Dasher! The big 'lighter had a Hooded Dasher tucked up under the bag!"

The remains of the Dasher struck the ground in a geyser of dust.

Now, the big 'lighter swerved left and its rock ballast scraped the side of another large rock on the plain. Sparks flew where the rocks met and Murdoch saw a line of fire spurt upward to the 'lighter which exploded in a flare of glowing yellow. Bits of the orange bag and a cloud of fine blue dust drifted and sailed all around.

The explosion ignited a wild frenzy of action on the plain. The other bags dropped their captives and soared upward. The demons on the ground spread out, some dashing and leaping to catch the remnants of the exploded 'lighter. Slower creatures such as the Spinnerets crept toward fallen rags of the orange bag.

And when it was over, the demons sped away or burrowed into the plain as was the particular habit of each.

Murdoch methodically described this into his recorder.

When it was done, he scanned the plain once more. All of the 'lighters had soared away. Not a demon remained. He shut down the observation post and signaled for a replacement to come up, then he headed back toward Lab One and the Garden. As he made his way along the more secure lighted passages, he thought about what he had seen and recorded. The visual record would go to Lewis and later to Oakes. Lewis would edit the verbal observations, adding his own comments.

What was it I saw and recorded out there?

Try as he might to understand the behavior of the Pandoran creatures, Murdoch could not do it.

Lewis is right. We should just wipe them out.

And as he thought of Lewis, Murdoch asked himself how long this most recent emergency at the Redoubt would keep the man out of touch. For all they really knew, Lewis might be dead. No one was completely immune to the threats of Pandora—not even Lewis. If Lewis were gone . . .

Murdoch tried to imagine himself elevated to a new position of power under Oakes. The images of such a change would not form.

Gods have plans, too.

—Morgan Oakes,
The Diaries

FOR A long time, Panille lay quietly beside Hali in the treedome, watching the plaz-filtered light draw radial beams on the air above the cedar tree. He knew Hali had been hurt by his rejection and he wondered why he did not feel guilty. He sighed. There was no sense in running away; this was the way he had to be.

Hali spoke first, her voice low, tentative.

"Nothing's changed, is it?"

"Talking about it doesn't change it," he said. "Why did you ask me out here—to revive our sexual debate?"

"Couldn't I just want to be with you for a while?"

She was close to tears. He spoke softly to avoid hurting her even more.

"I'm always with you, Hali." With his left hand he lifted her right hand, pressed the tips of his fingers against the tips of her fingers. "Here. We touch, right?"

She nodded like a child being coaxed from a tantrum.

"Which is *we* and which the material of our flesh?"

"I don't..."

He held their fingertips a few centimeters apart.

"All the atoms between us oscillate at incredible speeds. They bump into each other and shove each other around." He tapped the air with a fingertip, careful to keep from touching her.

37

"So I touch an atom; it bumps into the next one; that one nudges another, and so on until . . ." He closed the gap and brushed her fingertips. ". . . we touch and we were never separate."

"Those are just words!" She pulled her hand away from him.

"Much more than words, you know it, *Med-tech* Hali Ekel. We constantly exchange atoms with the universe, with the atmosphere, with food, with each other. There's no way we can be separated."

"But I don't want just *any* atoms!"

"You have more choice than you think, lovely Hali."

She studied him out of the corners of her eyes. "Are you just making these things up to entertain me?"

"I'm serious. Don't I always tell you when I make up something?"

"Do you?".

"Always, Hali. I will make up a poem to prove it." He tapped her wire ring lightly. "A poem about this."

"Why're you telling me your poems? You usually just lock them up on tapes or store them away in those old-fashioned glyph books of yours."

"I'm trying to please you in the only way I can."

"Then tell me your poem."

He brushed her cheek beside the ring, then:

"With delicate rings of the gods
in our noses
we do not root in their garden."

She stared at him, puzzled. "I don't understand."

"An ancient Earthside practice. Farmers put rings in the noses of their pigs to keep the pigs from digging out of their pens. Pigs dig with their noses as well as their feet. People called that kind of digging 'rooting.'"

"So you're comparing me to a pig."

"Is that all you see in my poem?"

She sighed, then smiled as much at herself as at Kerro. "We're a fine pair to be selected for breeding—the poet and the pig!"

He stared at her, met her gaze and, without knowing why, they were suddenly giggling, then laughing.

Presently, he lay back on the duff. "Ahhh, Hali, you are good for me."

"I thought you might need some distraction. What've you been studying that keeps you so shut away?''

He scratched his head, recovered a brown twig of dead cedar. ''I've been rooting into the 'lectrokelp.''

''That seaweed the Colony's been having all the trouble with? Why would that interest you?''

''I'm always amazed at what interests me, but this may be right down my hatchway. The kelp, or some phase of it, appears to be sentient.''

''You mean it thinks?''

''More than that . . . probably much more.''

''Why hasn't this been announced?''

''I don't know for sure. I came across part of the information by accident and pieced together the rest. There's a record of other teams sent out to study the kelp.''

''How did you find this report?''

''Well . . . I think it may be restricted for most people, but Ship seldom holds anything back from me.''

''You and Ship!''

''Hali . . .''

''Oh, all right. What's in this report?''

''The kelp appears to have a language transmitted by light but we can't understand it yet. And there's something even more interesting. I can't find out if there's a current project to contact and study this kelp.''

''Doesn't Ship . . .''

''Ship refers me to Colony HQ or to the Ceepee, but they don't acknowledge my inquiries.''

''That's nothing new. They don't acknowledge most inquiries.''

''You been having trouble with them, too?''

''Just that Medical can't get an explanation for all the gene sampling.''

''Gene sampling? How very curious.''

''Oakes is a very curious and very private person.''

''How about someone on the staff?''

''Lewis?'' Her tone was derisive.

Kerro scratched his cheek reflectively.

''The 'lectrokelp and gene sampling. Hali, I don't know about the gene sampling . . . that has a peculiar stink to it. But the kelp . . .''

She interrupted, excited: ''This creature could have a soul . . . and it could WorShip.''

''A soul? Perhaps. But I thought when I saw that record: 'Yes!

This is why Ship brought us to Pandora.' ''

"What if Oakes knows that the 'lectrokelp is the reason we're here?''

Panille shook his head.

She gripped his arm. "Think of all the times Oakes has called us prisoners of Ship. He tells us often enough that Ship won't let us leave. Why won't he tell us why Ship brought us here?"

"Maybe he doesn't know."

"Ohhh, he knows."

"Well, what can we do about it?"

She spoke without thinking: "We can't do anything without going groundside."

He pulled his arm away from her and dug his fingers into the humus. "What do we know about living groundside?"

"What do we know about living here?"

"Would you go down to the Colony with me, Hali?"

"You know I would but..."

"Then let's apply for..."

"They won't let me go. The groundside food shortage is critical; there are health problems. They've just increased our workload because they've sent some of our best people down."

"We're probably imagining monsters that don't exist, but I'd still like to see the 'lectrokelp for myself."

A high-pitched hum blurted from the ever-present pribox on the ground beside Hali. She pressed the response key.

"Hali..." There was a clatter, a buzz. Presently, the voice returned. "Sorry I dropped you. This is Winslow Ferry. Is that Kerro Panille with you, Hali?"

Hali stifled a laugh. The bumbling old fool could not even put in a call without stumbling over something. Kerro was caught by the direct reference to someone being with Hali. Had Ferry been listening? Many shipside suspected that sensors and portable communications equipment had been adapted for eavesdropping but this was his first direct clue. He took the pribox from her.

"This is Kerro Panille."

"Ahhh, Kerro. Please report to my office within the hour. We have an assignment for you."

"An assignment?"

There was no response. The connection had been broken.

"What do you suppose that's all about?" Hali asked.

For answer, Kerro drew a blank page from his notebook, scribbled on it with a fade-stylus, then pointed to the pribox. *'He was listening to us.'*

She stared at the note.

Kerro said: "Isn't that strange? I've never had an assignment before . . . except study assignments from Ship."

Hali took the stylus from him, wrote: "Look out. If they do not want it known that the kelp thinks, you could be in danger."

Kerro stood, blanked the page and restored it to his case. "Guess I'd better wander down to Ferry's office and find out what's happening."

They walked most of the way back in silence, intensely aware of every sensor they passed, of the pribox at Hali's hip. As they approached Medical, she stopped him.

"Kerro, teach me how to speak to Ship."

"Can't."

"But . . ."

"It's like your genotype or your color. Except for certain clones, you don't get much choice in the matter."

"Ship has to decide?"

"Isn't that always the way, even with you? Do you respond to everyone who wants to talk to you?"

"Well, I know Ship must be very busy with . . ."

"I don't think that has anything to do with it. Ship either speaks to you or doesn't."

She digested this for a moment, nodded, then: "Kerro, do you really talk to Ship?"

There was no mistaking the resentment in her voice.

"You know I wouldn't lie to you, Hali. Why're you so interested in talking to Ship?"

"It's the idea of Ship *answering* you. Not the commands we get over the 'coders, but . . ."

"A kind of unlimited encyclopedia?"

"That, yes, but more. Does Ship talk to you through the 'coders?"

"Not very often."

"What is it like when . . . ?"

"It's like a very distinctive voice in your head, just a bit clearer than your conscience."

"That's it?" She sounded disappointed.

"What did you expect? Trumpets and bells?"

"I don't even know what my conscience sounds like!"

"Keep listening." He brushed a finger against her ring, kissed her quickly, brotherly, then stepped through the hatch into the screening area for Ferry's office.

The fearful are often holders of the most dangerous power. They become demoniac when they see the workings of all the life around them. Seeing the strengths as well as the weaknesses, they fasten only on the weaknesses.

—Shipquotes

WINSLOW FERRY sat in his dimly lighted office unaware of the random chaos around him—the piles of tapes and software, the dirty clothes, the empty bottles and boxes, the papers with scribbled notes to himself. It had been a long, tense dayside for him, and the place smelled of stale, spilled wine and old perspiration. His entire attention focused on the sensor screen at the corner of his comdesk. He bent his sweaty face close to the screen which showed Panille walking down a passageway with that lithe and succulent med-tech, Hali Ekel.

A wisp of gray hair fell over his right eye and he brushed it aside when a deeply veined hand. His pale eyes glittered in the com light.

He watched Hali on the holo, watched the smoothness of her young body glide from passageway to hatch to passageway. But the musk that surrounded him there in his office was Rachel. At times Rachel Demarest seemed all bone and elbow to him, a hard woman hardly used. He developed an amused distance from her whine. She had dreams that included him because she wanted

42

him, even if he was a sack of graying wrinkles and sour breath. She wanted power and Ferry liked to snuggle up to power. They were good for each other and they tricked themselves into a personal distance by trading information for liquor, wine for position or a warm night together. This game of barter between them walled off the kind of hurt they'd both been dealt at the hands of whimsical lovers.

Rachel was asleep now in his cubby, dreaming herself Senior Chair of a new Council that would wrest power from Oakes, make the Colony self-sufficient and self-governing.

Ferry sat at his console, slightly drunk, dreaming of Hali Ekel.

He waited to shift to the next spy sensor until he could no longer make out the details of Hali's small, firm hips tight against her jumpsuit. What luscious hips! As he switched sensors to the one ahead of them, he forgot to change focus. The two were a blur as they approached the sensor's forward field limit. Ferry fumbled with the controls and lost them.

"Damn!" he whispered, and his old surgeon's hands were shaking like a wihi in a flare.

He touched the screen to steady himself, touched Hali's image blurring past the sensor and into a treedome.

"Enjoy, enjoy, my dears." He spoke aloud, his words absorbed by the piled confusion around him. Everyone knew why young couples went into the treedome. He checked to see that the holo was on record and that sound levels were satisfactory. Lewis and Oakes would want to see this, and Ferry anticipated making a special copy for himself.

"Give it to her, young fellow! Give it to her!"

He felt a pleasant swelling at his crotch and wondered if he could get away to visit Rachel Demarest.

"Get something on that poet," Lewis had ordered, and he'd had five liters of the new Pandoran wine delivered to Ferry's office from groundside by Rachel—a double gift. One of the empties lay across his mazed hookup to the Biocomputer. Another empty was still on the deck of the cubby temporarily occupied by Rachel. She was a clone (one of the better ones) and wine was the treasure to her that Ferry was not. Rachel was the treasure to him that Ekel was not.

Ferry watched the small touches between Panille and Ekel, imagining every one of them to be his own.

Perhaps with a little wine . . . he thought, and he leered at the faint, half-imagined nipples pressing her suit, shouting him out of her conversation with Panille.

Are they going to couple?

He was beginning to doubt it. Panille was not reacting correctly. *I should've told them about Panille's groundside orders sooner.* That was always a good lever for sex. "I'm going groundside soon, dear one. You know what the dangers are down there?"

"Go ahead, do it, fellow!"

Ferry wanted to watch Hali slip out of her singlesuit, wanted her to desire a horny old surgeon with that desire she had in her eyes for Panille.

"So you want to know about the kelp," Ferry slurred to Panille's reclining image in the viewscreen. "Well, you'll know it all soon enough, fellow. And Hali..." His clammy fingers caressed the screen. "...perhaps Lewis can see to it that you are assigned to us here at Classification and Processing. Yesss." And the *yes* was a feverish hiss through his yellow teeth.

Suddenly, the conversation on the screen jarred him out of his daydream. He was sure he had heard correctly. Panille had told Hali Ekel that the kelp was sentient.

"Damn you!" Ferry screamed at the viewer, and this became his low-voiced chant as the eavesdropping continued.

Yes, Panille was telling her everything. He was spoiling everything!

Panille was going groundside, was going to be out of the way. And all because of the kelp! Ferry was sure of it. The groundside orders must have been cut by Lewis or Oakes. That had to be because they were cut as soon as that mass of study-circuits on the kelp started showing up on Panille's program orders. Panille was onto something, but could be stopped. He was quiet, and could be removed quietly. The only logical reason for the delay in sending the fellow groundside had to be that order from Lewis: "Get something on 'im."

Well...orders said the delay ended if Panille started talking too much.

"But damn him, he told *her!*"

Ferry caught his breath and tried to calm himself. He opened his last bottle of wine, the fantasy bottle that he would have offered to Ekel, if only in his dreams. He had neither the key, the code, nor the technical expertise to alter the holorecording, to erase all evidence that Ekel, too, knew about the kelp.

He took a long swallow of the wine and slammed the *call* key coded to her.

"Hali . . ." He threw the bottle across his office in rage, then lost his balance and fell against the console, breaking the call-connection. He pushed himself back, calmed his voice and once more opened the channel.

"Sorry I dropped you. This is Winslow Ferry. Is that Kerro Panille with you, Hali?" How he loved the sound of her name on his tongue, the touch of her even in word.

She laughed at him!

Ferry had no recollection of ending the call, ordering Panille to his office, but he knew he had done it.

She laughed at him . . . and she knew about the kelp. When Lewis reviewed this holorecord (and he would certainly do that), then Lewis would know she had laughed at him and Lewis would laugh because he often laughed at Ferry.

But it's always old Winslow who gets him what he needs!

Yes . . . always. When no one else could manage it, Winslow knew someone who knew someone who knew something and had a price. Lewis would not care deeply that she laughed at old Winslow. Momentary amusement, that was all. But Lewis would care about the kelp. New orders would be cut for Ekel. Ferry knew that for certain. And wherever Ekel was assigned, it would not be to Classification and Processing.

*A good bureaucracy is the best tool of oppression
ever invented.*

—Jesus Lewis,
The Oakes Diaries

WHEN REGA had set behind the western hills, Waela TaoLini turned atop her craggy vantage to watch the red-orange ball of Alki cross the southern horizon in its first passage of the diurn. She had only been forced to kill three demons in the past hour and there seemed little more to do on this watch except mark the distant line of powdery red to the south where they had burned out a Nerve Runner boil just two diurns past. But it looked as though they had sterilized the area, although she could still detect an occasional whiff of burned acid from that direction. But Swift Grazers were already into the red, gorging on the dead Runners. The bulbous little multipeds would not venture anywhere near a live boil of Runners.

As usual, she stood tall and alert on watch. She did not feel unusually exposed on the crag. There was a 'scape hatch and slide tunnel one step away on her left. A sensor atop the tunnel's marker pole kept constant watch on her. She carried a gushburner and lasgun, but even more important, she knew her own reflexes. Conditioned by the harsh requirements of Pandora, she could match anything except a massed attack by the planet's predators.

And the Nerve Runner invasion had been turned back.

Waela crouched then and stared down across the southern plain

to the rim of hills. Without conscious volition. her gaze darted
left, right; she stood and turned, repeated this procedure. It was
all random, constant movement.

"Try to look everywhere at once." That was the watchword.

Her yellow flaresuit was damp with perspiration. She was tall
and slim and she knew this gave her an advantage here. On patrol,
she walked tall. Other times, she pulled in her shoulders and tried
to appear shorter. Men did not like taller women, a continually
bothersome fact which amplified her constant concern over her
unavoidable peculiarity; her skin changed color through a broad
spectrum from blue to orange in response to her moods, a system
not under conscious control. Right now, her exposed skin betrayed
the pale pink of repressed fear. Her hair was black and cropped
at the neck. Her eyes were brown and shaded in epicanthic folds,
but she felt that she had a slender and attractive nose which com-
plemented her broad chin and full lips.

"Waela, you're some kind of chameleon throwback," one of
her friends had said. But he was dead now, drowned under the
kelp.

She sighed.

"Rrrrrssss!"

She turned to the sound and, by reflex, gunned out two Flatwings, thin and multilegged ground racers about ten centimeters
long, *Poisonous things!*

Alki was four diameters above the southern horizon now, sending long shadows northward and painting a red-purple glow across
the distant sea to the west.

Waela liked this particular watch station for its view of the sea.
It was the highest vantage connected to Colony. They called it
simply "Peak."

A line of hylighters drifted through the sky along the distant
shoreline. Judging by their apparent size from this distance, they
were giants. As with others among the Shipmen/Colonists, she
had studied the native life carefully, making the usual comparisons
against Shiprecords. The hylighters were, indeed, like giant airborne Portuguese men-of-war, great orange creatures born in the
sea. Steadied by its long black tendrils, a hylighter could adjust
the great membrane atop its buoyant bag and tack into the wind.
They moved with a strange precision, usually in groups of twenty
or more, and Waela found herself on the side of those who argued
for some intelligence in these gentle creatures.

Hylighters were a nuisance, yes. They were buoyed by hydrogen and that, coupled with Pandora's frequent electrical storms, made the creatures into lethal firebombs. In common with the 'lectrokelp, they were useless as food. Even to touch them produced weird mental effects—hysteria and even, sometimes, convulsions. Standing orders were to explode them at a distance when they approached Colony.

Almost without thinking about it, she noted a Spinneret creeping up the Peak on her left. It was a big one. She guessed it would equal the five kilos of the largest ever taken. Because the high-density, molelike creature was Pandora's only slow mover, she took her time responding. Every opportunity to study Pandora's predators had to be used. It was as gray-black as the rocks and she guessed its length at about thirty centimeters, not counting the spinner tail. The first Colonists to encounter Spinnerets had been trapped in the sticky fog the things released through that tail appendage.

Waela chewed her lower lip, watching the Spinneret's purposeful approach. It had seen her; no doubt of that. The sticky mesh of the Spinneret's fog produced a peculiar paralysis. It rendered everything it touched immobile, but alive and alert. The nearsighted Spinneret, having trapped a victim, could suck the captive dry at a slow and agonizing pace.

"Close enough," she whispered as the thing paused fewer than five meters below her and started turning to bring its lethal spinner into play. A quick red wash of the gushburner incinerated the Spinneret. She watched the remains tumble off the Peak.

Alki was now eight diameters above the horizon and she knew her watch was almost over. She had been ordered to assess possible dangerous activity among the free-roaming predators. They all knew the reason for watching outside Colony's barriers. The visible human in a yellow flaresuit would attract predators.

"We're bait out there," one of her friends had said.

Waela resented the assignment, but in a place of common perils she knew she had to share every danger. That was Colony's social glue. Even though she would get extra food chits for this, she could not help resenting it.

There were other dangers more important to her, and she saw this assignment as a symptom of perilous change in Colony priorities. Her place was out studying the kelp. As the sole survivor of the original study teams, she was the perfect choice for assembling a new team.

Are they phasing out our research?

There were rumors all through Colony. The materials and energy could not be spared for construction of strong-enough submersibles. The LTAs could not be spared. Lighter-Than-Air was still the most reliable groundside transport for the mining and drilling outposts, and, because they had been built to simulate hylighters, they attracted minimal attention from predators. Hylighters appeared to be immune to the predators.

She could see the rationale of the arguments. Kelp interfered with the aquaculture project and food was short. The argument for extermination, though, she saw as one of dangerous ignorance.

We need more information.

Almost casually, she gunned out a Hooded Dasher, noting that it was the first one seen anywhere near the Peak in twenty diurns.

The kelp must be studied. We must learn.

What did they know about the kelp after all the lives spent and all the frustrating dives?

Fireflies in the night of the sea, someone called them.

The kelp extruded nodules from its giant stems and those nodules glowed with a million firecolors. She agreed with all the others who had seen it and lived to report: the pulsing and glowing nodules were a hypnotic symphony, and the lights *might,* just *might,* be a form of communication. There *did* seem to be purpose in the glowing play of light, discernible patterns.

The kelp covered the planet's seas except for the random patch of open water called "lagoons." In a planet with only two major land masses, this represented a gigantic spread of life.

Once again, she returned to that unavoidable argument: what did they really know about the kelp?

It's conscious, it thinks.

She was certain of it. The challenge of this problem engaged her imagination with a totality she had never dreamed possible. It had caught others as well. It was polarizing Colony. And the extermination arguments could not be thrown out.

Can you eat the kelp?

You could not eat it. The stuff was disorienting, probably hallucinogenic. The source of this effect had thus far defied Colony chemists to isolate it.

It had this in common with the hylighters. The illusive substance had been dubbed "fraggo" because "it fragments the psyche."

That alone said to Waela that the kelp should be preserved for study.

Once more, she was forced to kill a Hooded Dasher. The long black shape went tumbling down the Peak, green blood gushing from it.

That's too many of them, she thought.

Warily, she examined her surroundings, probing for movement below her in the rocks. Nothing. She was still scanning the area this way moments later when her relief stepped out of the hatch. She recognized him, Scott Burik, an LTA fitter on the nightside shift. He was a small man with prematurely aged features, but he was as quick as any other Colonist, already scanning the area around them. She told him about the two Dashers as she passed over the 'burner.

"Good rest," he said.

She slipped into the hatch, heard it slam behind her then slid down to debriefing where she turned in her kill count and made her assessment of COA—Current Outside Activity.

The debriefing room was windowless with pale yellow walls and a single comdesk. Ary Arenson, a blond, gray-eyed man who never seemed to change expression, sat behind it. Everyone said he worked for Jesus Lewis, a rumor which predisposed Waela to walk and talk softly with him. Odd things happened to people who displeased Lewis.

She was tired now with a fatigue which watch always produced, a drained feeling, as though she were victim of a psychic Spinneret. The routine questions bored her.

"Yes, the Nerve Runner area appears sterilized."

At the end of it, Arenson handed her a small square of brown Colony paper with a message which restored her energy. She read it at a glance:

"Report to Main Hangar for new kelp research team assignment."

Arenson was glancing at his Comscreen as she read the note and now he changed expression, a wry smile. "Your replacement..." He pointed upward toward the Peak with his chin. "...just got it. A Dasher chewed his guts out. Stand by a blink. They're sending another replacement."

Poetry, like consciousness, drops the insignificant digits.

—Raja Flattery,
Shiprecords

SHIP'S WARNING that this could be the end of humankind left Flattery with a sense of emptiness.

He stared into the blackness which surrounded him, trying to find some relief. Would Ship really break the . . . recording? What did Ship mean by a recording?

Last chance.

His emotional responses told Flattery he had touched a deep core of affinity with his own kind. The thought that in some faraway future on a line through infinity there might be other humans to enjoy life as he had enjoyed it—this thought filled him with warm affections for such descendants.

"Do You really mean this is our last chance?" he asked.

"Much as it pains Me." Ship's response did not surprise him.

The words were torn from him: "Why don't You just tell us how to . . . ?"

"Raj! How much of your free will would you give me!"

"How much would You take?"

"Believe Me, Raj, there are places where neither God nor Man dares intervene."

"And You want me to go down to this planet, put Your question to them, and help them answer Your demand?"

"Would you do that?"

"Could I refuse?"

"I seek choice, Raj, not compulsion or chance. Will you accept?"

Flattery thought about this. He could refuse. Why not? What did he owe these . . . these . . . Shipmen, these *replay* survivors? But they were sufficiently human that he could interbreed with them. *Human*. And he still sensed that core of pain when he thought about a universe devoid of humans.

One last chance for humankind? It might be interesting . . . play. Or it might be one of Ship's illusions.

"Is all this just illusion, Ship?"

"No. The flesh exists to feel the things that flesh feels. Doubt everything except that."

"I either doubt everything or nothing."

"So be it. Will you play despite your doubts?"

"Will You tell me more about this play?"

"If you ask a correct question."

"What role am I playing?"

"Ahhhh . . ." It was a sigh of beatific grace. "You play the living challenge."

Flattery knew that role. Living challenge. You made people find the best within themselves, a best which they might not suspect they possessed. But some would be destroyed by such a demand. Remembering the pain of responsibility for such destruction, he wanted to help in his decision but knew he dared not ask directly. Perhaps if he learned more about Ship's plans . . .

"Have You hidden in my memory things about the game that I should know?"

"Raj!" There was no mistaking the outrage. It flowed through him as though his body were a sudden sieve thrust beneath a hot cascade. Then, more softly: "I do not steal your memories, Raj."

"Then I'm to be something *different*, a new factor, in this game. What else is different?"

"The place of the test possesses a difference so profound it may test *you* beyond your capacities, Raj."

The many implications of this answer filled him with wonder. So there were things even an all-powerful being did not know, things even God or Satan might learn.

Ship made him fearful then by commenting on his unspoken thought.

"Given that marvelous and perilous condition which you call

Time, power can be a weakness."

"Then what's this *profound difference* which will test me?"

"An element of the game which you must discover for yourself."

Flattery saw the pattern of it then: The decision had to be his own. Not compulsion. It was the difference between choice and chance. It was the difference between the precision of a holorecord replay and a brand-new performance where free will dominated. And the prize was another chance for humankind. *The Chaplain/ Psychiatrists' Manual* said: "God does not play dice with Man." Obviously, someone had been wrong.

"Very well, Ship. I'll gamble with You."

"Excellent! And, Raj—when the dice roll there will be no outside interference to control how they fall."

He found the phraseology of this promise interesting, but sensed the futility of exploring it. Instead, he asked: "Where will we play?"

"On this planet which I call Pandora. A small frivolity."

"I presume Pandora's box already is open."

"Indeed. All the evils that can trouble Mankind have been released."

"I've accepted Your request. What happens now?"

For answer, Flattery felt the hyb locks release him, the soft restraints pulling away. Light glowed around him and he recognized a dehyb laboratory in one of the shipbays. The familiarity of the place dismayed him. He sat up and looked around. All of that time and this . . . this *lab* remained unchanged. But of course Ship was infinite and infinitely powerful. Nothing outside of Time was impossible for Ship.

Except getting humankind to decide on their manner of WorShip.

What if we fail this time?

Would Ship really break the *recording?* He felt it in his guts: Ship would erase them. No more humankind . . . ever. Ship would go on to new distractions.

If we fail, we'll mature without flowering, never to send our seed through Infinity. Human evolution will stop here.

Have I changed in hyb? All that time . . .

He slipped out of the tank enclosure and padded across to a full-length mirror set into one of the lab's curved walls. His naked flesh appeared unchanged from the last time he had seen it. His face retained its air of quizzical detachment, an expression others often thought calculating. The remote brown eyes and upraked black eyebrows had been both help and hindrance. Something in the human psyche said such features belonged only to superior creatures. But superiority could be an impossible burden.

"Ahhh, you sense a truth," Ship whispered.

Flattery tried to swallow in a dry throat. The mirror told him that his flesh had not aged. Time? He began to grasp what Ship meant by such a length of Time which was meaningless. Hyb held flesh in stasis no matter what the passage of Time. No maturity there. But what about his mind? What about that reflected construct for which his brain was the receiver? He felt that something had ripened in his awareness.

"I'm ready. How do I get down to Pandora?"

Ship spoke from a vocoder above the mirror. "There are several ways, transports which I have provided."

"So You deliver me to Pandora. I just walk in on them. 'Hi. I'm Raja Flattery. I've come to give you a big pain in the head.' "

"Flippancy does not suit you, Raj."

"I feel Your displeasure."

"Do you already regret your decision, Raj?"

"Can You tell me anything more about the problems on Pandora?"

"The most immediate problem is their encounter with an alien intelligence, the 'lectrokelp."

"Dangerous?"

"So they believe. The 'lectrokelp is close to infinite and humans fear . . ."

"Humans fear open spaces, never-ending open spaces. Humans fear their own intelligence because it's close to infinite."

"You delight Me, Raj!"

A feeling of joy washed over Flattery. It was so rich and powerful that he felt he might dissolve in it. He knew that the sensation did not originate with him, and it left him feeling drained, transparent . . . bloodless.

Flattery pressed the heels of his hands against his tightly closed eyes. What a terrible thing that joy was! Because when it was gone . . . when it was gone . . .

He whispered: "Unless You intend to kill me, don't do that again."

"As you choose." How cold and remote.

"I want to be human! That's what I was intended to be!"

"If that's the game you seek."

Flattery sensed Ship's disappointment, but this made him defensive and he turned to questions.

"Have Shipmen communicated with this alien intelligence, this 'lectrokelp?''

"No. They have studied it, but do not understand it.''

Flattery took his hands away from his eyes. "Have Shipmen ever heard of Raja Flattery?''

"That's a name in the history which I teach them.''

"Then I'd better take another name.'' He ruminated for a moment, then: "I'll call myself Raja Thomas.''

"Excellent. Thomas for your doubts and Raja for your origins.''

"Raja Thomas, communications expert—Ship's best friend. Here I come, ready or not.''

"A game, yes. A game. And . . . Raj?''

"What?''

"For an infinite being, Time produces boredom. Limits exist to how much Time I can tolerate.''

"How much Time are You giving us to decide the way we'll WorShip?''

"At the proper moment you will be told. And one more thing—''

"Yes?''

"Do not be dismayed if I refer to you occasionally as My Devil.''

He was a moment recovering his voice, then: "What can I do about it? You can call me whatever You like.''

"I merely asked that you not be dismayed.''

"Sure! And I'm King Canute telling the tides to stop!''

There was no response from Ship and Flattery wondered if he was to be left on his own to find his way down to this planet called Pandora. But presently, Ship spoke once more: "Now we will dress you in appropriate costume, Raj. There is a new Chaplain/Psychiatrist who rules the Shipmen. They call him Ceepee and, when he offends them, they call him The Boss. You can expect that The Boss will order you to attend him soon.''

Perhaps the immobility of the things that surround us is forced upon them by our conviction that they are themselves and not anything else, and by the immobility of our conceptions of them.

—Marcel Proust,
Shiprecords

OAKES STUDIED his own image reflected in the com-console at his elbow. The curved screen, he knew, was what made the reflection diminutive.

Reduced.

He felt jumpy. No telling what the ship might do to him next. Oakes swallowed in a dry throat.

He did not know how long he had sat there hypnotized by that reflection. It was still nightside. An unfinished glass of Pandoran wine sat on a low brown table in front of him. He glanced up and around. His opulent cubby remained a place of shadows and low illumination, but something had changed. He could feel the change. Something . . . someone watching . . .

The ship might refuse to talk to him, deny him elixir, but he was getting messages—many messages.

Change.

That unspoken question which hovered in his mind had changed something in the air. His skin tingled and there was a throbbing at his temples.

What if the ship's program is running down?

56

His reflection in the blank screen gave no answer. It showed only his own features and he began to feel pride in what he saw there. Not just fat, no. Here was a mature man in his middle years. The Boss. The silver at his temples spoke of dignity and importance. And although he was . . . *plump*, his skin remained soft and clear, testimony to the care he took preserving the appearance of youth.

Women liked that.

What if the ship is Ship . . . is truly God?

The air felt dirty in his lungs and he realized he was breathing much too rapidly.

Doubts.

The damned ship was not going to respond to his doubts. Never had. Wouldn't talk to him; wouldn't feed him. He had to feed himself from the ship's limited hydroponics gardens. How long could he continue to trust them? Not enough food for everyone. The very thought increased his appetite.

He stared at the unfinished glass of wine—dark amber, oily on the inner surface of the glass. There was a wet puddle under the glass, a stain on the brown surface.

I'm the Ceepee.

The Ceepee was supposed to believe in Ship. In his own cynical way, old Kingston had insisted on this.

I don't believe.

Was that why a new Ceepee was being sent groundside?

Oakes ground his teeth together.

I'll kill the bastard!

He spoke it aloud, intensely aware of how the words echoed in his cubby.

"Hear that, Ship? I'll kill the bastard!"

Oakes half expected a response to this blasphemy. He knew this because he caught himself holding his breath, listening hard to the shadows at the edges of his cubby.

How did you test for godhood?

How do you separate a powerful mechanical phenomenology, a trick of technological mirrors, from a . . . from a miracle?

If God did not play dice, as the Ceepees were always told, what might God play? Perhaps dice was not challenge enough for a god. What was risk enough to tempt a god out of silence or reverie . . . out of a god's lair?

It was a stupefying question—to challenge God at God's own game?

Oakes nodded to himself.

In the game, perhaps, is the miracle. Miracle of Consciousness? It was no trick to make a machine self-programming, self-perpetuating. Complex, true, and unimaginably costly . . .

Not unimaginably, he cautioned himself.

He shook his head to drive out the half-dream.

If people did it, then it's imaginable, tangible, somehow explainable. Gods move in other circles.

The question was: *which* circles? And if you could define those circles, their limits, you could know the limits of the god within them. What limits, then? He thought about energy. Energy remained a function of mass and speed. Even a god might have to be somewhere within the denominator of—what kind of mass, how much, how fast?

Maybe godhood is simply another expansion of limits. Because our vision dims is no reason to conclude that infinity lies beyond.

His training as a Chaplain had always been subservient to his training as a scientist and medical man. He knew that to test data truly he could not close the doors on experiment or assume that what he wished would necessarily be so.

It was what you *did* with data, not the data, that was important. Every king, every emperor had to know that one. Even his theology master had agreed.

"Sell 'em on God. It's for their own good. Pin the little everyday miracles on God and you've got 'em; you don't need to move mountains. If you're good enough, people will move the mountains for you in the name of God."

Ahh, yes. That had been Edmond Kingston, a real Chaplain/Psychiatrist out of the ship's oldest traditions, but still a cynic.

Oakes heaved a deep sigh. Those had been quiet days shipside, days of tolerance and security of purpose. The machinery of the monster around them ran smoothly. God had been remote and most Shipmen remained in hyb.

But that had been before Pandora. Bad luck for old Kingston that the ship had put them in orbit around Pandora. Good old Edmond, dead on Pandora with the fourth settlement attempt. Not a trace recovered, not a cell. Gone now, into whatever passed for eternity. And Morgan Oakes was the second cynical Chaplain to take on the burden of Ship.

The first Ceepee not chosen by the damned ship!

Except . . . there was this new Ceepee, he reminded himself, *this man without a name who was being sent groundside to talk to the damned vegetables . . . the 'lectrokelp.*

He will not be my successor!

There were many ways that a man in power could delay things to his own advantage. *Even as I am now delaying the ship's request that we send this poet . . . this whatsisname, Panille, groundside.*

Why did the ship want a poet groundside? Did that have anything to do with this new Ceepee? A drop of sweat trickled into his right eye.

Oakes grew aware that his breathing had become labored. *Heart attack?* He pushed himself off the low divan. *Have to get help.* There was pain all through his chest. Damn! He had too many unfinished plans. He couldn't just go this way. *Not now!* He staggered to the hatch but the hatch dogs refused to turn under his fingers. The air was cooler here, though, and he grew aware of a faint hissing from the equalizer valve over the hatch. *Pressure difference?* He did not understand how that could be. The ship controlled the interior environment. Everyone knew that.

"What're you doing, you damned mechanical monster?" he whispered. "Trying to kill me?"

It was getting easier to breathe. He pressed his head against the cool metal of the hatch, drew in several deep breaths. The pain in his chest receded. When he tried the hatch dogs again they turned, but he did not open the hatch. He knew his symptoms could be explained by asphyxia . . . or anxiety.

Asphyxia?

He opened the hatch and peered out into an empty corridor, the dim blue-violet illumination of nightside. Presently, he closed the hatch and stared across his cubby.

Another message from the ship? He would have to go groundside soon . . . as soon as Lewis made it safe for him down there.

Lewis, get that Redoubt ready for us!

Would the ship really kill him? No doubt it could. He would have to be very circumspect, very careful. And he would have to train a successor. Too many things unfinished to have them end with his own death.

I can't leave the choice of my successor to the ship.

Even if it killed him, the damned ship could not be allowed to beat him.

It's been a long time. Maybe the ship's original program has run out.

What if Pandora were the place for a long winding-down process? Kick the fledglings out of the nest a millimeter at a time.

His gaze picked out details of the cubby: erotic wall hangings, servopanels, the soft opulence of divans . . .

Who will move in here after me?

He had thought he might choose Lewis, provided Lewis worked out well. Lewis was bright enough for some dazzling lab work, but dull politically. A dedicated man.

Dedicated! He's a weasel and does what he's told.

Oakes crossed to his favorite divan, fawn soft cushions. He sat down and fluffed the cushions under the small of his back. What did he care about Lewis? This flesh that called itself Oakes would be long gone when the next Chaplain took over. At the very least he would be in hyb, dependent on the systems of the ship. And it may not be a good idea to tempt Lewis with that much power, power that would be contingent upon Oakes' own death. After all, death was the specialty of Jesus Lewis.

"No, no," Lewis had said to Oakes privately, "it's not death— I give them life. *I* give them *life*. They're engineered clones, Doctor, E-clones. I remind you of that. If I give them life, for whatever purpose, it is mine to take away."

"I don't want to hear it." He waved Lewis away with a brush of his hand.

"Have it your way," Lewis said, "but that doesn't change the facts. I do what I have to do. And I do it for you . . ."

Yes, Lewis was a brilliant man. He had learned many new and useful genetic manipulation techniques from the genetics of the 'lectrokelp, that most insidious indigent species on Pandora. And it had cost them dearly.

A successor? What *real* choice would he make, if he truly believed in the process and the godhood of Ship? If he could exclude all the nastiness of politics?

Legata Hamill.

The name caught him off guard, it came so quickly. Almost as though he did not think it himself. Yes, it was true. He would choose Legata if he believed, if he truly believed in Ship. There was no reason why a woman could not be Chaplain/Psychiatrist. No doubt of her diplomatic abilities.

Some wag had once said that Legata could tell you to go to hell and make you anticipate the trip with joy.

Oakes pushed aside the cushions and levered himself to his feet. The hatch out into the dim passages of nightside beckoned him—that maze of mazes which meant life to them all: the ship.

Had the ship really tried to asphyxiate him? Or had that been an accident?

I'll put myself through a medcheck first thing dayside.

The hatch dogs felt cold under his fingers, much colder than just moments before. The oval closure swung soundlessly aside to reveal once more nightside's blue-violet lighting in the corridor.

Damn the ship!

He strode out and, around the first corner, encountered the first few people of the Behavioral watch. He ignored them. The Behavioral complex was so familiar that he did not see it as he passed through. Biocomputer Study, Vitro Lab, Genetics—all were part of his daily routine and did not register on his nightside consciousness.

Where tonight?

He allowed his feet to find the way and realized belatedly that his wanderings were taking him farther and farther into the outlying regions, farther along the ship's confused twistings of passages and through mysterious hums and odd odors—farther out than he had ever wandered before.

Oakes sensed that he was walking into a peculiar personal danger, but he could not stop even as his tensions mounted. The ship was able to kill him at any moment, anywhere shipside, but he took a special private knowledge with him: he was Morgan Oakes, Ceepee. His detractors might call him "The Boss," but he was the only person here (with the possible exception of Lewis) who understood there were things the ship would not do.

Two of us among many. How many?

They had no real census shipside or groundside. The computers refused to function in this area, and attempts at manual counting varied so widely they were useless.

The ship showing its devious hand again.

Just as the ship's machinations could be sensed in this order for a poet groundside. He remembered the full name now: Kerro Panille. Why should a poet be ordered groundside to study the kelp?

If we could only eat the kelp without it driving us psychotic.

Too many people to feed. Too many.

Oakes guessed ten thousand shipside and ten times that groundside (not counting the special clones), but no matter the numbers, *he* was the only person who realized how little knowledge his people had about the workings and purposes of the ship or its parts.

His people!

Oakes liked it that way, recalling the cynical comment of his mentor, Edmond Kingston, who had been talking about the need to limit the awareness of the people: "*Appearing to know the unknown is almost as useful as actually knowing.*"

From his own historical studies, Oakes knew that this had been a political watchword for many civilizations. This one thing stood out even though the ship's records were not always clear and he did not completely trust the ship's versions of history. It often was difficult to distinguish between real history and contrived fictions. But from the odd literary references and the incompatible datings of such works—from internal clues and his own inspired guess-work—Oakes deduced that other worlds and other people existed . . . or *had* existed.

The ship could have countless murders on its conscience. If it had a conscience.

*As I am your creation, you are Mine. You are My
satellites and I am yours. Your personas are My im-
personations. We melt into ONE at the touch of infinity.*

—Raja Flattery,
The Book of Ship

FROM THE instant the Redoubt's first hatchway exploded, Jesus
Lewis stayed within arm's length of his bodyguard, Illuyank. It
was partly a conscious decision. Even in the worst of times, Illuyank inspired a certain confidence. He was a heavily muscled
man, dark-skinned, with black wavy hair and a stone-cut face
accented by three blue chevrons tattooed above his left eyebrow.
Three chevrons—Illuyank had run outside around the Colony Perimeter three times, naked, armed only with his wits and endur-
ance, "running the P" for a bet or a date.

Testing their luck, some called it. When the hatch blew, they
all needed luck. Some of them were barely awake and had not yet
eaten their first dayside meal.

"The clones got a lasgun!" Illuyank shouted. His clear, dark
eyes worked the area. "Dangerous. They don't know how to use
it."

The two men stood in a passage between the clones' quarters
and a random huddle of survivors who waited behind them near
a half-circle of hatches leading to the core of the Redoubt. Even
in this moment of peril, Lewis knew how he must appear to the

63

others. He was a short man, thin all the way—thin straw-colored hair, thin mouth, thin chin made even more so by a deep cleft, a thin nose, and oddly dark eyes which never seemed to reflect light in the thin compression of his lids. Beside him, Illuyank was everything Lewis was not.

Both stared toward the core of the Redoubt.

There was a real question in their minds whether the core of the Redoubt remained secure.

Knowing this, Lewis had deactivated the communications pellet buried in the flesh of his neck and refused to answer it even when insistent calls from Oakes tempted him.

No telling who might be able to listen!

There had been some disquieting indications lately that their private communications channel might not be as private as he had hoped. By now, Oakes would have received word about the new Ceepee. Discussion of that and the possible breach of their private communications system would have to wait.

Oakes would have to be patient.

At the first sign of trouble, Lewis had hit an emergency signal switch to alert Murdoch at Colony. There was no certainty, though, that the signal had gone through. He had not been allowed time for a retransmit-check. And the whole Redoubt had gone onto emergency power then. Lewis had no way of knowing which systems might be working and which not.

The damned clones!

A loud *whirr* sounded from the direction of the clones' quarters. Illuyank flattened himself on the floor and the others were showered with shards of passage wall.

"I thought they didn't know how to use that lasgun!" Lewis shouted. He pointed at a gaping hole in the wall as Illuyank leaped up and spun him around toward the others at the hatch circle.

"Downshaft!" Illuyank called.

One of the waiting group whirled the downshaft hatchdogs and opened the way into a passage lighted only by the blue flickering of emergency illumination.

Lewis sprinted blindly behind Illuyank, heard the others scrambling after them. Illuyank shouted back at him as he ran: "They don't know how to use it and that's what makes it dangerous!" Illuyank tucked and rolled across an open side passage as he spoke, firing a quick burst down the passage from his gusgun. "They could hit anything anywhere!"

Lewis glanced down the open passage as he ran past, glimpsed a scattering of bodies blazing there.

It soon became apparent where Illuyank was leading them and Lewis admired the wisdom of it. They took a left turn into a new passage, then a right turn and found themselves in the Redoubt's unfinished back corridors, skirting the native rock of the cliffside into the small Facilities Room on the beach side. One plasma-glass window overlooked the sea, the courtyard and the corner where the clones' quarters joined the Redoubt itself.

The last of the followers dogged the hatch behind them. Lewis took quick stock of his personnel—fifteen people, only six of them from his personally chosen crew. The others, rated reliable by Murdoch, had not yet been tested.

Illuyank had moved to the maze of controls at the cliff wall and was poring over the Redoubt's schematics etched into a master plate there. It occurred to Lewis then that Illuyank was the only survivor from Kingston's mission to this chunk of dirt and rock named Black Dragon.

"Is this how it was with Kingston?" Lewis asked. He forced his voice to an even calm while watching Illuyank trace a circuit with one stubby finger.

"Kingston cried and hid behind rocks while his people died. Runners got him. I cooked them out."

Cooked them out! Lewis shuddered at the euphemism. The grotesque image of Kingston's head crisped to char grinned across his mind.

"Tell us what to do." Lewis was surprised at his control under this fear.

"Good." Illuyank looked directly at him for the first time. "Good. Our weapons are these." He indicated the power switches and valve controls around them. "We can control every circuit, gas and liquid from here."

Lewis touched Illuyank's arm and pointed to a one-meter square panel beside him.

"Yes." Illuyank hesitated.

"We're blind otherwise," Lewis said.

For answer, Illuyank tapped out a code on the console beneath the square. The blank panel slid back to reveal four small view-screens.

"Sensors," one of those behind them said.

"Eyes and ears," Lewis said, still looking at Illuyank.

The dark man's expression did not change, but he whispered to Lewis: "We also will have to see and hear what we do to them."

Lewis swallowed and heard a faint *snap-snapping* at the hatch.

"They're cutting in!" a voice quavered behind them.

Lewis and Illuyank scanned the screens. One showed the rubble that had been the clones' quarters. *I'M HUNGRY NOW!*, the new rallying cry of the clones, was smeared in yellow grease across one wall. The adjoining screen scanned the courtyard. A crowd of mutated humans—E-clones all—scoured the grounds for rocks and bits of glass, anything for a weapon.

"Keep an eye on them" Illuyank whispered. "They can't hurt us with that stuff, but all that blood out there will bring demons. There are holes all over our perimeter. If demons hit, they'll catch that bunch first."

Lewis nodded. He could hear some of the others pressing close for a better view.

Once more, there was that *snap-snapping* at the hatch.

Lewis glanced at Illuyank.

"They're just pounding at us with rocks," Illuyank said. "What we have to do is find that lasgun. Meanwhile, keep an eye on the courtyard. The blood..."

The lower left-hand screen showed the clone mess hall, a shambles of security hatches broken open in the background, a turmoil of clones throughout the area. This screen suddenly went blank.

"Sensor's gone in the mess hall," Lewis said.

"Food will keep them busy there for a time," Illuyank said. He was busy searching through the Redoubt on the remaining screen. It showed a flash of the courtyard from a different angle, then a broken tangle of perimeter wall, cut to pieces by the lasgun and swarming with clones coming in from the outside where Lewis had ejected them, the action which had ignited this revolt.

We have to cull them somehow, Lewis told himself. *The food will go only so far.*

He turned his attention to the screen showing the courtyard. Yes...there was a lot of blood. It made him aware that he was badly cut himself. Celltape stopped his major bleeding, but small cuts began to ache as he thought of his condition. None of them was without injury. Even Illuyank bled slightly from a rock cut above his ear.

"There," Illuyank said.

His voice coincided with a new thump and crackling agitation at the hatch. But the COA screen Illuyank had been using now showed the passage outside their hatch. It was filled with a mass of clone flesh: furred bodies, strange limbs, oddly shaped heads. At the hatch two of the strongest clones were trying to maneuver a plasteel cutter, but their actions were impeded by the press of others behind them.

"That'll get them in here for sure," someone said. "We're cooked."

Illuyank turned and barked orders, pointing, waving a hand until all fifteen were busy in the Facilities Room—a valve to control, a switch to throw; each had some particular responsibility.

Lewis keyed for sound in the screen and a confused babble came over the speakers.

Illuyank signaled to a man at the remote valve controls across the room. "Dump the brine tanks into level two! That'll flood the outer passage."

The man worked his controls, muttering as he followed the schematics at his position.

Illuyank touched Lewis on the elbow, pointed to the screen which showed the courtyard. The clones there were looking away from the sensor, all of them at full alert, their attention on a broken segment of wall which led to the perimeter. Abruptly, almost as one organism, they dropped their rocks and glass weapons and ran screaming off-screen.

"Runners," Illuyank muttered.

Lewis saw them then, a waving swarm of tiny pale worm shapes cresting the rubble. He could almost smell the burned acid and tasted acid in his throat. Automatically, he gave the orders.

"Seal off."

"We can't," a timid voice from the edge of the room began. "Some of our people are still out there. If we seal off . . . if we . . . they'll all . . ."

"They'll all die," Lewis finished for him. "And our perimeter's full of holes. Runners are in the courtyard. If we don't seal off we die, too. Seal off!"

He crossed to a valve-control panel, punched the proper sequence. Lights above the panel showed that the indicated valve was closing. He could hear others around him obeying. Illuyank's voice intruded with a quiet warning: "Check the surface shafts." This brought another bustle of activity.

Lewis glanced at the courtyard screen. A clone stumbled back into the sensor's range, screaming and beating at his eyes with the blunt knobs which passed for his hands. As he moved into range, he fell and lay twisting on the ground. A blur of writhing shadows swept over him. The courtyard filled with fleeing clones and tiny, eel-like bodies. Behind Lewis, one of their group could be heard vomiting.

"They're in the passage," Illuyank said. He gestured at the sensor where the view outside their hatch showed brine rising in the passage with a swarming mass of Nerve Runners riding in on the wave.

Lewis shot a frantic glance at the hatch. What the sensor revealed was happening right out there!

The brine stopped short of the passage ceiling, but not before it had shorted out the plasteel cutter.

Clones were thrashing in the water, Nerve Runners covering them, but here and there dead Runners could be seen on the brine's surface. And where the plasteel cutter had shorted out, a milky gray gas clouded the thin space over the water. Wherever the gas touched, Runners died.

Lewis felt his mind leaping from item to item. Item: *brine*. Item: *electrical short*.

"Chlorine," he whispered. Then louder: "Chlorine!"

"What?" Illuyank was clearly puzzled.

Lewis pointed at the screen. "Clorine kills Nerve Runners!"

"What's chlorine?"

"A gas created when you throw an electrical charge through sodium chloride brine."

"But . . ."

"Chlorine kills Runners!" Lewis looked across the Facilities Room where the plaz-glass barrier showed a corner of clone area and the ocean beyond. "Are the sea pumps still working?"

The man at the pump console checked his keyboard, then: "Most of them."

"Sea water wherever we can put it," Lewis said. "We need a large container where we can dump it from here and throw an electrical charge through it."

"Water purification," Illuyank said. "The purification plant. We can pump almost everywhere from there."

"Wait a bit," Lewis said. "We want to attract as many Runners as we can; make them easier to wipe out."

He watched the screens, dragging it out, then: "All right, let's hit them."

Once more, Illuyank scanned his schematics, throwing orders

over his shoulder while the survivors in the Facilities Room obeyed.

Lewis fixed his attention on the sensor screens. The outer passage was quiet now—a few dead E-clones floating on the surface of the brine, many dead Runners among them. He tuned the mess-room screen to another sensor eye, found the exercise bay outside the clone labs. It was filled with a thrashing crowd of E-clones in absolute panic and, here and there among them, some of his own people caught outside when he had given the order to seal off. There were not many recognizable faces, but the colors of the uniforms could be identified. One by one, they died, their mouths frothing pink and their last stares turned upward toward the sensor.

Even as the last of them were dying, a milky cloud of gas had begun to sweep out of an open passage, drifting across the scene, blurring it.

"Watch their eyes," Illuyank said. "If we don't get all the Runners, they'll go for the eyes first."

All was quiet in the Facilities Room then as the survivors listened to their own precious breath, felt the comfort of their own live sweat and watched the eyes of the dead outside for some reflection of their own mortality.

Lewis leaned against the lip of the console, feeling cold metal under his fingers. Other screens showed more of the milky gas billowing through the Redoubt. There were even sensor eyes still alive to show the area outside their perimeter, the gas drifting across the open ground there. Illuyank scanned from sensor to sensor.

Someone behind Lewis heaved a shuddering sigh and Lewis echoed it.

"Chlorine," Illuyank muttered.

"We'll be able to sterilize the Runner boils right out of existence now," Lewis said. "If we'd only known . . ."

"A nasty way to learn," someone behind them said.

And someone else said: "It'll be a long wait."

"Waiting's that way," Illuyank said. "Think how long you live if you're always waiting."

It was an insightful comment, deeper than anything Lewis had ever expected from Illuyank. And it meant that Illuyank would have to be shifted to a tour of duty Colonyside. He saw too much, deduced too much. That could not be permitted. First, though, they had to get out of here. But there was no way out except into the Runner-contaminated open areas of the Redoubt. The chlorine would make that possible . . . in time.

"Can we get a message to Murdoch?" Lewis asked.

"Emergency transmitter only," Illuyank said.

"Send him the emergency shut-down signal. No one comes in here until we've cleaned up. It wouldn't do to have anyone see what's happened and . . ." Lewis directed a loaded look at Illuyank.

Illuyank nodded, and provided Lewis with the perfect opening for what had to be done. "Someone should go Colonyside, though, and see that they understand."

"That had better be you," Lewis said. "Make sure they don't try to explain anything to The Boss shipside. That's my job."

"Right."

"Don't tell them any more than you have to. And . . . while you're there, try to circulate in the Colony—everything normal, routine. Accept the usual assignments . . ."

"And try to find out if word of this . . ." Illuyank glanced at the sensor screens. ". . . has leaked out."

"Good man."

And Lewis thought: *too good.*

Just as a technician learns to use his tools, you can be taught to use other people to create whatever you desire. This becomes more potent when you can create the special person for your special purpose.

—Morgan Oakes,
The Diaries

LEGATA HAMILL knew groundside was to be their permanent home eventually, but she did not like these courier jobs on which Oakes sent her. There was a sense of power in them, though; no denying it. Her pass (often just an identifying look at her by a guard) admitted her anywhere. She was an arm of Morgan Oakes. She knew what they saw when they looked at her: a small woman with pale skin and ebon hair, a figure almost lush in its femininity. They saw a woman The Boss wanted and who, because of that, was powerful and dangerous.

Every inspection trip she took for Oakes created tension.

This time she was to inspect Lab One at Colony. And all of it would be on holo to make a full record for Oakes to review.

"Penetrate it," Oakes had said.

The way he said "penetrate" had distinctly sexual overtones.

She had never been into the Lab One depths before and that alone piqued her curiosity. Lewis had a trusted minion here, Sy Murdoch. She was to meet Murdoch. Usually, Lewis was to be found in the shiny plasteel environs of the lab which was entered

71

via a triple-lock system at the end of a long tunnel. Not today. *Lewis was out of communication.* A strange way of putting it; and there was no doubt that Oakes was disturbed by this development.

"Find out where the hell he is, what he's doing!"

Both suns had been in the sky when the shuttle brought her down. Maximum flare security had been in force. She had been hustled out of the landing complex and into a servo which deposited her at the tunnel. The Colony personnel were quick and harried today—rumors of perimeter difficulties with Pandora's many demons.

Legata shuddered. Any thought of the predatory creatures which roamed the landscape beyond Colony's barriers filled her with apprehension.

Murdoch himself met her in the brightly lighted and bustling area where the last lock sealed off the entrance within the lab. He was a blocky man, light complexion and blue eyes, with cropped brown hair. His fingers were short and stubby, the nails well trimmed. He always appeared recently scrubbed.

"What is it this time?" he demanded.

She liked the energy focus in his question. It said: *We're busy here. What does Oakes want now?*

Very well, she could match that mood. "Where's Lewis?"

Murdoch glanced around to see who might overhear them. Seeing no workers nearby, he said: "Redoubt."

"Why doesn't he answer our calls?"

"Don't know."

"What was his last message?"

"Emergency code. Hold all transports. No craft permitted to land at Redoubt. Wait for clearance signal."

Legata absorbed this. *Emergency.* What was happening across the waters at the Redoubt?

"Why wasn't Doctor Oakes informed?"

"The code signal called for complete security."

She understood this. No transmissions from Colony to Ship could carry a message involving that restriction. But that was two full Pandoran diurns ago. She sensed another restriction in the last message from the Redoubt, a private Lewis restriction to his own minions. It would be pointless to explore such a conjecture, but she felt its presence.

"Have you sent an overflight?"

"No."

So that was restricted, too. Bad . . . very bad. Well, then, she had to get on to the rest of her assignment.

"I'm here to inspect the lab."

"I know."

Murdoch had been studying this woman while they talked. The orders transmitted from The Boss were clear. She was to go into everything except the Scream Room. That would come later for her...as it came for everyone here. She was a pretty thing: a pocket Venus with a doll face and green eyes. She had a good brain, too, by all accounts.

"If you know, let's get going," she said.

"This way."

He led her down a passage between banked vats of primary clonewombs into the Micro-micro Processing section.

At first, Legata's interest was intellectual—she knew this and it comforted her. Murdoch even took her hand at one point, leading her past rows of special-application clonewombs. He was so intent in his rhapsody on equipment and techniques that she did not mind his touch. It was, after all, clinical. Or unintentional. Whichever, Murdoch's touch was not born out of affection; this she knew.

But he knew Lab One as few others could, even perhaps as well as Lewis, and she had never been told to go deep into it before.

"...but I've accepted that as true," Murdoch was saying, and she had missed the point, being more intent on an incomplete fetus of odd proportions floating behind a screen of transparent plaz.

She looked at Murdoch. "Accepted what? I'm sorry, I was...I mean, there's so much to see."

"Plasteel by the kilometer, tanks and fluids, pseudo-bodies, pseudo-minds..." He waved his hand in frustration.

She realized that Murdoch was in a particularly manic mood and this bothered her. She felt the need to suppress unspoken questions about that odd fetus floating behind the screen of plasma glass.

"So you've accepted all this," she said. "So what?"

"We *birth* here. We conceive people here, nurture them fetally, extract them, send some shipside for training...Doesn't it strike you as odd that we can't bring *natural* births groundside, too?"

"What Ship decides is for good reason, for the good of..."

"...of Shipmen everywhere. I know. I've heard it as often as you have. But Ship did *not* decide. Nowhere in the records can anyone—even you, the best Search Technician we have, so I'm told—find where Ship has demanded that all births take place shipside. Nowhere."

Without knowing how she knew it, Legata realized he was

repeating Lewis' words verbatim. This was not Murdoch's manner of speaking. Why was she supposed to hear this? Was it part of Oakes' scheme to do away with the shipside obstetrics force, the Natali?

"But we are required to WorShip," she said. "And what greater WorShip can we have than to entrust Ship with our children? It makes sense, too . . ."

"It makes sense, it has logic," he agreed. "But it is *not* a direct command. And it makes a good deal of our work here in Lab One unnecessarily limited. Why, we could . . ."

"Own this world? Morgan says you can do it anyway."

There, let him chew on that. *Morgan*, not The Boss, not Doctor Oakes.

Murdoch dropped her hand and the flush of elation washed out of his cheeks.

He knows we're on holo, she thought, *and I've ruined his act.*

It occurred to her then that Murdoch had been playing to another audience, to Oakes. If the emergency at the Redoubt over on Black Dragon turned out fatal for Lewis . . . yes, they would need a replacement. She imagined Oakes' attention on them later from some metallic scanner shipside. But she wanted Murdoch to squirm a bit more. She took his hand and said, "I'd like to see The Garden."

Her statement was only half-true. She had seen the catalogues which Oakes kept securely locked away, the wide selection of E-clones grown to special purposes here—any purpose, it seemed. Fewer than a dozen people shipside were even aware that such a process existed. And here at Colony, Lab One was a complex of its own, secreted away from the rest of the buildings, its purpose shrouded in the mystique of its name.

Lab One.

When asked what went on at Lab One, people usually said, "Ship only knows." Or they began some childish ghost story of hunchbacked scientists peering into the heart of life itself.

Legata knew that Oakes and Lewis even encouraged the mystery, often started their own rumors. The result was a fearsome aura about the place, and recently there had been mutterings about the disproportionate supply of food allotted to Lab One. To be assigned here, in the minds of Shipmen and Colonists alike, was to disappear forever. All workers moved into quarters at the complex and, with few exceptions, did not return shipside or to Colony proper.

These thoughts left her with a feeling of unsettled doubts, and she had to remind herself: *I'm not being assigned here*. No, that wouldn't happen, not as long as Oakes wanted to get her naked on his couch . . . to *penetrate* her.

Legata took a deep breath of warm air. As in all Colony buildings, temperature and humidity were identical with Ship's. Here in the lab, though, her flesh shuddered off a special kind of chill, a gooseflesh that made her stomach ache and jabbed needles of pain into the knots that her nipples made against her singlesuit. She spoke quickly to mask her disquiet.

"Your staff people, they look so old."

"Many of them have been with us from the start."

There was evasion in his voice and it did not go unnoticed, but Legata chose to watch, not push.

"But they . . . look even older than *that*. What . . ."

Murdoch interrupted her. "We have a higher fatality rate than Colony, did you know that?"

She shook her head. It was a lie; had to be a lie.

"It's being out here on the perimeter," Murdoch said. "We don't get the protection everyone else does. Nerve Runners are particularly heavy this close to the hills."

An uncontrollable shudder swept over her arms. *Nerve Runners*! Those darting little worms were the most feared of all Pandoran creatures. They had an affinity for nerve cells and would eat their way slowly, agonizingly along human nerve channels until they gorged on the brain, encysted and reproduced.

"Bad," Murdoch said, seeing her reaction. "And the workload we carry here, of course . . . but that's agreed on from the start. These are the most dedicated people groundside."

She looked across a bank of plaz vats at a group of these dedicated workers—blank, tight-lipped faces. Most of those she had seen here were wrinkled and drawn, pale. No one joked; not even a nervous giggle broke the monotony. All was the clink and click of instruments, the hum of tools, the aching distance between lives.

Murdoch flashed her a sudden smile. "But you wanted to see The Garden." He turned, waved a hand for her to follow. "This way."

He led her through another system of locks, only doubles this time, into what appeared to be a training area for young E-clones. There were several of them around the entrance, but they drew back at Murdoch's approach.

Fearful, Legata thought.

There was a circular barrier across the training area and she identified another lock entrance.

"What's over there?" She nodded.

"We won't be able to go in there today," Murdoch said. "We're sterilizing in there."

"Oh? What's in there?"

"Well . . . that's the core of The Garden. I call it the Flower Room." He turned toward a group of the young E-clones nearby. "Now, here we have some of the young products from the Flower Room. They . . ."

"Does your Flower Room have another name?" she asked. She did not like his answers. Too evasive. He was lying.

Murdoch turned to face her and she felt threatened by the pouncing glee in his eyes. Guilty knowledge lay there—dirty, guilty knowledge.

"Some call it the Scream Room," he said.

Scream Room?

"And we can't go in there?"

"Not . . . today. Perhaps if you made an appointment for later?"

She controlled a shudder. The way he watched her, the avaricious glint to his eyes.

"I'll come back to see your . . . Flower Room later," she said.

"Yes. You will."

From you, Avata learns of a great poet-philosopher
who said: "Until you meet an alien intelligence, you
will not know what it is to be human."

And Avata did not know what it was to be Avata.

True, and poetic. But poetry is what's lost in translation. Thus, we now permit you to call this place
Pandora and to call us Avata. The first among you,
though, called us vegetable. In this, Avata saw the
deeper meaning of your history and felt fear. You
ingest vegetable to use the energy gathered by others.
With you, the others end. With Avata, the others
live. Avata uses minerals, uses rock, uses sea, uses
the suns—and from all this, Avata nurses life. With
rock, Avata calms the sea and silences the turbulence
inherited from the rip of suns and moons.

Knowing human, Avata remembers all. It is best
to remember so Avata remembers. We eat our history
and it is not lost. We are one tongue and one mind;
the storms of confusions cannot steal us from one
another, cannot pry us from our grip to rock, to the
firmament that cups the sea around us and washes
us clean with the tides. This is so because we make
it so.

We fill the sea and calm it with our body. The
creatures of water find sanctuary in Avata's shadow,
feed in our light. They breathe the riches we exude.
They fight among themselves for what we discard.
They ignore us in their ravages and we watch them

grow, watch them flare in the sea like suns and disappear into the far side of night.

The sea feeds us; it washes in and out, and we return to the sea in kind. Rock is Avata's strength and as strength grows so grows the nest. Rock is Avata's communion, ballast and blood. With all this, Avata orders quiet in the sea and subdues the fitful rages of the tides. Without Avata, the sea screams its fury in rock and ice; it whips the winds of hot madness. Without Avata, the rage of the sea returns to smother this globe in blackness and a thin white horizon of death.

This is so because we make it so—Avata: barometer of life.

Atom to atom to molecule; molecule to chain and chain winding around and around the magnificence of light; then cell to cell, and cell to blastula, cilia to tentacle, and from stillness blossoms the motion of life.

Avata harvests the mysterious gas of the sea and is born into the world of clouds and mountains, into the world the stars walk in fear. Avata sails high with the gas from the sea to find the country of the spark of life. There, Avata gives self to love, thence back to the sea, and the circle is complete but unfinished.

Avata feeds and is fed. Sheltered, Avata shelters, eats and is eaten, loves and is loved. Growth is the Avata way. In growth is life. As death resides in stillness, Avata strives for stillness in growth, a balance of flux, and Avata lives.

This is so because Avata makes it so.

If you know this of the alien intelligence and still find it alien, you do not know what it is to be human.

—Kerro Panille,
Translations from the *Avata*

You are called Project Consciousness, but your true goal is to explore beyond the imprinted pattern of all humankind. Inevitably, you must ask: Is consciousness only a special kind of hallucination? Do you raise consciousness or lower its threshold? The danger in the latter course is that you bring up the military analogue: you are confined to action.

—Original Charge to the Voidship Chaplain/Psychiatrist

ON THESE nightside walks through the ship. Oakes liked to move without purpose, without the persona of Ceepee tagging along. He had worked long and hard to remain just a name both shipside and groundside. Few saw his face and most of his official duties were carried out by minions. There was the routine WorShip in the corridor chapels, the food allotments groundside, a minimal endorsement of the many functions that the ship carried out with no human intervention. Ceepee rule was supposed to be nominal. But he wanted more.

Kingston had once said: "We have too damned much idle time. We're idle hands and we can get into trouble."

Memories of Kingston were much with Oakes this night as he took his nocturnal prowl. Through the outer passages, sensor eyes and ears dotted corridor walls and ceilings. They strung themselves ahead and behind in diminishing vectors of attention, dim glistenings in the blue-violet nightside lighting.

Still no word from Lewis. This rankled. Legata's preliminary report left too many unanswered questions. Was Lewis striking out on his own? Impossible! Lewis did not have the guts for such a move. He was the eternal behind-the-scenes operator, not a front man.

What was the emergency, then?

Oakes felt that too many things were coming to a head around him. They could not delay much longer on sending this poet, this Kerro Panille, groundside. And the new Ceepee the ship had brought out of hyb! Both poet and Ceepee would have to be bundled into the same package and watched carefully. And it would soon be time to start an eradication project against the kelp. People were getting hungry enough groundside that they were ready for scapegoats.

And that disturbing incident with the air in his cubby. Had the ship really tried to asphyxiate him? Or poison him?

Oakes turned a corner and found himself in a long corridor with iridescent green arrows on the walls indicating that it led outward from shipcenter. The ceiling sensors were dots receding into a converging distance.

Out of habit he noticed the activation of each sensor as he neared it. Each mechanical eye followed his pace faithfully, and, as he approached the limits of its vision, the next one rolled its wary cyclopean pupil around to catch his approach. He had to admit that, in Shipman or machine, he appreciated this sense of guarded watchfulness, but the idea that a possibly malevolent intelligence waited behind that movement set his nerves on edge.

He had never known a sensor to malfunction. To tamper with one meant dealing with a robox unit—a single-minded repair and defense device that respected no life or limb save that of Ship.

THE ship, dammit!

Those years of programming, preparation—even he could not shake them. How did he expect others of lesser will, lesser intelligence, to do so?

He sighed. He expected to sway no one. What he expected was that he would use the tools at hand. With intelligence, he felt that one could turn anything to advantage. Even a dangerous tool such as Lewis.

Another pair of sensors caught his attention, this time outside the access to the Docking Bays. It was quiet here and pervaded by that odd smell compounded from uncounted sleeping people. Not even freight moved during Colony's nightside which some-

times coincided with Shiptime, but often did not. All the industry
of dayside was put away for the community of sleep.

Except in two places, he reminded himself: life-support and
the agraria.

Oakes stopped and studied the line of sensors. He, of all Shipmen, should appreciate them. He had access to the movements
they recorded. Every detail of shipside life was supposed to be
his. And he had seen to it that the groundside colony was similarly
equipped. Ship's watchfulness was his own.

"The more we know, the stronger we are in our choices."

Kingston's voice came to him from his training days.

*What a raw but marvelously trainable bit of human material
I was!*

Kingston had been almost a master of control. Almost. And
control was a function of strong choices. When it came down to
it, Kingston had refused certain choices.

I do not refuse.

Choices resulted from information. He had learned that lesson
well.

But how can you know the result of every choice?

Oakes shook his head and resumed his wandering. The sense
that he walked into new dangers was an acute pressure in his
breast. But there was no stopping this, short of death. His feet
turned him down a passageway which he saw led to an agrarium.
There was the peculiar *green* smell of the passage even if he had
not recognized the wide cart tracks leading through an automatic
lock ahead. He stepped across the track-dump, through the lock
and found himself in a dimly lighted and frighteningly unbounded
space.

It was nightside here too. Even plants required that diurnal
pulse. An internally illuminated yellow wall map at his left showed
him his location and the best access routes out. It also showed
this agrarium. The largest extrusions of the ship were monopolized
for food production, but he had not entered one of those complexes
for years—not since provisioning that first attempted colony on
Pandora's Black Dragon continent. Long before they had gained
their Colony foothold on the Egg.

Kingston's first big mistake.

Oakes stepped closer to the map, aware of distant movement
far out in the agrarium but more interested in this symbol. He was
not prepared for what the map told him. The agrarium he had
entered was almost as large as the central core of the ship. It

spread out, fanlike, from roots in the original hull. Ship and Colony maintenance figures he had been initialing took on a new reality here. And the map's explanatory footnote was an exclamation point.

As Oakes looked on, the nightside shift of agrarium workers broke for their mid-meal WorShip. They did so as one and no perceptible signal passed among them, no reluctance of any sort evident. They moved together into the dim blue light of the WorShip alcove.

They believe! Oakes thought, *they really believe that the ship is God!*

As the shift supervisor led them in their litany, Oakes found himself washed in a sadness that came so suddenly and so hard that it held him on the verge of tears. He realized then that he envied them their faith, their small comfort of the ritual that was so much bother to him.

The supervisor, a squat, bowlegged man with dirt on his hands and knees, led them in the Chant of Sure Growth.

"Behold the bed of dirt," and he dropped a pinch of dirt to the floor.

"And the seed asleep in it," the crew responded, lifting their bowls and setting them down.

"Behold water," he dribbled some from his glass.

"And the waking it brings," they raised their glasses.

"Behold light," he lifted his face to the U-V racks overhead.

"And the life it opens," they spread their hands, palms up.

"Behold the fullness of the grain, the thickness of the leaf," he spooned from the communal pot, into the bowl to his left.

"And the seed of life it plants in us," each worker spooned a helping for the Shipman on his left.

"Behold Ship and the food Ship gives." The supervisor sat down.

"And the joy of company to share it," they said, and sat to eat.

Oakes turned away unnoticed.

The joy of company! he snorted to himself. If there were less company and more food there would be a damn sight more joy!

He moved along the rim of the ship's outer hull then, raw space only a few meters away. His mind was racing.

That agrarium could feed thirty thousand people. Instead of counting people, they could count agraria and add the support figures! He knew that groundside shipments supplied eighty percent of Colony stores. Here was a key to real numbers! Why had they not seen that before?

Even as he experienced elation at this thought, Oakes knew the ship would frustrate such an attempt. The damned ship did not want them to know how many people it supported. It blocked their attempts to count; it hid hyb complexes and confused you with meaningless corridors.

It brought a nameless Ceepee out of hyb and announced a new groundside project outside of Shipman control.

Well . . . accidents could happen groundside, too. And even a precious Ceepee from *Ship* could walk into a fatality.

What difference did it make? The new Ceepee was probably a clone. Oakes had seen the earliest records: Clones were property. Somebody who signed with the initials MH had said it. And there was an aura of power around that statement. Clones were property.

A word of caution about our genetic programs. When we breed for speed, we breed as well for very specific kinds of decisions. Speed chops out, edits out certain kinds of reflexive choices and long-term considerations. Everything becomes the decision of the moment.

—Jesus Lewis,
The E-Clone Directive

WHEN TEMPORARY seals had closed off the breaks in the perimeter of the Redoubt, Lewis directed the careful dayside cleanup of the interior. It was a long frustrating job, and they worked through the night with emergency lighting. The entire Redoubt stank of chlorine, so strong in some areas that they were forced to wear filters and portable breathing equipment.

In the morning, they drenched the courtyard with chlorine several times before daring to touch the corpses there. Even then, they moved the bodies with hastily improvised claw grabs attached to mobile equipment.

Chlorine everywhere, and the inevitable burns of both flesh and fabrics made it an even slower task.

At Sub-level Four, they came on a welcome surprise: twenty-nine clones and five more of the Redoubt crew sealed in an unlighted storage chamber—all of them hungry, thirsty and terrified. The chamber contained spare charges for the gushguns, permitting Lewis to add fire to the chlorine for a final sterilization sweep.

Lewis was surprised to find that the E-clones had not attacked the five crewmen. Then he learned that the crewmen had sounded the alarm at the Nerve Runner attack and herded the clones into the chamber. A sense of fellowship between E-clones and normals had developed during the long confinement. Lewis noted it as they emerged—clones helping normals and vice versa. Very dangerous, that. He gave sharp orders to separate them, clones to the more dangerous task of courtyard cleanup, normals to their regular supervisory tasks.

One observation particularly annoyed him: the sight of a trusted guard, Pattersing, being solicitous over a delicate female E-clone of the new mix. She was tall and emaciated by human standards, a light brown skin and large eyes. Her whole series was flawed by fragile bones, and Lewis had almost decided to abandon it— except that now she was one of his remaining examples of the genetic mix between human and Pandoran.

Perhaps Pattersing was merely being careful with valuable material. He must know how fragile the bones of this series were. Yes . . . that could be it.

Lewis was pleased to note other more successful examples of the new E-clones, the breed incorporating native genetic material. There would be no need to go back through that long, slow and costly development program. The disaster here at the Redoubt had not been total.

A mood of euphoria came over him as it became increasingly clear that they had sterilized the Redoubt, and that they had a new weapon effective against Runners.

"At least we've solved the food problem," he told Illuyank.

Illuyank gave him a strange, measuring look which Lewis did not like.

"Counting E-clones, there are only fifty of us left," Illuyank said.

"But we've saved the heart of the project," Lewis said.

Too late, Lewis realized he had said too much to this perceptive aide. Illuyank had proved himself capable of making correct deductions on limited information.

Well . . . Illuyank was going Colonyside. Murdoch would see to things there.

"We'll need replacements, lots of them," Illuyank persisted.

"I expect us to be stronger because of this testing" Lewis said.

Lewis diverted Illuyank then by ordering a complete inspection of the Redoubt—every corner, every bay, no space missed—chlorine and/or fire everywhere. They moved slowly through the passages and across the open areas, their progress marked by the hissing flames of the gushguns and great splashing washes of chlorine. Lewis ordered a final purging with chlorine gas, opening all valves, all hatches within the Redoubt. They then made another inspection with sensor eyes.

Clean. When it was finished, they pumped the chlorine residue onto the surrounding ground, following it by waves of gas which swept around the rocks and hillocks where the clones had huddled when he had ordered them thrust from the safety of the Redoubt.

Inevitably, some of the chlorine spilled over the cliff into the sea. It ignited a violent, churning retreat by the hallucinogenic kelp in the cove. A pack of hylighters came to the excitement. They floated at a safe distance over the surrounding hills, spectators, while Lewis and his meager force sterilized the area around the Redoubt.

Later, Lewis went grinding out of a lock in an armored vehicle to direct the outside sterilizing team, taking Illuyank as his driver. At one point, Lewis ordered Illuyank to stop and shut down while they studied the arc of hylighters in the distance. It was a scene framed by the thick barrier of plazglass in the crawler. The giant orange bags floated in disconcerting silence, anchored by long black tendrils twining in the rocks of the hills. They were a perimeter of mystery about three kilometers distant and they filled Lewis with angry fear.

"We'll have to eliminate those damned things!" he said. "They're floating bombs!"

"And maybe more," Illuyank said.

One of the surviving clones took this moment to drop his chlorine backpack. The clone turned to face the arc of hylighters, spread his stumpy arms wide and called out in a voice heard through the area: "Avata! Avata! Avata!"

"Get that damned fool out of here and into confinement!" Lewis ordered. Illuyank relayed the order over their vehicle's external speakers. Two supervisors scrambled to obey.

Lewis watched in grumbling impatience. *Avata*—that had been the other cry of the clone revolt. *Avata*, and, *We're hungry now!*

If the particular clone out there had not been one of the precious new ones with the genetic mix, Lewis knew he would have ordered the stupid creature killed immediately.

New security precautions would have to be put into effect, he told himself. Tougher rules about clone behavior. Oakes would have to be brought into these decisions. They would have to raid Colony, and Ship, for replacements—more clones, more staff, more guards, more supervisors. Murdoch and the Scream Room were going to be very busy for a time. Very busy. Well, gardening had always been a brutal business: root out the weeds, kill off the predatory grazers, destroy the pests. Lab One's special-purpose area was correctly labeled: The Garden. Producing flowers for Pandora.

"We've used up the chlorine and it looks clean out here," Illuyank said.

"Take us back inside," Lewis ordered. Then: "When you get back to Colony, I don't want any mention of the chlorine."

"Right."

Lewis nodded to himself. It was time now to consider what he would tell Oakes, how this disaster would be explained to make it an important victory.

Clones are property and that's that!

**—Morgan Hempstead,
Moonbase Director**

"THANK YOU for complying with my invitation."

Thomas watched the seated speaker carefully, wondering at the sense of peril aroused by such a simple statement. This was Morgan Oakes, Chaplain/Psychiatrist—the Ceepee, The Boss?

It was late dayside on Ship and Thomas had not been long enough from hyb to feel completely awake and familiar with his long-dormant flesh.

I am no longer Raja Flattery. I am Raja Thomas.

There could be no slip in the new facade, especially here.

"I have been studying your dossier, Raja Thomas," Oakes said.

Thomas nodded. That was a lie! The stress in the man's voice was obvious. Didn't Oakes realize how much he betrayed himself to trained senses? You could not believe a word this man uttered! He was careless—that was it.

Perhaps there are no other trained senses to test him.

"I responded to a summons, not to an invitation," Thomas said.

There! That was the kind of thing a Raja Thomas would say.

Oakes merely smiled and tapped a folder of thin Shippaper in his lap. A dossier? Hardly. Thomas knew that it was in Ship's interest to conceal the real identity of this new player in the game.

88

Thomas! I am Thomas! He glanced around the Shipcell to which Oakes had *invited* him, realizing belatedly that this once had been a cubby. Oakes had taken out bulkheads to expand the cubby. Then, as Thomas recognized a mystical decorative motif between two dark-red woven wall hangings, he suffered one of the worst shocks in this awakening.

This was my cubby!

It was obvious that Ship had expanded enormously since those faraway Voidship days when it had housed only a few thousand hybernating humans and a minimal umbilicus crew. The changes he had seen on the trip here from hybernation hinted at even deeper changes behind them. What had happened to Ship?

This expanded cubby suggested an unsavory history. The space was sybaritic with exotic hangings, deep orange carpeting, soft divans. Except for a small holoprojection at Oakes' left hand, all the cubby's expected servosystems had been concealed.

Oakes was giving his visitor plenty of time to study the space around him, using the time to return that scrutiny. What was Ship's intent with this mysterious newcomer? The question was engraved large on Oakes' face.

Thomas found his own attention caught by the computer-driven projection at the holofocus. It was a familiar three-dimensional analogue of a ship orbiting a planet, all glittering green and orange and black. Only the planetary system was unfamiliar; it had two suns and several moons. And as he watched the slow progression of the ship's orbit, he felt an odd sense of déjà vu. He was in motion in a ship in motion in a universe in motion . . . and it had all happened before.

Replay?

Ship said not, but . . . Thomas shrugged off such doubts, reserving them for later. He did not have to be told that the planet in the focus was Pandora and that this projection represented a real-time version of Ship's position in the system. Some things did not change no matter the great passage of time. Bickel had once monitored such a projection on the Voidship *Earthling*.

Morgan Oakes sat on a deep divan of rust velvet while Raja Thomas stood—an unsubtle accent on their positions in a hierarchy which Thomas had not yet analyzed.

"I'm told you are a Chaplain/Psychiatrist," Oakes said. And he thought: *This man does not respond to his name in a quite normal way.*

"That was my training, yes."

"Expert in communication?"

Thomas shrugged.

"Ahhh, yes." Oakes was pleased with himself. "That remains to be tested. Tell me why you have asked for the poet."

"Ship asked for the poet."

"So you say."

Oakes allowed silence to follow this challenge.

Thomas studied the man. Oakes was portly-going-on-fat, dark complexion, faint odor of perfume. His gray-streaked hair had been combed forward to conceal a receding hairline. The nose was sharp and flared at the nostrils, the mouth thin and given to a tight, stretching grimace; the chin was wide and cleft. The man's eyes dominated this rather common Shipman face. They were light blue and they probed, boring in, always trying to penetrate every surface they found. Thomas had seen such eyes on people diagnosed as psychotic.

"Do you like what you see?" Oakes asked.

Again, Thomas shrugged.

Oakes did not like this response. "What is it you see in me which requires such scrutiny?"

Thomas stared at the man. The genotype was recognizable and that first name was suggestive. Oakes could have Lon as a middle name. If Oakes were a clone instead of a replay-survivor rescued from a dying planet... yes, that would be an interesting clue as to how Ship was playing this deadly game. Oakes bore a more than casual resemblance to Morgan Hempstead, the long-ago director of Moonbase. And there *was* that first name.

"I've just been very curious to meet The Boss," Thomas said. He found a seat facing Oakes and sat without invitation.

Oakes scowled. He knew what they called him shipside and groundside, but politeness (not to mention politics) dictated that the term not be used in this room. Best not precipitate conflict yet, however. This Raja Thomas posed too many mysteries. Aristocratic type! That damned better-than-you manner.

"I, too, am curious," Oakes said.

"I'm a servant of Ship."

"But what is it you're supposed to do?"

"I was told you have a communications problem on Pandora—something about an alien intelligence."

"How very interesting. What are your special capabilities in this respect?"

"Ship appears to think I'm the one for the job."

"I don't call the ship's process *thinking*. Besides, who cares what opinions come out of a system of electronic bits and pieces? I prefer a human assessment."

Oakes watched Thomas carefully for a response to this open blasphemy. Who was this man . . . really? You couldn't trust the damned ship to play fair. The only thing to believe was that the ship was not a god. Powerful, yes, but with limits which needed exploring.

"Well, I intend to have a go at the problem," Thomas said.

"If I permit it."

"That's between you and Ship," Thomas said. "I'm well satisfied to carry out Ship's suggestions."

"It offends me . . ." Oakes paused, leaned back into his cushions. " . . . when you refer to this mechanical construction . . ." He waved a hand to indicate the physical presence of Ship all around. " . . . as Ship. The implications . . ." He left it there.

"Have you issued an order prohibiting WorShip?" Thomas asked. He found this an interesting prospect. Would Ship interfere?

"I have my own accommodation with this physical monstrosity which human hands loosed on the universe," Oakes said. "We tolerate each other. You have an interesting first name, do you know that?"

"In my family for a . . . very long time."

"You have a family?"

"*Had* a family would be more proper."

"Strange. I took you for a clone."

"That's an interesting philosophical question," Thomas said. "Do clones have families?"

"Are you a clone?"

"What difference does that make?"

"No matter. As far as I'm concerned, you're another machination of the ship. I will tolerate you . . . for now." He waved a hand in dismissal.

Thomas was not ready to leave. "You, too, have an interesting first name."

Oakes had been turning toward the holo projection and its com-console at his side. He hesitated, glanced at Thomas without turning his head. The gesture said: *You still here?* But there was more in his eyes. His interest had been caught.

"Well?"

"You bear a striking physical resemblance to Morgan Hempstead and I coulnd't help but notice that you have the same first name."

"Who was Morgan Hempstead?"

"We often wondered if the Moonbase director had allowed a clone of himself. Are you that clone?"

"I'm not a clone! And what the hell is Moonbase?"

Thomas broke off, recalling what Ship had told him. These replay survivors had been picked up at a different stage in human development. The resemblance, even the name, could be coincidence. Did they come from a time before space travel? Was Ship their first experience in the many dimensions of the universe?

"I asked you a question!" Oakes was angry and not bothering to conceal it.

"Moonbase was the project center which created Ship."

"On Earth's moon? *My* Earth?" Oakes touched his breast with a thumb. And he thought about this revelation.

"Didn't you ever wonder where Ship originated?" Thomas asked.

"Many times. But I never thought we did this thing to ourselves."

Thomas remembered more of Ship's recital now and drew on it. "Some people had to be saved. The sun was going nova. It required a herculean effort."

"So we were told," Oakes said, "but that was later. I am considerably more interested in how a Moonbase was kept secret."

"If there's only one lifeboat, do you tell everyone where it is?"

Thomas felt rather proud of this creative lie. It was just the kind of thing Oakes might believe.

Oakes nodded to himself. "Yes...of course." He glanced at the com-console, then twisted himself more comfortably into the divan. Thomas was lying, obviously. Interesting lie, though. Everyone knew that the ship had landed in Aegypt. Could there be two ships? Perhaps...and there could have been many landings.

Thomas stood. "Where do I find transportation down to Pandora?"

"You don't. Not until you've told me more about Moonbase. Make yourself comfortable." He indicated the seat which Thomas had vacated.

There was no avoiding the threat. Thomas sank back. *What*

a tangled web we weave, he thought. *Truth is easier.* But Oakes could not be told the truth . . . no, not yet. The proper moment and place had to be found for laying Ship's command upon him. Shipmen were far gone in the puny play of WorShip. They would have to be shaken out of that before they could even contemplate Ship's real demand.

Thomas closed his eyes and thought for a moment, then opened his eyes and began recounting the physical facts of Moonbase as he knew them. The account was barbered only to the extent needed for illusion that Moonbase had been a project kept secret from Oakes' Earth.

Occasionally, Oakes stopped him, pressing for particular details.

"You were clones? All of you?"

"Yes."

Oakes could not conceal his delight at this revelation. "Why?"

"Some of us were sure to be lost. Cloning was a way of improving the project's chances of success. The best people were selected . . . each group had more data."

"That's the only reason?"

"Moonbase directives defined clones as property. You . . could do things to clones that you couldn't do to Natural Natals, the naturally born humans."

Oakes ruminated on this for a moment while a slow smile crept over his face. Then: "Do continue."

Thomas obeyed, wondering what it was that Oakes found so satisfying.

Presently, Oakes raised a hand to stop the recital. Small details were not of pressing interest. The broad picture carried the messages he wanted. Clones were property. There was precedent for this. And now, he knew the name behind those significant initials: MH—Morgan Hempstead! He decided to press for any other weaknesses in this Raja Thomas.

"You say Raja is a *family* name. Are you, ahhhh, *related* to the Raja Flattery mentioned in what passes for our history?"

"Distantly."

And Thomas thought: *That's true. We're related distantly in time. Once there was a man called Raja Flattery . . . but that was another eon.*

Already, he felt himself firmly seated in the identity of Raja Thomas. In some ways, the role suited him better than that of Flattery.

I was always the doubter. My failures were failures of doubt. I may be Ship's "living challenge," but the means are mine.

Oakes cleared his throat. "I found this a most edifying and gratifying exchange."

Once more, Thomas stood. He did not like this man's attitude, the feeling that people were only valuable in terms of their usefulness to Morgan Oakes.

Morgan. He has to be a Hempstead clone. Has to be!

"I'll be leaving now," Thomas said.

Was that challenge enough? He studied Oakes for a negative response. Oakes was merely amused.

"Yes, Raja *Lon* Thomas. Go. Pandora will welcome you. Perhaps you'll survive that welcome . . . for a time."

Not until much later when he was standing in the shipbay waiting to board the groundside 'lighter did Thomas pause to wonder at where and how Oakes had obtained those sybaritic furnishings for his expanded cubby.

From Ship?

The mind falls, the will drives on.

—Kerro Panille,
   The Collected Poems

PANILLE EMERGED from Ferry's office dazed and fearfully excited.

Groundside!

He knew what Hali thought of old Ferry—a bumbling fool, but there had been something else in the old man. Ferry had seemed sly and vindictive, consumed by unresolved hostilities. Even so, there was no evading his message.

I'm going groundside!

He had no time for dawdling—his orders required him to be at Shipbay Fifty in little more than an hour. Everything was controlled now by the time demands of Colony. It might be the last quarter of dayside here, but down at Colony it would soon be dawn, and the shuttles from Ship tried to make their groundside landings in the early hours there—less hylighter activity then.

Hylighters . . . dawn . . . groundside . . .

The very words conveyed a sense of the exotic to him. No more of Ship's passages and halls.

The full import of this change began to fill him. He could see and *touch* 'lectrokelp. He could test for himself how this alien intelligence performed.

Abruptly, Panille wanted to share his excitement with someone.

95

He looked around at the sterile reaches of Medical's corridors—
a few med-techs hurrying about their business. None of the faces
were friendly acquaintances.

Hali's face was nowhere among these impersonal passersby.
Everything he saw was just the bustle and movement of Medical's
ordinary comings and goings.

Panille headed toward the main corridors. Medical's bright
lights bothered him. It was a painful contrast with Ferry's office—
the clutter, the dank smells. Ferry kept his office too dim.

Probably hiding the clutter even from himself.

It occurred to Panille then that Ferry's mind probably was like
that office—dim and confused.

A poor, confused old man.

At the first main corridor, Panille turned left toward his quarters. No time to search out Hali and share this momentous change.
There would be time for sharing later—at the next shipside period
of rest and recuperation. He would have much more to share then,
too.

At his cubby, Panille shoved things into a shipcloth bag. He
was not sure what to take. No telling when he might return.
Recorder and spare charges, certainly; a few keepsakes
...clothes...notepads and a spare stylus. And the silver net,
of course. He stopped and held the net up to examine it—a
gift from Ship, flexible silver and big enough to cover his head.

Panille smiled as he rolled the net and confined it in its own
ties. Ship seldom refused to answer one of his questions; refusal
signaled a defect in the question. But the day of this net had been
memorable for refusals and shifting responses from Ship.

Insatiable curiosity—that was the hallmark of the poet and Ship
certainly knew this. He had been at the Instruction Terminal, his
request. "Tell me about Pandora."

Silence.

Ship wanted a specific question.

"What is the most dangerous creature on Pandora?"

Ship showed him a composite picture of a human.

Panille was irritated. "Why won't You satisfy my curisoty?"

"You were chosen for this special training because of your
curiosity."

"Not because I'm a poet?"

"When did you become a poet?"

Panille remembered staring at his own reflection in the glistening surface of the display screen where Ship revealed its symbolic patterns.

"Words are your tools but they are not enough," Ship said. "That is why there are poets."

Panille had continued to stare at his reflection in the screen, caught by the thought that it was a reflection but it also was displayed where Ship's symbols danced. *Am I a symbol?* His appearance, he knew, was striking: the only Shipman who wore a beard and long hair. As usual, the hair was plaited back and bound in a golden ring at the nape of his neck. He was the picture of a poet from the history holos.

"Ship, do You write my poetry?"

"You ask the question of the Zen placebo: 'How do I know I am me?' A nonsense question as you, a poet, should know."

"I have to be sure my poetry is my own!"

"You truly believe I might try to direct your poetry?"

"I have to be certain."

"Very well. Here is a shield which will isolate you from Me. When you wear it, your thoughts are your own."

"How can I be sure of that?"

"Try it."

The silvery net had come out of the pneumatic slot beside the screen. Fingers trembling, Panille opened the round carrier, examined the contents and put the net over his head, tucking his long black hair up into it. Immediately, he sensed a special silence in his head. It was frightening at first and then exciting.

I'm alone! Really alone!

The words which had flowed from him then had achieved extra energy, a compulsive rhythm whose power touched his fellow Shipmen in strange ways. One of the physicists refused to read or listen to his poetry.

"You twist my mind!" the old man shouted.

Panille chuckled at the memory and tucked the silver snood into his shipcloth bag.

Zen placebo?

Panille shook his head; no time for such thoughts.

When the bag was full he decided that solved his packing problem. He took up his bag and forced himself not to look back when he left. His cubby was the past—a place of furious writing periods and restless inner probings. He had spent many a sleepless night there and, for one period, had taken to wandering the corridors looking for a cool breeze from a ventilator. Ship had felt overly warm and uncommunicative then.

But it was really me; I was the uncommunicative one.

At Shipbay Fifty, he was told to wait in an alcove with no chair or bench. It was a tiny metal-walled space too small for him even to stretch out on the floor. There were two hatches: the one through which he had entered and another directly opposite. Sensor lenses glittered at him from above the hatches and he knew he was being watched.

Why? Could I have angered The Boss?

Waiting made him nervous.

Why did they tell me to get right out here if they were going to make me wait?

It was like that faraway time when his mother had taken him to the Shipmen. He had been five years old, a child of Earth. She had taken him by the hand up the ramp to Ship Reception. He had not even known what *Ship* meant then, but he had been sensitized to what was about to happen to him because his mother had explained it with great solemnity.

Panille remembered that day well—a green spring day full of musty earth smells which had not vanished from his memory in all the Shipdays since. Over one shoulder, he had carried a small cotton bag containing the things his mother had packed for him.

He looked down at the shipcloth bag into which he had crammed the things for his groundside trip. Much more durable . . . larger.

The small cotton bag of that long-gone day had been limited to four kilos—the posted maximum for Ship Reception. It had contained mostly clothing his mother had made for him herself. He still had the amber stocking cap. And there were four primitive photographs—one of the father he had never seen in the flesh, a father killed in a fishing accident. He was revealed as a redhaired man with dark skin and a smile which survived him to warm his son. One picture was his mother, unsmiling and workworn, but still with beautiful eyes; one showed his father's parents, two intense faces which stared directly into the recording lens; and one slightly larger picture showed "the family place" which was, Kerro reminded himself, a patch of land on a patch of planet lost long ago when its sun went nova.

Only the photo survived, wrapped with the others in the amber stocking cap within his shipcloth bag. He had found all of this preserved in a hyb locker when the Shipmen had revived him.

"I want my son to live," his mother had said, handing him over to the Shipmen. "You have refused to take the two of us as a family, but you had better take him!"

No mistaking the threat in her voice. She would do something desperate. There were many desperate people doing violent things in those days. The Shipmen had appeared more amused than disturbed, but they had accepted young Kerro and sent him into hyb.

"Kerro was *my* father's name," she had explained, rolling the r's. "That's the way you say it. He was Portuguese and Samoan, a beautiful man. My mother was ugly and ran away with another man but my father was always beautiful. A shark ate him."

Panille knew that his own father had been a fisherman. His father had been named Arlo and his father's people had escaped from Gaul to the Chin Islands of the south, far across a sea which insulated them from distant persecution.

How long ago was that? he wondered.

He knew that hybernation stopped time for the flesh, but something else went on and on and on . . . *Eternity*. That was the poet's candle. The people who were keeping him waiting now did not realize how a poet could adjust the candle's flame. He knew he was being tested, but these Shipmen hidden behind their sensors did not know the tests he had already surmounted with Ship.

Panille idled away the wait by recalling such a test. At the time he had not known it was a test; that awareness came later. He had been sixteen and proud of his ability to create emotions with words. In the secret room behind Records, Panille had activated the com-console for a study session—to explore his own curiosity.

Ship began the conversation, which was unusual. Usually, Ship only responded to his questions. Ship's first words had startled him.

"As has been the case with other poets, do you think you are God?"

Panille had reflected on this. "All the universe is God. I am of this universe."

"A reasonable answer. You are the most reasonable poet of My experience."

Panille remained silent, poised and watchful. He knew Ship did not always give simple answers, and never simple praise.

Ship's response had been, once more, unexpected. "Why are you not wearing your silver net?"

"I'm not making poems."

Then, back to the original subject: "Why is there God?"

The answer popped into his head the way some lines of poetry occurred to him. "Information, not decisions."

"Cannot God make decisions?"

"God is the source of information, not of decisions. Decisions are human. If God makes decisions, they are human decisions."

If Ship could be considered to *feel* excitement, that was the moment for it and Kerro sensed this. There had been a pattern to the way Ship supplied information to him, and it was a pattern which only a poet might recognize. He was being trained, sensitized, to ask the right questions . . . even of himself.

As he waited at Shipbay Fifty, the questions were obvious, but he did not like some of the answers those questions suggested.

Why were they keeping him waiting? It signaled a callous attitude toward their fellows. And what use had the Colony found for a poet? Communication? Or were Hali's fears to be believed?

The hatch in front of him scissored open with a faint swish of servosystems and a voice called out: "Hurry it up!"

Panille recognized the voice and tried not to show surprise as he stepped through into a reception room and heard the hatch seal behind him. *Automatics*. And yes, it was the bumbler, Doctor Winslow Ferry.

With his recent analysis of Ferry, Panille tried to see the man sympathetically. It was difficult. Painful powers centered on this room, which was functional shipside standard: two hatches in metal walls, instruments in their racks, no ports. The room was blocked by a low barrier and a large com-console behind which Ferry sat. A gate on the right led to a hatch in the far wall.

It occurred to Panille that Ferry was old for shipside. He had watery gray eyes full of false boredom, puffy cheeks. His breath gave off a heavy floral perfume. There was slyness in his voice.

"Brought your own recorder, I see." He punched a notation into the com-console which shielded him from the waist down.

Ferry glanced at the shipcloth bag on Panille's shoulder. "What else you bring?"

"Personal possessions, clothes . . . a few keepsakes."

"Hrrrm." Ferry made another notation. "Let's see."

The distrust in this order shocked Panille. He put the bag on a flat counter beside the com-console, watched while Ferry pawed through the contents. Panille resented every stranger-touch on

intimate possessions. It became obvious after a time that Ferry
was searching for things which could be used as weapons. The
rumors were true, then. The people around Oakes feared for their
own flesh.

Ferry held up the flexible net of silver rolled into its tie bands.
"Wha's 's?"

"I use that when I'm writing my poetry. Ship gave it to me."

Ferry put it onto the counter with care, went back to examining
the rest of the bag's contents. Some items of clothing he passed
beneath a lens behind him and studied details in a scanner whose
shields prevented anyone else from seeing what he saw. Occasionally, he made notations in the com-console.

Panille looked at the silver net. What was Ferry going to do
with it? He could not take it!

Ferry spoke over his shoulder while examining more of Panille's clothing under the scanner lens.

"You think the ship's God?"

The "ship"? The usage surprised Panille. "I . . . yes."

And he thought back to that one conversation he had had with
Ship on the subject. That had been a test, too. Ship was God and
God was Ship. Ship could do things mortal flesh could not . . . at
least while remaining mortal flesh. Normal dimensions of space
dissolved before Ship. Time carried no linear restrictions for Ship.

*I, too, am God, Doctor Winslow Ferry. But I am not Ship . . . Or
am I? And you, dear Doctor, what are you?*

No doubting the origin of Ferry's question. Ship's godhead
remained an open question with many. There had been a time
when Ship was *the ship*, of course. Everyone knew that from the
history which Ship taught. Ship had been a vehicle for mortal
intelligence once. The ship had existed in the limited dimensions
which any human could sense, and it had known a destination.
It also had known a history of madness and violence. Then . . . the
ship had encountered the Holy Void, that reservoir of chaos against
which all beings were required to measure themselves.

Ship's history was cloudy with migrations and hints at a paradise planet somewhere awaiting humankind.

But Ferry was revealed as one of the doubters, one who questioned Ship's version of history. Such doubts thrived because Ship
did not censure them. The only time Panille had referred to the
doubts, Ship had responded clearly and with a creative style to
inspire a poet.

"What is the purpose of doubts, Panille?"

"To test data."

"Can you test this historical data with your doubts?"

That required thought and Panille answered after a long pause. "You are my only source."

"Have I ever given you false data?"

"I've found no falsehoods."

"Does that silence these doubts?"

"No."

"Then what can you do with such doubts?"

That involved more careful thought and a longer pause before answering. "I put them aside until a moment arrives when they may be tested."

"Does that change your relationship with Me?"

"Relationships change constantly."

"Ahhh, I cherish the company of poets."

Panille was shaken out of this memory by the realization that Ferry had spoken to him several times.

"I said, 'Wha's 's?'"

Panille looked at the object in Ferry's hand.

"It was my mother's comb."

"The stuff! The material?"

"Tortoise shell. It came from Earth."

There was no mistaking the avaricious glint in Ferry's eyes. "Well . . . I dunno about this."

"It's a keepsake from my mother, one of the few things I have left. If you take it I'll lodge a formal complaint with Ship."

Ferry betrayed definite anger, his eyes squinted, his hand trembled with the comb. But his gaze strayed to the silver net. He knew the stories about this poet; this one talked to the ship in the quiet of the night and the ship answered.

Once more, Ferry made a notation within the shielded secrecy of his com-console, then delivered himself of his longest speech: "You're assigned groundside to Waela TaoLini and it serves you right. There's a freighter waiting in Fifty-B. Take it. She'll meet you groundside."

Panille stuffed his belongings back into the bag while Ferry watched with growing amusement. *Did he take something while I was daydreaming?* Panille wondered. He preferred the man's anger to his amusement but there was no way to take everything out of the bag once more to check it. No way. What had happened to the people around Oakes? Panille had never seen such slyness and greed in a Shipman. And the smell of that stuff on his breath! Dead flowers. Panille sealed the bag.

"Go on, they're waiting," Ferry said. "Don't waste our time."

Panille heard the hatch open once more behind him. He could feel Ferry's gaze on him all the way out of the reception room.

Waela TaoLini? He had never heard the name before. Then: *Serve me right?*

Beware, for I am fearless and therefore powerful.
I will watch with the wiliness of a snake, that I may
sting with its venom. You shall repent of the injuries
you inflict.

—**Frankenstein's Monster Speaks,**
Shiprecords

OAKES SAT in shadows watching the holographic replay. He
was nervous and irritated. Where was Lewis?

Behind him and slightly to his left stood Legata Hamill. The
dim glow of the projector underlighted their features. Both of
them stared intently at the action in the holofocus.

The scene holding their attention revealed the main finger passage behind Shipbay Nineteen and leading out to one of the treedomes. Kerro Panille accompanied by Hali Ekel walked toward
the pickup which had caught the scene. The treedome could be
glimpsed in the background framed by the end of the passage.
Ekel carried her pribox over one shoulder, its harness held loosely
by her right hand. Panille wore a recorder at his hip and a small
bag from which protruded notepad and stylus. He was dressed in
a white one-piece which set off his long hair and beard. The hair
was bound in a golden ring, plaited and with the tip draped down
his chest on the left. Issue boots covered his feet.

Oakes studied each detail carefully.

"This is the young man of Ferry's report?"

104

"The same."

The rich contralto of Legata's voice distracted Oakes and he was a few blinks replying. During that time, Panille and Ekel walked from the range of one sensor and into the range of another. The holographic point-of-view shifted.

"They seem a little nervous," he said. "I wish I knew what they wrote on that pad."

"Love notes."

"But why write them if..."

"He's a poet."

"And she is not a poet. What's more, *he* resists *her* sexual advances. I don't understand that. She appears quite pneumatic, eminently couchable."

"Do you want him picked up and the notepad examined?"

"No! We must move with discretion and subtlety. Damn! Where *is* Lewis?"

"Still incommunicado."

"Damn him!"

"His assistants now say Lewis is occupied with a special problem."

Oakes nodded. *Special problem.* That was their private code for something which could not be discussed in the clear. No telling who might eavesdrop. Were the neck pellets then no longer immune to spying?"

Panille and Ekel had stopped near the hatch to Ferry's office in Medical.

Oakes tried to remember all the times he had seen this young man shipside. Panille had not invited much interest until it had become clear that he really might be talking to the ship. Then that order from the ship for Panille to be sent groundside!

Why does the ship want him groundside?

A poet! What use could there be for a poet? Oakes decided that he really did not believe Panille talked to the ship.

But the ship, and possibly that Raja Thomas, wanted Panille groundside.

Why?

He turned the question over and found no shadow.

"You're sure the request for Panille came from the ship?" he asked.

"It's been six diurns since the request...and it didn't read like a request to me; it read like an order."

"But from the ship, you're certain?"

"As certain as you can be of anything." The irritation in her voice bordered on insubordination. "I used your code and made the complete cross-check. Everything scans."

Oakes sighed.

Why Panille?

Perhaps more attention should have been paid to the poet. He was one of the originals from Earthside. Have to dig deeper into his past. That was obvious.

The scene in the holofocus showed Panille and Ekel parting. Panille turned and they had a view of his back—a wide and muscular back, Legata noted. She called this to Oakes' attention.

"Do you find him attractive, Legata?"

"I merely point out that he's not some dainty flower-sniffer."

"Mmmmmm."

Oakes was intensely conscious of the musky odor coming from Legata. She had a magnificently proportioned body which she had kept from him so far. But Oakes knew himself to be a patient man. Patient and persistent.

Panille was entering the hatch to Ferry's office. Oakes slapped the switch to stop the replay, leaving the carrier light still glowing. He did not care to have another run through that scene with Ferry. Stupid, bumbling old fool!

Oakes glanced at Legata with only the barest turning of his head. Magnificent. She often presented a vapid mask but Oakes saw the consistent brilliance in her work. Few people knew that she was shockingly strong, a mutation. She concealed an extraordinary musculature under that smooth warm skin. He found this idea exciting. She was known shipwide as a history fanatic who frequently begged Records for style displays to copy in her clothing. Currently, she wore a short toga which exposed most of her right breast. The light fabric hung precariously from her nipple. Oakes felt the pulse of her strength, even there.

Taunting me?

"Tell me why the ship wants a poet groundside," he said.

"We'll have to wait and see."

"We can guess."

"It may be a very simple and open thing—communication with the 'lectro . . ."

"Nothing the ship does is open and simple! And do not use that high-sounding term with me. It's kelp, nothing but kelp. And it's a damned nuisance."

She cleared her throat, the first sign of nervousness that Oakes had detected in her. He found this pleasing. Yes . . . she would be ready for the Scream Room soon.

"There's still Thomas," she said, "perhaps he can . . ."

"*You* are not to question him about Panille."

She was startled. "You're satisfied with the answers he gave you?"

"I am satisfied that he's too much for you to handle."

"I think you're overly suspicious," she said.

"With this ship you cannot be too suspicious. You suspect everything and know you'll miss something."

"But they're just two. . . ."

"The ship ordered this." There was a long pause while Oakes continued to stare up at her. "Your term: *order*. Is that not so?"

"As far as we can determine."

"Do you have any indication, even a faint hint, that Thomas and not the ship initiated this?"

"There's only one order from Ship adding this . . . this Panille to the Colony roster."

"You hesitated over his name."

"It slipped my mind!"

Now she was nervous and angry. Oakes found himself enjoying that very much. This Legata Hamill had potential. She would have to be broken of that habit, however, saying *Ship* rather than *the* ship.

"You don't find the poet attractive?"

"Not particularly."

The fingers of her left hand twisted a corner of her toga.

"And there's no record of communication between Thomas and the ship?"

"Nothing."

"You don't find that odd?"

"What do you mean?"

"Thomas had to come from hyb. Who ordered it? Who briefed him?"

"There's no record of any such communication."

"How could there be no record of something we know took place?"

Now fear edged her anger. "I don't know!"

"Haven't I warned you to suspect everything?"

"Yes! You tell me to suspect everyone!"

"Good . . . very good."

He turned back to face the light of the empty holofocus.

"Now, go and look some more. Perhaps there's something you've missed."

"Do you know of something I've missed?"

"That's for you to find out, my dear!"

He listened to the whisk-whisk of her clothing as she hurried from the room. There was a brief flare of light from the outer passage as she opened the hatch, then shadows once more and she was gone.

Oakes switched from replay to real-time and coded in the passage pickups to follow her progress as she took the turn to Records. He switched from pickup to pickup, watching until she sat down at a scandesk in the command level of Records and called for the information she wanted. Oakes checked the readouts. She was asking for any messages between the ship and Pandora, all references to Raja Thomas and Kerro Panille. She did not overlook Hali Ekel.

Good.

Her next step would be to use some of Lewis' people for actual surveillance. Oakes knew she already had scanned the Records data once, but now she would look even harder, seeking codes or other subterfuge. At least, he hoped that was her intent. If the secret were there, she could find it. She simply needed to be challenged, driven, goaded into it.

Suspect everything and everyone.

He shut down the holo and scowled at the darkness. Soon, very soon, he would have to go groundside for good. No returning to the dangerous confines of the ship. Pandora was dangerous enough, but the need for his own hole, a nest where he could not be watched by the ship increased with terrifying speed. *This mechanical monster!* He knew it followed every move he made shipside. *It's what I would do.*

There were some who thought the ship's influence extended farther. But the Redoubt would solve all of that. Provided Lewis had not failed him. No . . . no chance of that. This long silence from Lewis had to be some internal problem with the clones. There were too many fail-safe signals for real disasters. None of the signals had been activated. Something else was happening down at the Redoubt. *Perhaps Lewis is preparing a pleasant surprise for me. Just like him.*

Oakes smiled to himself, nursing the privacy of his innermost thoughts. You do not know what I plan, Mechanical Monster. I have plans for you.

He had plans for Pandora, too, big plans. And the ship was no part of them. Other plans for Legata. She would have to go to the Scream Room soon. Yes. She had to be made more trustworthy.

Nostalgia represents an interesting illusion. Through nostalgia, humans wish for things that never were. The positive memory is the one that sticks. Over several generations, the positive memory tends to weed out more and more of what really existed, refining down to a distillation of haunted desires.

—*Shipquotes*

FOR THE first time, Waela considered refusing an assignment. Not out of fear—she had survived in the research subs where no one else had, and still she accepted the fact that this project must continue at all costs. Beyond instinct, she knew that the 'lectrokelp was the most important factor in Colony life. Survival.

I've been down there and I survived. I should lead the new team.

This thought dominated her awareness as she and Thomas approached the bustle of early dayside activity around the new sub he was having rushed to completion.

Thomas worried her. One blink he seemed like a nice-enough fellow; the next . . . what? His mind appeared to wander.

He hasn't been out of hyb long enough to handle himself here.

They stopped a few meters from the work perimeter and she stared at what was taking shape under the brilliant lights. All this energy—all those workers. They were like insects intent on a giant egg. She tried to fathom the sense of this thing. It *did* make a certain sense . . . but a transparent core of plaz? They had always used plasma glass in the subs, but this detachable core constructed entirely of plaz was a new concept. She could see that it was going to be crowded in there and didn't know if she would like that.

Why Thomas? Why did they put him in charge?

She recalled their walk across the compound and into the LTA hangar. He had been too busy giving orders to *her* for him to see the telltale shadow-flicker of a Hooded Dasher breaking past the sentries. She had cooked it in mid-leap with a hipshot from her lasgun—and immediately began to shiver when she realized that she had almost left the weapon in her cubby. This perimeter was supposed to be secure, the sentries the best.

Thomas had barely noticed.

"Quick little devils," he said, calmly. "By the way, there's a poet coming onto our team from Ship."

"A *poet?* But we need. . . ."

"We will get a poet because Ship is sending us a poet."

"But we asked for . . ."

"I *know* what we asked for!"

He sounded like a man suppressing his own misgivings.

She said: "Well, we still need a systems engineer for . . ."

"I want you to seduce this poet."

She had trouble believing what she had heard.

Thomas said: "Your skin's a regular rainbow when you get upset. Just consider this a team assignment. I've seen a holo of the poet. He's not unattractive in . . ."

"My body is my own!" She glared at him. "And nobody— not you, not Oakes, not Ship, tells me who I will or will not let into my body."

They were stopped in the compound by then and she was surprised to see his hands up and a grin on his face. She realized that she had instinctively raised her lasgun to focus between his eyes. Without reducing her furious glare, she lowered the gun and holstered it.

"Sorry," he said. And they resumed their walk toward the hangar. Presently, he asked: "How important is the kelp team to you?"

He should know that! Everyone knew, and since Thomas had been groundside he had shown amazing ability to seek out critical information.

"It's everything to me."

Words began to pour from him. He wanted to know if Panille

was a free agent. Was Panille really sent by Ship? Could Panille
be working for Oakes or this Lewis people mentioned in such
fearful tones. Who? Who? Doubts—a cascade of doubts.

But why the hell should she have to seduce Panille to find out?
There was no satisfaction in the answer Thomas gave.

"You have to get through all of Panille's barriers, all of his
masks."

Damn!

"Just how important *is* this project to you?" Thomas demanded.

"It's vital . . . not just to me but to the entire Colony."

"Of course it is. That's why you must seduce this poet. If he's
to be a working member of this very bizarre team, there are things
we must know about him."

"And a hold we must have on him!"

"There's no other way."

"Pull his records if you want to know whether he prefers
women. I will not . . ."

"That's not my question and you know it! You will not refuse
my orders and remain on this team!"

"I can't even question the wisdom of your decisions?"

"Ship sent me. There is no higher authority. And there are
things I must know for this project to succeed."

She could not deny the intensity of his emotions, but . . .

"Waela, you're right that the project's vital. We can't play
with time as we play here with words."

"And I have nothing to say about the team?" She was close
to tears and did not care that it showed.

"You have a . . ."

"After all I've been through? I watched them all die! All of
them! That buys me some say in how this team goes, or it buys
me the R & R I can collect shipside. You name it."

Thomas, aware of the deepening flush in her skin, felt the
intensity of her presence. Such a quick and perceptive person. He
felt himself giving over to feelings he had not experienced in eons.

It's been Shipcenturies!

He spoke softly: "We consult, we share data. But all key
decisions are mine and final. If that had been the case all along,
this project would not have been botched."

Waela keyed the hangar door and they stepped inside to the
brilliant focus of lights and activity, the noise and smell of torches.
She put a hand on his arm to stop him. How thin and wiry he felt!

"How will seducing the poet make our mission succeed?"

"I've told you. Get to the heart of him."

She stared across at the activity around the new sub. "And replacing the plasteel with plaz..."

"No single thing will make it for us. We're a team." He glanced down at her. "And we're going in by air."

"By..." Then she saw the stranded cables reaching up and out of the brilliant illumination into the upper shadows of the hangar—a gigantic LTA partly inflated there. The sub was being fitted to a Lighter-Than-Air in place of the usual armored gondola.

"But why..."

"Because the kelp has been strangling our subs."

She thought back to her own survival from a doomed sub— the writhing kelp near the shore, the bubble escape, her frantic swim to the rocks and the near-miraculous dive of the observation LTA which had plucked her away from predators.

As though he read her thoughts, Thomas said: "You've seen it yourself. At our first briefing, you said you believed the kelp to be sentient."

"It is."

"Those subs did not just get tangled. They were snatched."

She considered this. On every lost mission where they had the data they knew that the sub had been destroyed shortly after collecting samples.

Could the kelp think we were attacking?

Her own reasoning made this possible. *If the kelp is sentient...Yes, it would have an external sensory matrix to respond to pain. Not blind writhing, but sentient response.*

Thomas spoke in a flat voice: "The kelp is not an insensitive vegetable."

"I've said all along that we should be attempting to communicate with it."

"And so we shall."

"Then what difference does it make whether we drop in or dive in from shoreside? We're still there."

"We go by lagoon."

Thomas moved closer to the work, bending to inspect a line of welds along the plaz. "Good work; good work," he muttered. The welds were almost invisible. When the conversion was complete, the occupants would have close to three hundred and sixty degrees of visibility.

"Lagoons?" Waela asked as he stepped back.

"Yes. Isn't that what you call those vertical tunnels of open water?"

"Certainly, but..."

"We will be surrounded by the kelp, actually helpless if it wants to attack. But we will not touch it. This sub is being fitted to play back the kelplights—to record the patterns and play them back."

Again, he was making sense.

Thomas continued to speak as he watched the work: "We can approach a perimeter of kelp without making physical contact. As you've seen, when we go in from shore, that's impossible. Not sufficient room between the kelp strands."

She nodded her head slowly. There were many unanswered questions about this plan, but she could see the pattern of it.

"Subs are too unwieldly," he said, "but they're all we've got. We must find a sufficiently large pocket of open water, drop into it and anchor. Then we dive and study the kelp."

It sounded perilous but possible. And that idea of playing back the kelplights to the kelp: She had seen those coherent patterns herself, sometimes repetitive. Was that the way the kelp communicated?

Maybe Thomas really was chosen by Ship.

She heard him mutter something. Thomas was the only man she knew who talked to himself more or less constantly. He faded in and out of conversations. You could never be sure whether he had been thinking aloud or talking to you.

"What?"

"The plaz. Not as strong as plasteel. We had to do some buttressing inside. Makes things much more crowded than you might expect."

He moved through a group of workers to speak to their foreman, a low-voiced conversation which came through to her only in bits: "...then if you lattice the...and I'll want...where we..."

Presently, he returned to her side. "My design isn't as good as it might be, but it'll suffice."

So he has his little mistakes but he doesn't hide them.

She had heard a few snatches of talk among the workers. They stood a bit in awe of Thomas. The man showed a surprising ability at their work, no matter what the work—plaz welding, control design...He was a jack of all trades.

Master of none?

She sensed that this was a difficult man to influence: *a fearsome enemy, that one friend who does not mirror but mocks when mockery is needed.*

This recognition increased her uneasiness. She knew she could like this man, but she felt bad vibrations about the team . . . and it wasn't even a team yet.

And the sub will be crowded even with three of us.

She closed her eyes.

Should I tell him?

She had never told anyone, not in the debriefings, nor in friendly conversation. The kelp had a special hold over her. It was a thing that began happening as soon as the sub started slipping through the gigantic stems and tentacles: a sexual excitement very nearly impossible to control at times. Absurdity, in fact. She had managed a form of balance by hyperventilating but it remained troublesome and sometimes reduced her efficiency. When *that* happened, though, the shock of it cleared the effect.

Her old teammates had thought the hyperventilating a response to fear, a way of overcoming the terrors all of them felt and suppressed. And now they were all dead—nobody left to hear her confession.

The closeness, the strange sexual air that had taken over the background of the project—the unknowns in Thomas—all frustrated her. She had thought of taking Anti-s to relieve the sexual tensions, but Anti-s made her drowsy and slowed her reflexes. Deadly.

Thomas stood beside her, silently observing the work. She could almost see him making mental notes for changes. There were gears turning in his head.

"Why me?" she muttered.

"What?" He turned toward her.

"Why me? Why do I have to take on this poet?"

"I've told you what . . ."

"There are women paid well to do just what you . . ."

"I won't pay for this. It's a project thing, vital. Your own word. You will do it."

She turned her back on him.

Thomas sighed. This Waela TaoLini was an extraordinary person. He hated what he had asked her to do, but she was the only one he could trust. The project was *that* vital to her, too. Panille posed too many unanswered questions. Ship's words were plain and simple: "There will be a poet . . ." Not: "I have named a poet,'' or, ''I have assigned a poet...''

There will be...

Who was Panille working for? Doubts...doubts... doubts...

I have to know.

By the old rush in his veins, he already knew that Waela would follow his orders, and he would sink into a sadness the likes of which he had almost forgotten.

''Old fool,'' he muttered to himself.

''What?'' She turned back toward him and he could see the acceptance and the resolve on her face.

''Nothing.''

She stood facing Thomas a moment, then: ''It all depends on how much I like the poet.'' With that, she turned on her heel and left the hangar with characteristic Pandoran speed.

Religion begins where men seek to influence a god. The biblical scapegoat and Christian Redeemer are cast from the same ancient mould—the human subservient to an unpredictable universe (or unpredictable king) and seeking to rid himself of the guilt which brings down the wrath of the all-powerful.

—**Raja Flattery**
The Book of Ship

AGAIN, THE communications pellet in Oakes' neck, made no contact with Lewis. Static or silence, wild images projected onto his waking dreams—these were all he got. He wanted to reach into his neck and rip the thing out.

Why had Lewis ordered no physical contact with the Redoubt? Oakes chafed at his own inability to raise too much disturbance. The real purposes of the Redoubt remained a secret from most Shipmen; to most it was just a rumored exploratory attempt out on Black Dragon. He did not dare countermand the order which had isolated the Redoubt. Too many would see the size of the place.

Lewis can't do this to me.

Oakes paced his cubby, wishing it were even larger. He wanted to walk off his frustrations but it was full dayside out in the ship's passages and he knew he would be plagued by the need to make decisions once he stepped from his sanctum. Rumors were raging through the ship. Many had noted his upset. This could not go on much longer.

I would go down myself . . . except . . .

No, without Lewis to prepare the way, it is too dangerous.

Oakes shook his head. He was too valuable to risk down there yet.

Dammit, Lewis! You could send me some message . . .

Oakes had come increasingly to suspect that Lewis really was involved in a primary emergency. That or treachery. No . . . it had to be an emergency. Lewis was not a leader. Then it had to be a major threat from the planet itself.

Pandora.

In many ways, Pandora was a more immediate and dangerous adversary than the ship.

Oakes glanced at the blank holofocus beside his couch. A touch of the buttons would call up real-time images of the planet. To what avail? He had tried a sensor search of the Black Dragon coastline from space. Too many clouds . . . not enough detail.

He could identify the coastal bay where the Redoubt was being built, could even see glinting reflections during the diurn passages of Alki or Rega.

Oakes took a deep breath to calm himself. This planet was not going to beat him.

You're mine, Pandora!

As he had told Legata, anything was possible down there. They could fulfill any fantasy.

Oakes examined his hands, rubbed them across his bulging stomach. He was determined that he would never under any circumstances grub out a living on the surface of a planet. Especially on a planet he owned. This was only natural.

The ship conditioned me to be what I am.

More than any other person he had ever known, Oakes felt that he knew the nature of the ship's conditioning processes—the differences from what they had been when they had lived free to scatter on Earth's surface.

It's the crush of people . . . too many people too close together.

Shipside congestion had been transported groundside. This way of life demanded special adaptations. All Shipmen adjusted the same way at bottom. They drugged themselves, gambled—risked everything . . . even their own lives. Running the Colony perimeter naked except for thonged feet. And for what? A bet! A dare! To hide from themselves. In his long walks through the ship, Oakes knew how he screened out the comings and goings of others. Like most Shipmen, he could retreat into the deepest interior of his mind for privacy, for entertainment, for living.

In these times of food shortage, this faculty had been especially valuable to him. Oakes knew himself to be the . . . *heaviest* man shipside. He knew there was envy and angry questioning, but even so no one stared directly at him with such thoughts openly readable.

Yes, I know these people. They need me.

Under Edmond Kingston's tutelage, he had studied well for the psychiatric side of his specialty—all the banks of records handed down for generations . . . eons maybe. The way the ship had put them in and out of hyb, the passage of real time had been lost.

That unknown length of time bothered Oakes. And the translations from the records produced too many anomalies. Popular apology for the ship said the confusion arose from Ship's attempt to rescue as many people as possible. Oakes did not believe this. The translations hinted at too many other explanations. *Translation?* The ship controlled even that. You asked a computer to render the unintelligible intelligible. But linguists pointed out that among the languages found in Records were some which existed in a free-floating universe of their own—without discernible beginnings nor descendents.

What happened to the folk of those rich linguistic heritages?

I don't even know what happened to us.

His childhood memories told him things, though. Compared to the people of the Earth from which the ship had plucked them, Shipmen were freaks—all of them, clone and Natural Natal alike. Freaks. The shipside mind had become a place to live very quickly for those who had little space, few private possessions to call their own, for people torn between WorShip and dismay. Shipmen cultivated the skills of personalizing whatever the ship provided them. Functional simplicity did not bear the onus or sense of restriction that arbitrary simplicity carried. Each tool, each bowl and spoon and pair of chopsticks, each cubby bore the signature of the user in some small fashion.

My cubby is merely a larger manifestation of this.

The mind, too, was the outpost of privacy, a last place to sit and whittle something sensible out of an insane universe.

Only the Ceepee was above it all; even while he participated, he was above. Oakes felt that sometimes the people around him wore signs revealing their innermost thoughts.

And what about this Raja Thomas? Another Ceepee and he

studied me carefully . . . much the way I sometimes study others.

It occurred to Oakes then that he had grown careless. Since old Kingston's death, he had thought himself immune to the probing study of others, alone in the ability to snare a Shipman's psyche. It was dangerous for someone else to have that weapon. Just one more reason this Thomas would have to be eliminated. Oakes realized he had been pacing back and forth in his cubby— to the mandala, turn and back to the com-console, once more to the mandala . . . He was confronted by the com-console when this realization struck him. His hand went out to the keys and he brought into the holofocus a scene from Agrarium D-9 out on shiprim. He stared at the bustle of workers, at the filtered blue-violet light which set these peoples apart in a world of their own.

Yes . . . if independence from the ship were possible, it would begin with food and the cultivation of life. The axolotl tanks, the clone labs, the biocomputer itself—all were but sophisticated toys for the well fed, the sheltered and clothed.

"Feed men, then ask of them virtue."

That was an old voice from one of his training records. A wise voice, a practical one. The voice of a survivor.

Oakes continued to stare at the workers. They attended their plants with total attention, occupation and preoccupation linked in a particular reverence which he had sensed only among older Shipmen during WorShip.

These agrarium workers engaged in a kind of WorShip.

WorShip!

Oakes chuckled, amused by the thought of WorShip reduced to tending plants in an agrarium. What a grand sight they must be in the eyes of a god! A pack of sniveling beggars. What kind of a god kept its charges in poverty to hear them beg? Oakes could understand a touch of subjugation, but . . . this? This spoke to something else.

Someone had to be boss, and the rest have to be reminded of that occasionally. Otherwise, how can anything be organized to work?

No; he heard the message. It said that the ship's programs were running out. All of the problems were being dumped on the Cee-pee's shoulders.

Look at those workers!

He knew they did not have the time to make the ordering decisions for their own lives. When? After work? Then the body was tired and the mind was dulled into a personal reverie which precluded insightful judgments for the good of all.

The good of all—that's my job.

He freed them from the agony of the decisions which they were not well informed enough, not energetic enough, nor even intelligent enough to make. It was the Ceepee who gave them that more pleasant gift of drifting time, the time to seek their own ease and recreations.

Recreation . . . Re-creation.

The association flitted through his mind. Re-creation was where they were made new again, where all they worked for was made real, where they *lived*. Looking down at the agrarium workers in the holofocus, Oakes felt like the conductor of an intricate musical score. He reminded himself to remember that analogy for the next general meeting.

Conductor of a symphony.

He liked that. It was food for thought. Did the ship have such thoughts? He experienced a sudden feeling of affinity for the ship, his enemy.

What food are we that we deserve reverence and care? What manna? Could the ship . . . ?

His reverie was shattered by the abrupt opening hiss of his cubby hatch.

Who dared . . . ?

The hatch slammed back against the bulkhead and Lewis darted through, sealed the opening behind him and dogged it. He was breathing hard and, instead of his usual self-effacing brown fatigues, he wore a crisp new issue singlesuit of dark green.

"Lewis!"

Oakes was overjoyed to see the man . . . and then dismayed. When Lewis turned at the sealed hatch, it was apparent that his face bore signs of quick medical patchwork to cover numerous cuts and bruises. And he was limping.

Judgment prepares you to enter the stream of chance and use your will. You use judgment to modulate will. Thinking is the performance of the moment. You sit in judgment, a convection center for the currents where past prepares a future. It is a balancing act.

—**Kerro Panille,**
The Avata Argue

HALI EKEL, moving with her usual sure-footed grace, leaped up one-handed to grasp the lift bar for the ceiling hatch leading to the software storage section of Records. Her pribox, suspended on its shoulder harness, slapped her hip as she jumped. She had discovered less than an hour earlier that Kerro Panille was headed groundside. He had done this without farewell, not even a note . . . or a poem.

Not that I have any special hold on him!

She opened the hatch and levered herself up into the service tube.

He refuses the breeding match with me, he . . .

She pushed such thoughts aside. But his leaving this way hurt. They had come to maturity in the same creche section, were the same age (within days) and had remained friends. She had heard his stories of Earthside and he had heard her stories. Hali had no illusions about her own emotions. She thought Kerro the most attractive male shipside.

122

Why was he always so distant?

She crouched to scuttle up the curving oval of the tube. It was only one hundred and sixty centimeters in its longest diameter, eight centimeters short of her height, but she was used to moving around Ship through such little-known shortcuts.

It's not as though I were ugly.

Her shipcloth singlesuit, she knew, revealed an attractive feminine figure. Her skin was dark, eyes brown and she wore her black hair cropped short as all technicians did. All of the medtechs were acutely aware of the sanitary advantages of hair shorn to a bristly cap. Not that she had ever wanted Kerro to clip his hair or beard. She found his style exciting. But he did not have to deal with medical problems.

She found the Records access hatch locked but she had memorized the code and it took only seconds to work the latch. Ship buzzed at her from the interior sensor-eye as she stooped and slipped through into the storage area.

"Hali, what are you doing?"

She stopped in shock. *Vocal!* Everyone knew the flat, metallic work-voice of Ship, the means of necessary contacts, but this was something different... a resonant voice full of emotional overtones. And Ship had used her name!

"I...I want a software reader station. There's always one open in here."

"You are very unconventional, Hali."

"Have I done something wrong?" Her strong fingers worked to seal the hatchdogs as she spoke, and she hesitated there, fearful that she had offended Ship.

But Ship was talking to her! Really talking!

"Some would think your actions wrong."

"I was just in a hurry. No one will tell me why Kerro has gone groundside."

"Why did you not think to ask Me?"

"I was..." She glanced along the narrow passage between the rotary bins of software discs toward the reader station. Its keyboard and screen were blank, unoccupied as she had expected.

Ship would not leave it there. "I am never farther from you than the nearest monitor or com-console."

She peered up at the orange bulb of the sensor-eye. It was a baleful orb, a cyclopain pupil with its surrounding metal grid through which Ship's voice issued. Was Ship angry with her? The measured control of that awful voice filled her with awe.

"I am not angry with you. I merely suggest that you show more confidence in Me. I am concerned about you."

"I'm...confident of You, Ship. I WorShip. You know that. I just never thought You would talk to me like this."

"As I talk to Kerro Panille? You are jealous, Hali."

She was too honest to deny it, but words would not come. She shook her head.

"Hali, go to the keyboard at the end of this aisle. Depress the red cursor in the upper right-hand corner and I will open a door behind that station."

"A...door?"

"You will find a hidden room there with another instruction station which Kerro Panille often used. You may use it now."

Wondering and fearful, she obeyed.

The entire keyboard and its desk swung wide to reveal a low opening. She crouched to enter and found herself in a small room with a vaguely yellow couch. Muted green light came from concealed illuminators at the corners of the room. There was a large console with screen and keyboard, a familiar holofocus circle on the floor. She knew the setting—a small teaching lab, but one she had not even known existed. It was smaller than any other of her experience.

She heard the hatch seal itself behind her, but she felt unaccountably secure in this privacy. Kerro had used this place. Ship was concerned about her. There was the unmistakeable musk of Kerro's flesh on her sensitive nostrils. She rubbed at the gold ring in her nose. There was a stationary swivel seat at the keyboard. She slipped into it.

"No, Hali. Stretch out on the couch. You will not need the keyboard here."

Ship's voice came from all around her. She looked for the source of that awesomely-measured voice. There were no sensors visible or monitor-eyes.

"Do not fear, Hali. This room is within my protective shield. Go to the couch."

Hesitantly, she obeyed. The couch was covered with a slick material which felt cold against her neck and hands.

"Why did you come here looking for an unoccupied terminal, Hali?"

"I wanted to do something...definite."

"You love Kerro?"

"You know I do."

"It is your right to try to make him love you, Hali, but not by subterfuge."

"I . . . I want him."

"So you sought My help?"

"I'll take any help I can get."

"You have free access to information, Hali, but what you do with it is your own decision. You are making a life, do you understand that?"

"Making a life?" She could feel her own perspiration against the slick material of the couch.

"Your own life. It is your own . . . a gift. You should treat it well. Be happy with it."

"Would You match Kerro and me again?"

"Only if that really suits you both."

"I'd be happier with Kerro. And Kerro's gone groundside!" It came out almost a wail and she felt tears at the edges of her eyes.

"Can you not go groundside?"

"You know I have Shipside medical responsibilities!"

"Yes, the Shipmen must be kept healthy that Colony may eat. But I ask about your own decision."

"They need me here!"

"Hali, I ask that you trust Me."

She blinked at the empty screen across from the couch. What a strange statement! How could one *not* trust Ship? All people were creatures of Ship. The invocations of WorShip marked their lives forever. But she felt that some personal response was being demanded and she gave it.

"Of course I trust You."

"I find that gratifying, Hali. Because of that, I have something just for you. You are to learn about a man called Yaisuah. The name is in an ancient language which was known as Aramaic. Yaisuah is a form of the name Joshua and it is where Jesus Lewis gets his name."

In all of this, Hali was most startled by Ship's pronunciation of *Jesus*. Anyone shipside referring to Jesus called him Hesoos. But Ship's diction could not be questioned: "Geezus."

She stared at the screen. The lab lights suddenly flared to bright, glinting off the metal surfaces. She blinked and sneezed.

Maybe it isn't Ship talking to me, she thought. *What if it's someone playing a joke?* This was a frightening thought. *Who would dare such a prank?*

"I am here, Hali Ekel. It is Ship speaking to you."

"Do You . . . read my mind?"

"Reserve that question, Hali, but know that I can read your reactions. Do you not read the reactions of those around you?"

"Yes, but . . ."

"Do not fear. I mean you no harm."

She tried to swallow, recalling what Ship had said she could learn. *Yaisuah?*

"Who is this . . . this Yaisuah?"

"To learn that, you must travel."

"Travel? Wha . . . what . . . ?" She cleared her throat and forced herself to be calm. Kerro had used this lab often and had never shown fear of Ship. "Where will I travel?"

"Not *where*, but *when*. You will stroll into that which you humans call *Time*."

She took this to mean that Ship would show her a holo-record. "A projection? What are You going to . . . ?"

"Not that kind of projection. For this experience, *you* are the projection."

"Me . . . the . . . ?"

"It is important that Shipmen learn about Yaisuah, who was also called Jesus. I have chosen you for this journey."

She felt tightness in her chest, panic near. "How . . . ?"

"I know how, Hali Ekel, and so do you. Answer Me: How do your neurons function?"

Any med-tech knew that. She tossed it off without thinking: "A charged measure of acetylcholene across the synapses where . . ."

"A charged measure, yes. A bridge, a shortcut. You take shortcuts all the time."

"But I . . ."

"I am the universe, Hali Ekel. Every part of Me—each part in its entirety—the universe. All Mine—including the shortcuts."

"But my body . . . what . . . ?" She broke off, stopped by an intense fear for this precious flesh she wore.

"I will be with you, Hali Ekel. That *matrix* which is you, that also is part of the universe and Mine. You wish to know if I read your thoughts?"

She found the very idea deeply disturbing, an invasion of her privacy. "Do You?"

"Ekel . . ." Such sadness Ship put into her name. "Our powers are of the same universe. Your thought is My thought. How can I help but know what you think?"

She struggled for a deep breath. Ship's words spoke of things just beyond her grasp, but WorShip had taught her to accept.

"Very well."

"Now, are you ready to travel?"

She tried to swallow in a dry throat. Her mind searched for some logical objection to this thing which Ship proposed. *A projection?* The words represented such an insubstantial thing. Ship said *she* would be the projection. How threatening that sounded!

"Why...why must I go through...Time?"

"Through?" Ship's tone conveyed an exquisite reprimand. "You persist in thinking of Time as linear and a barrier. That is not even close to the reality, but I will play that game if it reassures you."

"What is...I mean, if it's not linear...?"

"Think of it as linear if you wish. Think of it as thousands of meters of computer tape unraveled and crammed into this little lab. You could move from one Time to another—a shortcut—just by reaching across the loops and folds."

"But...I mean if you actually go across, how can you get back to...?"

"You never let go of the *now*."

In spite of that deep and grinding fear, she was interested. "Two places at one Time?"

"All Time is one place, Ekel."

It occurred to her then that Ship had shifted from the personal and reassuring Hali to Ekel, subtly but definitely.

"Why are You calling me Ekel now?"

"Because I perceive that this is the *line* which you believe to be yourself. I do it to help you."

"But if You take me somewhere else...?"

"I have sealed this room, Ekel. You will have two bodies simultaneously, but separated by a very long Time and a very great distance."

"Will I know both...?"

"You will be conscious of only one flesh, but you will know both."

"Very well. What do I do?"

"Stay there on the lab couch and accept the fact that I will make another body for you at another Time."

"Will it...?"

"If you do what I tell you to do, it will not hurt. You will understand the speech of this other place and I will give you an old body, an old woman. Old bodies are not as threatening to others. No one bothers an old woman."

She tried to relax in obedience. *Accept.* But questions filled her mind. "Why are You sending me to...?"

"Eavesdrop, Ekel. Observe and learn. And no matter what you see, do not try to interfere. You would cause unnecessary pain, perhaps even to yourself."

"I just watch and..."

"Do not interfere. You will see the consequences presently of interfering with Time."

Before she could ask another question, she felt a prickling along the back of her neck; a slither of chill swept down her spine. Her heart slammed against her ribcage.

Ship's voice came from a long distance. "Ready, Ekel." It was a command, not a question, but she answered, and her own voice echoed in her skull.

"Yesssssss ..."

The mind is a mirror of the universe.
See the reflections?
The universe is no mirror for the mind.
Nothing out there
Nothing in here
Shows ourselves.

—Kerro Panille,
The Collected Poems

WAELA TAOLINI lay in her groundside cubby, fatigue in her body, fatigue in her mind, but unable to sleep. Thomas had no mercy. Everything must be done to his perfectionist demands. He was a fanatic. They had spent twenty-one hours going through the operational routine for the new sub. Thomas would not wait for the arrival of the poet, who was somewhere in the bowels of Processing. No. *We will use what time we have.*

She tried to take a deep breath. Pain yanked a knot behind her breastbone.

She wondered how Thomas came to them. How could he be from Ship? Things he did not know, things that Shipmen took for granted, worried her. There was the incident with the Hooded Dasher.

He was calm, though, I'll give him that.

What really surprised her was his ignorance of The Game.

A crowd had gathered behind the LTA hangar—off-shift crew, most of them drinking what Shipmen called Spinneret wine.

"What's this about?" Thomas pointed his clipboard at the group.

"It's The Game." She looked at him with a new amazement. "You mean you don't know The Game?"

"What Game? That's just a bunch of drunks having a good time . . . strange, there was nothing in my briefing about liquors of any kind."

"There have always been lab alcohols," she said, "and at one time there were wines and brandies. But officially we can't afford to give up any productive food for wine. Somehow, some do and the market is brisk. Those men," she nodded toward the group, "have traded away some of their food chits for it."

"So, they trade food for wine that costs food to make—maybe less food. Isn't that their right?" His eyes squinted at her.

"Yes, but food's short. They're going hungry. In this place, going hungry means you slow down and here, Raja Thomas, if you slow down you die. And maybe someone else dies because of it."

"Do you do it?" he asked softly.

"Yes," her skin glowed red, "when I can afford the time."

She followed Thomas as he strolled toward the crew, pulled the sleeve of his singlesuit to stop him short.

"There's more."

"What?"

"It requires an even number of players, men or women. Each one buys into The Game with a certain number of food chits. They pair off any way they wish, and each one draws a wihi stick from a basket. They compare, and the longest stick wins a round. The shorter stick of the pair is eliminated, so those drawing the longer sticks pair up. They draw again, and so on until there is only one couple."

"What about the food chits?"

"The players up the ante every round, so if there are a lot of people, The Game gets pretty expensive."

"Does the last couple divide the chits?"

"No, they draw again. The one who draws the longer stick wins the chits."

"That seems boring enough."

"Yes."

She hesitated, then: "The loser runs the perimeter."

She said it offhand, without as much as a blink.

"You mean they run around the outside . . . ?" his thumb hung in the air over his shoulder.

She nodded. "They run it naked."

"But they can't possibly . . . that's almost ten kilometers out in the open . . ."

"Some make it."

"But why? Not for food, it's not that bad yet, is it?"

"No, not for food. For favors, jobs, quarters, partners. For the thrill. For the chance to go out with a flash from a boring life. The long sticks are the losers. Food chits are a consolation prize. The winner gets to run the P."

Thomas let out a long breath.

"What are the odds?"

"By experience, they work out just like the rest of The Game— fifty-fifty. Half don't make it."

"And it's *legal?*"

It was her turn to look at him quizzically.

"They have the right to their own bodies."

He turned to watch the people playing this . . . this *game*.

The crew had paired up, drawn, paired up, drawn, and was now down to the last pair. A man and a woman this time. The man had no nose, but wrinkled slits in his forehead pulsed with the moisture that Thomas took for breath. The woman looked vaguely like someone he had known.

They drew, and the woman matched longer. The crowd cheered and helped her gather her winnings. They tucked them in her collar and sleeves and belt. The last of the wine was passed around and the group began moving toward the west quarter exterior hatch.

"He's really going out there?" Thomas followed them with his eyes.

"Did you notice his right eyebrow?"

"Yes," he looked up at her, "it looked as though he had two eyebrows above it. And the nose . . ."

"Those were tattoos, hash marks. You get one for running the P."

"Then this is his *third?*"

"That's right. His odds are still fifty-fifty. But there is a groundside saying: 'You go once, you've had your flirt with death. You go twice, you live twice. Go three times and go for me.' "

"Charming."

"It's a good game."

"You ever play it, TaoLini?"

She swallowed, and the glow faded out of her skin.

"No."

"A friend?"

She nodded.

"Let's get back to work," he said, and walked her slowly back to the hangar.

Waela remembered this exchange with the odd feeling that she had missed something in Thomas' responses.

Thomas would not even pause for WorShip. He permitted a grudging rest, hardly a hesitation, only when fatigue had them dropping programs and forgetting coordinates. During one of these rests he had started an odd conversation with her and it kept her awake now.

What was he trying to say to me?

They had been seated in the globe of plaz which would shield them in the depths of the sea. Workmen continued their activity all around the outside. She and Thomas sat so close to each other that they had been required to learn a special rhythm to keep from bumping elbows. Waela had missed the right sequence of keys for the dive train three times running.

"Take a rest."

There was accusation in his tone, but she sank back into the sheltered contours of her seat, thankful for any relief, thankful even for the crash-harness which supported her. Muscles did not have to do what the harness did.

Presently, Thomas' voice intruded on her consciousness.

"Once upon a time there was a fourteen-year-old girl. She lived on Earth, on a chicken farm."

I lived on a chicken farm, Waela thought, then: *He's talking about me!*

She opened her eyes.

"So, you've pried into my records."

"That's my job."

A fourteen-year-old girl on a chicken farm. His job!

She thought about that girl she had been—child of emigrants, grubbers in the dirt. Technopeasants. Gaulish middle-class.

I broke away from that.

No . . . to be honest, she had to admit that she had run away. A sun going nova meant little to a fourteen-year-old girl, a girl whose body had become a woman's much earlier than her contemporaries.

I ran away to Ship.

She had held such conversations with herself many times. Waela closed her eyes. It was as though two people occupied her consciousness. One of them she called "Runaway," and the other, "Honesty." Runaway had objected to Shipman life and railed against groundside dangers.

Runaway asked, "Why was I chosen for this damned risky life, anyway?"

Honesty replied, "As I recall it, you volunteered."

"Then I must've parked my brains somewhere. What in hell was I thinking?"

"What do you know about Hell?" Honesty asked.

"Yeah, I have to know Hell before I can understand Paradise. Isn't that what the Ceepee says?"

"You have it backwards, as usual."

"You know why I volunteered, dammit!" The Runaway voice was edged with tears.

"Yea—because he died. Ten years with him and then—poof."

"He died! That's all you have to say about it, 'He died.'"

"What else would there be to say?" Honesty's voice was level, sure.

"You're as bad as the Ceepee, always answering with questions. What'd Jim do to deserve that?"

"He tested for limits and found them when he ran the P."

"But why doesn't Ship or the Ceepee ever talk about it?"

"About death?" Honesty paused. "What's there to talk about? Jim is dead and you're alive, and that's much more important."

"Is it? Sometimes I wonder . . . I wonder what's going to happen to me."

"You live until you die."

"But what's going to *happen?*"

Honesty paused again, uncharacteristically, and said, "You fight to live."

Waela! Waela, wake up!

It was Thomas' voice. She opened her eyes, tipped her head onto the seatback and looked at him. Light glittered from the plaza above him and there was the sound of workmen pounding metal out in the hangar. She noted that Thomas, too, looked tired but was fighting it.

"I was telling you a story about Earth," he said.

"Why?"

"It's important to me. That fourteen-year-old girl had such dreams. Do you still have dreams about your life?"

Her skin began a nervous glow. *Does he read minds?*

"Dreams?" She closed her eyes and sighed. "What do I need with dreams? I have my work."

"Is that enough?"

"Enough?" she laughed. "That's not my worry. Ship is sending down my prince, remember?"

"Don't blaspheme!"

"I'm not blaspheming, you are. Why do I have to seduce this poor idiot poet when . . .?"

"We won't argue that again. Leave now. Quit. But no more arguments."

"I'm not a quitter!"

"So I've noticed."

"Why did you pry into my records?"

"I was trying to recapture that girl. If she won't start with dreams, maybe she'll get somewhere with dreamers. I want to tell her what's become of those dreams."

"Well, what's become of them?"

"She still has them; she always will."

You speak of gods. Very well. Avata speaks that language now. Avata says consciousness is the Species-God's gift to the individual. Conscience is the Individual-God's gift to the species. In conscience you find the structure, the form of consciousness, the beauty.

—Kerro Panille,
Translations from the *Avata*

HALI FELT no passage of time, but when the echoes of her own voice stopped reverberating in her consciousness, she found she was facing herself. She still sensed the tiny reaching lab which Ship had revealed behind the terminal in Records. And there was her own flesh in that lab. Her body lay stretched out on the yellow couch, and she stared down at it without knowing how she did this. Light filled the lab, splashed from every surface. It startled her how different she appeared from the mirror image she had known all of her life. The slick yellow material of the couch accented her brown skin. She thought the brilliance of the light should be dazzling, but could feel no discomfort. Where her short black hair stopped below her left ear there was a dark mole. Her nose ring caught the light and glittered against her skin. An odd aura surrounded her body.

She wanted to speak and for a panic-seized instant wondered

how she could do this. It was as though she struggled to get back into her body. Sudden calm washed her and she heard Ship's voice.

"I am here, Ekel."

"Is that like hybernation?" She had no sensation of speaking, but heard her own voice.

"Far more difficult, Ekel. I show you this because you must remember it."

"I'll remember."

Abruptly, she felt herself tumbling slowly in darkness. And at the front of her awareness was Ship's promise to give her another body for this experience. An old woman's body.

How will that feel?

There was no answer except the tunnel. It was a long, warm tunnel and the most disturbing thing was that it contained no heartbeat, no pulse at all. But there was a glimmer of light at some distance and she could glimpse a hillside beyond the light. Raised shipside, she understood corridors without thinking about them, but when she emerged through the oval whiteness it was a shock to find herself in an unconfined area.

Now, there was a pulsebeat, though. It was in her breast. She put a hand there, felt rough fabric and looked down. The hand was dark, old and wrinkled.

That's not my hand!

She looked around. It was a hillside. She felt the deep vulnerability of her presence here. There was sunlight, a golden glowing which felt good to this body. She looked at her feet, her arms: an old body. And there were other people at a distance.

Ship spoke in her mind: "It will take a moment for you to become acquainted with this body. Do not try to rush it."

Yes—she could feel her awareness creeping outward through halting linkages. Sandals covered her feet; she felt the straps. Rough ground underfoot when she tried two shuffling steps. Fabric swished against her ankles—a coarsely woven sack of a garment. She felt how it abraded her shoulders when she moved; it was the only garment covering her body . . . no. There was a piece of cloth wound around her hair. She reached up and touched it, turning as she did this to face downhill.

A crowd of several hundred people could be seen down there— perhaps as many as three hundred. She was not sure.

She felt that this body might have been running before she

assumed her place in it. Breathing was difficult. A stink of old perspiration assaulted her nostrils.

She could hear the crowd now: a murmurous animal noise. They were moving slowly uphill toward her. The people in it surrounded a man who dragged what appeared to be part of a tree over his shoulder. As he drew nearer, she saw blood on his face, an odd circlet at his brow . . . it looked like a spiney sweat band. The man appeared to have been beaten; bruises and cuts could be discerned through his shredded gray robe.

While the man still was at some distance from her, she saw him stumble and fall on his face in the dirt. A woman in a faded blue robe hurried to help him up but she was beaten back by two young men who wore crested helmets and stiff upper garments which glittered. There were many such men in the crowd. Two of them were kicking and prodding the fallen man, trying to force him to his feet.

Armor, she thought, recalling her history holos. *They're wearing armor.*

A sense of the great time which stretched between this moment and her shipside life threatened to overwhelm her. *Ship?*

Be calm, Ekel. Be calm.

She forced several deep, painful breaths into the old lungs. The armored men, she saw, wore dark skirts which covered them to the knees . . . heavy sandals on their feet, metal greaves over their shins. Each had a short sword sheathed at the shoulder with the handle sticking up beside his head. They used long staves to control the crowd . . . *No,* she corrected herself. They were using spears, clubbing the crowd back with the butt ends.

The crowd was milling around now, concealing the fallen figure from her. There was a great screaming and crying from them— a conflict which she did not understand.

Some called out: "Let him up! Please let him up!"

Others shouted: "Beat the bastard! Beat him!"

And there was one shrill voice heard above all the others: "Stone him here! He won't make it to the top."

A line of the armored men pushed the crowd back, leaving a tall dark man beside the fallen one. The dark man glanced all around, his fear obvious. He jerked to one side, trying to flee, but two of the armored men cut him off, swinging the butts of their spears at him. He dodged back to the side of the fallen man.

One of the soldiers shook the pointed tip of his spear at the dark one, shouted something which Hali could not make out. But the dark one stooped and picked up the tree, lifting it off the fallen one.

What is happening here?

Observe and do not interfere.

A cluster of women was wailing nearby. As the fallen man climbed to his feet and accompanied the dark one, who now dragged the tree, all moved up the hill toward Hali. She watched them carefully, seeking any clue to tell her what was happening. Obviously, it was something painful. Was it momentous? Why had Ship insisted she witness this scene?

They drew nearer. The beaten man lurched along and, presently, stopped near the wailing women. Hali saw that he was barely able to stand. One of the women slipped through the ring of soldiers and mopped the injured man's bloody face with a gray cloth. He coughed in long, hard spasms, holding his left side and grimacing with each cough.

Hali's med-tech training dominated her awareness. The man was badly injured—broken ribs at least, and perhaps a punctured lung. There was blood at the corner of his mouth. She wanted to run to him, use her sophisticated skills to ease his suffering.

Do not interfere!

Ship's presence was like a palpable thing, a wall between her and the injured man.

Steady, Ekel.

Ship was in her mind.

She gripped her hands into fists, took several deep gasping breaths. This brought the smell of the crowd into focus. It was the most disgusting sensory experience she had ever known. They were rank with an unwashed festering. How could they survive the things which her nostrils reported?

She heard the injured man speak then. His voice was soft and directed at the women who fell silent when he spoke.

"Weep not for me, but for your children."

Hali heard him clearly. Such tenderness in that voice!

One of the armored men struck the injured one in the back with a spear butt then, forcing him to resume that lurching march uphill. They drew nearer. The dark one dragged the section of tree.

What were they doing?

The injured one looked back at the cluster of women who once more were wailing. His voice was strong, much stronger than Hali had thought possible.

"If they do these things in a green tree, what will they do in a dry?"

Turning back, the injured one looked full at Hali. He still clutched his side and she saw the characteristic red froth of a lung puncture at his lips.

Ship! What are they doing to him?

Observe.

The injured one said: "You have traveled far to see this."

Ship intruded on her shock: "He's talking to you, Ekel. You can answer him."

The dust of the crowd welled up around her and she choked on it before being able to speak, then: "How . . . how do you know how far I've come?"

It was an old woman's cracked voice she heard issuing from her mouth.

"You are not hidden from me," the injured one said.

One of the soldiers laughed at her then and thrust his spear in her direction. He did it almost playfully. "Get along, old woman. You may've traveled far but I can send you farther."

His companions guffawed at the jest.

Hali recalled Ship's reassurance: *No one bothers an old woman.* The injured man called out to her: "Let them know it was done!"

Then the angry shouts of the crowd and the swirling, odorous dust engulfed her. She almost choked as they moved past, caught by a coughing spasm which cleared her throat. When she could, she turned to gaze after the crowd and a gasp was forced from her. At the top of the hill beyond the crowd two men were hanging on tree constructions with crosspieces such as that being dragged along with the injured man.

A momentary opening in the crowd gave her another glimpse of the injured one and, turning back toward her, he shouted: "If anyone understands God's will, you must."

Once more, the milling crowd hid him from her.

God's will?

A hand touched her arm and she jerked away in fright, whirling to see a young man in a long brown robe at her side. His breath smelled of sewage. And his voice was an unctuous whine.

"He says you come from afar, mother," the foul-breathed one said. "Do you know him?"

· The look in Foul-breath's eyes made her acutely aware of the vulnerable old flesh which housed her consciousness. This was a dangerous man ... very dangerous. The look in his eyes reminded her of Oakes. He could cause great pain.

"You had better answer me," he said, and there was poison in his voice.

*You call Avata "Firefly in the night of the sea."
Avata has doubts about such words because Avata
sees the landscape of your mind. Avata moves through
your landscape with difficulty. It shifts and twists
and changes as Avata goes through. But Avata has
made such journeys before. Avata is an explorer of
such landscapes. Your phantoms are Avata's guides.
We are linked in motion.*

*What is this thing you call "the natural universe"?
Is that something taken from your god? Ahhh, you
have separated your parts to create the unique. You
do not need this separation for your creations. This
fluid evasiveness of your landscape is your strength.
The patterns . . . ahhh, the patterns. From yourself
come the forces which shape the course of each
thought. Why do you confine your thought in a tiny
fixed landscape?*

You find a distinction between measurement and preparation of your landscape. You continually prepare, saying: "I am going to say something about..." But that limits what you say and it tells your listener to accept your limits. All such measurement and limiting date back to a common system in a simple, linear landscape. Look about you, Human! Where do your senses find such simplicity?

Does a second look at the landscape yield the same view as the first look? Why is your will so inflexible?

A magical affinity between object and likeness, between being and symbol, underlies all symbol systems. It is the assumed foundation of language. The word for thing or object in most languages is related to the word for say or speak and these, in turn, have their roots in magic.

—Kerro Panille,
I Sing to the Avata

OAKES STOOD in stunned silence, staring at Jesus Lewis standing just inside the Ceepee cubby's hatch. Somewhere, there was a background buzz. Oakes realized he had left the holofocus projecting Agrarium D-9. Yes...it was full dayside out there. He slapped the cut-off.

Lewis moved another step into the cubby. He was breathing heavily. His thin, straw-colored hair was disarrayed. His dark eyes moved left, right—probing the room. It was an eye movement which Oakes identified as characteristic of groundsiders. There was a patch of pseudoflesh over an injury on Lewis' narrow, cleft chin, another over the bridge of his sharp nose. His thin mouth was twisted into a wry smile.

"What happened to you?"

"Clones..." Deep breath. "...revolt."

142

"The Redoubt?" A sharp twinge of fear shot through Oakes. "It's all right."

Limping, Lewis crossed the room, sank into a divan. "Is there any of your special joy juice around? Every last drop was lost at the Redoubt."

Oakes hurried to a concealed locker, removed a bottle of raw Pandoran wine, opened it and handed the whole bottle to Lewis.

Lewis upended the wine and took four long swallows without a breath while he stared around the bottle at Oakes. The poor old Ceepee looked to be in bad shape. There were dark circles under his eyes. *Tough.*

For Oakes, the moment was welcome as a time to recover his wits. He did not mind serving Lewis and the sense of personal concern this conveyed would have a desired effect. Obviously, something very bad had happened at the Redoubt. Oakes waited until Lewis put down the bottle, then: "They revolted?"

"The discards from the Scream Room, the injured and the others we just can't support. Food's getting very short. I put all of them outside."

Oakes nodded. Clones thrown out of the Redoubt were, of course, condemned to death. Quick and efficient disposal by Pandora's demons...unless they had the misfortune to encounter Nerve Runners or a Spinneret. Messy business.

Lewis took another deep swallow of the wine, then: "We didn't realize that the area had become infested with Nerve Runners."

Oakes shuddered. To him, Nerve Runners were the ultimate Pandoran horror. He could imagine the darting, threadlike creatures clinging to his flesh, savaging his nerves, invading his eyes, worming their ravenous way through to his brain. The long agony of such an attack was well known groundside and the stories had made the rounds shipside. Everything Pandoran feared the Runners except, perhaps, the kelp. They seemed immune.

When he could control his voice, Oakes asked: "What happened?"

"The clones raised the usual fuss when we put them outside. They know what it's like out there, of course. I suppose we didn't pay as close attention as we should. Suddenly, they were screaming, 'Nerve Runners!' "

"Your people buttoned down, of course."

"Everything shut up tight while we tried to spot the boil."

"So?"

Lewis stared at the bottle in his hands, took a deep breath.

Oakes waited. Nerve Runners were horrible, yes; it took three or four minutes for them to do what other demons did in a few eyeblinks. Same result, though.

Lewis sighed, took another swallow of the wine. He appeared calmer, as though Oakes' presence told him that he really was safe at last.

"They attacked the Redoubt," Lewis said.

"Nerve Runners?"

"The clones."

"Attacked? But what weapons . . . ?"

"Stones, their own bodies. Some of them smashed the sewage baffle before we could stop them. Two clones got inside that way. They were infected by then."

"Nerve Runners in the Redoubt?"

Oakes stared at Lewis in horror. "What did you do?"

"There was a wild scramble. Our mop-up crew, mostly E-clones, locked themselves in the Aquaculture Lab but Runners were in the water lines by then. The lab's a shambles. No survivors there. I sealed myself in a Command room with fifteen aides. We were clean."

"How many did we lose?"

"Most of our effectives."

"Clones?"

"Almost all gone."

Oakes grimaced. "Why didn't you report, ask for help?" He tapped the pellet at his neck.

Lewis shook his head. "I tried. I got static or silence, then someone else trying to talk to me, trying to put pictures in my head."

Pictures in his head!

That was a good description of what Oakes had experienced. Their safe little secret communications channel had been penetrated! Who?

He voiced the question.

Lewis shrugged. "I'm still trying to find out."

Oakes put a hand over his own mouth. *The ship? Yes, the damned ship was interfering!*

He did not dare speak openly of that suspicion. The ship had eyes and ears everywhere. There were other fears, too. A Nerve Runner boil had to be met by fire. He envisioned the Redoubt a mass of cinders inside.

"You say the Redoubt's all right?"

"Clean. Sterilized, and we have a bonus." Lewis took another long swallow of wine and grinned at Oakes, savoring the suspense he read in the Ceepee's face. The Ceepee was *so* easy to read.

"How?" Oakes did not try to hide his impatience.

"Chlorine and heavily chlorinated water."

"Chlorine? You mean *that* kills Nerve Runners?"

"I saw it with my own eyes."

"That simple? It's that simple?" Oakes thought of all the years they had lived in terror of these tiniest demons. "Chlorinated water?"

"Heavily chlorinated, undrinkable. But it dissolves the Runners. As a liquid or a gas, it penetrates all the fine places to get every one. The Redoubts stinks, but it's clean."

"You're sure?"

"I'm here." Lewis tapped his chest, took another swallow of wine. Oakes was reacting strangely. It was unsettling. Lewis put down the bottle of wine and thought about the report he had read on the shuttle coming shipside. *Legata to the Scream Room!* Were there no limits to what the old bastard might do? Lewis hoped not. That was how to control Oakes—through his excesses.

"You are, indeed, here," Oakes agreed. "How did you get ... I mean, how did you discover ... ?"

"Those of us in the Facilities Room had all of the controls in front of us. We started dumping whatever we could find to ... "

"But chlorine; how did you get chlorine?"

"We were trying salt brine. There was an electrical short, a wide-scale electrolytic reaction in the brine and we had chlorine. I was on the sensors at the time and saw the chlorine kill some Runners."

"You're sure?"

"I saw it with my own eyes. They just shriveled up and died."

Oakes began to see the picture. Colony had never put chlorine and Nerve Runners together. Most shipside caustics had little effect groundside anyway. Potable water was produced with filters and flash heat from laser ovens. That was the cheapest way. Fire worked on Nerve Runners. Colony had always used fire. Another thought occurred to him.

"The survivors ... how ... ?"

"Only those locked into a sealed area before the infection spread were saved. We flushed everything else with chlorine gas and heavily chlorinated water."

Oakes imagined the gas killing people and Runners, the caustic water burning flesh...He shook his head to drive out such thoughts.

"You're absolutely sure the Redoubt is safe?"

Lewis stared up at him. *The precious Redoubt!* Nothing was more important.

"I'm going back dayside."

Belatedly, Oakes realized he should show more human concern. "But my dear fellow, you're wounded!"

"Nothing serious. But one of us will have to be at the Redoubt all of the time from now on."

"Why?"

"The clean-up was pretty bloody and that's causing trouble."

"What kind of trouble?"

"The surviving clones, even some of our people... well, you can imagine how I had to clean up the place. There were necessary losses. Some of the surviving clones and a few of the more irrational among our people have..." He shrugged.

"Have what? Explain yourself."

"We've had to handle several petitions from clones and there were even a few of our people who sympathized. I have Murdoch down there standing in for me while I came up to report."

"Clones? Petitions? How are you handling them?"

"The same way I handled the food problem."

Oakes scowled. "And... the sympathizers?"

Again, Lewis shrugged. "When we sterilized the area around the Redoubt, the other demons returned. They're a fast and efficient way to solve our problem."

Oakes touched the scar of the pellet at his neck. "But when...that is, why didn't you send someone up to...?"

"We stayed until we were sure we were clean."

"Yes...yes, of course. I see. Brave fellows."

"And can you imagine what would happen if word of this leaks out?"

"You're quite right." Oakes thought about what Lewis had said. As usual, Lewis made the right decisions. Astringent but efficient.

"Now, what's this I hear about Legata?" Lewis asked.

Oakes was outraged. "You have no right to question my..."

"Oh, simmer down. You're going to send her to the Scream Room. I just want to know if we prepare to replace her."

"Replace...Legata? I think not."

"Let me know in plenty of time if you need a replacement."

Oakes was still angry. "It strikes me, Lewis, that you've been very wasteful of lives."

"You know some other way I could've handled this?"

Oakes shook his head. "I meant no offense."

"I know. But this is why I don't report such things unless you ask or unless I have no choice."

Oakes did not like the tone Lewis took there, but another thought struck him. "One of us has to stay at the Redoubt all the time? What about . . . I mean, Colony?"

"You're going to have to wind things up here and come groundside to manage Colony. It's our only answer. You can use Legata for shipside liaison, provided she's still useful after the Scream Room."

Oakes thought about this. Go groundside among all of those vicious demons? The periodic demonstration-of-power trips were bad enough . . . but live there full time?

"That's why I asked about Legata," Lewis said.

Mollified, Oakes ventured a more important question: "How . . . are . . . conditions at Colony?"

"Safe enough as long as you stay inside or travel only in a servo or shuttle."

Oakes closed his eyes for a long blink, opened them. Once more, Lewis demonstrated impeccable reasoning. Who else could they trust as they trusted each other?

"Yes. I understand."

Oakes glanced around his cubby. No visible sensors, but this had never reassured him. The damned ship always knew what was happening shipside.

I will have to go groundside.

The reasons were compelling. Lewis would take Lab One to the Redoubt, of course. But there were too many other delicate matters in balance at Colony.

Groundside.

He had always known he would have to quit the ship one day. It did not help that circumstances had made the decision for him. The move was being forced and he felt vulnerable. This incident with the Nerve Runners did nothing to reassure him.

What a dilemma!

As he gathered more power and exercised it, shipside became increasingly untrustworthy. But Pandora remained equally dangerous and unknown.

It occurred to Oakes then that he had been hoping for a tranquilized and sterilized planet, a place made ready for him by Lewis, before going groundside.

Sterile. Yes.

Oakes stared at Lewis. Why did the man appear so smug? It was more than survival against odds. Lewis was holding something back.

"What else do you have to report?"

"The new E-clones. They were in an isolated chamber and all survived. They're clean, completely unprogrammed and beautiful. Just beautiful."

Oakes was distrustful. The statistical incidence of deviation among clones was a known factor. The body, after all, was transparent to cosmic bombardments which altered the genetic messages in human cells. Rebuilding the DNA structure was Lewis' specialty, yes, but still...

"No kinks?"

"I used 'lectrokelp cells and went back to recombinant DNA as a foundation for the changes." He rubbed the side of his nose with a forefinger. "We've succeeded."

"You said that last time."

"It worked last time, too. We simply couldn't keep up with the food supply necessary to..."

"No freaks?"

"A clean job. All we get is accelerated growth to maturity. And that kelp isn't easy to work with. Lab people hallucinating all over the damn place and aging faster than..."

"Are you still able to *waste* lab technicians on this?"

"They're not wasted!" Lewis was angry, exactly the reaction Oakes had sought.

Oakes smiled reassuringly. "I just want to know that it's working, Jesus, that's all."

"It's working."

"Good. I believe you're the only person who could make it work, but I am the only person who can give you the freedom in which to do this. What is the time frame?"

Lewis blinked at the sudden shift of the question. Cagey old bastard always kept you off balance. He took a deep breath, feeling the wine, the remembered sense of protective enclosure which Ship... *the* ship always gave him.

"How long?" Oakes insisted.

"We can continue an E-clone's growth, the aging, actually,

and arrive at any age you want. From conception to age fifty in fifty divons.''

"In good condition?''

"Top condition and completely receptive to our programming. They're mewling infants until they become our . . . ah, servants.''

"Then we can restore the Redoubt's working force rather rapidly.''

"Yes . . . but that's the problem. Most of our people know this and they . . . ahh, saw what I did with the clones and the sympathizers. They're beginning to see that they can be replaced.''

"I understand.'' Oakes nodded. "That's why you have to stay at the Redoubt.'' He studied Lewis. The man was still worried, still holding something back. "What else, Jesus?''

Lewis spoke too quickly. The answer had been right there in front of his awareness awaiting the question.

"An energy problem. We can work it out.''

"*You* can work it out.''

Lewis lowered his gaze. It was the answer he expected. Correct answer, of course. But they had to produce more burst, their own elixir.

"I will give you one suggestion,'' Oakes said. "Plenty of hard work precludes time for plotting and worry. Now that you've solved the clone problem, put your people to work eliminating the kelp. I want a neat, simple solution. Enzymes, virus, whatever. Tell them to wipe out the kelp.''

An infinite universe presents infinite examples of unreasoned acts, often capricious and threatening, godlike in their mystery. Without god-powers, conscious reasoning cannot explore and make this universe absolutely known; there must remain mysteries beyond what is explained. The only reason in this universe is that which you, in your ungodlike hubris, project onto the universe. In this, you retain kinship with your most primitive ancestors.

—Raja Thomas,
Shiprecords

AS SHE stood frozen in terror of the foul-breathed stranger, Hali tried to think of a safe response. The terrible *differences* of this place where Ship had projected her compounded her sense of helplessness. The dust of the throng which followed the beaten man, the malignant odors, the passions in the voices, the milling movements against a single sun...

"Do you know him?" The man was insistent.

Hali wanted to say she had never before seen the injured man but something told her this could not be true. There had been something disquietingly familiar about that man.

Why did he speak to me of God and knowing?

Could that have been another Shipman projected here? Why

had the wounded man seemed so familiar? And why had he addressed her directly?

"You can tell me." Foul-breath was slyly persistent.

"I came a long way to see him." The old voice which Ship had provided her sounded groveling, but the words were true. She felt it in these old bones she had borrowed. Ship would not lie to her and Ship had said this: . . . *a very great distance*. Whatever this event signified, Ship had brought her expressly to see it.

"I don't place your accent," Foul-breath said. "Are you from Sidon?"

She moved after the crowd and spoke distractedly to the inquisitor who kept pace with her. "I come from Ship."

What were those people doing with the wounded man?

"Ship? I've never heard of that place. Is it part of the Roman March?"

"Ship is far away. Far away."

What were they doing up on that hill? Some of the soldiers had taken the piece of tree and stretched it on the ground. She glimpsed the activity through the crowd.

"Then how can Yaisuah say that you know God's will?" Foul-breath demanded.

This caught her attention. *Yaisuah?* Ship had said that name. It was the name Ship said had become Geezus and then Hesoos. Jesus. She hesitated, stared at her inquisitor.

"You call that one Yaisuah?" she asked.

"You know him by some other name?"

He gripped her arm hard. There was no mistaking the avaricious cunning in his voice and manner.

Ship intruded on her then. *This one is a Roman spy, an informer who works for those who torture Yaisuah.*

"Do you know him?" Foul-breath demanded. He gave her arm a painful shake.

"I think this . . . Yaisuah is related to Ship," she said.

"Related to . . . How can someone be related to a place?"

"Isn't he related to You, Ship?" She spoke the question aloud without thinking.

Yes.

"Ship says that's true," she said.

Foul-breath dropped her arm and stepped back two paces. An angry scowl twisted his mouth.

"Crazy! You're nothing but a crazy old woman! You're just as crazy as that one!" He gestured up the hill where the armored men had taken Yaisuah. "See what happens to crazies?"

She looked where he had pointed.

The two men already hanging there were roped to the cross-pieces and she realized they were being left to die. That was going to happen to Yaisuah!

As the full realization hit her, Hali began to weep.

Ship spoke within her mind: *Tears do little to improve acuity. You must observe.*

She wiped her eyes on a corner of her robe, observing that Foul-breath had moved up into the crowd. She forced herself to climb up with him, pressing in among the people.

I must observe!

The armored ones were stripping the robe from Yaisuah. This exposed his wounds—cuts and bruises all over his body. He stood with a stolid watchfulness through all this, not even responding to the gasp which went up when the mob saw his wounds. There was an unguarded vulnerability to this moment, as though everyone here was participating in his own personal death.

Someone off to the left shouted: "He's a carpenter! Don't tie him on!"

Several large, crudely wrought nails were pressed up through that part of the crowd and thrust into the hands of an armored young man.

Others took up the cry: "Nail him on! Nail him on!"

Two of the armored men supported Yaisuah on either side now. His head swayed slightly from side to side, then bowed. Things were being thrown at him from the far side of the crowd but he made no attempt to dodge. Hali saw stones strike him . . . an occasional glob of spittle.

It was all so . . . so bizarre, played in an orange glow of mute sunlight coming through a high layer of thin clouds.

Hali blinked the tears from her eyes. Ship said she had to observe this! Very well . . . She estimated that she stood no more than six meters from Yaisuah's left shoulder. He appeared to be a wiry man, probably active through most of his adult life, but now he was near the point of exhaustion. Her med-tech training told her that Yaisuah could survive this, given proper care, but she had the impression that he did not want such care, that none of this surprised him. If anything, he seemed anxious to get on with it. Perhaps that was the reaction of a tortured animal, cornered and beyond all will to fight or flee.

As she watched, he lifted his head slowly and turned to face

her. She saw then the slight glow about him, an aura such as she
had seen around her own body when Ship had projected her away
from . . .

Is he also a projection of Ship?

She saw that there was a debate going on among the armored
men. The nails were being waved in front of one of them by the
one who had taken them from the crowd at the far side.

Yaisuah was looking at her, compelling her attention. She saw
recognition in his eyes, the lift of eyebrows . . . a suggestion of
surprise.

Ship intruded: *Yaisuah knows where you are from.*

Are You projecting him?

That flesh lives here as flesh, Ship said. *But there is something
more.*

Something more . . . That's why You brought me here.

What is it, Ekel? What is it?

There was no mistaking the eagerness in Ship.

He has another body somewhere?

No, Ekel. No!

She cringed before Ship's disappointment, forcing herself to
a peak of alertness which her fears demanded.

Something more . . . something more . . . She saw something
then, a significance of the aura. *Time does not confine him.*

That is very close, Ekel. Ship was pleased and this reassured
her, but it did not remove the pressure from the moment.

There is something of him which Time cannot hold, she thought.
Death will not release him!

You please Me, Ekel.

Joy washed through her to be cut off abruptly by Ship's demanding intrusion: *Now! Watch this!*

The armored men had settled their argument. Two of them
threw Yaisuah to the ground, stretching his arms along the timber.

Another took the nails and using a rock for a hammer began
nailing Yaisuah's wrists to the wood.

Someone shouted from the crowd: "If you're the son of God,
let's see you get yourself out of this!"

Hali heard jeering laughter all around her. She had to clasp
her hands across her breast, forcing herself not to rush forward.
This was barbarous! She trembled with frustration.

We are all children of Ship!

She wanted to shout this to these fools. It was the lesson of
her earliest WorShip classes, the admonition of the Chaplain.

Two soldiers lifted the length of wood, hoisting the man who was nailed to it by his wrists. He gasped as they moved him. Four soldiers, two on each side of him, lifted the timber on their spear points into a notch on a tall post which stood upright between the other two victims. Another soldier scrambled up a crude ladder behind the post and lashed the crosspiece into the notch. Two more soldiers moved up to Yaisuah's dangling feet. While one soldier crossed the ankles, the other nailed the feet to the upright. Blood ran down the wood from the wound.

She had to open her mouth wide and breathe in gulping gasps to keep from fainting.

She saw the brown eyes flash with sudden agony as a soldier shook the upright to test its firmness. Yaisuah slumped forward unconscious.

Why are they causing him such pain? What do they want him to do?

Hali pressed forward in the suddenly silent throng, elbowing her way through with a strength which she found surprising in this old body. She had to see it close. She had to see. Ship had commanded her to observe. It was difficult moving in the press of people even with the strength of her inner drive. And she suddenly became aware of the breath-held silence in the throng.

Why were they so silent?

It was as though the answer had been flashed on her eyes. They want Yaisuah to stop this by some secret power in him. They want a miracle! They still want a miracle from him. They want Ship . . . God to reach out of the sky and stop this brutal travesty. They do this thing and they want a god to stop it.

She pressed herself past two more people and found that she had achieved the inner ring of the crowd. There were only the three timber constructions now, the three bodies . . .

I could still save him, she thought.

I play the song to which you must dance. To you is left the freedom of improvisation. This improvisation is what you call free will.

—*The Oakes Covenant*

"THE MEETING will please come to order."

Oakes used his wand-amplifier to dominate the shuffling and buzzing in the Colony's central meeting hall. It was a domed and circular room truncated by a narrow platform against the south wall where he stood. When not being used for meetings, the room was taken over by manufacture of food-production equipment and the sub-assembly operations for the buoyant bags of the LTAs. Because of this, all meetings had to be called at least ten hours in advance to give workers time to clear away machines and fabrics.

He still felt beset by the tensions of moving from shipside to groundside. His time sense was upset by the diurnal shift and this meeting had been rushed. It was almost the hour of mid-meal here. There would be psychological pressures from the audience because of that.

This was the wrong hour for a meeting and there had been some muttering about interference with important work, but Murdoch had silenced that by leaking the announcement that Oakes had come groundside to stay. The implications were obvious. A major push was impending to make Colony secure; Oakes would command that push.

On the platform with Oakes stood Murdoch and Rachel Demarest. Murdoch's position as director of Lab One was well known, and the mystery surrounding that lab's purposes made his presence here a matter of intense curiosity.

Rachel Demarest was another matter. Oakes scowled when he thought about her. She had learned things while acting as a messenger between Ferry and groundside.

Sounds in the room were beginning to subside as the stragglers made their way in and took seats. Portable chairs had been provided, many constructed from the twisted Pandoran plant material. The unique appearance of each chair offended Oakes. Something would have to be done to standardize appearances here.

He scanned the room, noting that Raja Thomas was present in a seat down front. The woman beside Thomas fitted the description Murdoch had provided of one Waela TaoLini, a survivor of the original kelp-research projects. Her knowledge might be dangerous. Well . . . she and the poet would share Thomas' fate. End of that problem!

Oakes had been groundside for almost two diurns now and much of that time had been taken up in preparation for this meeting. There had been many eyes-only reports from Lewis and his minions. Murdoch had been quite useful in this. He would bear watching. Legata had provided some of the data and, even now, was back shipside gathering more.

This meeting represented a serious challenge to his powers, Oakes knew, and he intended to meet it head on. Lewis had estimated that about a thousand people were here. The larger part of Colony personnel could never be spared from guard and maintenance and building and rebuilding. Two steps forward, one step back—that was Pandora's way. Oakes was aware, though, that most of those facing him down on that floor carried the proxy votes of associates. There had been an unofficial election and this would be a real attempt at democracy. He recognized the dangers. Democracy had never been the shipside way and it could not be allowed groundside. It was a sobering thought and he felt adrenaline overcoming an earlier indulgence in wine.

The people were taking a devilish long time to get settled, moving about, forming groups. Oakes waited with what show of patience he could muster. There was a dank, metallic smell in the room which he did not like. And the lights had been tuned too far into the green. He glanced back at the Demarest woman. She was a slight figure with unremarkable features and dull brown hair. She was notable only for her intensely nervous mannerisms. Demarest had been the instigator of the election—a petition-bearer. Oakes managed a smile when he looked at her. Lewis had said he knew how to defuse her. Knowing Lewis, Oakes did not probe for details.

Presently, Rachel Demarest came forward on the platform. Leaving her wand-amplifier on its clip at her wrist, she raised both arms, twisting her palms rapidly. It was interesting that the room fell silent immediately.

Why didn't she use her amplifier? Oakes wondered. Was she an anti-tech?

"Thank you all for coming," she said. Her voice was high and squeaky with a whine at the edge. "We won't take much of your time. Our Ceepee has a copy of your petition and has agreed to answer it point by point."

Your petition! Oakes thought. *Not my petition. Oh, no.*

But evidence from Lewis and Murdoch was clear. This woman wanted a share in Colony power. And she had managed most cleverly. to say *Ceepee* with an emphasis which made the title appear foolish. Battle, therefore, was joined.

As Demarest stepped back, glancing at him, Oakes produced the petition from an inner pocket of his white singlesuit. Making it appear accidental, he dropped the petition. Several pages fluttered off the platform.

"No matter." He waved back people in the front row as they moved to recover the pages. "I remember everything in it."

A glance at Murdoch brought him a reassuring nod. Murdoch had found chairs for himself and Demarest. They sat well back on the platform now.

Oakes hunched forward toward his audience in a gesture of confidence, smiling. "Few of our people are here this morning and you all know the very good reasons for this. Pandora is unforgiving. We all lost loved ones in the four failures on Black Dragon."

He gestured vaguely westward where the rocky eminences of Black Dragon lay hidden beyond the mists of more than a thousand kilometers of ocean. Oakes knew that none of those failures could be laid at his hatch; he had been very careful about that. And his presence permanently groundside imparted a feeling of excitement about Colony prospects here on the undulating plains of The Egg. That sense of impending success had contributed to the confrontation brewing in this room. Colonists were beginning to think beyond the present state of siege, rubbing their wishes together, shaping their desires for personal futures.

"As most of you know," Oakes said, lifting his amplifier to make his voice carry, "I am groundside to stay, groundside to direct the final push for victory."

There was a polite spatter of applause, much less than he had expected. It was high time he came groundside! He had loyalties to weld, organization to improve.

"The Demarest petition, then," he said. "Point One: elimination of one-man patrols." He shook his head. "I wish it could be done. Perhaps you don't understand the reason for them. I'll put it plainly. We are conditioning the animals of Pandora to run like hell when they see a human!"

That brought a rewarding burst of applause.

Oakes waited for it to subside, then: "Your children will have a safer world because of your bravery. Yes, I said *your children*. It is my intent to bring the Natali groundside."

Shocked murmurs greeted this announcement.

"This will not happen immediately," Oakes said, "but it *will* happen. Now—Point Two of the Demarest petition." He pursed his lips in recollection. " 'No major decision about Colony risks or expansion shall be made without approval by a clear majority of Colonists voting in Council.' Do I have that right, Rachel?" He glanced back at her but did not wait for her to respond.

Glancing once more at the scattered papers of the petition on the floor below him, he looked hard at the front row and swept his gaze across the audience.

"Putting aside for the moment the vagueness in that word 'clear' and this unexplained concept of 'Council,' let me point out one thing we all know. It took ten hours to clear this room for a meeting. We have a choice. We keep this hall clear and ready at all times, thereby putting a dangerous strain on production facilities, or we accept a ten-hour delay for every major decision. I prefer to call those *survival* decisions, by the way." He made a show of looking back at the large wall chrono, then returned his attention to the audience. "We've already been here more than fifteen minutes and obviously we will use more time on this."

Oakes cleared his throat, giving them a moment in which to absorb what he had said. He noted a few squirmers in the audience sending signals that they would like to comment on this argument, and he had not missed the fact that Murdoch had taken Rachel

Demarest's arm, whispering in her ear and, incidentally, keeping her from interrupting.

"Point Three," Oakes said. "More rest and recuperation back on the ship. If we..."

"Ship!" Someone in the middle rows shouted. Oakes identified the speaker, a guard on the hangar perimeter squad, one of Demarest's supporters. "Not *the* ship, but Ship!" The man, half out of his seat, was pulled back by a companion.

"Let's face that then," Oakes said. "I presume that a Chaplain/ Psychiatrist has a modicum of expertise with which to address this question."

He glanced at Rachel Demarest who still was being held quietly but firmly by Murdoch. *You want to use titles? Very well, let us put this title into its proper perspective. Not Ceepee, but Chaplain/ Psychiatrist. All the traditions of THE ship stand behind me.*

"I will spell it out for you," Oakes said, turning once more to the audience. "We are a mixed bag of people. Most of us appear to have come from Earth where I was born. We were removed by the ship..."

"Ship saved you!" That damned guard would not stay silent. "Ship saved you! Our sun was going nova!"

"So the ship says!"

Oakes gave it a bit more volume by a touch on his wand's controls. "The facts are open to other interpretation."

"The facts..."

"What have we experienced?" Oakes drowned him out and then reduced the volume. "What have we experienced?" Lower volume still. "We found ourselves on the ship with other people whose origins are not clear, not clear at all. Some clones, some naturals. The ship taught us its language and controlled our history lessons. We learn what the ship wants us to learn. And what are the ship's motives?"

"Blasphemy!"

Oakes waited for the stir of this outcry to subside, then: "The ship also trained me as a doctor and a scientist. I depend on facts I can test for myself. What do I know about Shipmen? We can interbreed. In fact, this whole thing could be a genetic..."

"I know my origins and so does everyone else!" It was Rachel Demarest breaking away from Murdoch and leaping to her feet. She still was not using her wand, but she fumbled with it as she moved toward Oakes. "I'm a clone, but I'm from..."

"So the ship says!"

Again, Oakes hurled that challenge at them. Now, if Lewis and Murdoch had read the Colonists correctly, suspicions had been placed like barbs where they would do the most good when the vote was called.

"So the ship says," Oakes repeated. "I do not doubt your sincerity; I merely am aghast at your credulity."

She was angered by this and, still fumbling with her wand, failed to give herself enough amplification when she said: "That's just your interpretation." Her voice was lost on all but the first rows.

Oakes addressed the audience in his most reasonable manner: "She thinks that's just my interpretation. But I would be failing you as your Chaplain/Psychiatrist if I did not warn you that it is an interpretation you must consider. What *do* we know? Are we merely some cosmic experiment in genetics? We know only that the ship . . ." He gestured upward with his left thumb. ". . . brought us here and will not leave. We are told we must colonize this planet which the ship calls Pandora. You know the legend of Pandora because it's in the ship's educational records, but what do you know about this planet? You can at least suspect that the name is very appropriate!"

He let them absorb this for several blinks, knowing that many among them shared his suspicions.

"Four times we failed to plant a Colony over on Black Dragon!" he shouted. "Four times!"

Let them think about their lost loved ones.

He glanced at Rachel Demarest, who stood three paces to his left, staring at him aghast.

"Why this planet and not a better one?" Oakes demanded. "Look at Pandora! Only two land masses: this dirt under us which the ship calls The Egg, and that other one over there which killed our loved ones—Black Dragon! And what else has the ship given us? The rest of Pandora? What's that? A few islands too small and too dangerous for the risking. And an ocean which harbors the most dangerous life form on the planet. Should we give thanks for this? Should we . . . ?"

"You promised to take up the entire petition!"

It was Rachel Demarest again and this time with her amplifier turned up too far. The intrusion shocked the audience and there were clear signs that many found the shock offensive.

"I *will* take it up, Rachel." Very soft and reasonable. "Your petition was a needed and useful instrument. I agree that we should have better procedures for work assignments. Calling this deficiency to my attention strengthens us. Anything which strengthens us meets my immediate approval. I thank you for it.''

She got her wand under control.

"You imply that the 'lectrokelp is the most dangerous . . .''

"Rachel, I already have started a project which will try to determine if there is something useful to us about the kelp. The director of that project and one of his assistants are sitting right down there.''

Oakes pointed down at Thomas and Waela, saw heads turned, people craning to see.

"Despite the dangers,'' he said, "very potent and obvious dangers, as anyone will agree who has studied the data from these oceans, I have started this project. Your petition comes *after* the fact.''

"Then why couldn't we have learned this when . . .?''

"You want more open communication from those of us making the decisions?''

"We want to know whether we're succeeding or failing!'' Again, she had her amplifer turned too high.

"Reasonable,'' Oakes said. "That is one of the reasons I have moved myself and my staff permanently groundside. In my head . . .'' He tapped his skull. ". . . is the complete plan to make Pandora into a garden planet for . . .''

"We should have Council members on . . .''

"Rachel! You propose having *your* people at key positions? Why *your* people? What record of success do they have?''

"They've survived down here!''

Oakes fought to conceal anger. That had been a low blow. She implied that he had remained safely ensconced shipside while she and her friends risked Pandora's perils. A reasonable tone was the only way to meet that challenge.

"I'm down here now,'' he said. "I intend to stay. I will submit to your questions at any mutually acceptable time, despite the fact which we all know—time taken to debate our problems could be used to better advantage for Colony as a whole.''

"Will you answer our questions today?''

"That's why I called this meeting.''

"Then what's your objection to having an elected Council which . . .?''

"Debating time, just that. We don't have the time for such a luxury. I agreed with those who objected that *this* meeting took us away from more important work, from food. But you insisted, Rachel.''

"What're you doing over on Black Dragon?" That was the objectionable perimeter guard down in the audience, taking a new tack now.

"We are attempting to build another foothold for Colony over on Dragon."

Reasonable . . . reasonable, he reminded himself. *Keep your voice reasonable.*

"Dividing your energies?" Rachel Demarest demanded.

"We are using new clones provided by the ship's facilities," he said. "Jesus Lewis is out there now directing the effort. I assure you that we are risking only new clones who fully understand the nature of their involvement."

Oakes smiled at Rachel Demarest, recalling Murdoch's jocular admonition: "A few lies don't hurt when you've given them some truth to admire."

Turning back to face the audience, Oakes said: "But this diverts us from the orderly resolution of our meeting. Rather than waste our time this way, we should take the issues one at a time."

His announcement about the attempt at Dragon had served its purpose, though. His listeners (even Rachel Demarest) were absorbing the implications with varying degrees of shock.

Someone away in the right rear quadrant of the room shouted: "What do you mean *new* clones?"

Silence followed his demand, a waiting silence which said it spoke a question in the minds of most.

"I'll let Jesus Lewis speak to that at another meeting. It's a technical question about matters which have been under his direct supervision. For now, I can say that the new clones are being bred and conditioned to defeat the perils we all know exist out on Dragon."

There: Lewis was prepared with subtle lies and half truths. The injection of rumors and key elements of their prepared story into Colony's grapevine would tie this issue down. Most people would accept the prepared story. It was always better to know that someone else was going into danger, sparing you that necessity.

"You didn't answer our question about rest and recuperation," Rachel Demarest accused.

"You may not realize it, Rachel, but the schedule of shipside R & R is the most important issue before us today."

"You're not going to buy us off with shipside time!" she said. She was clenching her wand with both hands, pointing it at him like a weapon.

"Again, I am aghast at your limited perception," Oakes said. "You really are not *fit* to be making the decisions which you ask the power to make."

At this direct attack, she backed two steps away from him, glared into his eyes.

Oakes shook his head sadly. "You have a friend down there brave enough to state the essential problem..." Oakes pointed down at the perimeter guard who sat in red-faced anger. *(Have to watch that one. A fanatic for sure.)* "...but not brave enough nor perceptive enough to see the full implications of his emotional outburst."

That did it. The man was on his feet and shaking a fist at Oakes. "You're a false Chaplain! If we follow you, Ship will destroy us!"

"Oh, sit down!"

Oakes used almost the full amplification to drown out the man's voice. The sound-shock provided the man's companions with the interval to pull him back into his seat.

Turning down the amplifier, Oakes asked: "Who among you asks what I ask? An obvious question: Where did WorShip originate? With the ship. That ship!"

He thrust a pointing finger ceilingward. "You all know this. But you don't question it. As a scientist, I must ask the hard physical questions. Some among you argue that the ship has been motivated by the wish to save us—a beneficent savior. Some of you say WorShip is a natural response to our savior. Natural response? But what if we are guinea pigs?"

"What are *your* origins, Oakes?"

That was Rachel Demarest again. Beautiful. She could not have performed better for him had she been programmed. Didn't she know that by the best guess, the naturals outnumbered the clones almost four to one?—perhaps even more. And she already had admitted to being a clone.

"I was a child of Earth," Oakes said, and once more his voice was its most reasonable. He looked directly at her, then back at the audience. A little barbering of the truth was called for now. No need to bring up the fact that old Edmond Kingston had chosen him as successor. "Most of you know my history. I was taken by the ship and trained as Chaplain/Psychiatrist. Don't you understand what that means? The ship directed my training to lead WorShip! Don't any of you find something strange in this?''

Right on cue, Rachel intruded: "That seems the most natural . . .''

"Natural?" Oakes allowed free reign to his rage. "A mirror and recorder would have done just as good a job as such a Chaplain! If we have no free will, our WorShip is sham! How can the ship expect to condition *me* for such a task? No! I question what that ship tells us. I don't even doubt. I question! And I don't like some of the answers.''

This was public blasphemy on a scale few of them had ever imagined. Coming from the Chaplain/Psychiatrist it amounted to an open revolt. Oakes allowed the shock to become well seated in them before hammering it home. He raised his face to the domed ceiling and shouted: "Why don't you strike me dead, *Ship?*''

The hall became one long-held breath while Oakes turned and smiled at Murdoch, then turned the smile on his audience. He reduced the amplifier volume to the minimum required for reaching the hall's extremities.

"I obey the ship because the ship is powerful. We are told to colonize this planet? Very well. That is what we are doing and we are going to succeed. But who can doubt that the ship is dangerous to us? Have you had enough food lately? Why is the ship reducing our food supplies? *I* am not doing this. Send a deputation shipside if you wish to verify this.'' He shook his head from side to side. "No. Our survival requires that we depend as little as possible upon the ship, and . . . eventually, no dependence upon the ship at all. Buy you with shipside time, Rachel? Hell no! I intend to save you by freeing you from the ship!''

It was a simple matter to read the majority reaction to this challenge. He might appear to be a fat little man but he was braver than any of them, dared more than the bravest among them . . . and he was risking new clones (whatever they might be). He was also going to feed them. When it came time for the question: *"Put me out of office or continue me. But no more of this democracy and Council crap."* When it came time for that, it was clear they would support him by acclamation. He was their brave leader, even against *Ship*, and few could doubt it now.

Both Lewis and Murdoch argued for a bit more insurance, though, and Oakes knew it would do no harm to follow their script.

"It has been suggested that we introduce complicated and time-consuming forms into our survival efforts," Oakes said, his voice tired. "The ones who propose this may be sincere but they are dangerous. Slow reactions will kill us all. We are required to act more swiftly than the deadly creatures around us. We cannot wait for debate and group decisions."

As both Lewis and Murdoch had insisted she would do when faced with defeat, Rachel Demarest tried the personal attack. "What makes you think *your* decisions will save us?"

"We are alive and Colony prospers," Oakes said. "My first effort here, my primary reason for being here, is to direct a crash program to increase food production."

"No one else could do what . . ."

"But *I* will!" He allowed just a touch of mild reproof into his tone. Anyone who could defy *Ship* could certainly solve the food problem. "We all know that I did *not* make those decisions which killed our loved ones on Dragon. If I had been making those decisions, we might still be alive and growing out there."

"What decisions? You talk about . . ."

"I would not have wasted our energy trying to understand life forms which were killing us! Simple sterilization of the area was indicated and Edmond Kingston could not bring himself to order it. He paid for that failure with his life . . . but so did many innocents."

She still wanted her reasonable confrontation.

"How can you fight what you don't understand?"

"You kill it," Oakes said, facing her and lowering the amplification. "It's that simple: You kill it."

There is fear in the infinite, in the unlimited chaos of the unstructured. But this boundless "place" is the never-ending resource of that which you call talent, that ability which peels away the fear, exposing its structure and form, creating beauty. This is why the talented people among you are feared. And it is wise to fear the unknown, but only until you see the new-found fearlessness which identity beautifies.

—**Kerro Panille,
Translations from the *Avata***

FOR A concentrated surge of time, Hali Ekel stood at the inner ring of the throng and stared up at the three men so cruelly suspended. It was a nightmare scene—the blood, the dust, the orange light which threw grotesque shadows on the doomed men, the sense of latent violence in every movement around her.

I'm an observer, observer, observer . . .

Her chest hurt when she breathed and she could smell the blood dripping from Yaisuah's nailed feet.

I could save him. She took one shuffling half-step forward.

Don't interfere. Ship's command stopped her. It was not in her to disobey that command. The conditioning of WorShip was too strong.

But he'll die there and he's just like me!

166

He is not just like you.

But he's . . .

No, Ekel. When the time comes, he will remember who he is and he will go back just as you will go back. But you two are profoundly different.

Who is he?

He is Yaisuah, the man who speaks to God.

But he . . . I mean, why are they doing this to him? What did he do?

He reported his conversations. Now, they try to move God in this way. Observe. This is not the way.

God? But God is Ship and Ship is God.

And the infinite is infinite.

Why won't you let me save him?

You could not save him.

I could try.

You would only inflict pain on that old flesh which you have borrowed. That flesh has enough pains. Why would you want to make it suffer more?

It occurred to her then that there might be another consciousness waiting somewhere to re-enter this body. *Borrowed.* She had not thought of it that way. The idea made her intensely aware of responsibility toward the body. She forced her attention away from the dangling figure of Yaisuah—those bleeding feet and palms.

The other two men began struggling against their restraints. Hali saw the cruel reason behind this torture then. In time, they would smother. Their chest muscles would fail and respiration would stop. The roped men pushed their feet against the wooden uprights, trying for leverage, seeking another few blinks of life.

One of the armored men saw this and laughed. "Look at the thieves squirm!"

Someone in the crowd behind Hali jeered: "They're trying to steal a little more time!"

One of the roped men looked down at his armored tormentor and groaned: "You'd hang your own mother." He gasped for another breath, and Hali saw the effort of it in his chest muscles. As he exhaled, he moved his head feebly toward Yaisuah. "This man here did nothing illegal . . ."

The armored man swung his spear butt and smashed the speaker's knees. The thief sagged and writhed in a final rattling agony. As he did this, Yaisuah stirred and turned toward him.

"Today, you go home with me," Yaisuah said.

It was said in a low tone, but most of the crowd heard him. The words were repeated for some few on the outskirts who had missed it.

The armored man laughed, said: "Bullshit!" He swung his spear butt once more and broke the other thief's knees. This man, too, collapsed in a spasm of choking gasps.

Yaisuah lifted his head, then called out: "I'm thirsty."

The spear-swinger looked up at him. "The poor boy's thirsty! We should give him something nice to drink."

Hali wanted to turn away, but could not move. What had made these men into such beasts? She searched around her for something in which to give the dying man a drink.

Once more, Ship warned her: *Let this happen, Ekel! This is a necessary lesson. These people must learn how to live.*

Some of the crowd began to leave. The show was over. Hali found herself alone on one side of the dying man, only a few women across from her . . . and the armored guardians of this torment. A young boy came running up with a jug which he handed to the armored man who had smashed the knees of the thieves. Hali saw a coin passed to the boy. He bit it and turned away, not even looking at the condemned men.

The armored man fastened a rag to the end of his spear, poured some of the jug's contents on it and pushed the rag up to the dying man's mouth.

Hali detected the odor of ascetic acid. *Vinegar!*

But Yaisuah sucked at the rag hungrily. The moisture spread across his cracked asnd bloody mouth. As the rag was pulled away, he slumped forward, once more unconscious.

An older man across from Hali called out: "He'd better die before sundown. We can't leave him up there for the Sabbath."

"Easily done." The armored man had taken the rag from his spear. He turned, ready to swing it against Yaisuah's knees. In that instant, the light faded, darkness spread over the landscape. A moan spread through the crowd. Hali glanced up, saw a partial eclipse behind the clouds.

A young woman broke from the crowd opposite Hali and grabbed the soldier's spear.

"Don't!" she cried. "Let him be. He's nearly gone."

"What's it worth to you?"

The young woman looked up at Yaisuah, who took this moment

to twist in delirium. She looked back at the spearman. Her back was to her companions and she faced only Hali as she lifted the spearman's hand and placed it on her breast inside her robe. At that instant, Yaisuah arched his back against the wooden upright and called out: "Father! Father, why have you forsaken me?"

A great breath shuddered through him. His eyes opened, his gaze directly on Hali.

"It is finished," he said. He fell forward, eyes still open, and did not take another breath.

The abrupt hush was shattered by the wailing of a woman in the group across from Hali. Others joined in, tearing at their garments. The armored man took his hand away from the young woman's breast.

Hali stood fixed in place, staring up at the dead man. As she looked, the sunlight returned. A wind picked up the hem of her robe; it chilled her. She could see the armored men moving off, one of them with an arm around the shoulder of the young woman who had stopped the spear blow. Hali turned away and headed down the hill, unable to watch more. She spoke to Ship as she moved.

Ship?

Yes, Ekel?

Is there a history of this event in the shipside records?

It is there for the asking. You who were raised shipside have not had much reason to ask, especially those of you whose ancestors came from places where this was not common knowledge.

Is this real, him dying there just now?

As real as your flesh waiting shipside.

She felt the tug of that remembered flesh then. This tired old body was such a poor vehicle by comparison. She felt joints aching as she stumbled down the hillside.

I want to go back, Ship.

Not yet

If Yaisuah was a projection, why didn't his body disintegrate when he died?

Active imagination supports him. It is essential to such phenomena. If I were to forget about the you that is shipside or the you that is here, the forgotten flesh would disappear.

But he's dead. What good is it to keep his flesh intact?

The survivors require something to bury. They will return to his tomb one day and find it empty. It will be a marvel. They will say he returned to life and walked from his tomb.

Will he do that?

That is not part of your lesson, Ekel.

If this is a lesson, I want to know what happens to him!

Ahhhh, Ekel, you want so much!

Won't You tell me?

I will tell you this: Those who remember him travel this world over teaching peace and love. For this they suffer murder and torture and they incite great wars in his name, many bloody events even worse than what you have just seen.

She stopped. There were rude buildings just ahead and she felt that she would be more protected in among them. They were more like . . . corridors, like Ship's own passages. But she was filled with outrage. *What kind of a lesson is this? What good is it?*

Ekel, your kind cannot learn peace until you are drenched in violence. You have to disgust yourselves beyond all anger and fear until you learn that neither extortion nor exhortation moves a god. Then you need something to which you can cling. All this takes a long time. It is a difficult lesson.

Why?

Partly because of your doubts.

Is that why You brought me here? To settle my doubts?

There was no response and she felt suddenly bereft, as though Ship had abandoned her. Would Ship do that?

Ship?

What do you hear, Ekel?

She bent her head, listening. Hurried footsteps. She turned. A group of people rushed past her down the hillside. A young man hurried behind this group. He stopped beside Hali.

"You stayed the whole time and did not curse him. Did you love him, too?"

She nodded. The young man's voice was rich and compelling. He took her hand.

"I am called John. Will you pray with me in this hour of our sadness?"

She nodded and touched her lips pretending that she could not speak.

"Oh, dear woman. If he had but said the word, your affliction would have passed from you. He was a great man. They mocked him as the son of God, but all he claimed was a kinship to Man. 'The Son of Man,' he said. That is the difference between gods and men—gods do not murder their children. They do not exterminate themselves.''

She sensed then in this young man's manner and his voice the power of that event on the hillside. It frightened her, but she realized that this encounter was an important part of what Ship wanted her to experience.

Some things break free of Time, she thought.

You can come back to your own flesh now, Ekel, Ship said.

Wait!

John was praying, his eyes closed, his grip firm on her hand. She felt it was vital to hear his words.

"Lord," he said, "we are gathered here in your name. One in the foolishness of youth and the other infirm with age, we ask that you remember us as we remember you. As long as there are eyes to read and ears to hear, you will not be forgotten. . . ."

She listened to the earnestness of the prayer as it unraveled from his mind. The firm touch of his hand pleased her. There were faint veins on his eyelids which trembled as he spoke. She did not even mind the universal stink which came from him as it came from all of those she had encountered here. He was dark, like Kerro, but he had wild, wiry hair that framed his smooth face and accented his intensity.

I could love this man!

Careful, Ekel.

Ship's warning amused her as much as her own thought had surprised her. But one look at the old, liver-spotted hand that John held reminded her she walked in another time. This was an old woman's body which enclosed her awareness.

". . . we ask this in Yaisuah's name," John concluded. He released her hand, patted her shoulder. "It would not be good for you to be seen with us."

She nodded.

"Soon we will meet again," he said, "at this house or that, and we will talk more of the Master and the home to which he has returned."

She thanked him with her eyes and watched him until he turned a corner and was gone among the houses below her.

I want to go home, Ship.

There came a moment of blankness and, once more, the tunnel passage, then the lab's dazzling lights pained her eyes after the Earthside dusk.

But those other eyes weren't the same as these eyes!

She sat up, feeling the vital agility of this familiar flesh. It reassured her that Ship had kept the promise to return her to her own body.

Ship?

Ask, Ekel.

You said I would learn about interfering with Time. Did I interfere?

I interfered, Ekel. Do you understand the consequences?

She thought about John's voice in prayer, the power in him— the terrible power which Yaisuah's death had released. It was unleashed power, capable of joy or agony. The sense of that power terrified her. Ship interfered and this power resulted. What good was such power?

What is your choice, Ekel?

Joy or agony—the choice is mine?

What choice, Ekel?

How do I choose?

By choosing, by learning.

I do not want that power!

But now you have it.

Why?

Because you asked.

I didn't know..

That is often the case when you ask.

I want joy but I don't know how to choose!

You will learn.

She swung her feet off the yellow couch, crossed to the screen and keyboard where this terrifying experience had begun. Her mind felt ancient suddenly, an old mind in a young body.

I did ask; I started it . . . back in that ancient time when all I wanted was Kerro Panille.

She sat down at the keyboard and stared into the screen. Her fingers strayed over the keys. They felt familiar, yet strange. Kerro's fingers had touched these keys. She saw this instrument suddenly as a container which held raw experiences at a distance. You did not have to go in person. This machine made terrible things acceptable. She took a deep breath and punched the keys: ANCIENT HISTORY RECORDS—YAISUAH/JESUS.

But Ship was not through intruding.

If there is any of it you wish to see in person, Ekel, you have but to ask.

The very thought sent shudders through her body.
This is my body and I'm staying in it.
That, Ekel, is a choice which you may have to share.

My imagination was too much exalted by my first success to permit me to doubt of my ability to give life to an animal as complex and wonderful as man.

—Mary Shelley's *Frankenstein,*
   Shiprecords

"I LIKE to call this the Flower Room," Murdoch said, leading Rachel Demarest across the open area to the lock. It was bright there, and she did not like the way the younger clones pulled back from Murdoch. A clone herself, she had heard the stories about this place and wanted to hold back, to delay what was happening. But it was her only chance at the Oakes/Lewis political circle. Murdoch kept a strong grip on her arm just above the elbow and she knew the pain he could cause if she hesitated.

Murdoch stopped at the lock and glanced at his charge.

This one won't carry any more petitions, he thought.

The slightly blue cast to her skin, her nervous, gangly limbs made her appear cold.

"Perhaps you and I could work something out," she said, and pressed her hip against him.

Murdoch was tempted . . . but that blue skin!

"I'm sorry, but this is standard for everyone who works here. There are things we need to know—and things that you need to know, too."

He really was sorry, remembering dimly some of the things which had happened to him during his own Scream Room initiation. There were things which he did not remember, too—a disturbing fact in itself. But orders were orders.

"Is this the place you call the Scream Room?" Her voice was barely a whisper as she stared at the hatch into the lock.

"It's the Flower Room," he said. "All of these beautiful young clones..." He waved vaguely at the room behind her.

"All of them come from here."

She wanted to glance back. There had been some strangely shaped people hugging the rear of the throngs in the room, some with colors even stranger than her own. Something in Murdoch's manner prevented her from turning.

He took her hand then and placed her palm on the sensor-scribe beside the hatch—"To record your entry time." She felt an odd stinging sensation as her palm touched the scribe.

Murdoch smiled, but there was no mirth in it. His free hand went out to the lock-cycling switch. The hatch hissed open and he thrust her into it.

"In you go."

She heard the hatch seal behind her, but her attention was on the inner hatch as it opened. When it had swung wide, she realized that what she had thought was a grotesque statue standing there was actually a naked living creature framed by the open end of the lock. And... and there were tears streaming down the creature's cheeks.

"Come in, my dear." His voice was full of hoarse gruntings.

She moved toward him hesitantly, aware that Murdoch was watching through the sensors overhead. The room she entered was lighted by corner tubes which filled the entire space with a deep red illumination.

The gargoyle took her arm as the hatch sealed behind her and he swung her into the room.

His arms are too long.

"I am Jessup," he said. "Come to me when you are through."

Rachel looked around at a circle of grinning figures—some of them male, some female. There were among them creatures even more grotesque than Jessup. She saw that a male with short arms and bulbous head directly in front of her had an enormous erection. He bent over to grasp it and point it at her.

These people are real! she thought. *This is not a nightmare.*

The rumors she had heard did not even begin to describe this place.

"Clones," Jessup whispered beside her, as though he had been reading her mind. "All clones and they owe their lives to Jesus Lewis."

Clones? These aren't clones; they're recombinant mutants.

"But clones are people," she whispered.

Bulbous-head lurched one step toward her, still holding that enormous erection pointed at her.

"Clones are property," Jessup said, his voice firm but still with those odd gruntings in it. "Lewis says it and it must be true. You may develop an ... appreciation for certain of them."

Jessup started to move away, but she clutched his arm. How cold his flesh was! "No ... wait."

"Yes?" Grunting.

"What ... what happens here?"

Jessup looked at the waiting circle. "They are children, just children. Only weeks old."

"But they're ..."

"Lewis can grow a full clone in a matter of days."

"Days?" She was clutching at any delay. "How ... I mean, the energy ..."

"We eat a lot of *burst* in here. Lewis says this is the reason his people invented burst."

She nodded. The food shortage—it would be amplified enormously by the requirements of making burst.

Jessup leaned close to her ear, whispered: "And Lewis learned some beautiful tricks from the kelp."

She looked at him full at him—that too-wide face with its toothless mouth and high cheeks, the pinpoint eyes, the receding forehead and protruding chin. Her gaze traveled down his body—enormous chest, but sunken with incurving ... and narrow hips ... pipestem legs ... He was ... he was not just *he,* she saw, but both sexes. And now she understood the grunting. He was fucking himself ... herself! Little muscles at the crotch moved the ...

Rachel whirled away, her mind searching wildly for something, anything to say.

"Why are you crying?" Her voice was too high.

"Ohhh, I always cry. It doesn't mean anything."

Bulbous-head lurched another step toward her and the circle moved with him.

"Entertainment time," Jessup said and pushed her roughly toward Bulbous-head.

She felt hands clutching her, turning her, and, presently, her memory left her... but for a long time she felt that she heard screams and she wondered if they might be her screams.

Absolute dependence is the hallmark of religion. It posits the supplicant and the one who dispenses gifts. The supplicant employs ritual and prayer in the attempt to influence (control) the dispenser of gifts. The kinship between this relationship and the days of absolute monarchs cannot be overlooked. This dependence on supplication gives to the keeper of those two essentials—the ritual paraphernalia and the purity of prayerful forms (that is, to the Chaplain)—a power akin to that of the gift dispenser.

> **—"Training the Chaplain/Psychiatrist"**
> **Moonbase Documents**
> **(from *Shiprecords*)**

RAJA THOMAS strode along a Colony passage with Waela TaoLini at his side. They both wore insulated yellow singlesuits with collar attachments for breather-helmets. It was first-light of Rega outside, but in here was the soft gold of dayside illumination that any Colonist could remember from shipside.

The food of this diurn's first meal sat heavily in his stomach and he wondered at that. They were adding some odd filler to the food. What was happening to the shipside agraria? Could it be possible, as Oakes' people hinted, that Ship was cutting down on hydroponics output?

Waela was oddly silent as she matched his pace. He glanced

178

at her and found her studying him. Their eyes flicked past a confrontation too brief to call recognition, but an orange glow suffused her neck and face.

Waela stared straight ahead. They were bound for the test-launch apron to inspect the new submersible gondola and its carrier. It would be tried first in the enclosed and insulated tank at the hangar before being risked in Pandora's unpredictable ocean.

Why can't I just say no? she wondered. She did not have to get at the poet in the way Thomas ordered. There were other ways. It occurred to her then to ask herself about the society of Thomas' origins. *What was his conditioning that he thinks sex is the best way to lower the psyche's guards?*

As happened on rare occasions when she was with others, Honesty spoke within her head: "Men ruled and women were a subordinate class."

She knew this had to be true. It fitted his behavior.

Thomas was speaking silently to himself: *I am Thomas. I am Thomas. I am Thomas . . .*

The strange thing about this inner chant which he had adopted as his personal litany was that it increased his sensitivity to doubts. Could it be something built into the name?

Waela no longer trusts me . . . if she ever did.

What is this poet and where is he? Processing was taking an unconscionably long time with him. *Will he be an arm of Ship?*

Why were they getting a poet on their team? It had to be a clue to Ship's plans. Obscure, perhaps . . . convoluted . . . but a clue. This might be the element of the deadly game which he was required to discover for himself.

How much time do we have?

Ship did not always play the game by rules that were just and fair.

You're not always fair, are You, Ship?

If you mean even-handed, yes, I am fair. The answer surprised Thomas. He had not expected Ship to respond while he walked along this corridor.

Thomas glanced at Waela—silent woman. Her color had returned to its normal pale pink. Did Ship ever talk to her?

I talk to her quite often, Devil. She calls me Honesty.

Thomas missed a step in surprise.

Does she know it's You?

She is not conscious of that, no.

Do You talk to others without their knowing?

To many, very many.

Thomas and Waela turned a corner into another portless passage, this one illuminated by the pale blue of overhead strip lighting—the color code which told them that it led outside somewhere up ahead. He glanced at Waela's hip, saw the ever-present lasgun in its holster there.

Waela broke the silence.

"Those new clones that Oakes says are being used out on Dragon—what do you suppose they are?"

"People with faster responses."

"I don't trust that Lewis."

Thomas found himself in agreement. Lewis remained a mystery figure—the brutal alter-ego to Oakes? There were stories about Lewis which suggested that Ship had held nothing back when lifting the lid of Pandora's box.

They had come to the hatch into the hangar. Thomas hesitated before signaling the dogwatch to admit them. He glanced through the transparent port, saw that the sky doors of the hangar were closed. There should be little delay.

"What's eating you, Waela?"

She met his gaze. "I've been wondering if there's anyone I can trust."

Pandora's curse, he thought, and chose to direct her suspicions at Oakes.

"Why don't we insist on an inspection team to explore everything Oakes is doing?"

"Do you think they'd let us?"

"It's worth finding out."

"I'll suggest it to Rachel when I see her."

"Call her when we get inside."

"Can't. The roster says she's on vegetation patrol, south perimeter. I'll call her nightside."

Without knowing precisely why, Thomas felt a chill at hearing this. Was that stupid Demarest woman in danger? He shook his head. They were all in danger, every moment.

Again, Thomas peered through the port at activity in the hangar. There were bright lights around the sub. The LTA was lost in shadows above. Many workers moved around in the lighted area. He could see that they had opened the floorgate to expose the testing basin beneath the hangar. The lights glistened off exposed water beside the plaz gondola and its carrier-sub. Ahh, yes. They were mating the sub and gondola.

So Rachel would not be back from south perimeter until night-side. He was caught by the curious persistences in Waela's ship-style language.

Nightside.

The irregular diurns of a planet with two suns caused few circadian problems for Colonists. They had been Shipmen, and Shipmen had a ready referent at hand: Day and Night were not times, but sides. Was there a clue here, something to help him in his search for a way to the heart of these people? He had thought that if he succeeded in communicating with the 'lectrokelp, this would give him the desired status.

Anything to help us fit into the rhythms of Pandora.

If Colonists learn to trust me . . . if they look up to me . . . then I can tell them what Ship really wants of them. They will believe and they will follow.

That sub in there—would it be the key? *Persistent symbols.* What would persist in the symbols of an intelligent vegetable? It was intelligent. He was convinced of it. So was Waela. But the symbols remained a mystery.

Fireflies in the night of the sea.

Did they talk to each other beneath the waves?

We do.

Waela gestured at the signal switch beside the hatch.

"What's the delay?"

"They're mating the new gondola and the sub. I didn't want to call anyone away from that."

He nodded as he saw the gondola swing into place, then he depressed the switch.

Presently, a green-clad workman unsealed the inner locks and the hatch swung open. Slow procedure, but this was a dangerous area. Hatches could be locked either side—from inside when the skydoors were open. Everything groundside was designed to contain an attack.

There was a musty aroma of outside within the hangar which set Thomas' nerves on edge.

Waela preceded him across the hangar floor, striding out with that watchful swing which Colonists never put aside, head turning, gaze darting about. Her pale singlesuit fitted her body like another skin.

He had insisted they go through Stores for the new suits. As he had ordered, they were insulated against the sea's chill, elim-inating the need for insulation on the gondola. Plaz was an excellent conductor unless doubled or tripled. This decision gave them a few extra centimeters in the gondola core.

Waela had disconcerted him when they picked up the suits. In shipside style, there were no separate dressing rooms. She had moved right into the try-on area with him. That habit of bodily candor still bothered him. He always found it necessary to turn his back when dressing or undressing with a female companion. Waela, on the other hand, remained frankly direct.

"Raj, did you know that you have a funny-looking mole on your butt?"

Without thinking, he had turned his head toward her just in time to see her stepping into her suit—breasts and pubis exposed. There was just the slightest hesitation in her while she continued dressing, as though she spoke only to his eyes, saying: *"Of course I'm a woman. You knew that."*

He found himself intensely aware that she was a woman, and there was no denying the magnetic attraction she worked on him. There also was no denying that she knew this and was amused by it in an undefinably gentle way. This knowledge in her might even have contributed to her upset when he asked her to apply sexual pressure to the new team member.

She was right, too. It was cheating.

But what if Ship is cheating us?

Doubts—always doubts. He found himself in silent agreement with some of the things Oakes had said. On the other hand, he could not fault Waela's argument: "We don't help ourselves by cheating each other."

That open candor in her attracted him as much as the chemistry of her physical presence.

But I am the goad, the devil's advocate, the challenger. I am the knight among the pawns.

And he knew he did not have much time. Ship might hand him an impossible deadline at any moment. Or Oakes and his crew might make good on their unspoken threat to cut this project off at the pockets as soon as they dared.

There was no mistaking the latent anger in Waela—it betrayed itself in her stride (a bit too emphatic) and in the way she studied him now when she thought he was not looking. But she would get to Panille and ask all of the proper questions. That was the important thing.

Thomas still felt remnants of her anger as they stepped into the glaring light and bustle at the testing apron where the new sub was cradled. She was all business as she stared up at this creation which had emerged from Thomas' commands.

It was a fat metallic teardrop, slightly elongated, its LTA attachment eyelets extending along the top in a double ridge reminiscent of the backbone of an antedeluvian Earthside monster. The principle was relatively simple. Most of the external sub was carrier for the plaz globe of the gondola at the core. Only the drive motors and fuel storage were made strong against the sea's pressures. The carrier had one more important function now visible to her eyes: Vertical lines of plaz-bubble lights extended up and down its sides—each bubble four centimeters in diameter. The trigger system to light them in sequence passed through a computer/sensor feedback program. What the sensor-eyes *saw* in the ocean depths, these lights could play back. The kelp's patterns would be its patterns, the kelp's rhythms its rhythms.

The chief of Construction Services, Hapat Lavu, came out to meet them at the edge of the lighted area. He was a slender, driving man, completely bald. His gray eyes missed few details of his work and, despite a biting and accusatory tongue which delivered reprimands with thin-lipped fury, he was one of the best-liked Colonists. The common assessment was, "You can depend on Hap."

Dependability gained high marks groundside, and Hap Lavu was fighting for his reputation. Of all the equipment from his shops, only the subs had failed to match Pandora's demands. Sixteen had been lost without a trace; there had been survivors from four, and the wreckage of three others had been located on the bottom. All had been crushed or otherwise disabled by giant strands of kelp.

Lavu's assessment was the opinion of many: "That damn stuff can think and it's a killer."

He had become an admirer of Thomas during their short association. Thomas had taken the accepted sub-components and reworked them into this new design. The only parts of the plan Lavu distrusted involved communications and pickup. He spoke to that as he greeted Thomas: "You should have something better than the rocketsonde. They fail, y'know."

"We'll stick with it," Thomas said.

He knew what worried Lavu. The ubiquitous 'lectrokelp not only clogged the seas, but their electrical activity jammed the communications channels—sonar to radar. Hylighter exhibited similar phenomena. Was there a relationship? There was no pattern to the jamming; it was random squirts of signal activity. Because of this, they depended on high power and line-of-sight relays waterside. Even then, a cloud of hylighters rising from the sea could block transmissions.

"You'll have to surface before you can communicate," Lavu said. "Now, if you'd let me adapt the anchor cable to..."

"Too many lines to the sub," Thomas said. "We could tangle in them."

"Then pray that y'can lift above interference for the relays to take your talk-talk."

Thomas nodded agreement. The plan was to anchor the LTA in a lagoon, slip down the anchor cable in a vertical dive and stay clear of the kelp barriers.

"We'll observe, play back their light patterns and seek any new coherent patterns in the lights or their electrical activity," he had said.

It was a workable plan. Several subs had survived exploratory dives by giving a wide berth to the kelp. It was when the subs went in to take specimens that violence occurred.

Workable...but with unavoidable weaknesses.

Their LTA would hang at the surface, tethered on its anchor-line and awaiting the sub's return from the depths. A plan to have another LTA with a lift-gondola anchored or standing by aloft had been scratched. The winds were too unpredictable and it was argued that two LTAs anchored in the same lagoon would pose dangerous maneuvering problems. The necessary size of such an LTA made them difficult to handle in tight quarters. The standard procedure at the hangar was to winch them down after grappling the downhaul hawser. Instead, their LTA bag had been triple-reinforced with compartmented cells.

These arguments went through Thomas' mind as he studied the new submersible.

Was it worth the risk? He felt that he was challenging Ship, but the stakes were the highest.

Will You let me die here, Ship?

No answer, but Ship had said that his destiny was his own now. That was a rule of this game.

If the kelp is sentient and we can make contact, the rewards will be enormous. Intelligent vegetable! Did it WorShip? It could be the key to Ship's demands.

Ship called the kelp intelligent and that could be another twist of this game. Should he doubt?

It occurred to Thomas then that if Ship were telling the truth, the kelp might be close to immortal. Except for specimens damaged by human intrusion, they had never seen dead kelp.

Did it live forever?

"Do y'still reject a standby LTA?" Lavu asked.

"How long could you hold one in sight of us?" Thomas asked.

"Depends on the weather, as y'well know."

There was resentment in Lavu's voice. He took it personally that so many of his creations had been destroyed, all of them equipped as best he knew for underwater survival. The answer, of course, was that Pandora's planet-wide sea contained perils beyond those they knew. Lavu felt that the entire project was now a challenge to him. He did not want to quit. It was more than a concern about hardware. Lavu wanted to go out as crew.

"How else can I learn what's needed if I don't go out m'self?"

"No," Thomas said.

All right, Ship. This will be the big throw of the dice.

Devil, why do you persist in such overly dramatic poses? This time, he expected the response and was ready for it.

Because they won't listen to me here unless I become bigger than life to them.

Life can never be bigger than itself.

Lavu patted the outer surface of the sub as Waela moved up beside him. She had been listening to the undertones in the conversation between Thomas and Lavu.

What drives Thomas? she wondered.

She had only the barest details about him. Out of hyb and into command of this project. Ship's doing, he said.

Why?

"She's heavier than any of the others," Lavu said, thinking that the question in Waela's mind. "I defy any Pandoran monster to break it."

"Did you solve the problem of filling the LTA?" Thomas asked.

"You'll have to get your final inflation outside," Lavu said, "I've laid on extra perimeter guards because the skydoors'll be open longer'n I like."

"The sub itself?" Waela asked.

"We've rigged guide cables up through the doors. That's it."

Instinctively, Thomas glanced up at the iris closure of the skydoors.

"She'll be ready by oh-six hundred at the latest," Lavu said.

"You'll have a full nightside of rest before going out. Who's to ride with y'?"

"Not you, Hap," Thomas said.

"But I . . ."

"A new fellow named Panille is to go with us," Thomas said.

"So I've heard. Untrained. A poet? Is that the truth?"

"An expert in communication," Thomas said.

"Well, then, let's run the tank test," Lavu said. He turned and waved a hand signal at an aide.

"We'll ride it with you," Thomas said. "What pressure will you take it to?"

"Five hundred meters."

Thomas glanced at Waela. She gave the barest inclination of her head to indicate agreement, then returned her attention to the sub. It curved over her, more than three times her height at the thickest part of the teardrop near its bow. The outer carrier concealed all but the upper bubble of the plaz gondola within it. The induction propeller at the stern had been shielded in a complex baffle and screening system which reduced its effectiveness, but guarded it against kelp fouling.

Workers ran a ladder up the side of the hull now, cushioned it with a foam blanket to keep the exterior signal lights clean, and steadied it while Lavu mounted. He spoke as he climbed.

"We've installed the manual override to insure that no random signal opens your hatch. You'll have to undog it by hand every time y'open it."

No surprises there, Thomas thought. That had been Waela's idea. There were suspicions that the kelp could control signals in a wide scanning spectrum and that some of the lost subs had merely been opened underwater by scanner-activation of their hatch motors.

Waela scrambled up behind Lavu, leaving Thomas to follow. They were already inside when he reached the open hatch. He paused there to peer along this craft he would command. In a way, it was a small Voidship. The stabilizer fins were like solar panels. Exterior sensors for all of the cardinal dirctions were like a Voidship's hull eyes. And every known weak point had been multiple-reinforced.

Backup systems piled on backup systems.

He turned, found the top rung of the access ladder with a foot and stepped down into the gondola. It was red-lighted gloom there with Lavu and Waela already at their positions. Waela was bent over her console, checking her instruments, leaving the line of her left cheek visible to Thomas in the red light. How tender and beautiful that line was, he thought. Immediately, he suppressed a cynical laugh.

Well, my glands are still working.

Cain rose up against Abel, his brother, and slew him. And the Lord said unto Cain, "Where is Abel, thy brother?" and he said, "I know not: am I my brother's keeper?" and He said, "What hast thou done? The voice of thy brother's blood cries unto Me from the ground."

—Christian *Book of the Dead,*
Shiprecords

"ANYTHING GOES here?" Legata asked.

She studied Sy Murdoch carefully as he thought about the question. He was taking too long to answer. She did not like this man, the pale eyes which defied everything around them. He kept the lab too bright, especially this late in the dayside. The young E-clones huddled against a far wall were obviously terrified of him.

"Well?"

"That takes a little thought," Murdoch said.

Legata pursed her lips. This was her second visit to Lab One in three diurns. She did not believe the reasons for this one. Oakes had pretended anger that she had not *penetrated* every element of the lab, but she had sensed the flaws in his performance. He was lying.

Why had Oakes sent her back here? Lewis was no longer out of contact. What did those two know that they had not shared with her? Legata felt anger at the frustrating unknowns.

Murdoch moved cautiously. Oakes had ordered Legata sent through the Scream Room, an "exploratory," but had warned: "She is frighteningly strong."

188

How strong? Stronger than me?

He did not see how she could be. Such a bouncy little thing.

"I asked you a simple question," Legata said, not bothering to conceal her anger.

"Interesting question, but not simple. Why do you ask it that way?"

"Because I've seen the lab reports to Morgan. You're doing some strange things here."

"Well . . . I would say that there are few limits here, but isn't that the basis for discovery?"

She replied with a cold stare, and he went on.

"There are few limits here, so long as Doctor Oakes has a complete holorecord of what we do."

"He has us on holo right now," she said.

"I know."

The way he said that made Legata's skin crawl. Murdoch carried his powerful body like a dancer. He lifted his chin and she saw a scar beneath his jaw that she had not noticed before. It mingled with creases as he lowered his chin. There was no telling his age. Given the possibility that he might be a clone, there was no telling his chronological age either.

Have to look into him, she noted to herself.

The things Lewis was having done here . . .

She glanced around the room once more. Something was not right. She saw the usual holo, com-console, sensors, but the place offended her directly. She was one who appreciated beauty. Not decoration, but beauty. The two huge flowers flanking the hatch-way . . . she'd noticed them before. They were pink as tongues and their petals convoluted into one another like a line of mirrors.

Strange, she thought, *they smell like sweat.*

"Let's get on with it," she said.

"First, a formality requested by Doctor Oakes."

Murdoch swung a sensorscribe from a panel beside the lock. It appeared to be the standard identification reader of her shipside experience. She placed her hand on the flat plate to allow it to read her.

Stupid formality, everyone knew who she was.

A sudden tingling sensation shot up her arm from her palm and she realized that Murdoch had said something to her. What did he say?

"I'm sorry . . . what?"

She felt weak and disoriented. Something. . . .

She saw that the hatch was open and she had no memory of him opening it. What had he done to her?

Murdoch's hand was on her shoulder propelling her into the lock. As she passed through the hatchway she imagined that she heard a tiny voice pleading from the heart of one of the flowers: *Feed me, feed me.*

She heard the hatch seal behind her and realized that she was alone and the inner door was swinging open... slowly ... ponderous. What was all the red light? And those dim shapes moving...?

She walked toward the opening hatch.

So strange that Murdoch had not accompanied her. She peered at the shapes awash in the red glow beyond the inner hatch. Oh, yes—the new E-clones. Some of them she recognized from the lab reports. They were designed to match the synapse-quick demons of Pandora. There was a problem with breeding for speed, something she'd intended to investigate.

What was it she wanted to watch for?

A voice whispered in her ear: "I am Jessup. Come to me when you are through."

How did I get inside here?

Something was wrong with her time sense. She swallowed hard and felt the thickness of her dry tongue rasp against the roof of her mouth.

"Good and evil hang their uniforms at the door."

Did somebody say that or did I think it?

Oakes had said, "Anything goes on Pandora. Our every fancy is possible there."

That's why I asked Murdoch... where is Murdoch? The gargoyle clones were all around her now and she tried to focus on them. Her eyes were not tracking. Someone grabbed her left arm. Painful.

"Let go of me, you..."

She rippled her arm and heard the grunts of surprise. Peculiar things were happening to her sense of time and the awareness of her own flesh. Blood welled up on her arms and she had no memory of how it got there. And her body—it was naked. Her muscles corded reflexively and she crouched in defense.

What is happening to me?

More hands—rough hands. She responded in a slow-motion flex of power. And she distinctly heard someone screaming. How odd that no one responded to those screams!

*Humans spend their lives in mazes. If they escape
and cannot find another maze, they create one. What
is this passion for testing?*

—**Kerro Panille,
Questions from the** *Avata*

RAJA THOMAS awoke in darkness and it was like that most
recent time, awakening in hyb. He found himself disoriented in
darkness, waiting for dangers he could not locate. Slowly, it came
to him that he was in his groundside cubby . . . night. He glanced
at the luminous time display beside his pallet: two hours into the
midnight watch.

What awakened me?

His cubby was eight levels under the Pandoran surface, a choice
location cushioned from surface noises and perils by numerous
color-coded passages, locks, hatches, slide-tubes and seemingly
endless branchings. The Ship-trained found no difficulty recording
mental maps of such layouts, the more remote the address the
better. Thomas resented being buried in these depths. Too much
travel time to places which demanded his attention.

Lab One.

He had gone to sleep while wondering about that restricted
place. The source of so many odd rumors.

"They're breeding people who're faster than the demons."

That was the popular story.

"Oakes and Lewis want nothing but servile zombies!"

Thomas had heard that story from one of the new militants, a fiery young woman associate of Rachel Demarest.

Slowly, he sat up and tried to probe the darkness around him. *Odd I should awaken at this hour.*

He touched the light plate on the wall beside his head and a dim glow replaced the dark. The cubby appeared boringly normal: his singlesuit draped over a slideseat . . . sandals. Everything as it should be.

"I feel like a damned Spinneret down here."

He spoke it aloud while rubbing his face. Presently, he summoned a servo, then slipped into his clothing while waiting for it. The servo buzzed his hatch and he stepped out into an empty passage lighted by the widely spaced ceiling bulbs of nightside. Seating himself in the servo, he ordered it to take him topside. He felt oppressed by the travel time, the weight of construction overhead.

I never needed open spaces shipside. Maybe I'm going native.

The servo emitted an irritating hum full of subsonics.

At the surface autosentry checkpoint, he keyed his code into the system. With the green *go* signal came the blinking yellow light for *Condition 2*. He swore under his breath, then turned to the lockers beside the topside hatch and took out a lasgun. He knew the hatch would not open unless he did this. The weapon felt clumsy in his hands and, when he holstered it, he was intensely conscious of the weight at his waist.

"Doesn't take much sense to know you shouldn't live in a place if you have to carry a gun." He muttered it, but his voice was loud enough that the blue *acknowledge* light winked at him from the sentry plate.

Still the hatch remained sealed to him. His hand was moving toward the override switch when he saw the little blinker at the bottom of the plate demanding: "Purpose of movement?"

"Work inspection," he said.

The sytem digested this, then opened the hatch.

Thomas slipped off the servo and strode out into the topside corridors, sure now of why he had awakened at this hour.

Lab One.

It was a mystery of peculiar odor.

He found himself presently in the darkened perimeter halls, passing an occasional worker and the well-spaced extrusions of sentry posts, each with its armed occupant paying attention only to the nightside landscape.

Plaz ports showed Thomas that it was moonlight out there, two moons quartering the southern horizon. Pandora's night was a buzz of shadows.

After a space, the ring passage ramped downward into a hatch-distribution dome about thirty meters in diameter. The passage to Lab One was indicated by an "L-1" sign on his right. He had taken only two steps toward it when it opened and a woman emerged, slamming the hatch behind her. It was dim in the dome, lighted only by the moonlight coming in through plaz ports on his left, but there was no mistaking the almost disjointed agitation in her movements.

The woman darted toward him, grabbing his arm as he passed, dragging him along toward the external ports with a strength which astonished him.

"Come here! I need you."

Her voice was husky and full of odd undertones. Her face and arms were a mass of scratches and he sensed the unmistakable odor of blood on her light singlesuit.

"What . . ."

"Don't question me!"

There was wildness, a touch of insanity, in her voice.

And she was beautiful.

She released him when they reached the barrier wall, and he saw the dim outline of an emergency hatch to Pandora's perilous open air. Her hands were busy at the hatch controls, keying the override system in a way that did not set off the alarms. One of her hands reached out and grabbed his right wrist, guiding his hand to the lock mechanism. Such strength in her!

"When I say so, open this hatch. Wait twenty-three minutes, then look for me. Let me in."

Before he could find the words to protest, she slipped out of her singlesuit and thrust it at him. He caught it involuntarily with his free hand. She already was crouching to thong her feet and he saw that she had a magnificent body—smooth muscles, a supple perfection—but swatches of Celltape criss-crossed her skin.

"What's happened to you?"

"I warned you once not to question." She spoke without looking up, and he sensed the wild power in her. Dangerous. Very dangerous. No inhibitions.

"You're going to run the P," he said. He glanced around, looking for someone, anyone, to call on for help. The circle of the distribution dome contained no other people.

"Bet on me," she said, standing.

"How will I tell the twenty-three minutes?" he asked.

She crowded close to him and slapped a panel beside the emergency hatch. Immediately, he heard the sentry circuit's hum, then a deep male voice: "Post Nine clear."

A tiny screen above the circuit speaker glowed with red numerals: 2:29.

"The hatch," she said.

There was no way to avoid it; he had felt her wild strength. He undogged the hatch and she thrust past him, swinging it wide as she dashed out into the open, turning right. Her body was a silver blur in the moonlight and he saw a dark shadow coming up behind her. His gun was in his hand without thinking about it and he cooked a Hooded Dasher that was only a step behind her. She did not turn.

His hands were shaking as he resealed the hatch.

Running the P!

He glanced at the time signal: 2:29. She had said twenty-three minutes. That would put her back at the hatch by 2:52.

It occurred to him then that the perimeter was just under ten kilometers.

It can't be done! No one can run ten kilometers in twenty-three minutes!

But she had come from the passage to Lab One. He unwadded her singlesuit. Blood on it, no doubt of that. Her name was stitched over the left breast: *Legata*.

He wondered if it was a first or last name.

Or a title?

He peered out of the plaz port, looking to the left where she would have to appear if she really did run the perimeter.

What would a Legata be?

A voice on the sentry circuit startled him: "Someone's out there, pretty far out."

Another voice answered: "It's a woman running the P. She just rounded Post Thirty-Eight."

"Who is it?"

"Too far out to identify."

Thomas found himself praying for her to make it as he listened to each succeeding post report the runner. But he knew there was not much chance. Since learning about The Game from Waela, he had looked into the statistics. Fifty-fifty in dayside, yes. But nightside, fewer than one in fifty made it.

The timer beside his head moved with an agonizing slowness: 2:48. It seemed to him that it took an hour shifting to 2:49. The sentries were silent now.

Why didn't the sentries mark her passage?

As though to answer him, a voice on the circuit said: "She just rounded East Eighty-Nine!"

"Who the hell is that out there?"

"She's still too far out to identify."

Thomas drew his lasgun and put a hand on the hatchdog. The word was that the last minutes were the worst, Pandora's demons ganging up on the runner. He peered out into the moonshadows.

2:50.

He spun the hatchdog, opened it a crack. No movement. . . . Nothing. Not even a demon. He found that he was swearing under his breath, muttering: "Come on, Legata. Come on. You can do it. Don't blow the fucking run at the end!"

Something flickered in the shadows off to his left. He swung the hatch wide.

There she was!

It was like a dance—leaping, dodging. Something large and black swerved behind her. Thomas took careful aim and burned another Dasher as she sped past him without breaking her stride. There was a musky odor of perspiration from her. He slammed the hatch and dogged it. Something crashed into the barrier as he sealed it.

Too late, you fucker!

He turned to see her slipping through the Lab One hatchway, her singlesuit in hand. She waved to him as the hatch hissed shut.

Legata, he thought. Then: *Ten klicks in twenty-three minutes!*

There was a babble of conversation on the sentry circuit.

"Anybody know who that was?"

"Negative. Where'd she go?"

"Somewhere over near Lab One dome."

"Sheee-it! That must've been the fastest time ever."

Thomas slapped the switch to shut them off, but not before a male voice said: "I'd sure like to have that little honey chasing . . ."

Thomas crossed over to the Lab One hatch, heaved on the dog. It refused to move, sealed.

All that just to put a hashmark above her eyebrow?

No . . . it had to be much more than the mark of success.

What were they doing down there in Lab One?

Again, he tried the hatchdog. It refused to budge. He shook his head and walked slowly back to the autosentry gate where he picked up a servo and rode it to his quarters. All the way down he kept wondering:

What the hell's a Legata?

The clone of a clone does not necessarily stay closer to the original than a clone of the older original. It depends on cellular interference and other elements which may be introduced. Passage of time always introduces other elements.

—**Jesus Lewis,**
The New Cloning Manual

OAKES SNAPPED off the holo and swiveled his chair around to stare at the design on the wall of his groundside cubby.

He did not like this place. It was smaller than his quarters shipside. The air smelled strange. He did not like the casual way some of the Colonists treated him. He found himself constantly aware of Pandora's surface . . . right out there.

Never mind that it was many layers of Colony construction beyond his quarters, it was *right out there.*

Despite the few familiar furnishings he had brought groundside, this place would never feel as comfortable as his old shipside cubby.

Except that the dangers of the ship—the dangers which only he knew—were more distant.

Oakes sighed.

It was late dayside and he still had many things to do, but what he had seen on the holo compelled his attention.

A most unsatisfactory performance.

197

He chewed at his lower lip. *No . . . it was more than unsatisfactory. Disturbing.*

Oakes leaned back and tried to relax. The holo of Legata's visit to the Scream Room filled him with disquiet. He shook his head. In spite of the drug suppressing her cortical responses, she had resisted. Nothing in her Scream Room performance could be held against her . . . except . . . no. She had done nothing.

Nothing!

If he had not seen it for himself . . . Would she ask to see this holo? He thought not, but nothing was certain. None of the others had asked to see their holos, although everyone knew such a record was made.

Legata had not performed according to pattern. Things were done to her and she resisted other things. The holo gave him no absolutely secure hold on her.

If she sees that holo, she'll know.

How could he keep the record of it from the best-known Search Technician?

Was it a mistake . . . sending her into the Scream Room?

But he thought he still knew her. Yes. She would not take action against him unless she were in great pain. And she might not ask for the holo. Might . . . not.

Not once in the Scream Room had Legata sought her own pleasure. She had acted only in reaction to the application of pain.

Pain that I commanded.

This made him uncomfortable.

It was necessary!

Given an adversary as potent as the ship, he had to take extreme measures. He had to explore the limits.

I'm justified.

Legata had not even required sedation after emerging from the Scream Room.

Where did she go, dashing off like that with only the minimal Celltape on her wounds?

She had returned naked, carrying her singlesuit.

Oakes had heard the rumors that someone had run the perimeter in that interval. Surely not Legata. A coincidence, no more. And the proof of it was that she wore no hashmark.

Damn fool! Running in the open at night like that!

He would have liked to prohibit The Game, but Lewis had warned him off this, and his own good sense had agreed. There was no way to prevent The Game without wasting too much manpower policing all the hatches. Besides, The Game vented certain impulses of violence.

Legata running the perimeter?

Certainly not!

Efficient damned woman! She was expected back at work by evening, the physical marks of her Scream Room experience almost gone. He looked at the notes beside his left hand. Unconsciously, he had addressed them to her.

"Check on possible relationship between waxing of Alki and growth of 'lectrokelp. Have Lab One begin two LH clones. Map new data on dissidents—special attention to those associated with Rachel Demarest."

Would Legata even take his orders now?

The picture of Legata's face from the holorecord kept slipping back into his mind.

She trusted me.

Had she really trusted him? Why else would she go back to Lab One when her misgivings about it were all that apparent? With anyone else, he would have laughed at such musings, but not with Legata. She was painfully different from the others and he had already taken her too far.

Entertainment time.

It had not been as entertaining as he had expected. He recalled the first potent look of betrayal in her eyes when the sonics hit her. The sonics had driven away the clones; they already had taken their entertainment. But even heavy pain had not moved Legata. Despite sedation, she could hear Murdoch's commands. And the sedation had been designed to suppress her will . . . but she resisted. Murdoch's commands told her what to do, the clone was prepared, the equipment set—but even then, she had to be totally awash with pain before inflicting anything like her own agony on the clone. Most of the time, her gaze had sought out the holo scanner. She had stared directly into the scanner, and the dimming of her eyes gave him no pleasure, no pleasure at all.

She won't remember. They never do.

Most of the subjects begged, offered anything for the pain to stop. Legata simply stared at the scanner, wide-eyed. Somewhere in her, he knew, there had been awareness that she was totally helpless, totally subject to his every whim. It was a conditioning process. He wanted her to be like the rest. He could deal with that.

But he had been unprepared for the shock of her difference.

Yes, she was different. What a shock, finally discovering this magnificent difference, to know that he had destroyed it. Whatever private trust they might have had was gone forever.

Forever.

She would never again trust him completely. Oh, she would obey—perhaps even more promptly now. But no trust.

He felt himself shaking with this knowledge. Tense, distracted. He had to force himself to relax, to concentrate on something which comforted.

Nothing is forever, he thought.

Presently, he drifted into his own peculiar arena of sleep, but it was a sleep haunted by the design on his cubby wall. The design took on distorted shapes from the holo of Legata in the Scream Room.

And Pandora was *right out there* . . . and . . . and . . . *tomorrow* . . .

HUMANKERRO: *"Does the listener protect his own sense of understanding and consciousness?"*

AVATA: *"Ahhh, you are building barriers."*

HUMANKERRO: *"That's what you call the illusion of understanding, is it not?"*

AVATA: *"If you understand, then you cannot learn. By saying you understand, you construct barriers."*

HUMANKERRO: *"But I can remember understanding things."*

AVATA: *"Memory only understands the presence or absence of electrical signals."*

HUMANKERRO: *"Then what's the combination, the program for learning?"*

AVATA: *"Now you open the path. It is the program which counts in the most literal sense."*

HUMANKERRO: *"But what are the rules?"*

AVATA: *"Are there rules underlying every aspect of human life? Is that your question?"*

HUMANKERRO: *"That appears to be the question."*

AVATA: *"Then answer it. What are the rules for being human?"*

HUMANKERRO: *"But I asked you!"*

AVATA: *"But you are human and I am Avata."*

HUMANKERRO: *"Well, what are the rules for being Avata?"*

AVATA: *"Ahhhh, Humankerro, we embody such knowledge but we cannot know it."*

HUMANKERRO: *"You appear to be saying that such knowledge cannot be reduced to language."*

AVATA: *"Language cannot occur in a reference vacuum."*

HUMANKERRO: *"Don't we know what we're talking about?"*

AVATA: *"Using language involves much more than recognizing strings of words. Language and the world to which it refers . . ."*

HUMANKERRO: *"The script of the play."*

AVATA: *"The script, yes. The script of the game and its world must be interrelated. How can you substitute a word or some other symbol for every cellular element of your body?"*

HUMANKERRO: *"I can talk with my body."*

AVATA: *"For that, you do not need a script."*

—**Kerro Panille,**
The Avata, **"The Q & A Game"**

*The mystery of consciousness? Erroneous data—
significant results.*

—P. Weygand,
Voidship Med-tech

OAKES WATCHED the sentry on the Colony scanner. The man writhed and screamed in agony. The evening light of Alki cast long purple shadows which twisted as the man flopped and turned. The Current Outside Activity circuits reproduced the sounds of the sentry with clear fidelity, terrifyingly immediate. The man might be just outside this cubby's hatch instead of on Colony's north perimeter as the sensor log indicated.

The screams turned to a hoarse growl, like a turbine running down. There came a convulsive flopping, shudders, then quiet.

Oakes found that the sentry's first screams still echoed in memory and would not be silenced.

Runners! Runners!

There was no escaping Pandora anywhere groundside. Colony remained under constant siege. And at the Redoubt—sterilization was their only solution. Kill everything.

Oakes found that he had pressed his hands to his ears trying to quiet the memory of those screams. Slowly, he brought his hands down to the scanner controls, looking at them as though *they* had betrayed him. He had just been running through the available sensors, scanning for any random COA which might require his attention. And . . . and he had encountered horror.

Images continued to play in his mind.

The sentry had clawed at his own eyes, ripping out the nerve tissue which Runners found so succulent. But he must have known what every Colonist knew—there could be no help for him. Once Runners contacted nerve tissue they could not be stopped until they encysted their clutch of eggs in his brain.

Except that this particular sentry knew about chlorine. Had some residual hope clutched at his doomed awareness? Surely not. Once the Runners were in his flesh, that was too late even for chlorine.

To Oakes, the most horrible part of the incident was that he knew the sentry: Illuyank. Part of Murdoch's Lab One crew. And before that, the doomed sentry had been with Lewis on Black Dragon Redoubt. Illuyank had been a survivor—three times running the P . . . and one of those who came back from Edmond Kingston's team. Illuyank had even come shipside to report on Kingston's failure.

I heard his report.

Movement in the scanner riveted Oakes' attention. The sentry's backup stepped into view (not too close!) with lasgun at the ready. The backup was marked as an ultimate coward by Colony rules. He had not been able to shoot the doomed Illuyank. So the Runners' victim had died the most miserable death Pandora could offer.

Now, the backup aimed his gun and burned Illuyank's head to char. Standard procedure. *Cook them out.* Those eggs, at least, would never hatch.

Oakes found the strength to switch off the scanner. His body was shaking so hard he could not move himself away from the console.

It had just been a routine scan, the kind of thing he did regularly shipside. The horror of this place!

What has the ship done to us?

Groundside—nowhere to turn for escape. No release from the knowledge that he could not survive on this synapse-quick world without multiple barriers and constant guarding.

And there was no turning back. Lewis was right. Colony required constant attention. Delicate decisions about personnel movements and assignments, the shifting of supplies and equipment to Redoubt—none of this could be trusted to shipside-groundside communications channels. Pandora required swift action and reaction. Lewis could not divide his attention between Redoubt and Colony.

Oakes pressed a thumb against the lump of pellet in his neck. Useless now. Groundside static interference limited range . . . and when that impediment lifted, as it did for brief moments, the random signals which came through proved that their secrecy had been breached.

The ship had to be the source of those signals. The ship! Still interfering. The pellets would have to come out at the first opportunity.

Oakes lifted a bottle from the floor beside his console. His hand still shook from the shock of Illuyank's death. He tried to pour a glass of wine and slopped most of it over his console where the sticky red splash reminded him of blood pulsing out of the sentry's empty sockets . . . out of his nose . . . his mouth . . .

The three tattooed hashmarks over Illuyank's left eye remained burned in Oakes' memory.

Damn this place!

Gripping the glass with both hands, Oakes drained what little remained in it. Even that small swallow soothed his stomach.

At least I won't throw up.

He put the empty glass on the lip of his console, and his gaze swept around the confines of his cubby. It was not big enough. He longed for the space he'd enjoyed shipside. But there could be no retreat—no return to the slavery of the ship.

We're going to beat You, Ship!

Bravo!

Everything groundside reminded him that he did not belong here. The speed of the Colonists! There was nothing like that speed shipside. Oakes knew he was too heavy, too out of condition to consider keeping up, much less protecting himself. He needed constant guarding. It festered in him that Illuyank had been one of the people considered for his own guard force. Illuyank was supposed to be a survivor.

Even survivors die here.

He had to get out of this room, had to walk somewhere. But when he pushed himself away from the console to stand and turn around, he confronted another wall. It came to him then that the loss of his lavish shipside cubby was a greater blow than anticipated. He needed the Redoubt for physical and psychological reasons as well as for a secure base of command. This damned cubby was larger than any other groundside, but by the time they housed his command console, his holo equipment and the other accoutrements of the Ceepee, he was almost crowded out.

There's no room to breathe in here.

He put a hand to the hatchdogs, wanting the release of a walk in the corridors, but when his hand touched cold metal he realized how all of those corridors led to the open, unguarded surface of Pandora. The hatch was one more barrier against the ravages of this place.

I'll eat something.

And perhaps Legata could be summoned on some pretext. Practical Legata. Lovely Legata. How useful she remained ... except that he did not like what had happened deep in her eyes. Was it time to ask Lewis for a replacement? Oakes could not find the will to do this.

I made a mistake with her.

He could admit this only to himself. It had been a mistake sending Legata to the Scream Room.

She's changed.

She reminded him now of the shipside agrarium workers. What had really impressed him out there was the difference between those workers and other Shipmen. Agrarium workers were a tight-lipped lot and always busy—sometimes noisy in their work but silent in themselves.

That was it. Legata had become silent in herself.

She was like the agrarium workers, containing seriousness, almost a reverence ... not the grimness found in the Vitro labs or around the axolotl tanks where Lewis produced his miracles ... but something else.

It occurred to Oakes that the agraria were the only parts of the ship where he had felt out of place. This thought disturbed him.

Legata makes me feel out of place now.

And there was no escaping the choices he had made. He would have to live with the consequences. Choices resulted from information. He had acted on bad information.

Who gave me that bad information? Lewis?

What control systems reposed in the information, leading inevitably to certain choices?

Such a simple question.

He turned it over in his mind, feeling that it put him on the track of something vital. Perhaps it was the key to the ship's true nature. A key somewhere in the flow of information.

Information-to-choice-to-action.

Simple, always simple. The true scientist was required to suspect complexity.

Occam's razor really cuts.

What choices did the ship make and on the basis of what information? Would the ship openly oppose moving the Natali groundside, for instance? The move could not yet be made, but the possibility of open opposition excited him. He longed for such opposition.

Show your hand, you mechanical monster!

The ship can act without hands.

But could the ship act without curiosity and without leaving clues?

As an intelligent, questioning being, Oakes felt the constant need to sharpen his curiosity, to keep himself in motion. He might not always move smoothly—that business with Legata—but he had to move ... in jumps and fits and starts ... whatever. The success of his movements stayed relative to his own intelligence and the information available.

Better information.

Excitement shot through him. With the right information, could he design the test which would prove, once and for all, that the ship was not God? An end to the ship's pretenses forever!

What information did he possess? The ship's consciousness? It had to be conscious. To assume otherwise would be to move backward—bad choice. Whatever else it might be, the ship could only be viewed as a complex intelligence.

A truly intelligent being might move seldom, but it would move surely and on the basis of reliable information which had been tested somehow for predictability.

Testing by large numbers or over a long time.

One or the other.

How long had the ship been testing its Shipmen? In a pure-chance universe, past results could not always guarantee predictions. Could the ship's decisions be predicted?

Oakes felt his heart thumping hard and fast. In this game, he truly felt himself come alive. It was like sex ... but this could be even bigger—the biggest game in the universe.

If the ship's movements and choices could be predicted, they could be precipitated. He would have the key to quick and easy victory on Pandora. What action could he take to link the ship's powers to his own desires? Given the right information, he could control even a god.

Control!

What was prayer but a whining, sniveling attempt to control. Supplication? Threats?

If You don't get me assigned to Medical, Ship, I'll abandon WorShip!

So much for WorShip. The gods, if there were any, could have a good laugh.

Abruptly, he was sobered by memory of Illuyank's death.

Damn this place!

To walk in a shipside agrarium right now . . . or even in a treedome . . .

He remembered once nightside on the ship, walking out through the shutter-baffles to a dome on the rim, pressing his forehead against the plaz to stare into the void. Out there, stars whirled in their slow spin and he had known, beyond a doubt, that they spun around him. But, in the face of those uncounted stars, he had felt himself slipping into a maw of terrifying black. On the other side of that plasmaglass barrier, whole galaxies awoke and whole galaxies died every second. No call for help could carry beyond the tip of his own tongue. No caress could survive the cold.

Who else in that universe was this much alone?

Ship.

The voice of his mind had spoken the unexpected. But he had known it for the truth. In that instant he had seen, in the plaz, the reflection of his own eyes melting into the dark between the stars. He recalled that he had stepped back in mute surprise.

That look! That same expression!

It had been on the face of the black man back on Earth when they took the man away.

Remembering, he realized it was the same expression he now saw in Legata's eyes.

In my eyes . . . in her eyes . . . in the eyes of the black man from my childhood . . .

Now, feeling the groundside cubby around him, all of the concentric rings of walls and barriers which comprised Colony, he sensed how his unguarded body could be betrayed.

I could betray myself to myself.

And perhaps to others.

To Thomas?

To the ship?

No matter his denials, the mystery of deep space and inner space filled him with wonder and fear. This was a weakness and it required that he deal with it directly.

God or not, the ship was one of a kind. *As I am.*

And what if . . . *Ship* were really God?

Oakes passed his tongue over his lips. He stood alone in the center of his cubby and listened.

For what am I listening?

He could only move by testing, by forcing the exchange, by groping beyond the ken of all other Shipmen. The key to the ship lay in its movements. Why did any organism move?

To seek pleasure, to avoid pain.

Food was pleasure. He felt hunger knot his stomach. Sex was pleasure. Where was Legata right now? Victory was pleasure. That would have to wait.

Let the pains demand their own actions.

Always the pendulum swung: pleasure/pain . . . pleasure/pain. Intensity and period varied; the balance, the mean, did not.

What sweets would tempt a god? What thorn would lift a god's foot?

It came over Oakes that he had been standing for a long time in one position, his gaze fixed on the mandala pattern attached to his cubby wall. It copied the one he had left shipside. Legata had made this copy for him before . . . She had produced another in her finest hand and it already was displayed at the Redoubt. How he wished the Redoubt were ready! Demons gone, dayside and nightside safe. Many times he had dreamed of stepping out into Pandora's double-sunshine, a light breeze ruffling his hair, Legata on his arm for a walk through gardens down to a gentle sea.

A sudden image of Legata clawing at her eyes replaced this pastoral vision. Oakes fought for a deep breath, his gaze fixed on the mandala.

Lewis has to destroy all of the demons—the kelp, everything!

It required a physical effort for Oakes to break himself away from his fixation on the mandala. He turned, walked three steps, stopped . . . He was facing the mandala!

What's happening to my mind?

Daydreaming. That had to be it, letting his mind wander. The pressure of all those demons outside Colony's perimeter walls overwhelmed him with feelings of vulnerability. He had lost the insulation he had enjoyed shipside—exchanged the perils of the ship for the perils of Pandora.

Who would ever have thought I'd miss the ship?

The damned Colonists were too brash, too quick. They thought they could barge in any time, interrupt anything. They talked too fast. Everything had to be done right now!

His com-console buzzed at him.

Oakes depressed a key. Murdoch's thin face stared at him from the screen. Murdoch began speaking without asking leave, without any preamble.

"My dayside orders say you wanted Illuyank assigned to . . ."

"Illuyank's dead," Oakes said, his voice flat. He enjoyed the look of surprise on Murdoch's face. That was one of the reasons for secret random sampling among the spy sensors. No matter what horrors you found, the information could make you appear omnipotent.

"Find someone else for my guard squad," Oakes said. "Make it someone more suitable." He broke the connection.

There! That was the way they did it groundside. Quick decisions.

The reminder of Illuyank's death brought back the knot in his stomach. Food. He needed something to eat. He turned, and once more found himself looking at the mandala.

Things will simply have to slow down.

The mandala rippled before his eyes, myriad grotesque faces weaving in and out of the design, folding upon themselves.

Belatedly, he realized that one of the faces was that of Rachel Demarest. Silly bitch! The Scream Room had driven her out of her mind . . . what was left of her mind. Running outside like that! Enough people had seen the demons get her that no blame would be laid at his hatch. One problem gone . . . but running outside . . .

Everything reminds me of outside!

Someone else would have to be found to make the liquor deliveries to old Win Ferry. Pure grain spirits he wanted now. And Ferry would have to get the message—no more pestering questions about that Demarest woman.

Oakes found that his hands ached and he realized both fists were clenched. He forced himself to relax, began to rub at the beginnings of cramp in his fingers. Maybe another small drink of the wine . . . No!

All this frustration! For what?

Only one answer, the answer he had given Lewis so many times: *For this world.*

Victory would give them their own safe world. Unconsciously, his right hand went out and touched the mandala. What a price! And Legata—historian, search technician, beautiful woman—perhaps she would be his queen. He owed her that, at least. Empress. His finger traced the maze of lines in the mandala, flowing intricacies.

"Politics is your life, not mine" Lewis had said.

Lewis did not know what it cost. All Lewis wanted was his lab and the safety of the Redoubt.

"Leave me alone here. You can proclaim and make policy all you want."

They were a great team—one in front and one behind.

Maybe just a little bit of the wine. He picked up the bottle and sipped from it. This Raja Thomas would be eliminated soon. Another victim of the kelp.

Lewis ought to drink more of this wine. They've really improved it.

Oakes sipped the wine, aerated it across his tongue with a slurping sound which he knew always made Lewis uneasy.

"You really should treat yourself to some of this stuff, Jesus. You might smooth some of those lines out of your face."

"No thanks."

"All the more for me, then."

"You and Ferry."

"No. I can take it or leave it alone."

"We have urgent problems," Lewis kept saying.

But urgency should never mean hurry, incautious rushing about. He had told Lewis in no uncertain terms: "If we're relaxed and reasonable in our urgency to complete the Redoubt, the solutions we find will be relaxed and reasonable."

No need for chaos.

He slurped more of the wine while staring at the mandala. The way those lines twisted—they, too, appeared to come right out of chaos. But Legata had found the design of it, duplicated it twice. Design. Pandora had its design, too. He just had to find it. Peel away all of this dissonance, and there would be the foundations of order.

We'll finish off the kelp, the Runners. Chlorine. Lots of it.

Things will start making sense around here pretty soon.

He lifted the bottle to take another sip, found that there was no more wine in it. He let the bottle slip out of his hand, heard it thump on the floor. As though that were the signal, his com-console buzzed at him once more.

Murdoch again.

"Demarest's people are asking for another meeting, Doctor."

"Stall them! I told you to sh . . . stall them."

"I'll try."

Murdoch did not sound very happy with the decision.

Oakes took two stabs with a finger to break the connection. How many times did you have to give an order around this damned place?

Once more, he focused on the mandala.

"We'll have some order around here pretty soon," he told it.

He realized then that he had taken too much wine. It sounded ridiculous, talking to himself in quarters this way, but he enjoyed hearing certain things, even if he had to be the one who voiced them.

"Gonna get some order around here."

Where was that damned Legata? Had to tell her to get some order into things.

*As the rock silences the sea, the One in one silences
the universe.*

—**Kerro Panille,
Translations from the** *Avata*

LEGATA PUT her shuttle on automatic for its landing at the
Redoubt station. She leaned back into her couch and watched the
shoreline sweep past beneath her. This time was her own. It was
early dayside and she did not have to deal with Oakes or Lewis
just yet, nor with demons or clones. She had nothing to do but
watch, relax and breathe easy.

Hylighters!

She had seen them on holo, and a few had skirted Colony
while she was there, but these hung no more than two hundred
meters from the plaz in front of her.

Ship's teeth! They're huge!

She counted twelve of them, the largest one half again as big
as her shuttle. Their bronzed orange sails caught the wind and
they tacked in unison, almost escorting her. The sunlight through
the membrane of their sails shimmered rainbows all over them.
Most of their tentacles were tucked up against their bodies. They
each held a ballast-rock with their two longest tendrils. The larger
ones allowed the rocks to drag in the sea, forming a frothy wake.
They tacked, and tacked again, picking up on the shifts of wind.
As her shuttle settled into its final glide-path, she saw two of the
smaller hylighters separate from the rest, pick up speed and slam

213

the boulders they carried into the plaz shield surrounding Oakes' private garden.

Garden, she shuddered at the thought of the word.

The boulders had no effect on the plaz—she could crash her shuttle into it and it might shatter, but rocks . . .

The two hylighters disappeared in a flash so bright that for a few blinks she was blinded. When her vision cleared, she saw that her shuttle was down and linked with the entry lock, and that the two exploded hylighters had been a diversion. The others, all larger, slammed their rocks into the walls and plaz of the Redoubt where it had already been damaged by the clones. Each boulder chipped off a few more chunks of the buildings before the sentries focused on the sails. The other hylighters too, went up in a flash. The largest one was so close to the shuttle station when it exploded that it took part of the control tower and rigging with it.

They give their lives for this, she thought. *They are either very foolish or very noble.*

Several parts of the grounds were in flames and a work crew, covered by sentires, was busy fighting the fires. Lewis beckoned her from the plaz verandah at Oakes' quarters and it was only then that she noticed the scorchmarks across the dome of her shuttle.

She opened her hatch and stepped out between two sentries who escorted her along the covered way to the Redoubt. There was a strong taint of chlorine lingering over everything.

At least we don't have to worry about Runners, she thought.

Over the chlorine she caught the sea-smell from the beach, and saw that the tideline had moved down several meters from its usual mark. The damp sand left behind was warmed by the suns. A heavy mist rose from it, dissipating in wisps over the rocks and the sea. She did not look at Lewis until she stepped up to the verandah.

"Legata," he offered his hand, "how are you?"

The searching expression in his eyes told her all that she needed to know.

So that's why I'm here, she thought. *He wants to explore my current . . . utility before Oakes arrives.*

"Quite well," she said, "that was a wonderful display the hylighters put on. Did you arrange it just for me?"

"If I'd arranged it, it wouldn't have cost us damage we can't afford."

He led her inside and closed the hatch behind them.

"How much damage?"

He was leading her further inside, away from the plaz. She wanted to see the grounds, the repairs.

"Not irreparable. Would you care for something to eat?"

A woman with large, fanlike ears walked past them, accompanied by a normal crewman carrying a lasgun.

"No, thank you, I'm not hungry."

At Legata's response, the woman turned, looked her full into the eyes as if she wanted to say something, then turned quickly and went outside. Legata remembered that a rallying cry of the clone revolt had been *I'm hungry now!* and she was embarrassed.

"Those ears . . . why?"

"She can hear a Hooded Dasher at a hundred meters. That gives us a full second's advantage. Attractive, too, don't you think?"

"Yes," Legata said coldly, "quite."

She noticed that Lewis was still limping, but she did not sympathize with him. Although she was curious about details of the revolt, she didn't ask. She countered by not dropping the subject.

"How reparable is 'not irreparable'?"

Lewis dropped his cordiality and assumed his usual business-like air.

"We lost most of our clone work force. Fewer than half of those remaining are effective. We're getting replacements from Colony and the ship, but that's slow work. Two of the finished hangars are badly damaged—hatches missing, holes in the walls. The clones' quarters have their exterior walls and hatches intact, but the interiors are completely useless. Serves 'em right. Let 'em sleep on the piles of plaz."

"What about this building?"

"Took some damage back where the clones' quarters join with the storage area. They got into the kitchen but that's where we sealed them off . . ."

"You sealed them off?"

Lewis glanced away from her, then back. He rubbed his nose with his finger and she was reminded of Oakes when he was nervous. When it became obvious that he wouldn't answer, she nodded.

"After you discovered chlorine killed the Runners, how long before you released it among the people you had sealed off?"

"Now, Legata, you weren't here. You didn't see what they were . . ."

"How long?"

He looked her in the eyes, but did not answer.

"So, you killed them."

"Runners killed them."

"But you could've killed the Runners."

"Then the clones would've gotten inside and killed us. You weren't here. You don't know what it was like."

"Yes, I think I do. Show me to Morgan's Garden."

It took all of her nerve just to say that word. Whatever that horror she had confronted at Colony, the name of *The Garden* would not be shaken off, even though she could not remember. But she saw it made Lewis uneasy to think about it and she would be damned if she would ease anything for him.

Lewis was obviously shaken by the sudden reference to *The Garden*. It meant Scream Room to him, too. She could see the questions forming behind his eyes: *How much does she know? Why isn't she afraid?* She refused to allow herself the luxury of fear. Let him see that much. Until she herself remembered what had happened, she would not allow anyone else to capitalize on her experience there.

"Yes," he said, his voice almost hushed, "of course. The Garden. You can relax there until Morgan comes. This way."

Lewis led Legata through the finished parts of the resort and into the main dwelling, a mammoth structure carved entirely out of the mottled stone of the mountainside and lined with plasteel. She turned at the entryway and looked back over the grounds and out across the sea.

"This hatchway opens to Morgan's quarters. The study, library and cubby are all in this unit. Further back are the meeting and dining areas, all of that. I'll take you through them if you like."

She watched the pulse of waves explode against the seawall ahead of them and imagined she could hear the *slap* and *crash* of the water through the insulating plaz.

"Legata?"

"Yes. I mean, no, you don't have to guide me. I'd like to be alone."

"Very well." Lewis spoke abruptly, "Morgan said that you are to be comfortable. I suggest you check with me before wandering around. You may need a sentry for some of the more exposed areas. It's still early and I'm not due back at Colony until after midmeal. Call if you need me."

With that, the hatch hissed shut and she was alone.

Once more, she looked at the sea. It tumbled away forever,

drawing her consciousness outward, reaching.

There's a power here that even Morgan can't buy, she thought, and fought back the temptation to run past the plazzed-in trees, the flowers, and the pond, past the stream meandering through the grasses, past the protection of the compound itself and into the wild sea air of Pandora. Then she noticed the kelp. The great masses of it which had glutted the beaches and the bay outside the Redoubt were reduced to a few isolated clumps and some long, serpentine tendrils undulating at the Surface. *Lewis' doing!* A sudden sadness filled her eyes with tears and she whispered aloud to the kelp, "I hope they're wrong. I hope you make it."

She caught a movement out of the corner of her eye and turned to see two clones working on the tower at the shuttle station.

Morgan's expected in, she thought, *they'll want things looking as controlled as possible*.

She looked closer at the two men, her attention caught by the fact that they were lifting and welding plaz that was at least four meters off the ground—*and neither was using scaffolding*.

Those arms . . .

She wondered, coldly, where those workers fit within the clone index and price list.

"Cost is no object, my dear," Murdoch had said, and something in his inflection had terrified her. This terror was rekindled by the sight of the two workers busily welding plaz.

Anything went, she thought, *my every fantasy was possible*. *Why can't I remember?*

Whatever horrors or pleasures took place in the Scream Room were no longer a part of her consciousness. There were flashes, uncontrollable and swift, that struck her mute in mid-conversation or mid-thought. Those who worked with her attributed it to a growing absentmindedness, an offshoot of her apparent love affair with The Boss.

She knew she could find the Scream Room holo, and see for herself what she had done. Oakes taunted her with it.

"Dear Legata," his every corpulent pore oozed honey and oil, "sit here with me, have a nice drink, and we'll enjoy your games in the Scream Room."

He laughed at first when she shuddered and turned away. It was difficult for her to keep any personal control—he'd seen to that when he'd had her trapped and helpless down in Lab One. And now the Scream Room had been moved to the Redoubt.

The laughter died away and he had spoken to her directly and flatly, "Like it or not, you're one of us now. You can never go back. You may never walk into that room again, but you *did* walk into it once. Of your own free will, I might add."

"Free will!" her blue eyes flashed up at him. "You drugged me! And those . . . *monsters*. Where was their free will?"

"They would have no will at all, no existence at all, if it weren't for me. . . ."

"If it weren't for Ship, you mean."

He sighed overdramatically. She remembered that he glanced at his viewscreen and made a few adjustments on his console.

"Sometimes I really don't understand you, Legata. One day soon you'll be luxuriating in the Redoubt and its exquisite pleasures, and here you are mumbling dark-ages crap about the mystical powers of Ship."

He had shown her a holo, then, of this garden around her now. There was no question of its beauty. It was thick with vegetation and the perfumes of countless blossoms. She turned her eyes up to the dome. The immensity and wonder of the Pandoran sky pumped a strange surge of power through her. She experienced a feeling of . . . of . . .

Connection! she thought. *Yes, no matter what he does, somehow all of this is alive in me just as I live in it now.*

At Colony the nightside before, as she had been preparing to leave for the Redoubt, Oakes had escorted her into the tiny plaz dome far above his quarters.

"There," he had pointed out a large white glow slowly traversing the horizon, "there is your ship. Another pinpoint in the night. It takes no mysticism, no degree of godhood whatsoever, for one bit of mass to orbit another."

"That's blasphemy," she answered, because he expected it.

"Is it? Ship can defend itself. Nothing is out of the hearing or the reach of Ship. Ship could terminate my program at any instant—but chooses not to. *Or can't.* Either is the same to me. Blasphemy?"

He had squeezed her hand tight, then. *Convincing himself,* she thought, and she had enjoyed the power this observation gave her.

He gestured widely, indicating the entire display of stars.

"I have brought you to this, not Ship. Ship is a tool. Complexity to the fifth power, granted, but still a tool. Built by people, *thinking* people, for the use of thinking people. People who know how to take charge, how to see light in the darkening storm of confusion . . ."

As he had raved on into the night, Legata had realized that much of what he said held a surprising sense of truth. She knew that, at the bottom of whatever was happening to Shipmen both on and off Ship, it was a result of non-interference by Ship itself. But she had delved into the secrets of Ship's circuitry for too long and too deeply to believe that Ship was a piece of steel and molded plastics, that Ship didn't *care*.

She stood in the garden at the Redoubt and looked up at what she guessed to be Ship's position above them.

I wonder, she thought, *I wonder if we're a disappointment.*

Two patrol drones screamed over the dome and shattered Legata's reverie. She guessed that Oakes would be coming soon, they were gearing up for him. She realized that she should prepare too.

Nothing, she reminded herself, *is sacred.*

Then, in a sudden leap of insight during the heavy stillness following the drones, she added, *but something should be.* This thought was liberating, exhilarating.

The universe has no center.

—Shipquotes

RAJA THOMAS stood under the gigantic semi-inflated bag of the LTA in the main hangar. Lavu's crew had gone, turning off most of the lights. It was full nightside now. The bag was a dim orange bulk tugging gently at its tethers above him. There were great folds and concavities in it yet, but before Alki joined Rega dayside, they would be airborne, the bag as full and smooth as a hylighter.

Except that no hylighter of that size had ever been seen.

Thomas glanced across the dark hangar, impatient to leave. *Why does Oakes want to meet me here?*

The order had been succinct and simple. Oakes was coming out especially to inspect the LTA and its attached sub before allowing them to venture into the unprotected wilderness of Pandora's sea.

Is he about to veto the project?

The implications were clear: Too much Colony energy went into projects such as this one. It was contra-survival. The *exterminators* wanted their way. This might be the last scientific investigation permitted for a long time. Too many subs lost . . . too many LTAs. Such energy could be applied to food production.

The contrary argument of reason found fewer listeners with every passing hour of hunger.

Without the knowledge we gain there may never be dependable food production on Pandora. The kelp is sentient. It rules this planet.

What did the kelp call Pandora?

Home.

Was that Ship or my own imagination?

No response.

Thomas knew he was too keyed up, too full of uncertainties. *Doubts.* It would be so easy to share every viewpoint Oakes put forward. Agree with him. Even some of Lavu's crew had been picking up that muttered catch phrase which could be heard all through Colony: *I'm hungry now!*

Where was Oakes?

Keeping me waiting to teach me my place.

The self-constructed persona of Raja Thomas dominated this thought, but there were distant echoes of Flattery in it—distant but distinct. He felt like an actor well seated in his part after many performances. The Flattery self lay in his past like a childhood memory.

What have You hidden in the depths of the sea, Ship?

That is for you to discover.

There! That definitely was Ship talking to him.

The LTA creaked against its tethers. Thomas stepped from beneath it and peered up at the sphincter leaves of the skydoor—a vast shadowy circle in the dim light. His nostrils tasted a faint bitterness of Pandoran esters in the air. Colony had found that some volatile renderings from selected demons insulated the area around them against other ravening native predators—especially against Nerve Runners. Nothing was forever, though. The demons soon developed counter-responses.

Thomas looked back at the shadowed sub—a smooth black rock held in the tentacles of an articifical hylighter . . . a smooth black rock with glittering lines down its sides.

Again, the LTA creaked against its tethers. There was a draft in the hangar and he hoped this did not mean some unguarded opening to Pandora's dangerous exterior. He was unarmed and alone here except for perimeter guards at the ground-level hatches, and a watchman off somewhere brewing tea. Thomas could smell it faintly—a familiar thing but marked by the subtle differences of Pandoran chemistry.

Am I being set up to go the way Rachel Demarest went?

He was a doubting man but there was no doubt in his mind

about the way of Rachel's passing. It had been too convenient, the timing too good.

Who could question it, though?

Such things happened every day on perimeter patrol. Colony had a number for this attrition: one in seventy. It was like losses in a war. Soldiers knew. Except that most Shipmen appeared to know very little about war in the historic sense.

They knew soldiering, though.

He sniffed.

A faintly sweet undertone of native lubricants drifted on the air. This made him acutely aware of how grudgingly this planet gave up any of its substance to Colony. He had seen the reports— just cutting in the wells for those lubricants had cost them one life for every six diurns. And there was a general reluctance to go for cloned replacements—an unexplainable reluctance.

Fewer and fewer clones around, except out at that mysterious project on Dragon.

What was Lewis doing out there?

Why the growing split between clones and naturals? Was it something about being groundside?

We originated on a planet.

Was there some atavistic memory at work here?

Why don't You answer me, Ship?

When you need to know, you will know without asking.

Typical Ship answer!

What did Oakes mean by *new* clones? *Are You helping him on that project, Ship? Are these new clones Your project?*

Who helped you make Me, Devil?

Thomas felt his throat go dry. There had been barbs in that response. He glanced at the sub suspended off to his left. Quite suddenly, he saw it as representing a fragile and foolish venture. Sub and LTA had been shaped to simulate a hylighter carrying its characteristic rock ballast. No matter that the sub did not look much like rock.

I should be out preaching Ship's demand instead of risking my ancient flesh on this venture.

But Ship had given him no stature for this game, no platform upon which to stand.

How will you WorShip?

No matter the different ways Ship phrased the question, it came out the same.

Who would listen to an unknown, self-proclaimed Ceepee awakened from hyb? He was an admitted clone, member of a minority whose role was being redefined by Oakes.

Talk to the sentient vegetable. Did the kelp have an answer? Ship hinted at it, but refused to say definitely.

That's for you to discover, Devil.

No help there. No clues on how he could open a conversation with this alien sentience. In the abstract, it was an exciting idea— talk to a life form so different from humankind that few evolutionary parallels could be drawn.

What strange things could we learn from them?

What could the kelp learn from him?

Again, Thomas glanced at his chrono. This delay was getting ridiculous!

Why do I permit it?

By this time Waela will have our poet in her cubby.

A deep sigh shook him.

Processing had released Panille less than an hour before nightside. *They delayed him deliberately . . . the way Oakes is delaying now.* What did they have in mind?

Waela, if . . .

Could *that* be the cause of Oakes' delay? Had Oakes discovered that Waela . . . ?

Thomas shook his head sharply. *Foolish speculation!*

He felt cold and exposed waiting here in the hangar, and there was no denying his uneasiness at thoughts of Waela.

Waela and the poet.

Thomas felt torn by his own imagination. He had never before experienced such a powerful physical attraction toward a woman. And there was in his background, dredged up from that ancient conditioning process, a terrifying drive toward possession—private and exclusive possession. He knew this ran directly counter to much of the behavior Ship had allowed . . . or promoted.

Waela . . . Waela . . .

He had to force a mask of distant, deliberate coolness. *The delay with Panille could have been the time for preparing him to act against me. They could have been briefing him.* It was necessary that Waela become intimate with this poet, peel away his masks and find . . . What?

Panille . . . Pandora . . .

More of Ship's doing?

Waela would find out. She had her orders. She must turn this Panille inside out, peer at the center of his being. She would learn and report back to her commander.

Me.

Who obeyed Oakes that way? Lewis, certainly. And Murdoch. And that Legata. What a surprise to find she was the Hamill of Ship's briefing. Did they set traps the way he had set this one for Panille?

Waela would do it right. It must seem a fortuitous accident to Panille. The right time . . . the right conditions . . .

Dammit! How can I be jealous? I set this up!

He knew he was performing according to Ship's design. And probably according to Oakes' design. What was the relationship between Oakes and Ship?

Blasphemous man, Oakes. But Ship allowed the blasphemy. And Oakes might be right.

Thomas had come to suspect more and more that Ship might not be God.

What did we make when we created Ship?

Thomas knew his own hand in that creation. But had there been other, unseen hands in that construction?

Who helped you make Me, Devil?

God or Satan? What did we make?

At this moment, it did not much matter. He was tired in body and emotions and his dominant personal hope was that Panille would see through the sexual trap and defy it. Thomas did not really expect that to happen.

I'm doing Your job to the best of my ability, Ship.

"A function of my Devil is to frustrate good works. Shipmen must extend themselves beyond anything they believe possible."

Those had been Ship's words to him.

Why? Because frustration helped us to succeed with Project Consciousness?

Were they only replaying an old theme which had worked once and might work once more?

It occurred to him then that the Moonbase director who had supervised the building and the crew preparations for that original Voidship—old Morgan Hempstead—had served this identical function.

He was our Devil and we knew it. But now I'm Ship's Devil . . . and best friend.

Thomas found cynical delight in this thought. Being a friend of Ship carried special perils. Oakes might have chosen the better role. Enemy of Ship. Thomas knew his own role, though. Ship chided him with it often enough.

"Play the game, Devil."

Yes, he had to play the game even though he lost.

A scraping noise intruded on his awareness. The sound came from the locker area where the sub crews prepared for their flights. *Dead men's lockers,* the Colony called them.

Something moved in the shadows over there, a waddling figure clad in a white shipsuit. Thomas recognized Oakes. Alone. So it was going to be that kind of a meeting.

Thomas took a handlight from his pocket and waved it to show where he stood.

Responding to the light, Oakes changed his path slightly. Oakes always felt diminished by the hangar area. Too much space used for too little return.

Bad investment.

Thomas appeared dwarfed by the immensity of the semi-inflated bag overhead.

These thoughts firmed his resolve. It would not pay to cancel this project outright without a dramatic motive. There were still some who supported it. Oakes knew the arguments.

Learn to live with the kelp!

You did not live with a wild cobra; you killed it.

Yes, Thomas had to go . . . but dramatically, very dramatically. Two Ceepees could not co-exist in Colony.

Oakes did not want to know what Lewis and Murdoch had arranged. An accident with the submersible, perhaps. There already had been enough accidents without arrangement. The cost in Shipmen lives had reached abrasive levels. Colonists expected casualties while they subdued this planet, but the latest attrition rate went beyond the tolerable.

As he came up to Thomas, Oakes smiled openly. It was a gesture he could afford.

"Well, let's look at this *new* submersible," Oakes said.

He allowed himself to be guided to the sub's side hatch and into the cramped command gondola at the core, noting that Thomas offered no small talk, none of the unconscious obeisance of language which Oakes had come to expect from those around him. Everything was business, technical: Here were the new sonar instruments, the remote-recording sensors, the nephelometers...

Nephelometers?

Oakes had to cast back into his medical training for the association.

Oh, yes. Instruments for collecting and examining small particles suspended in the water.

Oakes almost laughed. It was not small particles which needed study but the giant kelp: fully visible and certainly vulnerable. In spite of his amusement, Oakes managed a few seemingly responsive questions.

"What makes you say that everything in the sea has to serve the kelp?"

"Because that's what we find, that's the condition of the sea. Everything from the grazing cycles of the biota to the distribution of trace metals, everything fits the growth demands of the kelp. We must find out why."

"Grazing cycles of ... ?"

"The biota—all the living matter... The mud-dwelling creatures and those on the surface, all appear to be in a profound symbiotic relationship with the kelp. The grazers, for example, stir the toxic products cast off by the kelp into a layer of highly absorbent sediment where other creatures restore these substances to the food chain. They..."

"You mean the kelp shits and this is processed by animals on the bottom?"

"That would be one way of stating it, but the total implication of the sea system is disturbing. There are leaf grazers, for instance, whose only function is to keep the kelp's leaves clean. The few predators all have large fins, much larger than you'd expect for their size, and..."

"What does that have to do with ...?"

"They stir the water around the kelp."

"Huh?" For a moment, Oakes had found his interest aroused, but Thomas had all the earmarks of a specialist blowing his own private horn—even to the esoteric language of the specialty. This was supposed to be a communications expert?

Just to keep things moving, Oakes asked the expected question: "What disturbing implications?"

"The kelp is influencing the sea far more than simple evolutionary processes can explain. Perhaps it supports the marine community. The only historical comparisons we can make lead us to believe that a sentient force is at work here."

"Sentient!" Oakes put as much disdain as he could muster into the word. That damned report on kelp-hylighter relationships! Lewis was supposed to have made it inaccessible. Was the ship interfering?

"A conscious design," Thomas said.

"Or an extremely long-lived adaptation and evolution."

Thomas shook his head. There was another possibility, but he did not care to discuss it with Oakes. What if Ship had created this planet precisely the way they found it? Why would Ship do such a thing?

Oakes had absorbed enough from this encounter. He had made the gesture. Everyone would see that he was concerned. His guards were waiting back there at the hatch. They would talk. Losses were too high and the Ceepee had to look into it himself. Time to end it.

Oakes relaxed visibly. How nicely things were working.

And Thomas thought: *He's going to let us go without a struggle. All right, Ship. I'm going to pry into one of Your secret places. If You made this planet to teach us Your WorShip, there have to be clues in the sea.*

"Well, I'll want a complete report when you return," Oakes said. "Some of your data may help us begin a useful aquaculture project."

He left then, muttering loud enough to be heard: "Sentient kelp!"

As he walked back across the hangar, Oakes thought it had been one of his best performances, and all of it caught by the sensors, all of it recorded and stored. When . . . whatever Lewis had arranged happened, they would be able to edit excerpts from the record.

See how concerned I was?

From the sub's hatch, Thomas watched Oakes leave, then slipped back down for a final inspection of the core. Had Oakes sabotaged something? All appeared normal. His gaze fell on the central command seat, then on the secondary position to the left where Waela would sit. He caressed the back of the seat.

I'm an old fool. What would I do? Waste precious time with a useless dalliance? And what if she refused to respond to me? What then, old fool?

Old!

Who but Ship even suspected how old? Original material. A clone, a doppelganger—but original material. Nothing like it alive and moving anywhere else in the universe.

So Ship said.

Don't you believe Me, Devil?

The thought was a static burst in Thomas' awareness. He spoke as he often did to answer Ship when alone. No matter that some thought him slightly mad.

"Does it matter whether I believe You?"

It matters to Me.

"Then that's an edge I have and You don't."

You regret your decision to play this game?

"I keep *my* word."

And you gave Me your word.

Thomas knew it did not matter whether he said this aloud or merely thought it, but he found himself unable to prevent the outburst.

"Did I give my word to Satan or to God?"

Who can settle that question to your satisfaction?

"Maybe You're Satan and I'm God."

That is very close, My Doubting Thomas!

"Close to what?"

Only you can tell.

As usual, nothing was settled in such an exchange except the re-establishment of the master-servant relationship. Thomas slipped into the command seat, sighed. Presently, he began going through the instrument checklist, more to distract himself than for any other reason. Oakes had not come to sabotage but to make a show of some kind.

Devil?

So Ship was not through with him.

"Yes, Ship?"

There is something you need to know.

Thomas felt his heartbeat quicken. Ship seldom volunteered information. It must be something momentous.

"What is it?"

You recall Hali Ekel?

That name was familiar . . . yes; he had seen it in the Panille dossier which Waela had supplied.

"Panille's med-tech friend, yes. What about her?"

I have exposed her to a segment of a dominant human past.

"A replay? But You said..."

A segment, Devil, not a replay. You must learn the distinction. When there is a lesson someone needs, you do not have to show the entire record; you can show only a marked passage, a segment.

"Am I living in a marked passage right now?"

This is an original play, a true sequel.

"Why tell me this? What are you doing?"

Because you were trained as a Chaplain. It is important that you know what Hali has experienced. I have shown her the Jesus incident.

Thomas felt his mouth go dry. He was a moment recovering, then: "The Hill of Skulls? Why?"

Her life has been too tame. She must learn how far holy violence can extend. You, too, need this reminder.

Thomas thought about a sheltered young woman from the ship-side life being exposed suddenly to the crucifixion. It angered him and he let that anger appear in his voice.

"You're interfering, aren't You!"

This is My universe, too, Devil. Never forget that.

"Why did you do that?"

Prelude to other data. Panille has recognized the trap you set for him and avoided it. Waela failed.

Thomas knew he could not conceal his elation and did not try. But a question remained: "Is Panille Your pawn?"

Are you My pawn?

Thomas felt a tight band across his chest. Nothing worked the way he expected. Presently, he found his voice.

"How did he recognize the trap?"

By being open to his peril.

"What does that mean?"

You are not open, as My Devil should be.

"And You told me You wouldn't interfere with the roll of the dice!"

I never said I would not interfere; I said there would be no outside interference.

Thomas thought about that while he fought to overcome a deep sense of frustration. It was too much and he spoke his feelings: "You're in the game: You can do anything You want and You don't call that..."

You, too, can do anything you want.

This froze him. What powers had Ship imparted to him? He

did not *feel* powerful. He felt helpless before Ship's omnipresence. And this business of Hali Ekel and the Jesus *incident*? What did it mean?

Once more, Ship intruded: *Devil, I tell you that some things take their own course only if you fail to detect that course. Waela really feels a powerful attraction toward young Panille.*

Young Panille!

Thomas spoke past an emptiness in his breast: "Why do You torture me?"

You torture yourself.

"So You say!"

When will you awaken? There was no mistaking Ship's frustrated emphasis.

Thomas found that he did not fear this. He was much too tired and there was no more reason for him to stay here in the sub. Oakes had approved the venture. They would go out on schedule—Waela and Panille with him.

"Ship, I'll awaken early tomorrow and take out this LTA and its sub."

Would that this were true.

"You intend to stop me?" Thomas found himself oddly delighted at the prospect of Ship interfering in this particular way.

Stop you? No. The play must run its course apparently.

Was that sadness in Ship's projection? Thomas could not be certain. He sat back. There was a stabbing ache between his shoulderblades. He closed his eyes, sent his fatigue and frustrations out in thought.

"Ship, I know I can't hide anything from You. And You know why I'm going out to the sea tomorrow."

Yes, I know even what you hide from yourself.

"Are You *my* psychiatrist now?"

Which of us usurps the function of the other? That has always been the question.

Thomas opened his eyes. "I have to do it."

That is the origin of the illusion men call kismet.

"I'm too tired to play word games."

Thomas slipped out of the command seat and stood up. He kept one hand on the seat back, spoke as much to himself as to Ship.

"We could all die tomorrow, Waela, Panille and I."

I must warn you that truisms represent the most boring of all human indulgences.

Thomas felt Ship's intrusive presence withdraw, but he knew that nothing had been taken away. Wherever he went, whatever he did, Ship was there.

He found his thoughts winging back to that faraway time when he had been trained (conditioned, really) not merely as a Psychiatrist, but as a Chaplain/Psychiatrist.

"Fear him which is able to destroy both soul and body in hell."

Old Matthew knew how to put the fear of God in you!

Thomas found it took him several blinks to overcome a sense of panic so deep that it kept him locked in place.

Early training is the most powerful, he reminded himself.

Man also knows not his time: as the fishes that are taken in an evil net, and as the birds that are caught in the snare; so are the sons of men snared in an evil time, when it falls suddenly upon them.

—**Christian** *Book of the Dead,* *Shiprecords*

FOR A long time after returning to Ship from the Hill of Skulls, Hali could not find the will to leave the room. She stared up and around at the softly illuminated space—this secret place where Kerro had spent so many hours communing with Ship. She remembered the borrowed flesh of the old woman, the painful and halting steps. The ache of aging shoulders. A feeling of profound sensitivity to her familiar body pervaded her awareness; each tiny movement became electric with immediacy.

She remembered the man who had been nailed to the rigid crosspiece on the hill. *Barbaric!*

Yaisuah.

She whispered it: "*Yaisuah.*"

It was understandable how this name had evolved into that of Jesus . . . and even to the Hesoos of Jesus Lewis.

But nowhere could she find understanding of why she had been taken to witness that agonizing scene. *Nowhere*. And she found it odd that she had never encountered historical records of that faraway event—not in Ship's teachings nor in the memories of Shipmen who came from Earth.

In the first moments of her return, she had asked Ship why she had been shown that brutal incident, and had received an enigmatic response.

Because there are things from the human past that no creature should forget.

"But why me? Why now?"

The rest was silence. She assumed that the answers were her own to find.

She stared at the com-console. The seat there at the instruction terminal was her seat now; she knew it. Kerro was gone . . . groundside. Ship had introduced her to this place, had given it to her.

The message was clear: *No more Kerro Panille here.*

A shuddering wave of loss shot through her, and she shook tears from her eyes. This was no place to stay now. She stood, took up her pribox and slipped out the way she had entered.

Why me?

She wound her way out of softwares and into D passage leading back to Medical, into the workings of Ship's body.

The *beep* of her pribox startled her.

"Ekel here," she said, surprised at the youthfulness of her own voice—not at all like the ancient quavering of that old woman's voice she had borrowed.

Her pribox crackled, then: "Ekel, report to Dr. Ferry's office."

She found a servo and, instead of walking, rode to Medical.

Ferry, she thought. *Could it mean reassignment? Could I be joining Kerro groundside?*

The thought excited her, but the idea of groundside duty remained fearful. So many nasty rumors. And lately, all groundside assignments seemed permanent. Except for the tight-knit political circle at Medical, no one made the return trip. Pressures of work had kept her from thinking much about this before, but suddenly it became vital.

What are they doing with all our people?

The drain on equipment and food from Ship was a topic for constant anxious conversation; recurrent dayside orders exhorted greater production efforts . . . but few speculated about missing people.

We've been conditioned not to face the finality of absolute endings. Is that why Ship showed me Yaisuah?

The thought stood there in her awareness, riding on the hum of the servo carrying her toward Medical and Ferry.

It was clear to her that Yaisuah had ended, but his influence had not ended. Pandora was a place of endings. It gulped food and people and equipment. What influences were about to be sent reverberating from that place?

Endings.

The servo fell silent, stopped. She looked up to see Medical's servo gate and, across the passage, the hatch to Ferry's offices. She did not want to go through that hatch. Her body still throbbed with sensitivities ignited by what Ship had shown her. She did not want Ferry touching her body. It was more than her dislike for him—the silly old fool! He drank too much of the alcohol which came up from Colony and he always reached out to put a hand on her somewhere.

Everyone knew the Demarest woman brought him his wine from groundside. He always had plenty of it after her visits.

His food chits can't support that kind of drinking.

She stared at the dogged hatch across the way. Something was definitely wrong—shipside *and* groundside. Why did Rachel Demarest bring wine up to Ferry?

If she brings him wine, what does she get in return?

Love? Why not? Even neurotics like Ferry and Demarest needed love. Or . . . if not love, at least an occasional couch partner.

A remembered image of Foul-breath shuddered through her mind. She could almost feel the touch of his hand translated to her own young flesh. Involuntarily, she brushed her arm.

Maybe that's how they get so foul. No love . . . no lovers.

There was no evading the summons, though. She slid off the servo and crossed to Ferry's hatch. It snicked open at her approach. Why was she reminded of a sword leaving its scabbard?

"Ahhh, dear Hali." Ferry opened his palms to her as she entered.

She nodded. "Dr. Ferry."

"Sit down wherever you like." His hand rested on the arm of a couch, inviting her to the place beside him. She chose a seat facing him, cleared off the mess of papers and computer discs that covered it. The whole office smelled sour in spite of Ship's air filtration. Ferry appeared to be drunk . . . at least happy.

"Hali," he said, and recrossed his legs so one foot reached out to touch hers. "You're being reassigned."

Again, she nodded. *Groundside?*

"You're going to the Natali," Ferry said.

It was totally unexpected, and she blinked at him stupidly. *To the Natali?* The elite corps which handled all natural births had never been her ambition. Not even her hope. A dream, yes . . . but she was not the type to hope for the impossible.

"How do you feel about that?" Ferry asked, moving her foot with his.

The Natali! Working daily with the sacrament of WorShip!

She nodded to herself as the reality of it seeped through her. She would join the elite who opened the hatchway to the mystery of life . . . she would help rear the children shipside until they were assigned to their own schools and quarters at the age of seven annos.

Ferry smiled a red-stained smile. "You look stunned. Don't you believe me?"

She spoke slowly. "I believe you. I suspected that this . . ." She waved a hand at his office. ". . . was for reassignment, but . . ."

Ferry made no move to respond, so she went on.

"I thought I'd be going groundside. Everyone seems to be going there, lately."

He steepled his fingers and rested his chin on them.

"You're not happy with this assignment?"

"Ohhh, I'm very happy with it. It's just . . ." She put a hand to her throat. "I never thought I . . . I mean . . . Why me?"

"Because you deserve it, my dear." He chuckled. "And there's talk of moving the Natali groundside. You may get the best of both worlds."

"Groundside?" She shook her head. Too many shocks were coming at her one after the other.

"Yes, groundside." He spoke as though explaining something simple to an errant child.

"But I thought . . . I mean, the foremost provision of WorShip is that we give our children to Ship until they're seven. Ship designated the Natali as the trustees of birth . . . and their quarters are here, the estate . . ."

"Not Ship!" Ferry's interruption was gutteral. "Some Ceepee did it. This is a matter for our determination."

"But doesn't Ship . . ."

"There's no record of Ship doing this. Now, our Ceepee has ruled that it is no violation of WorShip to move the Natali groundside."

"How . . . how long . . . until . . .?"

"Perhaps a Pandoran anno. You know—quarters, supplies, politics." He waved it all off.

"When do I go to the Natali?"

"Next diurn. Take a break. Get your things moved over. Talk toooo . . ." He picked up a note from the jumble on his desk, squinted. ". . . Usija. She'll take care of you from there."

His foot brushed the back of her heel, then rubbed her instep.

"Thank you, Doctor." She pulled her foot back.

"I don't feel your gratitude."

"But I do thank you, especially for the time off. I have some notes to catch up on."

He held up an empty glass. "We could have a drink . . . to celebrate."

She shook her head, but before she could say *no*, he leaned forward, grinning.

"We'll be neighbors, soon, Hali. We could celebrate *that*."

"What do you mean?"

"Groundside." He pushed the glass toward her. "After the Natali go . . ."

"But who'll be left here?"

"Production facilities, mostly."

"Ship? A factory?" She felt her face blaze red.

"Why not? What other use will we have for Ship when we're groundside?"

She jumped to her feet. "You would lobotomize your own mother!" Whirling from his startled gaze, she fled.

All the way back to her quarters, she heard the drum of Yaisuah's voice in her ears: *If they do these things in a green tree, what will they do in a dry?*

I like seeing things fall into place.

—**Kerro Panille,**
The Notebooks

NIGHTSIDE AFTER nightside, always nightside! The horror! Legata awoke on the deck in a shipside cubby, her hammock hanging around her like the torn shreds of her nightmares. Sweat and fear chilled her in the dark.

Slowly, reason returned. She felt the remnants of the hammock on and under her, the cold of the deck against her palms.

I'm shipside.

She had come up earlier at Oakes' command to check out reports that Ferry was too far gone on alcohol to be effective. It had shocked her, getting off the shuttle in a familiar shipbay, to see how few Shipmen formed the arrival crew. Staffing raids by Lewis were decimating the shipside work force to replace losses at the Redoubt.

How many people did they really lose?

She tugged pieces of hammock out from under her, hurled them into the darkness.

Ferry, warned of her approach, had gulped too many 'wakepills and had been a jittering mess when she found him. She had dressed him down in fury which had surprised even her, and had removed

237

the last of his Colony liquor supply.

At least, she hoped it was the last of it.

I have to do something about these nightmares.

Some details remained unclear upon waking, but she knew she dreamed of blood and her most tender flesh peeled back by dozens of needlenosed instruments—all of this backed by the feverish glitter of Morgan Oakes' smile. Oakes' thick-lipped smile . . . but Murdoch's eyes. And . . . somewhere in the background . . . Lewis laughing.

She found pieces of her bedding, an intact cushion, pulled them together and, still in the dark, dragged herself across the cubby to a mat. Only once before had she felt this beaten, this empty . . . this helpless.

The Scream Room.

It was why she had run the P—to regain some pieces of her self-respect. Self-respect regained . . . but no important memories.

What happened in that room? What kind of a game is Morgan playing? Why did he send me in there?

She remembered the preliminaries. Innocent enough. Oakes had given her a few drinks, left her with a holo cannister which detailed as he put it, "a few of the treats available to those who can afford them."

He had begun by showing her technical summaries and graphs of the work Lewis was doing on E-clones. The drinks fuzzed her thinking, but most of it remained in memory.

"Lewis has made remarkable modifications in the cloning system," Oakes said.

Remarkable, indeed.

Lewis could grow a clone to age thirty annos in ten diurns.

He could *engineer* clones for special functions.

It had occurred to her as she watched the holo display of Lab One's clones that she could begin playing this game with Oakes, but that they must switch to *her* rules.

I didn't even know the game!

When Oakes had suggested she inspect Lab One, she had not suspected that he wanted her to . . . that she was expected to . . .

Nothing is sacred!

The thought kept returning. She breathed in a deep lungful of the sweetly filtered shipside air. How different it was from groundside. She knew she was wasting time. There were things she must remember before returning to Oakes.

*He believes he has nothing to fear from me now. I had better
keep it that way.*

His powers were not diminished. But after all he had done to
her, after the Scream room, she still felt that she was the only
person who knew him well enough to beat him. There would be
no opposition from him as long as he did not consider her a
threat . . . or a challenge.

*As long as he wants my body . . . and now that I know the game
we're really playing . . .*

Anxiety began to build in her—the nightmares . . . the lost
memories . . .

She pounded the deck beside her with both fists. The anxiety
rose in her like some *thing*, like a bastard child got by rape. The
unresolved emotions in her were a *place*, immediately demanding,
and she felt that she looked down upon her present upset as the
dying were said to look down upon themselves from some high
and unresolved corner.

Her hands pained her where she had pounded the deck.

A Chaplain is supposed to ease anxiety, not cause it!

Chaplain—she had searched the word out once and the readout
had surprised her: *Keeper of the sacred relics.*

What were Ship's sacred relics?

Humans?

Slowly, she forced herself to relax in the darkness of the shipside cubby, but her mind remained a blur of unanswered questions,
and once more she caught herself gasping for breath. In sudden
dizziness, she saw a memory image of herself touching a dial in
the Scream Room. Just a glimpse, and across from her, that twisted
clone face . . . those wide terrified eyes . . .

Did I turn that dial? I have to know!

She hugged her knees to keep herself from pounding the deck.

Did I turn that dial myself or did Oakes force my hand?

She held her breath, knowing that she had to remember. She
had to. And she knew she would have to destroy Oakes, that she
was the only one who could do it.

Even Ship cannot destroy him. She peered up into the cubby's
darkness. *You can't do it, can You, Ship?*

She felt that someone else's thoughts spun in her head—dizziness, dizziness. She shook her head sharply to rid it of the
feeling.

Nothing . . . is . . . sacred.

Violent trembling shook her body.

The Scream Room.-She had to remember what happened there! She would have to know her own limits before she went after someone else's limits. She had to face the blank places in her mind or Oakes would continue to own her—not her body, but her most private self. He would *own* her.

Her hands clenched into fists against her legs. Her palms ached from the bite of her own fingernails.

I must remember . . . I must . . .

There was one fogged memory and she clung to it: Jessup kneading her maimed flesh with oddly gentle fingers whose deformity she had not even minded.

That memory was real.

She forced herself to open her clenched fists, relax her legs. She sat cross-legged on the mat, sweating and nude. One hand went out in the dark and groped for one of the bottles of wine she had taken from Ferry. Her hands were shaking so badly she was afraid she would crush a glass—besides, that would require her to stand, turn on lights, open a locker. She uncapped the raw wine and drank straight from the bottle.

Presently, a semblance of calm restored, she found the light control, tuned it for a low yellow, and returned to the bottle she had left on the deck. *More of that?* She had visions of herself reduced to Ferry's condition. *No!* There had to be a better way. She recapped the bottle, stuffed it in a locker, and sat on her mat, feet stretched out straight.

What to do?

Her gaze fell on her reflection in the mirror beside her hatch and what she saw made her groan. She liked her body—the suppleness, the firmness. To men, it appeared intensely female and soft, an illusion attributable to large breasts. But even her breasts were firm to touch, toned by a rigorous physical program which few besides herself and Oakes knew she enjoyed. Now, though, she saw red marks across her stomach, down one arm—the beginnings of softness down her thighs where there were more red streaks from her nightmare struggle with the hammock.

She held up her left hand and stared at it. The fingers ached. In that slender arm and those fingers she held the strength of five men. She had discovered this early and, afraid it would mean a life of body-work instead of mind-work, she had concealed this genetic gift. But she could not hide from what the mirror showed—

the shambles she had made of her hammock and the marks on her
flesh.

What to do?

She refused to go back to the wine. Sweat was beginning to
cool on her skin. Her thick hair was stuck to her face and neck—
damp dark at the ends. She no longer felt perspiration trickle down
the small of her back.

Her green eyes stared back at her from the mirror and pried
into her like Oakes' spying sensors.

Damn him!

She closed her eyes in a grimace. There had to be some way
of breaking through the memory barrier! *What happened to me?*

Scream Room.

She spoke it aloud: "Scream Room."

Jessup's terrible fingers kneaded her neck, her back.

Abruptly, images began to rush through her mind like a storm.
Bits and shards at first: a glimpse of a face here, an agony there.
Writhings and couplings. There was a rainbow of sad clones
mounting each other, always sweating, their freak organs slick,
waving...

I took none of them!

Her terrible strength had stunned the clones.

Blood! She saw blood on her arms.

But I did not join them! None of it! She knew it. And because
she knew it, there was a new strength in her. An objectifying
freedom glared from her eyes when she stared once more into the
mirror.

The holorecord!

Oakes had offered to play it for her, amusement in his
eyes... and something else there... a fearful watching. She had
refused.

"No-o-o. Perhaps some other time."

And her stomach was a knot of terror.

The wine or the holorecord? There was a certainty in her that
it had to be one or the other, and she experienced an abrupt wave
of sympathy for old Win Ferry.

What did they do to that poor old bastard?

There was no doubt about her choice. It had to be the holo,
not the bottle. She had to see herself as she had appeared to Oakes.
This was the horror required of her before the nightmares could
be stopped.

Before Oakes and Lewis and Murdoch could be stopped.
If they're stopped, who keeps Colony alive?

Shipmen had tried four times—four leaders, four failures. "Failure" was the Shipman euphemism for the reality—revolt, slaughter, suicide, massacre. The records were there for a good Search Technician to winkle out.

The present Colony had suffered setbacks, true, but nothing even close to total wipeout—no retreat en masse back to the insulated corridors of Ship. Pandora had become no friendlier. Shipmen had grown wiser. And the wisest of all, beyond question, were Oakes and Lewis.

Ship only knew how many Shipmen crawled the surface of Pandora or the myriad passageways of Ship. And all survived, to whatever degree of comfort or discomfort, because of Oakes and the efficiency of his management . . . and because Lewis knew how to carry out orders with brutal efficiency. To her knowledge, no other Ceepee team could make such a claim in all the histories of Ship.

Ship will care for us.

She felt Ship around her now, the faint hummings and susurrations of nightside.

But Ship had never agreed to care for Shipmen.

At one time, she had been interested in Shipman's place in the Ship scheme of things. She had pored through a confusing lot of histories seeking some agreement, a covenant, some evidence of even rudimentary formal relationship between the people and their god.

Ship who is God.

All agreements save one had been made by Ceepees on behalf of Ship. Back in the earliest accounts, she had come on one recorded line, a direct demand from Ship: *You must decide how you will WorShip Me.*

That had to be the origin of present WorShip. It could be traced to Ship. But the demand appeared suitably vague and, when she had recounted it to Oakes, he had seen it as emphasizing the powers of the Ceepees.

"We, after all, command the WorShip."

If Ship *were* God . . . well, Ship still appeared to be unwilling to interfere directly in the management of Shipman affairs. Every visible thing Ship did could be attributed to work at maintaining itself.

Some Shipmen claimed they talked to Ship, and she had studied these people. They fell into two obvious categories: fools and non-fools. Most of the claimants had a history of talking to walls, bowls, items of clothing and such. But perhaps one out of every twenty who said they talked to Ship were Ship's best. For them, talking with Ship represented the single rare absurdity of their records. It fascinated her that, for this small group, the talking incidents were isolated and seemingly innocuous—almost as though Ship were checking in from time to time.

Unlike Oakes and Lewis, she did not count herself a disbeliever.

But God or not, Ship apparently refused to interfere in the private decisions of Shipmen.

So what if I decide to destroy Oakes?

Did Ship *care* for him, too?

Oakes was too cautious, too painstakingly right about the things he did. What if he were the only reason Colony had survived? Could she watch Colony wither and die, knowing she had done it?

Was the Scream Room right?

Only the holorecord could decide that for her. She had to see it.

She levered herself to her feet, found a singlesuit and slipped into it. There was a sense of urgency about her motions now compounded of the late hour and the terrors she knew she was holding at bay. A glance at her chrono showed only six hours to dayside. Six hours to call up those records, review them and cover her tracks. And those records spanned most of a diurn—perhaps forty hours. All she needed was to see the essence of it, though.

What did he do to me?

Without conscious decision, she headed for Oakes' abandoned shipside cubby, realizing her own choice only when she grasped the hatchdogs. Yes, the com-console would still be here. It was a good place to search out the record and review it. She knew the code which would call up the Scream Room holo. Her priority number would insure that she got it. And there was something exquisitely right about the choice of the place to do it.

As she keyed the hatchdogs on the cubby, she reminded herself: *Whatever he wanted me to do, I did not do it.* Some part of her knew that neither the pleasures nor the curiosities of the Scream Room had tempted her—neither ecstasy nor pain. But Oakes wanted her to believe in some willing debasement. He required that she believe.

He'll see.

She released the hatchdogs and stepped inside.

The family feeds its fledgling, and under the nest weaves twigs—Intelligence is a poor cousin to understanding.

—Kerro Panille,
The Collected Poems

THE DULL crimson of instruments and telltales filled the sub's core gondola with red shadows and played firelight flickers off every movement of the three people strapped in their seats around the tight arc of controls.

Thomas, intensely aware of the crushing pressure of water around them, glanced up at the depth repeater. This was not completely like a Voidship, after all. Instead of empty space, he sensed the inward pressing of the Pandoran sea. All he had to do was look directly up through the transparent dome of the gondola where it protruded from the carrier-sub and he could see the diminishing circle of glowing light which was the surface of the lagoon.

As he moved his head, he glimpsed Waela engaged in the same reflexive check of the repeater. She appeared to be taking it well. No residual fugue from her bad experiences down here.

He looked then at Kerro Panille. This poet was not what he had expected—young, yes—barely past twenty according to the records—but there was something more mature in Panille's manner.

The poet had been quiet during the descent, not even asking the expected questions, but his eyes missed very little. The way he cocked his head at new sounds betrayed his alertness. There had been no time really to train him for this. Waela had set Panille to watching the monitors on their communications program to signal when it began accepting the firefly patterns of the kelp. She had reserved for herself the instruments which reported the status of their linkage to the anchor cable. The anchor had been dropped in the center of a lagoon and now the cable guided their descent. The LTA rode close to the sea surface overhead, tightly tethered to the cable.

"He's very sensitive to unconscious communication," she had told Thomas before Panille's arrival at the hangar.

Thomas did not ask how she knew this. She already had confirmed the failure of her attempt to seduce Panille.

"Was he too naive? Did he know what you . . . ?"

"Oh, he knew. But he has this thing about his body being his own. Rather refreshing in a man."

"Is he . . . do you think he's really working for Oakes?"

"He's not the type."

Thomas had to agree. Panille displayed an almost childlike openness.

Since the abortive and (she had to admit it) rather amateurish attempt at seduction, Waela had felt restrained with Panille. But the poet showed no such inhibition. He had shipside candor and, she suspected, would be rather more apt than not to walk openly into some deadly Pandoran peril out of curiosity.

I like him, she thought. *I really like him.*

But he would have to be educated swiftly to the dangers here or he would not last long enough to write another poem.

Ship really did send him, then, Thomas thought. *Is he supposed to keep watch on me?*

Thomas had reserved for himself the visual observation of the kelp-free pocket through which they were descending. It was a column of clear water about four hundred meters in diameter, a Pandoran "lagoon." They had not yet descended into the dark regions where the kelp played its light show.

Panille had been fascinated by the name *lagoon* when he had heard it. Ship had displayed an Earthside lagoon for him once— palm trees, an outrigger with white sails. Would Pandora ever see such play upon its seas?

He found himself acutely aware of every sensory impression about this experience. It was the stuff of countless poems. There was the faint hiss of air being recycled, the smell of human bodies too close and exuding their unspoken fears. He liked the way the red light played off the ladder which ran up to the hatch.

When Thomas had used the word *lagoon* to describe their destination, Panille had said: "The persistence of atavism." The remark had provoked a startled glance from Thomas.

Waela marked their descent past eighty-five meters and called it out. She leaned close to the screen which displayed the lagoon's nearest wall of encaging kelp. The long strands angled down into darkness with an occasional black tentacle reaching out toward the sub. The external dive lights played green shadows on the pale kelp, revealing small dark extrusions, bubbles whose purpose remained undiscovered. Farther down, such bubbles played their bright patterns of light.

The water around the kelp strand and in the upper lagoon was aswarm with darting and slow-moving shapes, some with many eyes and some with none. Some were thin and worm-like, some fat and ponderous with long fleshy fins and toothless gaping jaws. None had ever been known to attack Shipmen and it was thought they lived in symbiosis with the kelp. Taking them for specimens aroused the kelp to violence and when they were removed from the sea, they melted so rapidly that mobile labs appeared to be the only way to examine them. But mobile labs did not survive long here.

Farther down, Waela knew, there would be fewer and fewer of these creatures. Then the sub would enter the zone of crawlers, things which moved along the kelp and across the sea floor. A few large swimmers there, but crawlers dominated.

On the flight out to the lagoon, Waela had kept herself busy, fearing that she might break down when the moment came to make another dive. It had helped to recall the strong construction of this sub, but the actual moment of the dive had loomed ahead, mingled with a return to dark memories of terror. Colony's last dive had been a disaster. The sub had been seventy meters long, studded with knives and cutters. It had cost Colony a terrible toll in lives to transport it across The Egg's undulating plains to the one area on the south coast where they could skid the sub into a wave-washed bay of kelp. She had been one of the nine on the crew, the only survivor.

For a time, they had thought sheer size and weight would bring them success. Water doors were opened remotely and stuffed with kelp specimens. But the kelp's cable-strands released themselves from the rocks on the seafloor and, tendrils waving, swept over the sub. There seemed no end to the attack. More and more kelp came at them, wrapping around the sub, overwhelming the cutters by weight of numbers, drawing them deeper and deeper while tendrils probed for any weak point. Leaves blinded their external sensors. Static crackled in their communications system. They were blind and dumb. Then water had jetted into the hull near a hatch, a stream so strong it cut the flesh in its path.

Thinking about those moments made Walea's breath come faster. She had been operating a cutter, her station a plaz bubble extruded from the hull. Leaves covered the bubble except for straining strands of kelp trying to crush the sub. Through the crashing static in her earphones, she had heard a crewmate describe the water jet cutting one of their companions in half. Abruptly, a warping of the hull and the explosive shift of pressure within the sub had blasted her bubble free. It shot out and clear of the blinding leaves, then upward as the kelp spread aside to permit her passage. She had never been able to explain that phenomenon. The kelp had opened a way to the surface for her!

Once into the glare of double-dayside, she had forced open the hatch, dived clear to an undulant sea covered by broad fans of kelp leaves. She remembered touching the leaves, fearing them and needing them to support her; they were a pale green cushion which dampened the waves. Then she had felt a tingling all through her body. Her mind had been invaded by wild images of demons and humans locked in death struggles. She remembered screaming, swallowing salty water and screaming. Within seconds, the images overwhelmed her and she rolled across a kelp leaf unconscious.

An observation LTA had snatched her from the sea. She had spent many diurns recovering, awakening to acclaim because she had proved that the kelp not only was dangerous because of its physical abilities, but that its hallucinogenic capacity worked havoc when enough of it contacted enough of a Shipman's body in a liquid medium.

"Is something wrong, Waela?"

That was Panille staring at her, concerned by her introspection.

"No. We're leaving the active surface waters. We'll begin to see the lights soon."

"You've been down here before, they tell me."

"Yes."

"We'll be safe as long as we don't threaten the kelp," Thomas said. "You know that."

"Thanks."

"The records say that attempts to establish a shoreside harvester were defeated when the kelp actually came ashore to attack," Panille said.

"People and machines were snatched from the shore, yes," she said. "The people drowned and were thrown back. Machines just disappeared."

"Then why won't it attack us here?"

"It never has when we just come down and observe."

Saying this helped her restore a measure of calm. She returned to observation of sensors and telltales.

Panille peered over his shoulder at her screen, saw the angled strands of kelp, the fluting leaves and the curious bubble extrusions which reflected starbursts from the sub's dive lights. When he looked up past the ladder to the top hatch, he could see the luminous circle of the lagoon's surface—a receding moon populated by the darting shapes of the creatures who shared the sea with the kelp.

The lagoon was a place of magic and mystery with a beauty so profound he felt thankful to Ship just to have seen it. The kelp strands were pale gray-green cables, thicker than a Shipman's torso in places. They reached up from darkness into the distant mercuric pool of light overhead.

Light reaches for stars and, seeing the stars, fears to grasp them, floats in wonder. Oh, stars, you burn my mind.

The kelp aimed itself at Rega, the only sun in their sky at the moment. Alki would join Rega later. Even under clouds, the kelp aligned itself perpendicular to the passage of a sun. When two suns were present, this tropism adjusted to the radiation balance. It was a precise adjustment.

Panille thought about this, reviewing what he had learned from Ship. These were observations which perilous ventures into the sea had gleaned. Sparse information, and nowhere as intense as what he learned by being here. He knew some of the things he would see at the bottom: kelp tendrils wrapped around and through large rocks. Crawling creatures and burrowing ones. Slow currents, drifting sediments. Lagoons were ventilators, passages for exchange between surface and bottom waters. Near the surface, they provided light for creatures other than kelp.

The lagoons were cages.

"These lagoons are where the kelp engages in aquaculture," he said.

Thomas blinked. That was so close to his own surmise about how kelp fitted into the sea system that he wondered if Panille had been eavesdropping on his thoughts.

Is Ship talking to him even now?

Panille's words fascinated Waela. "You think the kelp follows a conscious paln?"

"Perhaps."

To Thomas, the poet's words pulled a veil from the kelp domain. He began to sense the sea in a different way. Here was rich living space free of Pandora's other dangerous demons. Was it right then to rid the sea of kelp? He knew it could be done—disrupt the ecosystem, break the internal chain of the kelp's own life. Was that the decision of Oakes and Lewis?

"The lights!" Panille said. "Ohhh, yes."

They had reached the dark zone where the sub's external sensors began to pick up the flickering lights. Jewels danced in the blackness beyond the range of the dive lights—tiny bursts of color . . . red, yellow, orange, green, purple . . . There appeared to be no pattern to them, just bursts of brillance which dazzled the awareness.

"Bottom coming up," Waela said.

Panille, every sense alert, shot a glance at her screen. Yes—the bottom appeared to be moving while they remained stationary. *Coming up.*

Thomas adjusted the rate of descent—slower, slower. The sub came to rest with a slight jar which stirred sediment into a gray fog around them. When the fog settled, the screens showed a plastering of ripples out to the limits of their illumination. Bottom grazers moved through the ripples—inverted bowls with gulping lips all around the rim. At the extreme forward edge of illumination, the flukes of the sub's anchor dug into the sediment. The cable sagged back over them and out of light range. Off to the port side, they could glimpse black mounds of rock with kelp tendrils lacing over and through them. Dark shapes swam deep in the kelp jungle—more attendants of the sea's rulers.

Tiny crawlers already were working their way along the anchor and the cable. Panille knew that the anchor tackle had been made of native iron and steel—substances which would be etched away to lace in a few diurns. Only plaz and plasteel resisted the erosive powers in Pandora's seas.

This knowledge filled him with a sense of how fragile was their link to safety. He watched the jewel brilliants flickering in the gloom beyond the sub's dive lights. They seemed to speak to him: "We are here. We are here. We are here..."

To Thomas, the lights were like the play of a computer board. Watching holorecords of them had formed this association in his mind. He had proposed it to Waela during one of the sessions when she had been teaching him the ways of Pandora's deeps. "A computer could crunch far greater numbers, form so many more associations so much faster."

Out of this had been born his proposal: Record them, scan for patterns and play those patterns back to the kelp.

Waela had admired the elegant simplicity of it: Leap beyond the perilous collection and analysis of specimens, beyond the organic speculations. Strike directly for the communications patterns!

Say to the kelp: "We see you and know you are aware and intelligent. We, too, are aware. Teach us your speech."

As he watched the play of lights, Thomas wanted to say they were like Christmas lights twinkling in the dark. But he knew neither of his crew would understand.

Christmas!

The very thought made him feel ancient. Shipmen did not know Christmas. They played other religious games. Perhaps the only person in his universe who might understand Christmas was Hali Ekel. She had seen the Hill of Skulls.

What did the Hill of Skulls and the passion of Jesus have to do with these lights flickering in a sea?

Thomas stared at the screen in front of him. What was he supposed to see here?

Aquaculture?

Would Shipmen be forced to exterminate the kelp? Crucify it for their own survival?

Christmas and aquaculture...

The play of lights was hypnotic. He felt the silent wonder of watchfulness throughout the command gondola. A sense of revelatory awe crept over him. Here on the bottom was the record of Pandora's budget, all the transactions which the planet's life had made. This was more than the bourse, it was the deposit vault where Pandora's grand geochemical and biolchemical circuit of exchange lay open to view.

What do you here, mighty kelp?

Was this what Ship wanted them to see?

He did not expect Ship to answer that question. Such an answer did not fit into the rules of this game. He was on his own down here.

Play the game, Devil.

The pressure of the water around their gondola filled his awareness. They remained here by the sufferance of the kelp. By the kelp's own tolerance could they survive. Others had come into this sea and survived by careful restraint. What might the kelp interpret as a threat? Those jeweled blinkings in the gloom took on a malevolent aspect to him then.

We trust too much.

In the silence of his fears, Panille's voice came as a jarring intrusion.

"We're beginning to get some pattern indicators."

Thomas shot a glance at the recording board to the left of his console. The load-sensors indicated preparation for playback. This would control the sub's exterior bubbles to replay any light patterns which the computer counted as repetitive and significant. Any such patterns would be played to the kelp.

"See! Now, we talk to you. What are we saying?"

That would catch its attention. But what would it do?

"The kelp's watching us," Panille said. "Can you feel it?"

Thomas found himself in silent agreement. The kelp around them was watching and waiting. He felt like the child of that faraway day at Moonbase when he had entered the creche school for the first time. There was a truth revealed here which most educators ignored: You could learn dangerous things.

"If it's watching us, where are its eyes?" Waela whispered.

Thomas thought this a nonsense question. The kelp could possess senses which Shipmen had never imagined. You might just as well ask about Ship's eyes. But he could not deny that sense of watchfulness around the sub. The *presence* which the kelp proejcted onto the intruders was an almost palpable thing.

The recorder buzzed beside him and he saw the green lights which signaled the shift to replay. Now, the extruded bubbles on the carrier surface were playing back something, he had no idea what. Exterior sensors revealed only a glow of many colors reflecting off particles in the water.

He could see no discernible change in the light play from the kelp.

"Ignoring us." That was Waela.

"Too soon to say," Panille objected. "What's the response time of the kelp? Or maybe we're not even *speaking* to it yet."

"Try the pattern display," Waela said.

Thomas nodded, punched for the prepared program. This had been the alternate approach. The small screen above the recorder board began to show what was being displayed on the sub's hull: first Pythagorean squares, then the counting of the sticks, the galactic spiral, the pebble game . . .

No response from the kelp.

The dim shapes of swimmers among the kelp did not change their movements dramatically. All appeared to be the same.

Waela, studying her own screens, asked: "Am I mistaken or are the lights brighter?"

"A bit brighter perhaps," Thomas said.

"They are brighter," Panille said. "It seems to me that the water is . . . murkier. If . . . Look at the anchor cable!"

Thomas flicked to the view Panille's screen displayed, saw the sensors signaling the approach of some large object from above.

"The cable's gone slack," Waela said. "It's sinking!"

As she spoke, they all saw the first remnants of the LTA bag settling around them into the range of the dive lights—dull orange reflections from the fabric, black edges. It pulled a curtain over the bubble dome above them. This disturbed the creatures among the kelp and ignited a wild flickering in the kelp lights which vanished as the curtain settled around the sub.

"Lightning hit the bag," Waela said. "It . . ."

"Stand by to drop the carrier and blow all tanks," Thomas said. He reached for the controls, fighting to suppress panic.

"Wait!" Panille called. "Wait for all of the bag to settle. We could be trapped in it, but the sub can cut a way through it."

I should've thought of that, Thomas thought. *The bag could trap us down here.*

Hittite law emphasized restitution rather than re-
venge. Humankind lost a certain useful practicality
when it chose the other Semitic response—never to
forgive and never to forget.

—**Lost People,**
Shiprecords

LEGATA SAT back, her whole body shaking and trembling. She could tell by the flickering cursor on the com-console that it was almost dayside. Familiar activities soon would begin out in Ship's corridors—familiar but with a feeling of sparseness because of the diminished crew. She had kept illumination low during nightside, wanting no distractions from the holorecord playing at the focus in front of Oakes' old divan.

Her gaze lifted and she saw the mandala she had copied for Oakes' quarters at the Redoubt. Looking at the patterns helped restore her, but she saw that her hands still shook.

Fatigue, rage or disgust?

It required a conscious effort to still the trembling. Knots of tension remained in her muscles, and she knew it would be dangerous for Oakes to walk into his old cubby right now.

I'd strangle him.

No reason for Oakes to come shipside now. He was permanently groundside.

The prisoner of his terrors.

As I was . . . until . . .

She took a deep, clear breath. Yes, she was free of the Scream Room.

It happened, but I am here now.

What to do about Oakes? *Humiliation.* That had to be the response. Not physical destruction, but humiliation. A particular humiliation. It would have to be at once political and sexual. Something more than embarrassment. Something *he* might think of to do against someone else. The sexual part was easy enough; that was no challenge to a woman of her beauty and genius. But the politics . . .

Should I conceal the evidence that I've seen this holo?

Save that information for the proper moment.

That was a good thought. Trust her own inspiration. She keyed the com-console and typed in: SHIPRECORDS EYES ONLY LEGATA HAMILL. Then the little addition which she had discovered for herself: SCRAMBLE IN OX.

There. No matter who thought to search for such a datum, it would be lose in that strange computer which she had discovered in one of her history hunts.

I'll stay shipside this diurn. She would not feel well. That would be the message to Oakes. He would grant her a rest period without question. She would spend her time here pulling every trick of computer wizardry she could to get the complete record on Morgan Oakes.

Political humiliation. Political and sexual. That had to be the way of it.

Perhaps that other Ceepee brought out of hyb, that Thomas, might hold a clue. Something in the way he looked at Oakes . . . as though he saw an old acquaintance in a new role . . .

And she owed a debt to Thomas. Strange that he should be the only one to know she had run the P. He had kept the secret without being asked . . . or asking. Rare discretion.

She had no thought of fatigue now. There was food shipside when she needed it. The power of Oakes' position made that no problem. She sent her message to Oakes groundside, turned to the console.

Somewhere in the records there would be a useful fact or two. Something Oakes had hidden or that he did not even know about himself—perhaps something he had done and did not want revealed. He was good at this concealment game but she knew herself to be better at it.

She began at the main computer—Ship's major interface with Shipmen.

Would it take fancy programming? A painstaking search through coded relationships which could hide bits of data far in the recesses of offshoot circuitry such as that Ox gate? How about the Ox gate? She hid things there, but had never asked it about Oakes.

She tapped out a test routine, keyed it and waited.

Presently, data began flowing across the small screen on the console. She stared. That simple? It was as though the material were waiting for her to ask. As though someone had prepared a bio for her to discover. Everything she needed was there—facts and figures.

"Suspect everyone," Oakes had said. "Trust no one."

And here he was being proved right beyond his wildest fears. The text kept rolling out. She backed it up, keyed for printout, and set it in motion once more.

The heading of the record was the most surprising thing of all. *MORGAN LON OAKES.*

Cloned. Raised, as he would put it, "like a common vegetable." Out of the axolotl tanks and into an Earthside womb.

Why?

There it was even as she asked. "To conceal the fact that it could be done, the birth was made to appear natural."

It was a feat of politics worthy of Ship . . . or Oakes. Did he know? How could he know? She stopped the printout and asked who else had called up this data.

"Ship."

It was an answer she had never before seen. Ship had worked with this data. Fearfully, she asked why Ship had called up the bio on Oakes.

"To store it in a special record for Kerro Panille should he ever desire to write a history."

She pulled her hands away from the keys. *Am I talking to Ship?*

Panille was one of those who said he talked to Ship. Not one of the fools, then.

Am I a fool?

She found herself more fearful of this discovery than she had been of the Scream Room. Ship dealt in powers far beyond those of Oakes and Lewis and Murdoch. She glanced around the enlarged cubby—pretentious damned place. Her gaze fell on the mandala. He had taken the movable hangings. The mystical design lay exposed against a bare metal bulkhead of silvery gray. It appeared lifeless to her, robbed of some original breath.

I'm not worthy of talking to Ship.

This had been an accident . . . a dangerous accident. Hesitantly, she started the Oakes bio printing once more. Words again flowed across the screen and the printer rattled with its text.

Legata heaved a deep sigh of relief. Perilous ground. But she had escaped.

This time.

She felt that something strange was happening, some new program awakening in Ship. It was a feeling in her shoulderblades. Something even more awesome might happen and she was right in the middle of it.

Her attention returned to the Oakes bio. That had been a time of great scurrying about Earthside, great secrets. Salvation and survival—whatever the label—the arrival of Ship and the desperation of doomed people.

Desperation breeds extremes if nothing else.

"Legata."

It was Oakes calling her name and she felt her heart skip a beat. But it was the console override. He was calling her from groundside.

"Yes?"

"What are you doing?"

"My job."

She glanced at the com-console telltales to see if he could find out what she was reading. It was still blocked by the Ox gate.

He recognized the sound of the printer, though.

"What are you printing out?"

"Some data you'll find interesting."

"Ahhhh, yes."

She could almost see his mind working on this. Legata had something she would not trust to the open channels between Ship and ground. She would show it to him, though. It must be interesting.

I'll have to find something juicy, she thought. *Something about Ferry. That's why I'm here.*

"What do you want?" she asked.

"I've been expecting you groundside."

"I'm not feeling well. Didn't you get my signal?"

"Yes, my dear, but we have urgent matters demanding our attention."

"But it's not full dayside yet, Morgan. I couldn't sleep and I still have work here."

"Is everything all right?"

"Just busy," she said.

"This cannot wait. We need you."

"Very well. I'm coming down."

"Wait for me at the Redoubt."

At the Redoubt!

He broke the connection and it was only then that she realized he had spoken of needing her. Was that possible? *Alliance or love?* She did not think there was much room for love in the convoluted patterns of Morgan Oakes.

Sooner expect Lewis to start raising a pet Runner.

Either way, Oakes wanted her presence. That gave her a wedge into the power she needed. Something still nagged at her, though— the one fear above all other: *What if he does love me?*

Once, she had thought she wanted him to love her. There was no question that he was the most interesting man she had ever met. Unpredictably terrifying, but interesting. There was much to be said for that.

Will I destroy him?

The printer finished producing the Oakes bio. She folded it, crossed to the mandala looking for a place to conceal the thick wad of Shipscript. The mandala was fixed solidly to the bulkhead. She turned and glanced around the cubby. Where to hide this?

Do I need to hide it?

Yes. Until the right moment.

The divan? She crossed to the divan and knelt beside it. The thing was fixed to the deck by bolts. Could she call a serviceman? No . . . she didn't dare let anyone suspect what she was doing. Gritting her teeth, she put two fingers on a bolt and twisted. The bolt turned.

Strength has its purposes!

The bolts removed, she lifted the end of the divan. My! It was heavy. She doubted that three men could lift it. She slipped the text under the divan, restored the bolts, twisting them tight.

Now for something juicy about Win Ferry.

She stood up and returned to the console. Ferry gave her no difficulty either. He practiced no discretion whatsoever.

Poor old fool! I'm going to destroy Oakes for you, Win.

No! Don't trick yourself into nobility. You're doing it on your own and for yourself. Let's keep love and the glory of others out of it.

Remember that I have power; you believe yourself miserable, but I can make you so wretched that the light of day will be hateful to you. You are my creator, but I am your master.

—Frankenstein's Monster Speaks,
Shiprecords

OAKES WOKE out of his first sound sleep groundside to muffled pounding outside his cubby.

His fingers reached his com-console before he was even awake and the viewscreen showed complete madness up and down Colony's corridors.

Even outside his own locked hatchway!

"I'm hungry now! I'm hungry *now*! I'm hungry *now*!"

The chant was a snarl in the throat of the night.

There were no guns in evidence, but plenty of rocks.

In a matter of blinks, Lewis was on the line.

"Morgan, we've lost them for now. This thing will have to run its course until..."

"What the hell is happening?" Oakes did not like it that his voice cracked.

"It started out as a round of The Game down in the 'ponicsways. Lots of drinking. Now it's a food riot. We can flood 'em out with..."

"Wait a minute! Are the perimeters still secure?"

"Yes. My people out there."

"Then why . . .?"

"Water in the passages will slow 'em down until we . . ."

"No!" Oakes took a deep breath. "You're out of your league, Jesus. What we'll do is let them go. If they seize food, then it'll be *their* responsibility when food gets even shorter. The supply does not change, you hear me? No extra food!"

"But they're running wild through . . ."

"Let them rip things up. The repairs afterward will keep them busy. And a good riot will purge emotions for a time, wear them out physically. *Then* we turn it to our advantage, but only after well-reasoned consideration."

Oakes listened for some response from Lewis, but the 'coder remained silent.

"Jesus?"

"Yes, Morgan." Lewis sounded out of breath. "I think that you . . . had better move . . . to the Redoubt immediately. We can't wait for dayside, but you'll . . ."

"Where are you, Jesus?"

"Old Lab One complex. We were moving out the last of . . ."

"Why must I go to the Redoubt now?" Oakes blinked and turned up the illumination in his cubby. "The riots will pass. As long as the perimeter's secure we can . . ."

"They're not stamping their feet and whining, Morgan. They're killing people. We've sealed off the gun lockers but some of the rioters . . ."

"The Redoubt cannot be ready yet! The damage there was . . . I mean, is it safe?"

"It's ready enough. And the crew there is handpicked by Murdoch. They're the best. You can rely on them. And, Morgan . . ."

Oakes tried to swallow, then: "Yes?"

Another long pause, garbled snatches of conversation.

"Morgan?"

"I'm still on."

"You should go now. I've arranged everything. We'll flood 'em out of the necessary passages. My people will be there within minutes: our usual signal. You should be at the shuttle hangar within fifteen minutes."

"But my records here! I haven't finished the . . ."

"We'll get that later. I'll leave a briefing disc for you with the shuttle crew. I'll expect to hear from you as soon as you get to the Redoubt."

"But . . . I mean . . . what about Legata?"

"She's safe shipside! Call her when you get to the Redoubt."

"It's . . . that bad?"

"Yes."

The connection went dead.

Though a pendulum's arc may vary, its period does not. Each swing requires the same amount of time. Consider the last swing and its infinitesimal arc. That is where we are truly alive: in the last period of the pendulum.

—Kerro Panille,
The Notebooks

LEGATA LOOKED past Oakes to the sea below the Redoubt. It was an orderly suns-set out there, Rega following Alki below the rim of the sea. A distant line of clouds boiled along the horizon's curve. Long waves rolled in to crash on the beach of their small bay. The surf lay out of sight beneath the cliffs upon which the Redoubt perched. Double walls of plaz plus an insulated foundation screened out most of the sounds, but she could feel the surf through her feet. She certainly could see the spray misting her view and beading the plaz along the view porch.

Orderly suns-set and disorderly sea.

She experienced a sense of calm which she knew to be false. Oakes had bolstered himself with alcohol, Lewis with work. They were still getting reports from Colony, but the last word suggested that the old Lab One site was under siege. Lucky thing Murdoch had been sent shipside.

Disorderly sea.

Only thin rags of kelp remained on the surface, and she found the absence of it a loss which she could not explain. Once kelp had dampened the surf. Now, wind whipped white froth across the wavetops. Had Lewis allowed for that?

"Why do you link the kelp and hylighters?" she asked. "You've seen the reports. They're vectors of the same creature or symbiotic partners."

"But it doesn't follow that they think."

Oakes directed a lidded stare at her, swirled an amber drink in a small glass. "Touch one of them and the other responds. They act together. They think." He gestured at the cliffs across the Redoubt's bay where a scattered line of hylighters hovered like watchful sentries.

"They're not attacking now," she said.

"They're planning."

"How can you be sure?"

"*We* plan."

"Maybe they're not like us. Maybe they're not very bright."

"Bright enough to pull out and regroup when they're losing."

"But they're only violent when we threaten them. They're just a . . . a nuisance."

"Nuisance! They're a threat to our survival."

"But . . . so beautiful." She stared across the small bay at the drifting orange bags, the stately way they tacked and turned, touching the cliff with their tendrils to steady themselves, avoiding their fellows.

Turning only her head, she shifted her attention to Oakes, and tried to swallow in a dry throat. He was staring down into his drink, gently swirling the liquid. Why wouldn't he talk about what was happening at Colony? She felt nervous precisely because Oakes no longer appeared nervous. It had been two full diurns since the food riot. What was happening? She sensed new powers being invoked—the bustling activity all through the Redoubt while Oakes stood here drinking and admiring the view with her. Not once in this period had Oakes turned to her with an assignment. She felt that she might be on probation for a new position. He could be testing her.

Does he suspect what I discovered about him shipside? Morgan Lon *Oakes*.

Impossible! He could not appear this calm in the face of that knowledge.

Oakes raised his eyebrows at her and tossed back his drink.

"They're beautiful, yes," he said. "Very pretty. So's a sun going nova, but you don't invite it into your life."

He turned back to the ever-present dispenser for another drink, and something about the mural on the inner wall of the porch caught his eyes, startling him. The thing seemed to move . . . like the waves of the sea.

"Morgan, may I have a drink, too?"

Her voice sounded small and weak against the background of the mural—yet she had created this mural. A gift. He had thought: *She wants to please me.* But now . . . there was always something other than pleasing in the way she looked at him. What had she really meant with this painting? Was it to please him or disturb him? He stared at it. The painting was a splash of colors, much larger than the mandala for his new offices here. She called it: "Struggle at suns-set."

The mural recreated a scene they had witnessed earlier on holo: Colonists at a construction site near the sea fighting back a sudden swarm of hylighters. One Colonist dangled by a leg in mid-air, wide-eyed . . . Horror or hallucination? The doomed man pointed an accusing finger out of the painting directly at the observer. This detail had escaped Oakes before. He stared at it.

All the construction sites, the drilling sites, the mine heads—all of them were shut down now. Everything depended on the Redoubt.

Why did that figure in the painting look accusing?

"A drink, please, Morgan?"

He did not have to turn to know her expression, the tongue flickering out to wet her lips. What was she planning? He pressed the dispenser key for two drinks. The Scream Room had left its imprint on her, no doubt of that, but instead of making her more trustworthy . . . it had . . . What? He did not like the eagerness in her request for a drink. Was she going the way of that damned Win Ferry? Her report on Ferry was unsettling. They had to have somebody shipside they could trust!

Oakes returned to her side, handed her one of the drinks. The suns-set was shading into dark purples with a few streaks of rose higher in the sky.

"Is this the way I have to buy your favors now?" He focused on her drink.

She managed a smile. What did he mean by that question?

Coming here had been far more difficult than she had imagined. Even armed with the new knowledge in her possession . . . even fleeing the turmoil at Colony—very difficult. A New Lab One with Lewis in charge was being built only a few blinks away, buried in the rocks of the Redoubt.

I'm free of that. I'm free.

But now she knew it would take more than conscious awareness of what had happened to her, much more, before she could feel completely liberated. Oakes still had his grasping hand in her psyche.

Her fingers trembled as she sipped from the glass he had handed her. It was pungent and bitter, a distillation, but she could feel it soothing her.

When the right time comes, Morgan Lon Oakes.

Oakes touched her hair, stroked her head. She did not lean toward him or away.

"In another few diurns," he said, "all that will remain of the kelp will be holo approximations and our memories. If we're right about the hylighters, they won't endure much longer." He glanced out the plaz where the after-glow of the setting suns had left golden luminescence in the sky and two fans of shadowy lines radiating upward from beyond the curve of the sea. "None too fond, eh, Legata?"

She shuddered as his fingers touched a nerve in her neck.

"Cold, Legata?"

"No."

She turned and her gaze fell on the mural. Sensors had ignited low illumination to compensate for the shadows filling the porch. The mural. It drank her mind.

I did that. Was it real or dream?

She stared into the mural at the world of her dreams, that peculiar soothsayer of the mind called *imagination*—a world Oakes could never see without the intervention of someone like herself.

Again, she shuddered, recalling the holorecord which had inspired the painting: the eerie moanings of the hylighters and the *whoosh* and *thump* when they exploded, the tortured screams of burning Colonists. Even as she recalled the scene, she imagined the smell of burning hair. It seemed to fill the porch. She tore her attention away from the mural and stared out at the sea—all darkness out there except for a distant white line glowing along the horizon. It looked threatening, more threatening than her memories.

"Why did we have to build so near the sea?" she asked.

The question was out before she could think about it and she wished she had suppressed it.

The drink. It loosens the tongue.

"We're high above the sea, my dear, not very near at all."

"But it's so big and..."

"Legata! You helped draw the plans for our Redoubt. You agreed. I recall your words clearly: 'What we need is a place to get away, a safe place.' "

But that was before the Scream Room, she thought.

She forced herself to look at him. The dim illumination erased the soft edges of his features and left the shadows controlled by his skull.

What other plans does he have for me?

As though he heard the question in her mind, Oakes began to speak, addressing her reflection in the plaz.

"As soon as we get matters orderly down here, Legata, I'll want you to make a few trips back to the ship. We'll have to keep an eye on Ferry until we can find a replacement."

So he still needs me.

It was clear now that he feared going shipside more than he feared the terrors groundside. Why? How does *Ship* threaten him? She tried to imagine herself as Oakes back in his cubby shipside, completely surrounded by the presence of Ship. Not *the* ship. Ship! Did Oakes, after all, believe in Ship?

He put an arm around her waist. "You agreed, my dear."

She forced herself not to cringe, fearful of the artificial kindness in his tone, afraid of unknown plans he might have for her. What was the reasoning behind his decisions?

Perhaps there is no reason.

The futility of this thought frightened her even more than Morgan Oakes did. Morgan *Lon* Oakes. Could it be that... clones and the wild creatures of Pandora... and Shipmen—that so many died merely because Oakes acted without reason?

He has his reasons.

Once more, she looked at her mural. *What did I paint there?* The doomed man stared back at her—the eyes, the melting flesh, the pointing finger, all screamed: *You agreed! You agreed!*

"You can't kill all of the creatures on this planet," she whispered, and shut her eyes tight.

He removed his arm from her waist. "Pardon me, Legata. I thought you said 'can't.'"

"I . . ." She could not continue.

He took her arm above the elbow the way Murdoch had grasped her at the Scream Room! She felt him guide her across the porch, and she opened her eyes only when her shins touched the red couch. Firmly, he pressed her down into the cushions. She saw that she still clutched her drink, some of it still sloshing in the glass. She could not look up at Oakes. She was shaking so hard that small splashes of the drink jumped out of the glass to settle on her hand and thigh.

"Do I make you nervous, Legata?" He reached down to stroke her forehead, her cheek.

She could not answer. She remembered the last time he did this and began to cry silently, her shoulders stiff, tears flowing quietly down her cheeks.

Oakes dropped to the couch beside her, took the drink from her hand and put it somewhere aside on the floor. He began to massage the back of her neck, working the stiffness out of her shoulders. His fingers, his precise medical touch, knew where to reach her and how to ease through her defenses.

How can he touch me like this and be wrong?

She leaned forward, almost totally relaxed, and her elbow touched a damp spot on her thigh where she had spilled her drink. She knew in that instant that she could resist him . . . and that he would not expect the way of her resistance.

He does not know about the record I hid shipside.

His fingers continued to move so expertly, so full of pseudo-love.

He doesn't love me. If he loved me he wouldn't . . . he wouldn't . . . She shuddered at a memory of the Scream Room.

"Still cold, my dear?"

His practiced hands pulled her gently down onto the couch, eased the tensions from her throat and breast.

If he loved me, he wouldn't touch me this way and frighten me the way he does. What does he really want?

It had to be more than sex, more than her body which he knew how to ignite with such sureness. It had to be something far more profound.

How strange, the way he could go on talking to her at a time like this. His words seemed to make no sense whatsoever.

"... and in the recombinant process itself, we have gained an interesting side effect to the degeneration of the kelp."

Degeneration! Always degeneration!

Avata informs through the esoteric symbols of Avata's history reduced to dreams and to images which often can be translated only by the dreamer, not by Avata.

—**Kerro Panille,**
History of the Avata

THERE'S NO *reason to panic yet*, Waela told herself.

Others subs had lost their LTAs and survived. The drill was spelled out by those experiences.

Still, she found herself trembling uncontrollably, her memory focused on her escape from the depths at the south shore of The Egg.

I escaped before. I'm a survivor. Ship, save us!

Save yourself. That was the unmistakable voice of her own Honesty. *Certainly*. She knew how to do it. She had taught the procedure to Thomas by repeated drill. And Panille appeared to be a cool one. No panic there. He was watching the screens, estimating the extent that the downed LTA bag was covering them.

Strange that it drifted straight down.

"There has to be a vertical current in this lagoon," Panille said, as though answering her thought. "See how the fabric has draped itself over us."

Thomas had watched the fabric cover them, sinking all around

270

the sub to enclose them in an orange curtain which cut off their view of the kelp.

There's no way the LTA could have been brought down by lightning, he thought. The bag was grounded to its anchor cable. It was compartmented. Breaking half the compartments would not have brought it down. There still would have been enough lift to take off the stripped-down gondola.

Somebody doesn't want us back.

"I think we could begin cutting away the fabric now," Panille said. He touched Thomas on the shoulder, not liking the way the man sat staring fixedly at the screens.

"Yes . . . yes. Thank you."

Thomas lifted the nose of the sub then and extruded the cutters. Whiplike arc burners, they slipped from hull-top compartments and began their work. The plaz dome above them glowed with silvery blue light from the burner. Thomas saw the orange curtain part and drift down, stirring up a fog of sediment.

"Do you want me to do it?" Waela asked.

He shook his head abruptly, realizing that she too must have noted his funk. "No. I can handle it."

The procedure was direct: release the slip-tackle which linked them to the anchor cable, fire the blast bolts which freed the command gondola from the carrier, blow the tanks and ride the gondola to the surface. Once on the surface, the gondola would stabilize automatically. They could fire their radiosonde then and set their locator beacon. From there, it was a matter of waiting out the arrival of a relief LTA.

The sense of failure was large in Thomas as he began the escape procedure. They had barely started the communications routine . . . and the plan had been a good one.

The kelp could've answered.

They all felt the jolt of the blast bolts. The gondola began to lift from the split carrier. *Rising out of it like a pearl from an oyster*, Thomas thought.

As they lifted, the kelp lights once more came into view through the open areas of the plaz walls.

Waela stared out at the winking lights. They pulsed and glowed in spasmodic bursts which sparked a memory just at the edge of awareness.

Where have I seen that before?

It was so familiar! Lights almost all green and purple winking at her . . .

Where? I was only down in the . . .

The memory returned in a rush and she spoke without thinking.

"This is just like the other time when I escaped. The kelp lights were very much like that."

"Are you sure?" Thomas asked.

"I'm sure. I can still see them there—the kelp separating and opening a way to the surface for me."

"Hylighters are born in the sea," Panille said. "Maybe they think we're a hylighter."

"It may be," Thomas said. And he thought: *Is that what we were supposed to see, Ship?*

There was a certain elegant sense in the idea. Colony had copied the hylighters to give the LTAs free access to Pandora's skies. Hylighters did not attack an LTA. Perhaps the kelp could be fooled in the same way. It would bear investigation. There were more important considerations of survival right now, however. Suspecting sabotage, he had to share that suspicion with his team.

"Nothing ordinary could have brought down that LTA," he said.

Panille turned from looking out at the firefly lights of the kelp.

"Sabotage," Thomas said. He produced the arguments.

"You don't really believe that!" Waela protested.

Thomas shrugged. He stared out at the descending cables of kelp. The gondola was almost into the biologically active zone near the surface.

"You don't," she insisted.

"I do."

He thought back through his conversation with Oakes. Had the man come out to inspect a sabotage device? He certainly had done nothing discernible. But there had been discrepancies in his responses—lapses.

Panille stared out through the gondola's plaz walls at the enclosing cage of kelp. Illumination was increasing rapidly now. The surface dome of light expanded and expanded as they entered sun-washed waters. Swimming creatures darted out of their path and circled close. Dazzling rays of light shot through the enclosing kelp barrier. The flickering nodules dimmed and were gone. Within a few heartbeats, the gondola broke free on the surface.

Thomas activated the surface program as the gondola began to bob and turn in the currents of the lagoon, rising and settling on a low swell. The sky overhead was cloudless but a mass of hylighters could be seen downwind.

A sea anchor popped from its external package below them, spread its funnel shape and snubbed the capsule around. The plaz-filtered light of both suns filled the gondola with brilliant reflections.

Panille exhaled a long sigh, realized he had been holding his breath to see if they really had stabilized on the surface.

Sabotage?

Waela, too, thought about Thomas' suspicions. He had to be wrong! A few remnants of the LTA bag drifted in the kelp leaves around the downwind edge of the lagoon. It was all consistent with a lightning strike.

In a cloudless sky?

Honesty *would* have to focus on the big discrepancy!

The hylighters, then?

Hylighters do not attack LTAs. You know that.

Thomas armed the radiosonde, punched the firing key. There was a popping sound overhead and a red glow arced over them, swerved left and dove into the sea. Boiling orange smoke lifted from the water where it had gone and was whipped toward the mass of hylighters tacking across the downwind horizon.

They all saw the kelp leaves twist and lift in agitation where the radiosonde had gone.

Thomas nodded to himself. A faulty radiosonde.

Waela freed herself from her seat restraints and reached for the release handle to the top hatch, but Panille grabbed her arm. "No! Wait."

"What?" She twisted free of him.

It embarrassed her to touch him after that scene the previous nightside. She found her skin glowing a hot and velvety purple which she was unable to control.

"He's right," Thomas said. "Touch nothing yet."

Thomas unlocked his own seat restraints, found the gondola's toolkit and removed a unipry. With the unipry, he began removing the cover to the hatch mechanism. The cover came off with a snapping sound and fell to the deck below. They all saw the odd green package nested in the controls where it would be crushed by a lever when the hatch was undogged and opened. Thomas took nippers from the toolkit and released the green package. He handled it gently.

Very amateur work, he thought, recalling the training which his Voidship crew had undergone in detecting and defusing dangerous devices. *Ship did much better than this even before it was Ship*. That had been good training and necessary. There had been no telling how a rogue Voidship might attack its umbilicus crew.

Did we create a rogue Voidship of more subtle powers?

The evidence of sabotage which he had seen thus far did not feel like Ship. It reeked of Oakes . . . or Lewis.

"What's that package?" Waela asked.

"My guess is it's a poison vapor set to start fuming when we tried to undog the hatch," Thomas said.

Handling it with caution in the bobbing gondola, Thomas set the package aside and returned his attention to the hatch controls. The system appeared to be free of other tampering. Slowly, gingerly, he undogged the hatch, folded down the screw handle and began turning it. The hatch lifted to expose the rim of gaskets and a sky unfiltered by the enclosing plaz.

When he had the hatch fully open, Thomas took the green package in one hand, climbed part way up the ladder and threw the package downwind. When it touched the water, lime-yellow smoke erupted from it, was caught by the wind and blown across the kelp-covered waves. The surface leaves writhed away from the smoke, curling and withering as he watched.

Waela clutched a stanchion for support and put one hand across her mouth.

"Who?"

"Oakes," Thomas said.

"Why?" Panille asked. He found himself more fascinated than fearful at these developments. Ship could save them if it came to that.

"He may want no more than one Ceepee alive in Colony."

"You're a Ceepee?" Panille was surprised.

"Didn't Waela tell you?" Thomas came back down the ladder.

"I . . ." She blushed a deep purple. "It slipped my mind."

"Perhaps The Boss has his own plans for the kelp," Panille said.

Thomas pounced on this. "What do you mean?"

Panille repeated what Hali Ekel had told him about the threat to exterminate the kelp.

"Why didn't you tell us?" Waela demanded.

"I thought Hali might be mistaken and . . . the opportunity to tell you did not arise."

"Everybody stay put," Thomas said, "while I see if there are any more little surprises in here."

He bent to his examination.

"You seem to know what you're looking for," Waela said.

"I've had some training in this."

She found this a disturbing idea: Thomas trained to locate sabotage?

Panille listened to them with only part of his attention. He released himself from his seat and looked up at the open hatch. There was a sweet smell to the salt-washed air blowing in the hatchway. He found the smell invigorating. Through an unblocked area beside his console, he could see the flock of hylighters tacking closer across the wind. The motions of the gondola, the smells—even the survival from the perils of the dive—all charged him with a sense of being intensely alive.

Thomas finished his examination.

"Nothing," he said.

Waela said: "I still find it difficult to . . ."

"Believe it anyway," Panille said. "There are things happening around Oakes that the rest of us are not supposed to learn."

She was outraged. "Ship wouldn't allow . . ."

"Hah!" Thomas grimaced. "Oakes may be right. Ship or *the* ship? How can we be sure?"

Such open blasphemy intrigued Panille. From another Ceepee, too! But it was the old philosophical question he had debated many times with Ship, merely cast in a more direct form. As he thought about this, Panille watched the approach of the hylighters, and now he pointed downwind.

"Look at those hylighters!"

Waela glanced over her shoulder. "A lot of them and big ones. What're they doing?"

"Probably coming to investigate us," Thomas said.

"They won't get too close, do you think?"

Panille stared at the orange flock. They were alive, perhaps sentient. "Have they ever attacked?"

"There's argument about that," Waela said. "They use hydrogen for buoyancy, you know, very explosive if ignited. There have been incidents . . ."

"Lewis argues that they sacrifice themselves as living bombs," Thomas said. "I think they're just curious."

"Could they wreck us?" Panille asked. He stared all around the horizon. No land in sight. He knew they had food and water

in the compartments under their feet. Waela had inspected those
before takeoff while he held a handlight.

"They could blacken the gondola's skin a bit," Thomas said.
He spoke while working at his console. "I've activated the locator
beacon, but there's a lot of static on those frequencies. Radio
appears to be working..."

"But we can't punch past the interference without the 'sonde,"
Waela said. "We're marooned."

Panille, holding himself against the pitching of the gondola,
climbed several steps of the ladder until his shoulders cleared the
hatch. One glance showed the hylighters still working their way
toward the gondola. He turned his attention to the 'sonde-release
package attached to the plaz beside the hatch.

"What're you doing?" Thomas demanded.

"There's a lot of the 'sonde's antenna wire still in its reel."

Thomas moved to the foot of the ladder, peered up. "What're
you thinking?"

Panille stared at the hylighters, at the wind-whipped sea surface. He felt an unexpected freedom here, as though all of that
time confined in Ship's artificial environment had merely been
preparation for this release. All of the holorecords, the history and
the intense hours of study could not touch one blink of this reality.
The preparations had, however, armed him with knowledge. He
looked down at Thomas.

"A kite could lift our antenna high enough."

"Kite?" Waela stared up through the plaz at him. Kites were
carrion-eating birds.

Thomas, knowing the other meaning, looked thoughtful. "Do
we have the material?"

"What are you talking about?" Waela demanded.

Thomas explained.

"Ohhh, festival flyers," she said. She glanced around the gondola. "We have fabrics. What're these?" She unsnapped a sealing
strip from an instrument panel, flexed it. "Here's material for the
bracing."

Panille, looking down at them, said: "Then let's..." He broke
off as a shadow passed over him.

They all looked up.

Two large hylighters passed directly over the gondola, some
of their tendrils tucked up while others held large rocks in the
water to steady them. The ballast tendrils of one hylighter rubbed

across the gondola, rocking it sharply.

Panille clutched the hatch rim for support. The ballast rock sped past below him in a foaming wake.

"What're they doing?" Waela shouted.

"That gas we threw out killed a lot of the kelp," Thomas said. "You don't suppose hylighters protect the kelp?"

"Here come some more of them!" Panille called.

Thomas and Waela looked where he was pointing. A swarm of hylighters glowing golden orange tacked across the wind perhaps a hundred meters away, turning in unison.

Panille climbed farther out of the hatch to sit on the rim. From this vantage, he could see the ballast rocks draw foaming lines across the waves, skipping over the kelp's leaves. The giant sail-crests of the hylighters billowed and flapped as they turned, then stiffened as they took their new heading.

Standing below him to peer over the top of an instrument bank, Thomas could see some of this.

"Don't tell *me* they're brainless," he said.

"I wonder if we've angered them?" Waela asked.

Panille, the wind tugging at his hair and beard, heard this as though it came from the ancient world of Ship. He felt exhilarated—free at last. Pandora was wonderful!

"They're beautiful!" he cried. "Beautiful!"

A sharp crackling sound from behind Thomas brought him whirling around. It was the speaker of a radio he had left on after testing it. Another sharp crackling erupted from the speaker. Hylighters and kelp both were blamed for this phenomenon which made radio undependable here, but how did they do it?

The swarm was almost at the gondola now. A giant specimen in the lead aimed its rock ballast directly at the gondola. Thomas held his breath. How much of *that* could the plaz withstand?

"They're attacking!" Waela shouted.

Panille had climbed farther out, standing now on the ladder's topmost rung while he steadied himself with a knee against the open hatch cover. He waved both arms wide, shouting: "Look at them! They're gorgeous! Magnificent!"

Thomas shouted to Waela who stood at the foot of the ladder: "Get that fool down here!"

As he shouted, the tucked tendrils of the leading hylighter slid over the gondola and the rock smashed into the plaz directly in front of Waela. She clutched the ladder for support and screamed at Panille as the gondola tipped, but her warning came too late. Arms still waving, Panille was knocked off his feet and spilled out of the gondola. She saw one of his hands clutch a hylighter tendril and he was jerked skyward. Other tendrils quickly enfolded him, almost concealing his body which was now glimpsed only in places through the hylighter's grasp. She saw all of this in bits and pieces as the gondola went through a series of wildly twisting gyrations under the massed onslaught of hylighters.

They were attacking!

Thomas had wedged himself into a corner where the arc of controls joined the communications board. He saw only Panille's feet disappear and heard Waela scream: "They've got Kerro!"

In your terms, Self may be called Avata. Not hylighter, not kelp, not 'lectrokelp, but Avata. That is
the Great Self in the language from your animal past.
Avata. Finding this label in you, Avata knows we
sing the same song. Through each other, Avata and
human know Self. No second measurement for Avata.
Same value every time. No separate qualities or forms.
Thus with human.

Avata. But not Avata.

To name is to limit, to control. To name without
knowing your limit is to hinder the knowing. At best,
it is a diversion. At worst, it is a misrepresentation,
a stolen label, a death. To name a thing falsely and
to act thereafter on the name—that is killing, a cutting
of the spiritual leaf, the death of the stem. A thing
is Self or it is Other. The naming is a matter of
proximity.

Avata identifies the speciesfold magnetification, the
magnetism of proximity; the wavelength of space:
humanthomas humankerro, humanjessup, human-
oakes. Avata concludes lack of sensory organ necessary to differentiate between clone and human. Avata
does not consider this lack a weakness or misrepresentation.

Avata is one in hylighter and kelp, not separate
in either, nor the same. Cells differ but share the One.
Before humans, Avata did not distinguish. Both are
Self. Avata would teach you the self of Other, the
human in clone.

Some things are because you name them. You per-petuate them in your language, you commiserate over the woe they have wrought you.

Say simply that these things are not so. Do not change the label but the labelness. Eliminate them from your life by washing them first from your tongue. Ignoring that which is false is also a knowing. Thus—learning. To learn is to grow and to grow is to live. You may practice forgetting and thus learn.

"Home."

That is your label for this place, humankerro. Avata washes your tongue here that you may properly inflect the name and then forget it. Avata brings you this to cleanse you of expectancies, that you may learn the cues to which Avata responds or refuses to respond.

This is how you learn Avata. You are both lower level and higher level, and the continuity is the con-tinuity of your will. Observe the vine which is all Avata winding through "Home." Grasp the vine. Cup the waters in your hands and drink.

You are the observer-effect.

—**Kerro Panille,
Translations from the *Avata***

And the Lord God said, "Behold the man is become
as one of us, to know good and evil: and now, lest
he put forth his hand, and take also of the tree of life,
and eat, and live forever: Therefore the Lord God sent
him forth from the Garden of Eden to till the ground
from whence he was taken. So he drove out the man;
and he placed at the east of the Garden of Eden Cher-
ubims, and a flaming sword which turned every way,
to keep the way of the tree of life.

—Christian *Book of the Dead,*
Shiprecords

FOR KERRO Panille, his last sensible thought was the beauty of
the lead hylighter passing within two meters overhead. He felt the
presence of the sea and the wind, saw the black twisting mass of
tendrils and the long rope of them which he knew linked the
magnificent creature to its ballast rock. Then he was knocked off
his feet and clutched at the only possible handhold—that long rope
of guiding tendrils.

From his study of them, Panille knew that the creatures were
considered to be dangerously hallucinogenic, explosive and poisonous to Shipmen, but nothing could have prepared him for the
actual experience. As his hand touched the hylighter he experienced an electric buzzing which climbed to a crescendo in every

sense of his body. He tasted bitter iron. The musk of uncounted flowers savaged his nostrils. His ears were the citadel of the fiercest attack—cymbals and twanging strings competed with horns and the cries of birds. Behind this assault, he heard the choral singing of a multitude.

Then his sense of balance went crazy.

Silence.

The sensations were turned off as though by a switch.

Am I dead? Is this real?

You live, humankerro.

In a way, it was like the voice of Ship. It was calm, faintly amused, and he knew it occurred only in his head.

How do I know that?

Because you are a poet.

Who . . . who are you?

I am that which you call hylighter. I save you from the sea.

The beautiful . . .

Yes! The beautiful, gorgeous, magnificent hylighter!

There was pride in this announcement, but still that sense of amusement.

You called me . . . humankerro.

Yes—humankerro-poet.

What does being a poet have to do with my knowing this is real?

Because you trust your senses.

As though these words opened a door to his body, he felt the enclosing tendrils, the sharp bite of wind between them, and his inner ears registered the roll of a sweeping turn as the hylighter tacked. His eyes reported a shadowy golden area millimeters from his nose and he knew he lay on his back in a cradle of tendrils, the body of the hylighter close above him.

What did you do to me?

I touched your being.

How . . .

Again, he experienced the savage assault on his senses, but this time there was pattern in it. He detected bursts of modulation too fast for him to separate into coherent bits. His sense of sight registered pictures and he knew he was looking down with hylighter vision upon the sea . . . and the gondola from which he had been snatched. He felt that he must cling to these sensations as he clung to his sanity. Madness lurked at the edges of his awareness . . .

And once more, the assault stopped with shocking abruptness.

Panille lay gasping. It was like being immersed in all the most beautiful poetry that humankind had ever produced—everything simultaneous.

You are my first poet, and all poets are known through you.

Panille sensed an elemental truth in this.

What are you doing with me? he asked. It was very much like talking to Ship in his head.

I strive to prevent the death of human and of Self.

That was reasonable.

Panille could make no response to this. All the thoughts which occurred to him felt inadequate. Poison from the gondola had killed kelp. The hylighters, known to originate in the sea, obviously resented this. Yet, this hylighter would save a human. It occurred to him then that he was talking to a source which could explain the relationship between kelp and hylighter. Before he could think through his question, the voice filled his head, a single thoughtburst: *Hylighterself-kelpself-all-one.*

It was like Ship asking him about God. He sensed another elemental truth.

Poet knows . . . This thought twined around in his mind until he could not tell if it originated with the hylighter or with himself. *Poet knows . . . poet knows . . .*

Panille felt himself washed in this thought. It was still with him when he realized that he was conversing with the hylighter in no language he could recall. The thoughts occurred . . . he understood them . . . but of all the languages he knew, none coincided with the structure of this exchange.

Humankerro, you speak the forgotten language of your animal past. As I speak rock, you speak this language.

Before Panille could respond he felt the tendrils opening around him. It was a most curious sensation: He was both the tendrils and himself, and he knew he was clinging to the Avata as he was clinging to his own sanity. Curiosity was his grip upon his being. How curious this experience! What poetry it would make! Then he knew he was being dangled over the sea: The foam at the edge of a kelp's fan leaf caught his attention and held it. He was not afraid; there was only that enormous curiosity. He wanted to drink in everything that was happening and preserve it to share with others.

Wind whipped past him. He smelled it, saw it, felt it. He was turning in the grasp of the hylighter and he saw a mounded mass of hylighters directly below. They opened like flower petals expanding to reveal the gondola in their midst—orange petals and the glistening gondola.

With gentle sureness, tendrils lowered him into the flower, into the gondola's hatch. They followed him, spreading around the interior of the gondola. He knew he was there with Waela and Thomas, yet still saw the flower as its petals closed.

An orange blaze surrounded him and he saw through the plaz, the hylighters all around, holding the gondola in a basket of tendrils.

Again, the wild play of his senses resumed, but now it was slower and he could think between the beats of it. Yes, there were Thomas and Waela, eyes glazed—terrified or unconscious.

Help them, Avata.

*Even the seemingly immortal gods survive only
as long as they are required by mortal men.*

—The Oakes Covenant

OAKES BEGAN to sputter and snore. His body lay half-melted
into cushions of the long divan which stretched beneath Legata's
mural on the porch of the Redoubt. The light was dull red, the
early dayside of Rega coming in through the plaz above the sea.

Legata untangled herself from Oakes, slowly eased the sleeve
of her singlesuit from under his naked thigh. She stepped over to
the plaz and looked out at the dayside light flickering off the tops
of waves. The sea was wild turmoil and the horizon a thick line
of milky white. She found the uncontrolled violence of the sea
repellent.

Perhaps I was not made for a natural world.

She pulled her singlesuit on, zipped it.

Oakes continued to snore and snort.

*I could have crushed him there in those cushions, thrown his
body to the demons. Who would suspect?*

No one except Lewis.

The thought had very nearly become reality back there on the
divan. Oakes had been satyric all through the dark hours. Once,
she had slipped her arms up around his ribs while he worked at
her, sweating and mumbling, but she could not bring herself to
kill. Not even Oakes.

285

Waves whipped high onto the beach across the bay as she scanned the scene. The water slashed high this morning. The pounding surf echoed a deeper trembling of the earth and she could hear the clatter of rock against rock. The sound must be frighteningly loud outside for it to be heard that well in here.

It's the job of waves and rocks to make sand, she thought. *Why can't I do my job that well . . . without question?*

The answer came immediately, as though she had thought it through countless times: *Because changing rock into sand is not killing. It is change, not extermination.*

Her artist's eye wanted to find order in the view out the plaz, but all was disorder. Beautiful disorder, but frightening. What a contrast with the peaceful bustle of a shipside agrarium.

She could see the shuttle station off on the isolated point of land to her left, an arc of the bay between, and the low line of the protected passage leading from Redoubt to Station. That had been Lewis' idea: Keep the Station remote, easy to cut off should attackers come from Colony.

She found herself wanting the roll and toss of kelp leaves in the bay, but the kelp was going . . . going . . .

A chill crawled up her spine and down her arms.

A few diurns, Oakes had said.

She closed her eyes and the picture that haunted her was her own mural, the accusing finger which pointed straight at her heart.

You are killing me! it said.

No matter how hard she shook her head, the voice would not be still. Against her better judgment, she crossed to the dispenser and keyed it for a drink. Her hand was steady. She returned to the plaz-guarded view, and sipped slowly while watching the waves bite their way up the beach across the bay. The waves had buried the previous high-tide mark at least a dozen meters back. She wondered whether she should wake Oakes.

A hylighter suddenly valved itself low across the beach below the shuttle station. A sentry appeared at the beachside guardpost and snapped her heavy lasgun to her shoulder, then hesitated. Legata held her breath, expecting the bright orange flash and concussion. But the woman did not fire; she lowered her weapon and watched as the delicate hylighter drifted out of sight around the point.

Legata let out her breath in a long sigh.

What happens when we have no others to kill?

Oakes' desire for a paradise planet vanished when she confronted that seascape. He could make it sound so plausible, so natural, but . . .

What about the Scream Room?

It was a symptom. Would people turn on each other, band together in tribes and attack each other in the absence of Dashers or Runners . . . or kelp?

Another hylighter drifted past farther out.

It thinks.

And the vanishing kelp. Oakes was right that she had seen the reports from the disastrous undersea research project.

It thinks.

There was a sentience here which touched her where cell walls left off, somewhere within that realm of creative imagination which Oakes distrusted and would never enter.

Almost eighty percent of this planet is wrapped in seas and we don't even know what's under there.

She found herself envying the researchers who had risked (and lost) their lives groping beneath these seas. What had they found?

A pair of huge boulders down on the beach beneath her smashed together with a jarring *crack* that caused her to jump. She glanced at the beach across the bay. As quickly as it crossed the high-tide mark, the waters began their ebb.

Curious.

Tons of boulders had been rolled up against the cliff barrier across the compound. More of them obviously must be on the beach beneath her. The boulders she could see were gigantic.

That much power in the waves.

"Legata . . ."

The abruptness of Oakes' voice and touch upon her shoulder startled her, and she crushed the glass in her hand. She stared down at the hand, the cuts, her own blood, shards of glass glinting in her flesh.

"Sit over here, my dear."

He was the doctor then, and she felt thankful for it. He plucked out broken glass, then unrolled strips of Celltape from a dispenser at his com-console to stop the bleeding. His hands were firm and gentle as he worked. He patted her shoulder when he had finished.

"There. You should . . ."

The buzz of the console interrupted.

"Colony's gone." It was Lewis.

"What do you mean, *gone*?" Oakes raged. "How can the entire . . ."

"A shuttle overflight shows nothing but a hole where Lab One was. Plenty of demons, hatchways to all lower levels blown . . ." He shrugged, a tiny gesture in the console screen.

"That's . . . that's thousands of people. All . . . dead?"

Legata could not face Lewis, even on the screen. She crossed to the divan silently and stared out the plaz.

"There could be survivors holed up behind some of the hatches," Lewis went on. "That's how we made it here when . . ."

"I know how you made it here!" Oakes shouted. "What are you suggesting?"

"I'm not suggesting anything."

Oakes gritted his teeth and pounded the console. "You don't think we should have Murdoch try to save anyone?"

"Why risk the shuttles? Why risk one of our last good people?"

"Of course. A hole, you say?"

"Nothing but rubble. Looks to've been the work of lasguns and plasteel cutters."

"Do they . . . I mean, are there any shuttles left over there?"

"We disabled everything before leaving."

"Yes . . . yes, of course," Oakes murmured. Then: "LTAs?"

"Nothing."

"Didn't you and Murdoch say that you cleared everything out of that Lab One site? Moved it all here?"

"Apparently the rioters thought there might be some burst hidden away there. They captured the only remaining communications equipment. They were demanding help from . . . the ship."

"They didn't . . ." Oakes could not complete the question.

"The ship didn't answer. We were listening."

A deep sigh shook Oakes.

Without turning to face him or the viewscreen, Legata called out, "How many people did we lose there?"

"Ship knows!" Lewis threw back his head, laughing.

Oakes hit the key to shut him off.

Legata clenched her fists. "How could he laugh that way at . . . ?" She shook her head.

"Nervous," Oakes said. "Hysteria."

"He was not hysterical! He was enjoying it!"

"Calm yourself, Legata. You should get some rest. We have much to do and I'll need your help. We've saved the Redoubt. We have most of the food that was at Colony and far fewer people to eat it. Be thankful that you're among the living."

That worry in his tone, in his eyes.

It was almost possible to believe he felt genuine love for her.

"Legata . . ." He put out a hand to touch her arm.

She pulled away. "Colony's gone. The hylighters and kelp are next. Then what? Me?"

She knew it was her own voice speaking, but she had no control over it.

"Really, Legata! If you can't handle alcohol, you should not drink it."

His gaze went to the broken glass on the floor.

"Especially this early in the dayside."

She whirled away from him and heard him press the console key and summon a clone worker to clean up the broken glass. As he spoke, Legata felt the last of her hope shatter in the morning air, lost on the wild glinting of the waves she could see out there.

What can I do against him?

Human, do you know how interesting it is, this thing you describe? Avata does not have a god. How is it that you have a god? Avata has Self, has this universe. But you have a god. Where did you find this god?

**—Kerro Panille,
Translations from the *Avata***

FOR THOMAS and Waela, the return of the hylighters had appeared another concerted attack. Thomas tried to close the gondola's hatch and found it jammed. Waela was shouting up at him to hurry, and asking if he saw Kerro.

Both suns were up now. And the light on the sea was dazzling.

Waela's head was still spinning from the gondola's gyrations.

"What'll they do with him?" she called.

"Ship knows!" He jerked at the hatch cover, but it would not move. Something had hit the mechanism while the gondola was twisted and tilted in the first attacks.

Thomas peered at the tacking hylighters. One of them had its tendrils tucked up tightly. It could be holding Panille in there. He saw that the gondola had been pushed out of the dead kelp into a patch of living green. The sea all around was subdued by a carpet of gently pulsing leaves.

"They're coming back!" Waela shouted.

Thomas abandoned his attempts on the hatch, slid back into the gondola.

"Brace yourself in your seat!" he called. And he followed his own order while he watched the advancing swarm of orange.

"What're they doing?" Waela asked.

It was a rhetorical question. They could both see the hylighters slow their advance at the last instant. In concert, they turned their great sail membranes into the wind and cupped the gondola in dangling tendrils.

Waela freed herself from her seat, but before she could move, the massed hylighters opened a way overhead and Panille was lowered through the hatch.

She tried to avoid the questing mass of tendrils which accompanied Panille, but they found her. They enfolded her face with a sensation of tingling dryness which immediately gave way to a drunken sense of abandon. She knew her body; she knew where she was: right here in the gondola which was being held steady in a cupped hammock of hylighter tendrils. But nothing mattered except a feeling of joy which insinuated itself all through her. She felt that the sensation came from Panille and not from the hylighters.

Avata? What are Avata?

That thought had seemed her own, but she could not be certain. She was not aware of up or down. There was no spatial solidity.

I'm going crazy!

All of the horror stories about poisonous and hallucinogenic hylighters crashed through her barriers and she tried to scream but could not locate her voice.

Still, the joy persisted. Panille was right there saying things to soothe her. "It's all right, Lini."

Where did he get that name for me? That was my childhood name! I hate that name.

"Don't hate any part of yourself, Lini."

The joy would not be denied. She began to laugh but could not hear her own laughter.

Quite suddenly, an island of clarity opened around her and she knew Kerro Panille lay nude beside her. She felt his warm flesh against her.

Where did my clothing go?

It was not important.

I'm hallucinating.

This was a product of Thomas' command that she seduce the poet. She gave herself up to the dream, to the warmth and hardness of him as he slid into her, rocking her. And she sensed all around the questing tendrils as they explored, joining her with images of flaring stars. That, too, was unimportant—more hallucination. There was only the joy, the ecstasy.

For Panille, the slowed play of the sense-attack wavered when he first saw Waela. He felt his own body and he felt the hylighter's. Wind whipped his sail membranes. Then he heard music, a slow and sensual chant which moved his flesh in time to the dance of tendrils around him. He found himself drawn to Waela, his hands upon her neck. How electric her flesh! His hands unsnapped her singlesuit. She made no move to assist or resist, but kept time to the sensory beat with a soft swaying of her hips which did not stop even when the singlesuit slid off her body.

Strangest sensation of all: He could see her flesh, the lovely body, yet he saw also a golden-orange hylighter rise from the sea and spring free into the sky, and he saw Hali stretched out in warm yellow light beneath a cedar of a treedome. Wonder filled him as he dropped his own suit and drew Waela down to the deck.

Ship? Ship, is this the woman for whom I saved myself?

How is it that you call upon Ship when you could call your human-self?

Was that Ship or Avata? No matter. He could not listen for an answer. There was only the hard beat of sexual magnetism which told him every movement his body should make. Waela became not-Waela, not-Hali, not-Avata, but part of his own flesh entwined with a sensation of enormous involvement by countless others. Somewhere in this, he felt that he lost even himself.

Thomas, still restrained securely by his seat straps when Panille returned, was caught there by entwining tendrils. He tried to fight them off, but . . .

Voices! There were voices . . . he thought he heard old Morgan Hempstead back at Moonbase, christening their Voidship. Momentous day. There was a buzzing in his nostrils and he smelled the musk of Pandora but he was crouched within his own nostrils recording this. *Tendrils!* They moved all over his body, under his suit, avoiding no intimate contact. As they moved, they sucked out his identity. First he was Raja Flattery, then Thomas, then he did not know who he was. This amused him and he thought he laughed.

I'm hallucinating.

That was not even his own thought because he was not there to have such a thought. There was a head somewhere spinning out of control. He thought he felt brains rattle and slosh in their cage of skull. He knew he ought to breathe but he could not find where to breathe. He was sliding through a passage which no clone had ever known—the womb of all wombs.

That's how it is to be born.

Panic threatened to overcome him. I was never born! *The hylighters are killing me!*

Avata does not kill you!

That was a voice echoing in a metal barrel. *Avata?* He knew that from his Chaplain studies—ancient superego of the Hindu oversoul.

Who am I who knows this?

He glimpsed Panille and Waela, their naked bodies entwined in lovemaking. The ultimate biological principle. Clones don't have that link with their past.

Am I a clone? Who am I?

He knew what clones were, whoever he was; he knew that. Clones were property. Morgan Hempstead said so. Again, panic threatened him, but it was stifled instantly while he tried to follow a silvery thread of awareness which moved faster and faster as he sped to overtake it.

Waela . . . Panille . . .

He knew those had to be people, but he did not know who, except that the names filled him with rage. Something fought him to calmness.

The mandala on his cubby wall. Yes. He stared at it.

Who was Waela?

A sense of loss flooded through him. He was forever out of his time, far gone from someplace where he had grown, stripped of past and without his own future.

Damn You, Ship!

He knew who Ship was—the keeper of his soul, but this thought made him feel that he was Ship and he had damned himself. No reality remained. Everything was confusion, everything gone to chaos.

It's you damned Avata/hylighters! Keep that Panille out of my mind! Yes, I said MY mind.

Darkness. He was aware of darkness and of motion, sensations of controlled movement, glimpses of light and a glaring sun, then craggy rocks. He could see Rega low on a castellated rock horizon. There was flesh around him and he knew it for his own.

I'm Raja Flattery, Chaplain/Psychiatrist on . . . No! I'm Raja Thomas, Ship's Devil!

He looked down to find himself strapped into his command couch. There was no motion to the gondola. When he looked out through the plaz he could see solid ground—a damp stretch of Pandoran soil studded with native plants: odd spikey things with fluting silver leaves. He turned his head and there was Waela seated on the deck, completely naked. She was staring at two singlesuits. One of them, Thomas saw, carried Waela's shoulder badge of the LTA service, and the other . . . the other was Panille's.

Thomas looked all around the gondola. Panille was not there.

Waela turned to look up at Thomas. "I think it was real. I think we really did make love. And I was in his head while he was in me."

Thomas pushed himself hard against the back of his seat, his memory struggling for the bits and pieces of what had happened to them. Where was the damned poet? He could not survive out there.

Waela moved her tongue against her teeth. She felt that she had lost track of time. She had been out of her body in some new place, but now she knew her body better than ever before. *Images.* She recalled the earlier, more terrible moments off the south coast of The Egg when she had sprawled on a kelp leaf, fighting for her sanity. This recent experience in the gondola was not the same, but one partook of the other. In both, she felt the aftermath as a loosening of her identity and a mixing of linear memories, shaking bits of her past out of place.

Thomas unfastened his seat restraints, stood and peered out through the filtering plaz. He felt that something had reached into his psyche and drained away the energy. *What are we doing here? How did we get here?*

There was no sign of hylighters.

What are Avata?

The gondola had been deposited in a broad pocket of flat land surrounded by a rock rim. The place looked vaguely familiar. The outline of the west rim . . . He stared at it, caught up in a fugue state of attempted recollection.

"Where are we?" That was Waela.

His throat was too dry to respond. It took a moment of con-vulsive attempts to swallow before he could speak.

"I . . . think we're somewhere near Oakes' Redoubt. Those rocks—" He pointed.

"Where's Kerro?"

"Not here."

"He can't be outside. The demons!"

She stood and stared all around over the obstructing panels of instruments, craning her neck to peer every direction. *That fool poet!* She looked up at the hatch. It was still open.

In that instant an LTA drifted over the rim of rocks to the west; the glare of Rega setting ringed it in a golden halo. The LTA was valved down to a landing beside the gondola, the hiss of its loud vents stirred up the dust. The gondola was a conventional landside type, armored against demons and studded with weapons. The side hatch opened a crack and a voice called from within: "You can make it if you run! No demons near."

Hastily, Waela stood and slipped into her suit. It was like putting on familiar flesh. She felt her sense of identity firming.

I must not think about what has happened. I'm alive. We're rescued.

But somewhere within her she thought she heard a voice crying names: "Kerro . . . Jim . . . Kerro . . . where are you?"

There was no answer, just Thomas insisting that she follow only after he had tested the outside. *Damn fool! I'm faster than he is.* But she went quietly up the ladder behind him, watched him slide down the smooth plaz curve of the gondola, then fol-lowed on his heels. The rescue hatch of the other gondola swung wide as they reached it, and they were jerked inside by two pairs of hands. They were in familiar red shadows with the Shipmen at defensive stations all around the interior.

Waela heard the hatch slammed and dogged behind her, felt the gondola lift, swinging. There was the humming of a scanner as it passed over her body. A voice at her ear said: "They're clean."

Only then did she realize that she stood in a sealed-off bubble within the rescue gondola. This spoke of only one threat: *Nerve Runners!*

There were Runners in the area.

She felt a deep sense of gratitude for the Shipman who had scanned them, risking contact with Runners. Turning, she saw a long-armed monstrosity only vaguely Shipman in shape.

"We take you Lab Oneside," he said and his mouth was a toothless black hole.

*In a fit of enthusiastic madness I created a rational
creature and was bound towards him to assure, as far
as was in my power, his happiness and well-being.
This was my duty, but there was another still para-
mount to that. My duties towards the beings of my
own species had greater claims to my attention because
they included a greater proportion of happiness or
misery.*

—**Dr. Frankenstein Speaks,**
Shiprecords

THOMAS STRETCHED himself in the hammock of a cell and
watched a fly creep its way across his ceiling. There were no ports
in this cell, no chrono. He had no way of estimating the time.

The fly skirted the protrusion of a sensor eye.

"So we brought you, too." Thomas spoke aloud to the fly.
"It wouldn't surprise me to find a few rats skulking around this
place. Non-human rats, that is."

The fly stopped and rubbed its wings. Thomas listened. There
was a steady stream of footsteps up and down the passage outside
his locked hatch. It had been locked from the outside, no handle
in here.

He knew he was somewhere within Oakes' infamous Redoubt,
the fortress outpost on Black Dragon. They had taken all of his

297

clothing, every possession, leaving him with a poorly fitted green singlesuit.

"Quarantine!" he snorted, still talking aloud. "At Moonbase we called it 'the hole.'"

Some of those footsteps outside were running. Everything was rush-rush here. He wondered what was happening. What was going on over at Colony? Where had they taken Waela? They had told him he was headed for debriefing. It turned out to be a quick once-over by a strange med-tech and isolation in this cell. *Quarantine!* Before they had closed the hatch, he had glimpsed a sign across the way: "Lab One." So they had a Lab One here, too . . . or they had moved the other one from Colony.

He was aware of the sensor eye prying at him from the ceiling. The cell was spartan—the hammock, a fixed desk, a sink, an old-style composting toilet without seat.

Once more, he looked at the fly. It had progressed to the far corner of the cell.

"Ishmael," he said. "I think I'll call you Ishmael."

. . . his hand will be against every man and every man's hand against him, and he shall dwell in the presence of all his brethren.

Ship's unmistakable presence filled Thomas' head so suddenly that he clapped his hands over his ears in reflex.

"Ship!" He closed his eyes and found that he was near tears. *I can't give in to hysteria! I can't!*

Why not, Devil? Hysteria has its moments. Particularly among humans.

"There isn't time for hysteria." He opened his eyes, brought his hands away from his ears, and spoke in the general direction of the ceiling sensor. "We have to solve Your problem of WorShip. They won't listen to me. I'll have to take direct action."

Ship was relentless: *Not MY problem! Your problem.*

"My problem, then. I'm going to share it with the others."

It is time to talk of endings, Raj.

He glared at the sensor, as though that were the origin of the presence in his head.

"You mean . . . break the recording?"

Yes, it is the time of times.

Was that sadness in Ship?

"Must You?"

Yes.

So Ship really meant it. This was not just another diversion, another replay. Thomas closed his eyes, feeling his voice go slack in his throat, his mouth dry. He opened his eyes and the fly was gone.

"How . . . long do we . . . how long?"

There was a noticeable pause.

Seven diurns.

"That's not enough! I might do it in sixty. Give me sixty diurns. What's such a sliver of time to You?"

Just that, Raj: a sliver. Annoying, the way it works its way into the most sensitive area. Seven diurns, Raj, then I must be about other business.

"How can we discover the right way to WorShip in seven diurns? We haven't satisfied You for centuries and . . ."

The kelp is dying. It has seven diurns until extinction. Oakes thinks it will be longer, but he is mistaken. Seven diurns, then, for you all.

"What will You do?"

Leave you to the certainty that you will wipe yourselves out.

Thomas leaped from his hammock, shouted: "I can't do anything about it in here! What do You expect from . . . ?"

"You in there! Thomas!"

It was a male voice from a hidden vocoder. Thomas thought he recognized the voice of Jesus Lewis.

"Is that you, Lewis?"

"Yes. Who are you talking to?"

Thomas looked up at the sensor in the ceiling. "I have to talk to Oakes."

"Why?"

"Ship is going to destroy us."

Let you destroy yourselves. The correction was gentle but firm in his awareness.

"Was that what you were shouting about? You think you were talking to the ship?" There was derision in Lewis' tone.

"I *was* talking to Ship! Our WorShip is all wrong. Ship demands that we learn how to . . ."

"*Ship* demands! *The* ship is about to be put in its proper place, a functional . . ."

"Where's Waela?" He shouted it in desperation. He had to have help. Waela might understand.

"Waela's pregnant and she's been sent shipside to the Natali. We don't have birthing facilities here yet."

"Lewis, please listen to me, please believe. Ship awakened me from hyb to put you all on notice. You don't have much time left to..."

"We have all the time in this world!"

"That's it! And this world has only seven more diurns. Ship demands that we learn the proper WorShip before..."

"WorShip! We can't waste time on such nonsense. We have to make a whole planet safe to live on!"

"Lewis, I have to talk to Oakes."

"You think I'm going to bother the Ceepee with your babblings?"

"You forget that I'm a Ceepee."

"You're insane and you're a clone."

"Unless you listen to me, you're headed for destruction. Ship will break the... it will be the end of humankind forever."

"I have my orders about you, Thomas, and I'm going to obey them. There's only room for one Ceepee here."

The hatch behind Thomas popped open and he whirled to see the yellow dayside lights of the passage framing an E-clone sentry there—giant head, round black hole for a mouth, huge arms that hung nearly to his ankles. The eyes were glaring red and bulbous.

"You!" A growling voice issued from the round black hole. "Out here!"

One of the massive hands reached in, closed around Thomas' neck and jerked him out into the passage.

"WorShip. We have to learn how to WorShip," Thomas croaked.

"I get tired a hearin' that WorShip crap," the sentry said. "You're movin' out." The sentry released his neck and gave Thomas a violent push down the passage.

"Where are we going? I have to talk to Oakes."

The sentry lifted one of his arms, pointed down the passage. "Out!"

"But I..."

Another push sent Thomas stumbling. There was no resisting the strength of this clone. Thomas allowed himself to be herded down the passage. It curved to the right and ended at a locked hatch. The sentry took one of Thomas' arms in a relentless grip, opened the hatch. It swung wide to reveal the open ground of Pandora in the harsh cross-lighting of Alki swinging low on the horizon to his left. A sudden push from the clone sent Thomas sprawling into the open and took his breath away. He heard the hatch slam closed. Somewhere above him, he heard the distant fluting of a flock of hylighters.

They've sent me into the open to die!

*And the Lord said, "Behold, the people is one, and
they have all one language . . . and now nothing will
be restrained from them which they have imagined to
do. Let us go down and confound their language that
they may not understand one another's speech."*

—Christian *Book of the Dead,
Shiprecords*

FROM THE instant the first tentacles brushed her face to the
moment she boarded the shuttle for Ship, Waela lived in a blur
of past-present-future which she could not control. Kerro was gone
and Thomas was not available, this much she knew. And contact
with the hylighters had left her with a voice in her mind. It flared
there in flashes of total demand. She wavered between accepting
the voice and believing herself insane.

The voice of Honesty would not answer, but this new voice
intruded without warning. When it came, she felt herself filled
with the same conceptual ecstasy she had felt in the gondola.

It is the Avata way of learning.

The voice kept repeating this. When she questioned, answers
came, but in a jargon which confused her.

*Like electricity, humanwaela, knowledge flows between poles.
It activates and charges all that it touches. It changes that which
moves it and moves within it. You are such a pole.*

302

She knew what the words meant, but they went together in a confusing way.

And all the while, she remained vaguely aware of the processing procedure when the rescue gondola deposited them at Colony. Thomas was taken away somewhere and she was rushed into a medical unit for debriefing. The session was run by Lewis—astonishing!

It was right there that the first demanding flash hit her.

Waela. I have found the Avata.

She knew there was no sound, but the voice filled her sense of hearing. It was Kerro Panille, no denying it. Not his voice, but his identity recognized in an internal way which could not be disguised. She knew it as she knew herself. But she didn't even know that Kerro was alive!

I'm alive.

Then he had found some way of reaching out ... or of reaching in.

Either that or I'm insane, she thought.

She did not feel insane as she stood in the Medical section's glaring tile-white cubicle looking across a metal table at Lewis. Hands supported her. It was nightside; she knew this. Rega had been setting and they had brought her directly in here. Lewis was speaking to her and she kept shaking her head, unable to answer him because of that voice in her mind. An older med-tech said something to Lewis. She heard three words. "... too soon for ..."

Then the whirl of that intruding voice returned. She was uncertain whether she recognized words—or whether it really could be called a *voice*—but she knew what was being said. It was a non-language, and she knew this when she found that she could not distinguish between "I" and "We" in Kerro's communication. A language barrier was down.

In that instant of recognition, she knew Avata as Kerro Panille knew Avata. She wondered how she learned this lesson, this ancient bit of human history.

How did I learn, Kerro Panille?

What is done to one is felt by all, humanwaela.

"Why am I *humanwaela*?" She asked it aloud and saw an odd expression come over the face of Lewis as he turned from talking to the med-tech. This did not bother her. She felt her mind drifting lazily in Pandoran wind. There were mutterings and headshakings among people around her—med-techs, several of them ... an entire team. She filtered them out. Nothing was more important than the voice in her mind.

You are humanwaela because you are at once human and at once Waela. There may be such a time as this is not so. Then you will be human.

"When will that be?"

The cold node of a pribox drilled the back of her left hand, tingled up her arm and sent her down a whirlwind of dis-timed memories which were not her own.

When you know all that otherhumans know, and otherhumans know all of you, then you are human.

She concentrated on that magnificent universe of the interior which this concept opened before her. *Avata.* She had no sensation of time while she floated in the arms of Avata, or whether Avata was really with her. If it was just a dream, she wanted it never to end.

Only you can end it, humanwaela. See?

Memories poured into her—from that first sensory awareness of the first Avata to the coming of Shipmen to Pandora and then to her rescue from the gondola—everything poured into her through a timeless flash, a non-linear stream of sensations.

This is not hallucination!

She saw humans, *Shipman/humans* of many suns, and un-counted histories which died with them. It baffled her how she understood this. *How . . . ?*

She heard the voice in her mind: *This we trade with those we touch. Lives of all humans alive in each of you. But you and humankerro are the first to recognize the trade. Others resist and fear. Fear erases. Humanthomas resists, but out of humanfear, not out of humanthomas fear. There is something he will not trade.*

Waela found herself eavesdropping through another's eyes. She was looking in a mirror and the face that looked back was Raja Thomas. A shaking hand explored the face, a wan face, tired. She heard a voice which she knew to be Ship's.

Raj.

Then there were no more mind pictures. He blanked her out. Rejected.

She found herself alone on a gurney in a Redoubt passage.

So Thomas is on speaking terms with Ship.

"Why?" The question was a dry crackle in her throat and a nearby med-tech bent over her. "You'll be shipside soon, dear.

Don't worry." The gurney's straps hurt her breasts.

This is Pandora, humanwaela. All evil has been released here.
There was that voice again. Not Kerro. *Avata?*

The word tingled on her tongue as med-techs began to roll her gurney onto a shuttle. There was another face above her then— dream or reality? Small, a face like Lewis, but not Lewis. The voices all around were babble. She was being wheeled, pushed and probed, but her attention remained with the voice in her mind and the link she had seen to that intricate chain of humanity.

"She's pregnant. That means shipside, the Natali. Orders."

"How long's she been pregnant?"

"Looks like more'n a month."

That can't be! she thought. *I've just arrived here and Kerro and I . . .*

She felt a doubled awareness of time then—one told her she had arrived at the Redoubt late in the same diurn that had seen their sub enter the lagoon. The other time-sense lived in her abdomen, and the clock there had gone mad . . . spinning, spinning, spinning. It raced completely out of pace with the clock in her head.

"She'll be the Natali's problem pretty soon," someone said. Those were words in her ears. Time out of sync was more important. From the time Kerro had slipped into her. . . .

The time was out of phase. She knew only that she must be delivered shipside to the Natali. That was the way of WorShip.

How can that be, Avata?

She felt that she was meant to be pregnant and the act of conception was an Avata formality.

As the hatchway opened to the shuttle the lean-faced man took hold of the gurney and she saw that it was one of Murdoch's people, a long-fingered clone who spoke in a falsetto. A shock of fear jolted her body.

Am I going shipside?"

She couldn't bring herself to ask the other half of the question, *Or to Lab One?*

Yes," he said, as she thumped across the threshold of the shuttle.

What do we do now?" she asked aloud. And the voice from her mind said, *Save the world.*

Then the hatchdogs were secured and she slept.

CONSCIOUS: *from Latin* com, *with* scire (*to know*).
CONSCIENCE: *from Latin* com (*intensive*), *with* scire.
Conscious—to know; conscience—to know well (or, in the vernacular, to know better).

—Shiprecords

"SHIPSIDE!" OAKES screamed into the vocoder on his console. "Who ordered the TaoLini woman shipside?"

The med-tech facing him on the screen looked terrified and small. His little mouth worked itself into a stumble of words.

"You did, sir. I mean . . . orders. She's pregnant, sir, and you signed the WorShip order sending all . . ."

"Don't tell me what I signed!"

"No, sir. Are you ordering her back, sir?"

Oakes pressed a hand against his forehead.

Too late, now. The Natali have her. Reprocessing her groundside would mean an executive order and that would mean attention. The Redoubt was problem enough. Better to let the matter rest until something could be arranged . . . Damn! Why couldn't we have moved the Natali down here . . . ?

"I want to talk to Murdoch."

"He is shipside, sir."

"I know he's shipside! Get him on a line to me as soon as you can!"

He smacked the key on the console with the side of his fist and the frightened little med-tech's face faded.

Damn! Just when things were going right!

He looked out over the clear bay beside the shuttle station. No more kelp there anyway. The perimeter lights and the arcs from the nightside crew's torches reflected the flat calm of the water.

No kelp. It'll be gone from Pandora before we know it.

That left Ship.

The ship.

And now, that TaoLini woman. No telling what she knows. Thomas could have convinced her of anything. After all, he was a Ceepee....

Oakes turned back to his console and activated the holo of Thomas' debriefing.

Thomas sat in the center of the room, a cell three meters square. He faced the sensor. A tall woman from Behavioral stood facing Thomas and he was shaking his head from side to side.

"No time. No time. 'You must decide how you will WorShip,' Ship says and the clue is in the sea. I know it's in the sea. WorShip... WorShip. And there is no time, after all the eons and all these worlds... no time. No time...." Oakes switched off the holo in disgust.

The kelp got to him, that's for sure. Maybe it's just as well.

He paced back to the plaz which screened the ocean view, and watched the dazzle of the welders and cutters play across the water.

The kelp is a trade, he thought. *Thomas wasn't all that far off. With the kelp gone, we buy ourselves time and with time we buy a world. Not a bad barter.*

He retraced his steps again and again, plaz to console, console to plaz.... Having that TaoLini woman shipside was too big a variable—something would have to be done.

Damn that tech! his fist came down again. *He should've double-talked her into Lab One instead of letting her go shipside. Can't the fool think for himself? Do I have to make every decision?*

He knew Murdoch was up there in a power-scrimmage with Ferry, but they were Lewis' people and it was Lewis' business. This whole fiasco was really Lewis' fault.

"Until they interfere with the Ceepee," he said aloud, pointing an affirmative finger at his reflection in the plaz. On the other side of the reflection, the quiet bay began to pick up the rhythmic *rush rush* of small waves licking at the beach.

Inflection is the adjective of language. It carries the subtleties of delight and horror, the essence of culture and social process. Such is the light-pattern displayed by the kelp; such is the song of the hylighter.

—**Kerro Panille,**
History of the Avata
(from the "Preface")

WAELA SAT watching a holo of Panille as a child. Except for the projected action at the holofocus, it was quiet in the small teaching study where Hali Ekel had put her. The chair, a simple sling in a metal frame, presented the holocontrols on its arm beneath her right hand. Soft blue light suffused the room, down-toned to increase resolution at the holofocus. Each time the holosound subsided, a low sussuration of venting air could be heard.

At frequent intervals, Waela turned her head slightly to the left and drank from a tube leading into a shiptit. Her left hand rested lightly on her abdomen and she was certain that the hand felt the growth of the fetus. There was no concealing the rapidity of that growth, but she tried not to think about it. Every time she was forced to confront the mystery of what was happening within her, she felt a hiccup of terror—a sensation which subsided in a blink as something dampened it.

A sense of isolation permeated the study—an accent on her awareness that she was being kept out of contact with ordinary

309

shipside life. The Natali were doing this deliberately.

The pangs of terrible hunger controlled the movement of her mouth to the shiptit. She drank greedily and with feelings of guilt. Hali Ekel had not explained why there was a shiptit here, nor why Ship fed her from it when others were denied. Feelings of rebellion welled up in Waela from time to time, but these, too, were dampened by some automatic response. She continued to sit and stare at the holo of the young Panille.

At the moment, the holo showed him sleeping in his cubby. The register gave his age as only twelve standard annos at the time, and there was no mention of who had authorized this holo.

A Ship 'coder rattled in the sleeping child's cubby then, waking Panille. He sat up, stretched and yawned, then increased the cubby's light level with one hand while rubbing his eyes with the other.

Ship's voice filled the cubby with its awful clarity: "Last night-side, you claimed kinship with God. Why do you sleep? Gods need not sleep."

Panille shrugged and stared at the 'coder from which Ship's voice issued. "Ship, have You ever stretched out as long as You can reach and yawned?"

Waela held her breath at the audacity of the child. This question suggested blasphemy and there was no reply.

Panille waited. Waela thought him patient for one so young.

"Well?" he asked, finally, smug in his adolescent logic.

"I'm sorry, young Kerro. I nodded my head but apparently you did not see it."

"How could you nod? You don't have a head to put on a pillow."

Waela gasped. The child was challenging Ship because of Ship's question about kinship with God. She waited for Ship's response and marveled at it.

"Perhaps the head I nod and the muscles I stretch are simply not within your field of vision."

Panille took a glass of water from his cubby spigot and drank before replying.

"You're just imagining what it's like to stretch. That's not the same at all."

"I actually stretched. Perhaps it is you who imagines what it is to stretch."

"I really stretch because I have a body and that body sometimes wants to sleep."

Waela thought he sounded defensive, but there were plain hints at amusement in Ship's tones.

"Never underestimate the power of imagination, Kerro. Notice the word itself: creator of images. Is that not the essence of your human experience?"

"But images are . . . just images."

"And the artistry in your images, what is that? If, someday, you compose an account of all your experiences, will that be artistry? Tell me how you know that you exist."

Waela slapped the shut-off switch. The holo image of young Panille held itself in the negative, like an afterthought, then died. But she thought he had been nodding as she stopped the replay, as though he had acquired sudden insight.

What *did* he acquire in his odd way of relating to Ship? She felt herself inadequate to the task of understanding Panille, despite these mysterious recordings. How had Hali Ekel known about these holos? Waela glanced around the tiny study cubby. What a strange little place hidden away here behind a secret hatch.

Why did Hali want me to look at these recordings? Will I really find him there in his past—lay the ghost of his childhood to rest or drive his voice from my mind?

Waela pressed her palms against her temples. That voice! In her most unguarded moments of panic, that voice came into her mind, telling her to be calm, to accept, telling her eerie things about someone called Avata.

I'm going mad. I know I am.

She dropped her hands and pressed them against her abdomen, as though this pressure would stop the terrible speed of that growth within her.

Hali Ekel's diffident knock sounded at the hatch. It opened just enough to let her slip through. She sealed the hatch, swung her pribox around to her hip.

"What have you learned?" Hali asked.

Waela indicated the jumble of holo recordings around her chair. "Who made these?"

"Ship." Hali put her pribox on the arm of Waela's chair.

"They don't tell me what I want to know."

"Ship is not a fortuneteller."

Waela wondered at the oddity of that response. There were times when Hali seemed at the point of saying something important about Ship, something private and secret, but the disclosure never came—just these odd statements.

Hali attached the cold platinum node of the pribox to the back of Waela's left hand. There was a moment of painful itching at the contact, but it subsided quickly.

"Why is the baby growing so fast in me?" Waela asked. The hiccup of terror leered in her mind, vanished.

"We don't know," Hali said.

"There's something wrong. I know it." The words came out flat, absolutely devoid of emotion.

Hali studied the instruments of her pribox, looked at Waela's eyes, her skin. "We can't explain this, but I can assure you that everything except the speed of it is normal. Your body has done months of work in only a few hours."

"Why? Is the baby . . . ?"

"Everything we scan shows the baby is normal."

"But it can't be normal to . . ."

"Ship says you're being fed everything you need." Hali indicated the tube into the shiptit.

"Ship says!" Waela looked down at the linkage between her hand and the pribox.

Hali keyed a cardiac scan. "Heart normal, blood pressure normal, blood chemistry normal. Everything normal."

"It is not!"

Waela panted with the exertion required to put emotion into her voice. Something did not want her excited, upset or frustrated.

"This child is growing at a rate of about twenty-three hours for every hour of the gestation," Hali said. "That is the only abnormal thing about this."

"Why?"

"We don't know."

Tears welled up in Waela's eyes, slipped down her cheeks.

"I trust Ship," Hali said.

"I don't know what to trust."

Without conscious volition, Waela turned to the shiptit, drank in long sucking gulps. The tears stopped while she drank. She watched Hali at the same time, how purposefully the young woman moved, changing the settings on the pribox. What a strange creature, this Hali Ekel—shipcut hair as black as Panille's, that odd ring in her nostril.

So mature for one so young.

That was the real oddity about Hali Ekel. She said she had never been groundside. Life was not rendered down to raw survival here the way it was groundside. There was time here for softer things, more sophisticated dalliances. Ship's records at your fingertips. But Hali Ekel had groundside eyes.

Waela stopped drinking, her hunger satisfied. She turned and stared directly at Hali.

Could I tell her about Kerro's voice in my head?

"You scattered the graphs there," Hali said. "What were you thinking?"

Waela felt a warm flush spread up her neck.

"You were thinking about Kerro," Hali said.

Waela nodded. She still felt a tightening of her throat when she tried to talk about him.

"Why do you say hylighters took him?" Hali asked. "Groundside says he's dead."

"The hylighters rescued us," Waela said. "Why should they turn around and kill him?"

Waela closed her eyes as Hali remained silent and watchful. *You see, Hali, I hear Kerro's voice in my head. No, Hali, I'm not insane. I really hear him.*

"What does it mean to run the P?" Hali asked.

Waela's eyes snapped open. "What?"

"Records says you once lost a lover because he ran the P. His name was Jim. What does it mean to run the P?"

Slowly at first, then in bursts, Waela described The Game, then, seeing the reason for Hali's question, added: "That has nothing to do with why I believe Kerro's alive."

"Why would the hylighters take him away?"

"They didn't tell me."

"I want him to be alive, too, Waela, but..." Hali shook her head and Waela thought she detected tears in the med-tech's eyes.

"You were fond of him, too, Hali?"

"We had our moments." She glanced at Aaela's swelling abdomen. "Not *those* moments, but good just the same."

With a quick shake of her head, Hali turned her attention to the pribox, keyed another scan, converted it to code, stored it.

"Why are you storing that record?"

She's watching me carefully, Hali thought. *Do I dare lie to her?*

Something had to be done, though, to allay the obvious fears aroused by this examination and the questions which could not be answered.

"I'll show you," Hali said. She called back the record and shunted it to the study screen beyond the holofocus. With an internal pointer, she indicated a red line oscillating across a green matrix.

"Your heart. Note the long, low rhythm."

Hali keyed another sequence. A yellow line wove its way through the red, pulsing faster and with lower intensity.

"The baby's heart."

Again, Hali's fingers moved over the keys. "Here's what happened when you thought about Kerro."

The two lines formed identical undulations. They merged and pulsed as one for a dozen beats, then separated.

"What does that mean?" Waela asked.

Hali removed the node from Waela's hand, began restoring the pribox to its case at her hip.

"It's called synchronous biology and we don't know exactly what it means. Ship's records associate it with certain psychic phenomena—faith healing, for example."

"*Faith* healing?"

"Without the intervention of accepted scientific medicine."

"But I've never . . ."

"Kerro showed me the records once. The healer achieves a steady physiological state, sometimes in a trance. Kerro called it 'a symphony of the mind.' "

"I don't see how that . . ."

"The patient's body assumes an identical state, in complete harmony with the healer's. When it ends, the patient is healed."

"I don't believe it."

"It's in the records."

"Are you trying to tell me my baby is *healing* me?"

"Given the unknowns about this rapid gestation," Hali said, "I would expect greater upset from you. But you don't seem capable of maintaining long periods of physiological imbalance."

"Whatever else she may be, she's still an unformed infant," Waela said. "She could not do that."

"She?"

Waela felt pressure against one of her lower ribs, the baby shifting.

"I've known all along that it's female."

"That's what the chromosome scan says," Hali agreed. "But the odds were even that you could guess right. Your guess doesn't impress me."

"No more than your faith healing."

Waela stood up slowly and felt the baby adjust to this new position.

"Unborn infants have been known to compensate for deficiencies in the mother," Hali said, "but I'm not selling faith healing."

"But you said . . ."

"I say a lot of things." She patted her pribox case. "We've set up a special exercise cubby down in P-T. You have to keep up your body tone even if . . ."

"If you're right, this baby will be born in a matter of diurns. What can I do to . . ."

"Just get down to P-T, Waela."

Hali slipped back out through the hatch before Waela could raise more objections. That was an alert and intelligent woman in there. Waela knew how to search records, and her curiosity would not be dampened by inadequate answers. *Now, what do we do?*

Hali turned at the creche hatch and saw one of the children staring out at her from the open bubble of the play area. Hali knew the child, Raul Andrit, age five. She had treated him for nightmares. She bent toward him. "Hi. Remember me?"

Raul turned his face up to her, wan and listless. Before he could answer, he fell out of the bubble into the passage.

Setting her alarm signal on *call*, Hali turned the child onto his back and attached the pribox. The emergency readout buzzed and, for the first time, Hali doubted a computer diagnosis. In the snarl of facts blurring past her eyes she read: *fatigue . . . exhaustion . . . 10.2 . . .*

"Yes?" The voice of a responding medic was thin in her pribox speaker. She briefed him and set the boy up for a glucose and vitamin series from her emergency packet.

"I'll send a cart." The speaker blipped as the medic broke the connection.

Hali put a question to her computer: "Raul Andrit: age?"

The screen flashed *5.5*.

"What is the age of the subject just tested?"

10.2.

Her fingers scurried across the keys: "The last subject tested *was* Raul Andrit. How could he be 5.5 *and* 10.2?

He has lived 5.5 standard annos. His body exhibits the characteristic intracellular structures of one who is 10.2. For medical purposes, cellular age is the more important.

Hali sat back on her heels and stared down at the unconscious child—dark circles under his eyes, pale skin. His chest appeared too thin and it heaved convulsively when he breathed. What the computer had just told her was that this little boy had doubled his age in a matter of diurns. She heard the cart pull up, a young attendant with it.

"Get this child to sickbay. Notify his Natali sponsor and continue treatment for fatigue," she said. "I'll be along shortly."

She hurried toward Physical Therapy and, at the passage turn, bumped into a breathless medic rushing out. "Ekel! I was just coming for you. You signaled with a child who fainted? There's another one in the Secondary play area. This way."

She followed on his heels, listening to the description. "He's a seven-anno in Polly Side's section. Kid can barely stay awake. Eating too much lately and, what with food monitoring, that's a problem; but he was weighed today and found to be down two kilos from last week."

She did not have to be told that this was a significant drop for a child of that age.

The boy was lying on a stretch of thick green lawn in the freeplay area, a shutter-shielded dome overhead. As she crouched beside him to set up her case, she smelled the fresh-clipped grass and thought how incongruous that was—the enticing green odor and this boy ill.

The pribox readout did not surprise her after Raul Andrit. *Fatigue . . . exhaustion . . . signs of aging . . .*

"Should we move him?"

That was a new voice. She turned and looked up at a thin-faced man in groundside blue standing beside the medic.

"Oh, this is Sy Murdoch," the medic said. "He came up to ask some questions of the TaoLini woman. You sent her down to P-T, didn't you?"

Hali stood up, recalling the grapevine stories about Murdoch: *Kelp and clones. Lab One director. One of Lewis' people.*

"Why would *you* want to move him?" she asked.

"I understand from the medics that Raul Andrit has been taken to sickbay with a similar seizure. It occurred to me that . . ."

"You say Raul Andrit with a certain familiarity," she said. "You're wearing groundside. What do you know about . . .?"

"Now, see here! I don't have to answer your . . ."

"You'll answer me or a medical board. This could be a disease brought up from groundside. What's your association with Raul Andrit?"

His face went blank, completely unreadable, then: "I know his father."

"That's all?"

"That's all. I've never seen the child before. I just . . . knew he was here, shipside."

Hali, trained from childhood to be a med-tech, to support life and see that Shipmen survived, knew each bodily muscle, nerve, gland and blood vessel by name and often spoke to them quietly as she worked. Instinctively, she knew that Murdoch was trained otherwise. He repelled her. And he was lying.

"What's your business with Waela TaoLini?"

"That concerns the Ceepee, not you."

"Waela TaoLini has been put in my charge by the Natali. That's Ship's business. Anything concerning her concerns me."

"It's just routine," Murdoch said.

Every mannerism said it was not *just routine*, but before she could respond, she saw Waela walk into the play area.

While she was still at some distance, Waela called: "They said somebody here was looking for me. Do you . . .?"

"Stay back there!" Hali called. "We've some sick boys and we don't want them near any expectant mothers. Wait for me over in the Natali Section. I'll join you in . . ."

"Forget it!" That was Murdoch speaking with a new forcefulness. He gave every indication of someone who had come to an important decision. "We'll meet with Ferry in Medical. Immediately."

Hali protested: "With Ferry? He doesn't . . ."

"Oakes left him in charge shipside. That should be good enough for you." He turned on his heel and strode from the area.

Myths are not fiction, but history seen with a poet's eyes and recounted in a poet's terms.

—*Shipquotes*

FERRY SAT at his command couch sipping a pale liquid which reeked of mint. He had been reviewing biostats on a shielded viewscreen when Hali and Waela entered and he did not lower the shields.

The command cubby, which had been tacked onto the Processing complex after Oakes' departure, was brightly illuminated by corner remotes which filled the room with yellow light. There was a sharp smell of caustic cleaner in the air.

Hali noted two things immediately: Ferry was not yet overcome by the drink and he appeared fearful. Then she saw that the command center had been tidied recently. Anywhere Ferry worked was soon a scattered mess—a notorious situation shipside where instincts of neatness equated with survival. But things had been made neat here. Unusual.

She saw Murdoch then and realized that Ferry feared what Murdoch might report to Oakes. Murdoch stood at one side of the command center, arms folded, impassive.

Ferry closed down his screen with a conscious flourish, swiveled to face the newcomers.

"Thank you for coming along so quickly."

Ferry's voice was reedy with controlled emotions. He stroked

318

the bridge of his nose once, an unconscious imitation of Oakes.

Waela noted that his fingers were trembling.

What does he fear? she wondered.

The man's furtiveness spoke of terrified concealments.

Is it something to do with my baby?

The characteristic blip of her own fears lifted and fell. And there was Kerro's voice: *"Trust Hali and Ship, Waela. Trust them."*

Waela tried to swallow in a dry throat. Could no one else hear him? She shot a furtive glance around the room. When she heard the voice, she felt sure of it. The instant it was gone, she doubted. Her real-time perceptions were demanding full attention, though. Physical senses honed to high sensitivity by the necessities of survival on Pandora—these she trusted. And Ferry demanded her attention. The man was a menace, operating on several levels of deception. She had heard the stories about Ferry, a competent-enough medical man with a few eccentricities, but not to be trusted alone with a young woman.

Her eyes told her something else.

A bumbler, Waela told herself, *who sits in the command seat. Interesting. Why did Oakes choose a bumbler?*

Waela's Pandora-sensitized nostrils detected alcohol in Jerry's drink. She put on her best impassive mask to conceal the recognition. The groundside uses of alcohol and tetrahydracannabinol in their various forms were generally accepted in Colony. But somehow she had not expected this shipside. With Ship to protect them . . . well, Shipmen had long held that alcohol was a risky and undesirable poison shipside. But then again, she knew that Ferry, like herself, had spent his early years Earthside. His reversion might not be all that unusual.

Still, Ferry's actions interested her. If the fact of her impregnation outside Ship's regular breeding program were taken seriously in certain circles . . .? Well, why else would Ferry be using viewscreen shields? And alcohol! She did not want her life, nor her baby's life, depending on someone who deliberately lowered his acuities.

Drinking, she thought. The word was dredged up out of her childhood and she had a bottomless-pit feeling about the hyb-plus-waking time which had passed since she had equated that word with alcohol.

The shielded screen bothered her. It was time someone invaded Ferry's privacy, she thought.

"That drink smells like fresh mint. Could I taste it?"

"Yes . . . of course."

It was not *of course*, but he offered her the glass. "Just a taste. It's not the kind of thing a prospective mother should have."

The glass was cold against her fingers. She sipped the drink and closed her eyes, recalling a scorched afternoon in Earthside summer when her mother had let her have a diluted mint julep with the grownups. The color of this drink was paler, but it was definitely bourbon with mint. She opened her eyes and saw Ferry's gaze fixed on the glass.

Hungry for it, she saw. *He's nearly drooling.*

"It's quite good," she said. "Where did you get it?"

He reached for the glass, but Waela handed it to Hali, who hesitated and looked at Ferry, then at Waela.

"Go ahead," Waela said. "Everyone should have one sometime. I had my first when I was twelve."

When Hali still hesitated, Ferry said, "Perhaps she shouldn't, what with this strange illness going around. What if it's catching?"

He treats it like a precious jewel, Waela thought. *It must be hard to get.*

She said: "If it's that contagious, we've caught it. Go ahead, Hali."

The younger woman sipped, swallowed and immediately bent her head in a fit of coughing, the glass thrust out for someone to take it. Ferry grabbed it from her hand.

Eyes watering, Hali said: "That's terrible!"

"It's all in knowing what to expect," Ferry said.

"And lots of practice," Waela said. "You never told us where you got it. Not one of our lab alcohols, is it?"

Ferry placed the glass carefully on the deck beside his seat.

"It's from Pandora."

"Must be hard to get."

"Don't we have more important things to discuss?" Murdoch asked.

They were his first words, and they transfixed Ferry. He reached down for the drink, drew his hand back without it. He turned and fussed with the controls for his screen, dropped the shield, hesitated, then left it down.

Waela promised herself that she would use the first opportunity to call up the records Ferry found so interesting. With unrestricted use of Ship's research facilities, it would not be difficult.

Murdoch moved around behind Ferry, an action which increased Ferry's nervousness.

Waela found herself sympathizing with the old man. Murdoch in that position would make anyone's shoulderblades twitch.

Ferry sputtered, then: "I was ... ahh, waiting for some ahhh, others to come up before, ahhh, taking up the, ahh business we ... I mean ..."

"What *are* we doing here?" Hali asked. She did not like the undercurrents flowing through this room. Unspoken threats lay heavy on Ferry's shoulders and it was obvious they came from Murdoch.

Ferry reached for the drink with a convulsive motion, but before he could put it to his lips, Murdoch reached over Ferry's shoulder and removed the glass from his hand.

"This'll wait."

Murdoch put the glass on a ledge behind him. As he turned back toward the others, the hatch opened and three people entered.

Hali recognized Brulagi from Medical, a heavy-set woman with fat arms and a thick lower lip. She wore her auburn hair in the regular close-cropped style, and her eyes shone bright blue above a flat nose. Right behind her came Andrit from Behavioral, a large dark man with quick almond eyes of deep brown and a nervous, darting manner. Behind these two was Usija, gray-haired, a thin-lipped, soft-spoken woman from the Natali, who had assigned Hali to monitor Waela TaoLini.

"Ahhh, here you are," Ferry said. "Please be seated, everyone. Please be seated."

Hali was glad to sit. She found a sling chair for Waela and another for herself. Waela moved her own chair to seat herself directly across from Ferry. It put her apart from the others, an observer's distance, and let her focus on Ferry and Murdoch without having to turn. Ferry would notice and it would annoy him, she thought. He wanted attention, not investigation.

What is it with you, old man? Waela wondered. *What do you fear?*

The three latecomers perched on a couch at right angles to Ferry. Murdoch remained standing.

Hali, noting Waela's move, wondered about it, but was distracted by the sudden realization that Andrit from Behavioral must be the father of young Raul. What was going on here?

Murdoch touched Ferry's shoulder and the older man jumped. "Show them the map."

Ferry swallowed, turned to his keyboard, punched at it clumsily. A miniature projection of Ship's schematic materialized at the holofocus beside him.

Hali recognized the special Natali area outship from Behavioral and noted a number of red dots through the projection. Brulagi from Medical leaned forward with her thick arms on her legs and stared at the three-dimensional map. Andrit appeared agitated by it. Usija merely nodded.

"What are the red markers?" Hali asked.

"Each dot represents a stricken child," Ferry said. "If you connect them, they form a spiral and you'll note that they increase in density as they reach the spiral's center."

"A vortex," Murdoch said.

Waela peered closely at the schematic. She caught her breath and glanced up to catch a look of unguarded fury on Andrit's face. He was clenching and unclenching his fists. She saw the heavy muscles of his forearms knotting under his singlesuit.

Ferry pulled some papers from the ledge beside his keyboard and shuffled through them while he spoke: "For the sake of those who might not know, ahh, where is your cubby, Waela?"

Andrit leaned forward, almost falling from the couch as he glared at Waela. She saw Murdoch repress a smile. What amused him?

"You all know where I sleep, *Doctor*. My cubby's at the center of the spiral."

Andrit lunged as quickly as anyone Waela had ever seen shipside. But even though she felt heavily pregnant, Pandora had conditioned her reflexes to blurring speed. When Andrit hit the space where Waela had been sitting, she no longer was there. Before he could recover, Waela felled him with a blow to his carotid—every move automatic.

She felt strength flowing through her. It gushed from the fetus within her and out through every fiber of her body.

Hali, out of her chair by this time, looked from Andrit sprawled unconscious on the deck to Waela who stood poised and breathing easily in front of them. The sudden exertion had fanned the reddish glow under her skin to a blaze. As she turned slowly on one heel to see if there would be more attack, she was an awesome sight.

Dazed, Hali asked: "Why did he do that?"

Waela confronted Ferry. "Why?" She stood balanced on the

balls of her feet. Andrit had threatened not her but her unborn child! Let any of them try to harm her child!

Murdoch chose to answer, an odd glint in his eyes. He appeared to be enjoying this.

"He was . . . personally upset, you understand? One of the stricken children is his son."

"What do those red dots really mean?" Hali demanded.

"Ahh, there have been some energy problems, we believe," Murdoch said. "We saw a similar thing in Lab One."

Waela took a step toward Ferry. "I want to hear it from you. Oakes left you in charge here. What's going on?"

"I, uhh, don't really know much about it." Ferry licked his lips, shot a glance over his shoulder at Murdoch.

"You mean you're not supposed to know anything about it," Waela said. "Tell us what you *do* know."

"Now, let's change our tone a bit," Murdoch said. "There's an injured man on the deck and this whole unfortunate matter does not require more passion."

He truned toward the Natali representative. "Doctor Usija, since the med-tech appears unable to respond . . ."

Hali looked down at Andrit who was beginning to stir.

"He'll recover," Waela said. "I pulled my blow."

Hali stared at her. The implication was obvious: She could have killed the man. Belatedly, Hali bent to examine him. Her pribox showed a bruise on his neck, some nerve damage, but Waela was right: He would recover.

"What happened in Lab One?" Waela directed her question to Murdoch.

"An . . . artificial form of this phenomenon. You are the first *natural* example of this we've seen."

"Natural example of what?" Waela forced the words out.

"The draining of energy from . . . other people."

Waela glared at him. What was he saying? She took a step toward him and felt Hali's hand on her arm. Waela whirled on the med-tech and almost brought her down. Sensing this, Hali jerked her hand back.

"Waela? Just a moment. I'm beginning to understand."

"Understand what?"

"They think you're responsible for the sick children."

"Me? How?" She turned back toward Ferry. "Explain."

Murdoch started to speak, but she snapped an angry glare at him. "Not you! Him."

"Now, Waela, calm yourself," Ferry said. "This has all been an unfortunate mistake."

"What do you mean *unfortunate mistake*, you drunk? You set this up. You invited Andrit here. You knew about that spiral in your schematic. What were you trying to do?"

"I will not take that tone from you," Ferry said. "This is my . . ."

"This is your funeral if you don't tell me what's going on here!"

Hali stared at Waela. What was happening to the woman? Murdoch, Hali noted, was standing very still—no threatening movements at all. Usija and Brulagi were frozen in their seats.

"Now, don't you threaten me, Waela," Ferry said. There was a plaintive note in his voice.

She's perfectly capable of killing him if he doesn't satisfy her demand, Hali thought. *Ship, save us! What has come over her?*

Usija began to speak very softly, but her voice was compelling in the tense air of the room.

"Doctor Ferry, you are looking at the phenomenon of the threatened feral mother. It goes very deep. It is dangerous to you. Since Waela is Pandora-conditioned, I advise you to answer her."

Ferry pushed himself back in his seat as far as he could go. He wet his lips with his tongue.

"I, ahhh . . . your circumstances shipside, Waela. There has been some, ahhh, let us call it superstition."

"About what?"

"About, ahhh, you. We have tested you since your return and . . . ahhh, we do not find usable answers. Even Ship is no help. Whatever it is, Ship has locked it away—*Restricted*. Or . . ." He shot a venomous glance at Hali. ". . . we are referred to Med-tech Hali Ekel."

Hali could not repress a gasp.

Waela whirled and glared at her.

Hali realized suddenly that now she was a target.

"Waela, I swear to you that I don't know what he's talking about. I'm here to protect you and your baby, not to hurt you."

Waela gave a curt nod, returned her attention to Ferry.

Andrit groaned and pushed himself upright. Waela bent and, with one hand, hoisted him to his feet. In the same motion, she hurled him toward the couch where he narrowly missed Brulagi and Usija. The effortless way Waela did this made Hali hold her breath, then exhale slowly. *Very dangerous, indeed.*

"Tell us the circumstances where Ship refers you to Hali Ekel,"

Waela said. Her voice was like a bubbling volcano.

Andrit leaned forward abruptly and vomited, but no one looked.

"When we asked if it was the child causing this or if it was you," Ferry said.

Hali gasped, her vision suddenly blurred by memory of a dusty hillside, the setting of a blazing yellow sun, and three figures tortured on crosses. What kind of a child was Waela carrying?

Waela spoke without turning. "Hali, does that mean anything to you?"

"How was your child conceived?" Hali asked.

Waela turned a startled look toward her. "Kerro and I . . . for Ship's sake, you know how babies are made! Do you think we carry axolotl tanks on those subs?"

Hali looked at the deck. The legend said immaculate conception—no man involved. A god . . . But it was only a legend, a myth. Why would Ship refer the questioners to her? Many times since that trip through time, Hali had asked herself why? *What was I supposed to learn?* Ship spoke of holy violence. The accounts concerning the Hill of Skulls which she had scanned since the experience certainly confirmed this. *Holy violence and Waela's child?*

Waela continued to stare at her. "Well, Hali?"

"Perhaps your child is not confined to this time." She shrugged. "I can't explain, but that's what occurs to me."

Apparently, this satisfied Waela. She glanced at Andrit, who was holding his head and remaining quiet. She turned back to Ferry.

"What is it about my baby? What're you afraid of?"

"Murdoch?" It was a desperate plea from Ferry. Murdoch crossed his arms and said, "We got the reports from Ferry and . . ."

"What reports?"

Murdoch swallowed, nodded at the holoprojection with its spiral of red dots.

"What were you supposed to do to me?" Waela asked.

"Nothing. I swear it. Nothing."

He's terrified, Hali thought. *Has he seen this feral threatened-mother phenomenon before?*

"Questions?" Waela asked.

"Oh, yes, of course—questions."

"Ask them."

"Well, I was . . . I mean, I discussed this with the Natali and, we, that is, Oakes, wanted me to ask if you would return ground-side to have your baby?"

"Violate our rules of WorShip?" Waela looked at Usija.

"You do not have to go groundside," Usija said. "We merely agreed that he could ask."

Waela returned her attention to Murdoch. "Why groundside? What did you hope to do there?"

"We have stockpiled a large supply of burst," Murdoch said. "It's my belief you will need every ounce of it you can get."

"Why?"

"Your baby is growing at an accelerated rate. The physical requirements for the cellular growth are . . . very large."

"But what about the sick children?" She turned toward Andrit. "What have they told *you*?"

He lifted his head, glared at her. "That you're responsible! That they've seen this before groundside."

"Do you want me to go groundside?"

They could see him battling with his WorShip conditioning. He swallowed hard, then: "I just want *it* to go away, whatever's making my son sick."

"How do they explain my responsibility for this?"

"They say it's a . . . *psychic* drain, often observed but never explained. Perhaps Ship . . . " He was incapable of repeating outright blasphemy.

They chose a poor tool to attack me, Waela thought.

The pattern of the plot was clear now: Andrit was to demon-strate potential violence in shipside opposition to her. She would be forced to go groundside *"for your own good,* my dear." They wanted her down there badly.

Why? How am I dangerous to them?

"Hali, have you ever heard of this phenomenon?"

"No, but I would agree that the evidence points at you or your baby. You don't need burst, though."

"Why?" Murdoch demanded.

"Ship is feeding her from the shiptits."

Murdoch glared at her, then: "How long have you Natali known that this baby was growing too rapidly?"

"How do *you* know it?" Usija countered.

"It's part of this phenomenon—rapid growth, abnormal de-mand for energy."

"We've known since our first examinations of her," Hali said.

"You kept it under wraps and proceeded with caution," Murdoch said. "Precisely what we did groundside."

"Why would you want to feed me on burst?" Waela asked.

"If the fetus gets enough energy from burst, the psychic drain does not take place."

"You're lying," Waela said.

"What!"

"You're as transparent as a piece of plaz," Waela said. "Burst cannot be better than elixir."

Usija cleared her throat. "Tell us, Murdoch, about your experience with this phenomenon."

"We were doing some DNA work with kelp samples. We found this . . . this survival characteristic. The organism absorbs energy from the nearest available source," Hali said.

"The mother's the nearest available source," Hali said.

"The mother's the host and immune. The organism takes from other organisms around it which are, ahhh, similar to the hungry one."

"I'm not aging," Hali said. "And I'm around her more than anyone."

"It does that," Murdoch said. "It takes from some people and not from others."

"Why from children?" Hali asked.

"Because they're defenseless!" That was Andrit, fearful but still angry.

Waela felt energy charging every muscle in her body. "I'm not going groundside."

Andrit started to get to his feet, but Usija restrained him. "What are you going to do?" Usija asked.

"I'll move out to the Rim beyond one of the agraria. We'll keep people, especially children, away from me while Hali studies this condition." She looked at Hali, who nodded.

Murdoch did not want to accept this. "It would be far better if you came groundside where we've had experience with . . ."

"Would you try to force me?"

"No, oh no."

"Perhaps if you sent us a supply of burst," Usija said.

"We would not be able to justify shipment of such a precious food at this time," Murdoch said.

"Tell us what you know about the phenomenon," Hali said. "Can we develop an immunity? Does it recur or is it chronic? Does . . . ?"

"This is the first time we've seen it outside a lab. We know that Waela TaoLini conceived outside the breeding program and outside Colony's protective barriers, but...."

"Why don't I get answers from Colony?" Ferry asked. He had been sliding his chair slowly to one side while Murdoch spoke, and now he looked up at the man.

"That has nothing to do with..."

"You speak of not shipping burst at this time" Ferry said. "What is special about this time?"

Waela heard desperation in the old man's voice. *What is Ferry doing?* Something deep in him was driving these questions out.

"Your questions do not relate to this problem," Murdoch said, and Waela heard death in his voice.

Ferry heard it, too, because he fell into abashed silence.

"What do you mean about the conception being outside of Colony's barriers?" Usija asked. It was the scientist's voice gnawing at an interesting question.

Murdoch appeared thankful for the interruption. "They were floating in a...in a kind of plaz bubble. It was in the sea, completely surrounded by the kelp. We don't know all of the details, but some of our people have suggested that Waela *and* her child may no longer be humantype."

"Don't try to get me groundside!" Waela said.

Usija climbed to her feet. "Humans bred freely Earthside and anywhere they liked. We're merely seeing it happen again...plus an unknown which must be studied."

Murdoch directed his glare at her. "You said..."

"I said you could ask her. She has made her decision. Her plan is a sensible one. Isolate her from children, put her under constant monitoring..."

Usija's voice droned on outlining specifics to implement Waela's decision—a place with a shiptit, a rotation of Natali medtechs...

Waela tuned out the droning voice. The babe was turning again. Waela felt dizzy.

None of this is normal. Nothing is as it should be.

Blip. The fear lifted in her awareness, then dropped.

What did Murdoch mean that she might no longer be humantype?

Waela tried to recall details of what had happened in the gondola as it floated on Pandora's sea. All she could remember was the ecstatic wash of her union with something awesome. This shipside command cubby, Usija's voice—none of this was important any longer. Only the baby growing at its terrible pace within her was important.

I need a shiptit.

An image of Ferry pressed itself into her awareness. He was somewhere else with his inevitable drink in his hand. Murdoch was talking to him. Ferry was trying to protest without success. She heard faint voices, distant and muffled as though they came from a sealed room. There was a high view of Pandora's sea glowing in the light of two suns. It was replaced by a blurred vision of Oakes and Legata Hamill. They were making love. Oakes lay on his back on a brown woven mat. She was astride him . . . slow movement . . . very slow . . . an insane look of joy on her face, her hands clenching and unclenching the fat of his chest. In the vision, Legata leaned back, trembling and Oakes caught her as she fell.

It's a dream, a strange waking dream, Waela told herself.

Now, the dream shifted to Hali on her knees in her own cubby. Atop a ledge in front of Hali stood an odd construction of wood— two smooth sticks, one of them fixed off-center across the other. Hali leaned her head close to the crossed sticks and, as she did this, Waela experienced the unmistakable fragrance of cedar, as fresh as anything she had ever smelled in a treedome.

Abruptly, she was back in the command cubby. Hali's arm was around her shoulder, leading her out the hatch while Usija and Brulagi argued with Murdoch behind them.

"You need food and rest," Hali said. "You've overstressed yourself."

"Shiptit," Waela whispered. "Ship will feed me."

The prophets of Israel who preached the idea of the nucleus of ten good men required for a city's survival, built this concept on the Talmudic idea of the Thirty-Six Just Ones *whose existence in each generation is necessary for the survival of Humankind.*

—Judaism's *Book of the Dead,*
Shiprecords

UNTIL SHE saw him sprint across the east plain, a Hooded Dasher close behind, Legata did not know Thomas was at the Redoubt. She stood at the giant screen in the Command Center, the hum of late dayside activity going on all around. Oakes and Lewis were conferring off to her left. The big screen had been set on a scan program, ready to lock onto any unusual activity. She took over the controls and zoomed in on the running man. The Dasher was only a few leaps behind him. The scene was outlined in the harsh cross-light of the evening suns.

"Morgan, look!"

Oakes rushed to her side, stared up at the screen.

"The fool," he muttered.

Thomas swerved abruptly to the left, made a desperate leap off a dangerously high rock onto the sand at the high tide mark. The Dasher leaped after him, misjudged and landed in a patch of dead kelp washed up by the surf. It immediately began gulping rags of kelp while Thomas ran off down the beach. Another Dasher appeared behind him then, dropping from a high rock, running as it landed. Thomas dodged around a boulder and sped off along the high tide mark. His boots kicked up globs of damp sand. There was no doubt that he heard the Dasher closing on him.

"He'll never make it, no one can," Oakes' trembling voice betrayed his nervousness.

Afraid he won't get away? Legata asked herself. *Or afraid he will?*

"Why did you turn him out?" she asked. She kept her attention on the figure darting and weaving away from her, and she remembered that nightside meeting with him outside Colony's Lab One. She found herself silently urging him on: *Into the surf! Dodge into the water!*

"I didn't turn him out, my dear," Oakes said. "He must've escaped." Oakes turned and called out to Lewis across the room. "Make sure nothing's been left open to the outside."

"He was a prisoner. Why?"

"He and the TaoLini woman came back from their undersea venture without Panille, a wild story about hylighters rescuing them. That requires more than simple debriefing."

Lewis came up to stand beside Oakes. "All secure."

Thomas had swerved toward the water once more, diving under ragged scraps of dead kelp. He surfaced draped with the stuff, and the second Dasher remained behind to feed on the scraps. Thomas was visibly tiring now, his stride irregular.

"Can't we do anything for him?" Legata asked.

"What would you have us do?" Oakes asked.

"Send a rescue party!"

"That area's full of Dashers and Flatwings. We can't afford to lose any more people."

"If he was foolish enough to go outside, he takes his own chances," Lewis said. "Isn't that the rule for running the P?" He stared at Legata.

"He's not running the P," she said, and she wondered if Lewis had somehow learned about her own mad run.

"Whatever he's doing, he's on his own," Oakes said.

"Ohhh, no . . ." The gasp escaped her as the black figure of another Hooded Dasher, two Flatwings close behind it, took up the chase. Thomas was staggering now and the Dasher closed rapidly. In the last blink, as the Dasher stretched for the final blurring leap, it swerved abruptly aside. A mass of tentacles dropped from the air and a hylighter soared across Thomas, scooping him up.

Oakes worked the screen controls, zooming back for a general view. Someone behind them said: "Would you look at that!" It was almost a sigh.

The hills and cliffs inland from the Redoubt displayed tier upon tier of hylighters, great mobs of them gathered in a siege arc beyond the range of the Redoubt's weapons.

"Goodbye, Raja Thomas," Oakes said. "Too bad the hylighters got him. A Dasher would've ended it quickly."

"What do the hylighters do to you?" Legata asked.

Before Oakes could answer, Lewis turned to the room and said: "All right, everybody. Show's over. Back to work."

"We only have evidence from some demon carcasses," Oakes said. "They were sucked dry."

"I . . . wish we could've saved him," she said.

"He took his chances and he lost."

Oakes reached out to the controls, his finger poised over the scan program, stopped. He stepped backward to bring the whole screen into view. The hylighter carrying Thomas had lost itself in the distant mobs. The great billowing bags now danced on the air, underlighted by the orange glow of the suns, their sail membranes rippling and filling.

Legata saw what had stopped Oakes. More hylighters were coming up, climbing higher and higher, filling in the sky.

"Ship's eyes!" another voice behind them said. "They're blocking out the suns!"

"Split screen," Oakes said. "Activate all perimeter sensors."

It took several blinks for Legata to realize he was addressing her. She flipped the switches and the screen went gray, then reformed in measured squares of the different views, a locator number under each. Hylighters englobed the sky all around the Redoubt—over the sea, over the land.

"Look there." It was Lewis pointing to a screen showing the base of the inland cliffs. "Demons."

They became aware then that the entire rim of cliffs, as far as the sensors could reach, writhed with life. Legata felt certain that never before had such a mass of teeth and claws and stings assembled in one place on the face of Pandora.

"What are they doing?" Oakes asked, and his voice trembled.

"They look like they're waiting for something," Legata said.

"Waiting for orders to attack," Lewis said.

"Check security!" Oakes barked.

Legata keyed for the proper sensors and the screens flickered to re-form with views of the clean-up work on the damage left by the E-clone revolt. Orders from whom? she wondered. Crews were busy in every screen, mostly E-clones guarded by armed normals. Some worked in the open courtyard where the Nerve Runners had left nothing alive; others toiled along the shattered sections of the perimeter where temporary barriers had been erected. There were even some heavily guarded crews outside. No demons or hylighters interfered.

"Why aren't they attacking?" Legata asked.

"We seem to be at a stand-off," Lewis said.

"We're saving our energy," Oakes said. "My orders are not to shoot them at random. We cook them now only if they come within twenty-five meters of our people or equipment."

"They can think," Lewis said. "They think and plan."

"But what are they planning?" Legata asked. She noticed that Oakes was going paler by the blink.

Oakes turned. "Jesus, we'd better do some planning of our own. Come with me."

They left, but Legata did not notice. She remained at the screen, working through the outside sensors. The whole landscape had turned into a golden dazzle of suns and hylighters, black cliffs aswarm with demons, and a surging sea capped with white foam and spray.

Presently, Legata turned, realized that Oakes and Lewis no longer were in the Command Center.

I'll have to act soon, she thought. *And I have to be ready.*

She worked her way through the activity in the Center, opened a main corridor hatch and hurried toward her own quarters.

Poet
You see bones up ahead
where there are none.
By the time we get there
so do they.. . .

—Hali Ekel
Private Letters

HALI STUDIED the monitors on the reclining Waela with care. It was well into dayside, but Waela appeared to be asleep, her body quiet on the tightly stretched hammock which they had rigged in one of Ship's rim compartments. Her abdomen was a mounded hillock. There was no hatch to this cubicle, only a fabric curtain which rustled in faint stirrings from the agrarium to which this extrusion was attached.

This is not normal sleep, Hali thought.

Waela's breathing was too shallow, the passivity of her body too profound. It was as though she had slipped back into something approaching hyb. What did that mean for the fetus?

The compartment was slightly larger than a regular cubby, and Hali had brought in a small wheeled cart to support the monitor screen. The screen showed Waela's vital signs as visible undulating curves with synchronous time-blips. A secondary set of lines reported on the child developing in Waela's womb. A simple twist of a dial could superimpose one set of lines on the other.

Hali had been checking the synchronous beat for almost an hour. Waela had come to this Natali retreat without protest, o-beying every suggestion Hali made with a sleepwalker's passivity. She had appeared to gain some energy after feeding at a corridor shiptit—a process which still filled Hali with confusion. So few ever received elixir at the shiptits anymore that most Shipmen ignored them, taking this as a sign of Ship's deeper intents or displeasure. Attendance at WorShip had never been more punctual.

Why was Ship feeding Waela?

While Waela drank from the shiptit container, Hali had tried to get a response from the same corridor station. No elixir.

Why, Ship?

No answer. Ship had not been easily responsive since sending her to see the crucifixion of Yaisuah.

The lines on the monitor screen were merging once more—fetus and mother in synchronous beat. As the lines merged, Waela opened her eyes. There was no consciousness in the eyes, only an unmoving stare at the compartment ceiling.

"Fly us back to Jesus."

As she spoke, the synchronous lines separated and Waela closed her eyes to sink back into the geography of her mysterious sleep.

Hali stood in astonished contemplation of the unconscious woman. Waela had said "Jesus" the way Ship pronounced the name. Not *Yaisuah* or *Hesoos*, but *Geezuz*.

Had Ship sent Waela, too, on that odd journey to the Hill of Skulls? Hali thought not. *I would recognize the signs of that shared experience.* Hali knew the marks on herself which came from that trip to Golgotha.

My eyes are older.

And there was a new quietude in her manner, a wish to share this thing with someone. But she lived with the knowledge that no other person might understand . . . except possibly . . . just *possibly*, Kerro Panille.

Hali stared at the pregnant mound of Waela's abdomen.

Why had he bred with this . . . this older woman?

Fly us back to Jesus?

Could that be just delirious muttering? Then why *Geezuz*?

A deep sense of uneasiness moved itself through Hali. She used her pribox to call down to Shipcore and arranged for a relief watch on the monitor. The relief showed up presently, a young

Natali intern named Latina. Her official green pribox hung at her hip as she hurried into the compartment.

"What's the rush?" Hali asked.

"Ferry sent word that he wants to see you right away down at WorShip Nine."

"He could've called me." Hali tapped her own pribox.

"Yes . . . well, he just said for me to tell you to hurry."

Hali nodded and gathered her things. Her own pribox and recorder were beyond habit, a part of her physical self. She briefed Latina on the routine as she gathered her equipment, noting the log of synchronous beats, then ducked out through the curtain. The agrarium was a scene of intense dayside activity, a harvest in process. Hali wove her way through the dance of workers and found a servo going coreside. At Old Hull she took the slide to Central and dropped off at the Study passage which led to Wor-Ship Nine.

The red numeral winked at her as she found the hatch and slipped into the controlled blue gloom. She could not see Ferry anywhere, but there were perhaps thirty children in the five-to-seven age range sitting cross-legged around a holofocus at the center of the WorShip area. The focus showed a projection of a man in shipcloth white who was lying on bare ground and covering his eyes with both hands in great pain or fear.

"What is the lesson, children?"

The question was asked in the flat and emotionless tone of Ship's ordinary instruction programs.

One of the boys pointed to another boy beside him and said: "He wants to know where the man's name came from."

The projected figure stood, appearing dazed, and a hand reached from outside the focus to steady him. The hand became another man in a long beige robe as the focus widened. Beside this other man, skittish and wild-eyed, danced a large white horse.

The children gasped as the horse stepped into, then out, then back into the holo. They clapped when the robed man got it under control.

Hali moved across to a WorShip couch overlooking this performance and sank into the cushions. She glanced around once more for Ferry. No sign of him. Typical. Tell her to hurry, then he was not here.

Neither of the projected figures was speaking, but now a voice in a strange tongue boomed from the holofocus. How familiar that tongue sounded! Hali felt that she could almost understand it—as though she had learned it in a dream. She tapped the *translate* switch on the arm of the couch beside her and the voice boomed once more: "Saul, Saul, why do you persecute me?"

That voice! Where had she heard that voice?

The white-clad figure, still with hands over his eyes and concealing most of his face, rolled over and climbed to his feet with his back to Hali. She saw that he was not wearing a shipsuit after all, but a white robe which had clung to his long legs. The man stumbled back two steps now and fell once more. As he fell, he cried: "Who are you?"

The booming voice said: "I am Yaisuah, whom you persecute. It is hard for you to kick against the thorns."

Hali sat in breathless quiet: *Yaisuah . . . Hesoos . . . Geezuz.*

The holofocus blipped out and the WorShip lights came up to a warm yellow. Hali saw that she was the only adult in the room— this had been a session for young children. Why had Ferry ordered her to meet him here?

One of the children still seated on the floor spoke directly to Hali: "Do you know where that man got his name?"

"It was a mixture from two ancient cultures Earthside," she said. "Why were you watching that?"

"Ship said that was today's lesson. It started with the man on the horse. He rode very fast. Do we have horses in hyb?"

"The manifest says we have horses but we have no place for them yet."

"I'd like to ride a horse sometime."

"What did you learn from today's lesson?" Hali asked.

"Ship is everywhere, has been everywhere and has done and seen everything," the boy said. Other children nodded.

Was that why You showed me Yaisuah, Ship?

No answer, but she had not expected one.

I didn't learn my lesson. Whatever it was Ship wanted me to learn . . . I failed.

Distraught, she stood and glanced at the boy who had addressed her. Why weren't there any adults here? It was children's WorShip, but not even a guide?

"Has Doctor Ferry been here?" she asked.

"He was here but someone called him away," a little girl in

the background said. "Is he supposed to leave WorShip?"

"When it's the business of Ship," Hali said. The apology sounded empty, but the girl accepted it.

Abruptly, Hali turned away and slipped out of the room. As she left, she heard the little girl call: "But who's going to lead us in lesson study?"

Not me, little girl. I have my own studying to do.

Something was going very wrong shipside. Waela's odd pregnancy was merely one symptom among many. Hali ran down the side passage coreside from the WorShip area, found a service access plate and slipped it aside. She wormed her way down a dimly lighted tube to a cross-tube where she slipped out through another service plate into the main passage to Records. There was activity in Records—a teener group learning how to handle the more sophisticated equipment, but she found her aisle between the storage racks unoccupied and no one at the console which concealed Kerro's small study lab.

Hali opened the concealed hatch, saw pale pink light in the lab. She slid inside and sat at the control seat. The hatch snicked closed behind her. She was breathless from the rush of getting here, but wanted no delay. Where to begin? Vocoder? Projection?

Hali chewed at her lip. Nothing could be hidden from Ship. The lesson for the children had been a true one. She knew this.

I don't even need this equipment to address Ship.

Then why did Ship use this place at all?

"Most of you find it less disturbing than when I speak in your mind."

Ship's intimate voice issued from the vocoder in front of her. For some reason, the calm and rational tone angered her.

"We're just pets! What happens when we become a nuisance?"

"How could you become a nuisance?"

The answer was there without considering it: "By losing our respect for Ship."

There was no reply.

This cooled her anger. She sat in silent contemplation for a moment, then: "Who are You, Ship?"

"Who? Not quite the proper term, Hali. I was alive in the minds of the first humans. It required time for the right events to occur, but *only* time."

"What do *You* respect, Ship?"

"I respect the consciousness which brought Me into your awareness. My respect is made manifest by My decision to interfere as little as possible in that consciousness."

"Is that how I'm supposed to respect You, Ship?"

"Do you believe you can interfere with My consciousness, Hali?"

She let out a long breath.

"I do interfere, don't I." It was a statement, not a question.

With a sudden sensation of sinking, as though the realization occurred because she let it happen and not because she willed it, Hali saw the lesson of the Hill of Skulls.

"The consequences of too much interference," she whispered.

"You please Me, Hali. You please Me as much as Kerro Panille ever pleased Me."

"Hali!"

It was Ferry's voice shouting at her over the pribox speaker at her hip. "Get to Sickbay!"

She was out the concealed hatch and halfway down the storage aisle before she realized she had broken away from Ship in mid-conversation. Ship had spoken personally with very few people, and she had the impudence to jump up and leave. Even as this thought flashed through her mind, she laughed at herself. She couldn't leave Ship.

Ferry met her at the main hatchway into Sickbay. He was wearing the heavier groundside blue and carried another suit of it under his arm. He thrust it at her and Hali saw then that the suits had been fitted for helmets of hazardous flight.

She accepted the suit as Ferry thrust it at her. The old man appeared to be in the grip of deep agitation, his face flushed, hands trembling.

The groundside fabric felt rough in her hands, so different from the shipcloth. The detachable slicker and hood were contrastingly slippery.

"What's . . . what's happening?" she asked.

"We have to get Waela offship. Murdoch's going to kill her."

She was a blink accepting the import of his words. Then doubts filled her. Why would this fearful old man oppose Murdoch? And by implication oppose Oakes!

"Why would you help?" she asked.

"They're demoting me groundside, sending me to Lab One."

Hali had heard the rumors of Lab One—clone experiments, some wild stories, but Ferry was visibly terrified. Did he know something definite about Lab One?

"We have to hurry," he said.

"But how . . . they'll catch us."

"Please! Put on the groundsides and help me."

She slipped the clothing over her shipsuit and noted how bulky it made her feel. Her fingers fumbled with the slicker's catches as Ferry hurried her into Sickbay.

"We'll be gone by the time they suspect," he said. "There's a freighter leaving in four minutes from Docking Bay Eight. It's carrying hardware, no crew—everything on automatic."

They were at a Sickbay alcove by now and, as he pulled aside the curtains, Hali suppressed a startled question. Waela lay on a gurney, already clad in groundside slicker with the hood pulled down over her brow. Her swollen abdomen was a blue mound under the slicker. How had Ferry brought her here?

"Murdoch had her brought down here as soon as you were relieved," Ferry said, grunting as he wrestled the gurney out of its alcove. Hali moved to unhook the monitor connections.

"Not yet!" Ferry snapped. "That's the signal to Bio that something's wrong."

Hali drew back. Of course; she should've thought of that.

"Now, hook up your pribox," Ferry said. "People will think we're moving her somewhere for more tests." Ferry folded the groundside hood under Waela's head and covered her with a gray blanket. She stirred sleepily as he lifted her head.

"What did they give her?" Hali asked.

"A sedative, I think."

Hali looked down at her groundsides, then at Ferry. "People will take one look at our clothes and know something's wrong."

"We'll just act as though we know what we're doing."

Waela jerked in her sleep, mumbled something, opened her eyes and said: "Now. Now." Just as quickly she was back in her sedated sleep.

"I hear you," Hali muttered.

"Ready?" Ferry asked. He gripped the head of the gurney.

Hali nodded.

"Unhook her."

Hali removed the monitor connections and they wheeled Waela out into the passageway, moving as fast as they could.

Docking Bay Eight, Hali thought. *Four minutes*. They could make it if they were not delayed too long anywhere along the way.

She saw that Ferry was guiding the gurney toward the tangent passage to the docking bays. Good choice.

They had taken fewer than a dozen hurried steps when Hali was paged.

"Ekel to Sickbay. Ekel to Sickbay."

Hali estimated two hundred meters from Sickbay to their goal. They could not trust shiptransport internally. If Murdoch was a killer, if she had figured him for less than what he revealed himself, then placing themselves in a transit tube would be disaster. He could override the controls and have them delivered like salad to his hatchway.

The gurney's wheels squeaked and Hali found this irritating. Ferry was panting with unaccustomed exertion. The few people they passed merely observed the obvious rush on medical business and squeezed aside to let them pass.

Once more, she was paged: "Ekel! Emergency in Sickbay!"

They skidded around the corner into the passage to the Docking Bay and nearly overturned the gurney. Ferry grabbed for it and prevented Waela from sliding off.

Hali helped to settle Waela as they continued pushing toward Number Eight. They were passing Number Five and she could see the Eight down the passage ahead of them.

Ferry, reaching under Waela's shoulder as they moved, pulled out something which had caught his eye.

Hali saw him go pale. "What's that?"

He held it up for her to see.

The thing looked insidious—a small pale tube of silver.

"Tracer," Ferry gasped.

"Where was it?"

"Murdoch must've tried to feed it to her, but he didn't stick around long enough to be sure she swallowed it. She must've spit it out."

"But . . ."

"They know where we are. The biocomputer can track this through the body, yes, but it can also track it anywhere in Ship."

Hali grabbed it out of his hand and threw it behind her as far as she could.

"All we need's a little delay."

"This is as far as you go, Ekel!"

It was Murdoch's shrill voice almost paralyzing her as he stepped out of the Number Eight hatch just ahead of Ferry. She glimpsed a laser scalpel in his hand, realizing he could use it as a weapon. That thing under full power could sever a leg at ten meters!

As the Jesuits recognized, a key function of logic limits argument and, therefore, confines the thinking process. As far back as the Vedanta, this way of tying down the wild creativity of thought was codified into seven logic-directing categories: Quality, Substance, Action, Generality, Particularity, Intimate Relation and Non-existence (or Negation). These were thought to define the true limits of the symbolic universe. The recognition that all symbol processes are inherently open-ended and infinite came much later.

— **Raja Thomas,**
Shiprecords

THE HYLIGHTER with Thomas cradled in its tentacles vented a brief undulating song and began a slow drop into blue haze. Thomas felt the tentacles enfolding him, heard the song—was even aware that Alki was beginning its long slide into sunset. He saw the dark purple of the meridian sky, saw the side-lighted brilliance of the blue haze and a surrounding rim of steep crags. He saw all of this and still was not sure of what he saw, nor was he entirely sure of his own sanity.

The haze enclosed him then, warm and moist.

His memories were confused, like something seen through swirling water. They moved and shifted, combining in ways that frightened him.

Calm. Be calm.

He could not be sure this was his own thought.

Where was I?

He thought he remembered being thrust into the open outside Oakes' Redoubt. The land beneath him, then, could still be Black Dragon. He could not, however, remember being picked up by a hylighter.

How did I get here?

As though his confusion ignited some remote explanation, he saw a distant view of himself sprinting across a plain, a Hooded Dasher close behind, then the swoop of a hylighter as it lifted him to safety. The images played in his mind without his volition.

Rescue? What am I doing here? Ballast? Food? Maybe the hylighter is taking me to its nest and a bunch of hungry . . . hungry what?

"Nest!"

He heard the word clearly as though someone spoke directly into his ear, but there was no one. He knew the voice was not his, not Ship's.

Ship!

They had fewer than seven diruns left! Ship was about to break the recording. End of humankind.

I've gone insane, that's it. I'm not really being carried through blue haze by a hylighter.

In his mind, a hatch opened and he heard a babble of voices, Panille's among them. Memories . . . he felt his mind lock onto memories that had been sealed away until this babble of voices. The gondola—the hylighters reaching into the surfaced gondola . . . Waela and Panille making love, tentacles all around like long black snakes slithering . . . questing. He heard his own hysterical laughter. Was that another memory? He recalled the LTA carrying them to the Redoubt . . . the cell—those odd E-clones . . . more laughter. *I'm hallucinating . . . and remembering hallucinating.*

"Not hallucinating."

That voice again! The cradling tentacles shifted, but he still saw only blue haze and . . . and . . . Nothing else was certain.

The chatter continued in his mind—memories or present, he did not know. His head whirled. Fragments of what appeared to be holorecords danced behind his eyes.

I've finally gone all the way—really insane.

"Not insane."

No . . . I just talk to myself.

The chatter had begun to separate into discriminate pieces. He thought he recognized specific snatches of conversation, but the internal holorecord terrified him. He felt that the entire planet had become eyes and ears just for him, that he was . . . everywhere.

In fits and starts, silence returned. He felt it wash through his mind. Slowly—the creep of some small creature up a gigantic wall—he felt those other eyes and ears remove themselves from his awareness.

He was alone.

What the hell is happening to me?

No answer.

But he sensed the cadences of his mind's voice echo down a long, dark system of tunnels and corridors. He was in darkness. And somewhere in this dark was an ear to hear and a voice to answer. Waela was there. He sensed her as though he could reach out with one hand and touch . . .

The tentacles no longer enclosed him!

One palm touched the ground . . . rock, sand. Darkness all around. Waela remained there—calm, receptive.

I've turned into some kind of a damned mystic.

"Live mystic."

That voice! It was as real as the wind he felt abruptly on his face. He knew then that he knelt on some dark ground with . . . with haze turning luminous blue all around. And he remembered, really remembered being picked up by a hylighter. Most precious memory: He nursed it as though it were his only child. Memory: a shimmering expanse of sea, narrow ribbon of coast winding itself out of sight, the most rugged mountains of Pandora lifting from the sea and plain—Black Dragon.

"Look up, Raja Thomas, and see how the child becomes father to the man."

He tipped his head and saw ripplings of bright yellow and orange in the blue mist. A whistling song astounded his ears. It was a small hylighter directly overhead in the mist. Tentacles brushed the ground around him. The mist began to thin, pushed by the breeze he could feel on his skin. He smelled floral perfumes. Visibility moved outward through air thick and warm with water vapor. He looked right and left.

Jungle.

Without knowing how it came about, he understood his surroundings: a large crater nestled in black rock, a captive cloud
layer creating an inversion with protected warmth beneath the
crater's rim.

One of the hovering hylighter's tentacles snaked toward him,
touched the back of his left hand. It felt as warm and soft as his
own flesh. A small trickle of condensation ran down the back of
his neck. He looked up at the hylighter. Another tentacle dripping
condensation dangled directly above him.

Calmness fled.

What's it going to do to me?

His gaze moved all around: warm blue mist.

Crack!

Far overhead, a bright flash of lightning flared horizontally
across the haze. He felt the prickling presence of it along the hairs
on the back of his neck and arms.

Where is this place?

"Nest."

He felt that he was not really hearing that voice. No... it
played on his aural centers the way Ship's voice played, but it
was not Ship.

Still, he sensed reality in what his eyes reported. A hylighter
tentacle touched his hand; another hovered over him. The jungle
remained right out there. Perhaps he was seeing what he desired
most: the legendary refuge, the place of the horn of plenty, where
there were no worries and no passage of time: Eden.

*I've taken refuge in my own mind because of Ship's decision
to end us.*

He ventured another look at the mist-wrapped jungle all
around—mottled clumps of trees and vines with odd colors hidden
in the green.

"Your senses do not lie, Raja Thomas. Those are real trees and
vines. Do you see the flowers?"

The colors were blossoms—red, magenta, draping cascades of
golden yellow. It was all too perfect, a delicate fiction.

"We find the flowers quite pleasant."

"Who... is... talking... to... me?"

"Avata talks to you. Avata also admires the wheat and corn,
the apple trees and cedars. Avata planted here what was swept
away and abandoned by your kind."

"Who is Avata?"

Thomas stared up at the hovering hylighter, afraid of the answer he might get.

"This is Avata!"

Visions flooded his senses: the planet in light and darkness, the crags of Black Dragon and the plains of The Egg, seas and horizons—a confusion which overwhelmed his ability to discriminate. He tried to cringe away from it, but the visions persisted.

"The hylighters," he whispered.

"We choose to be called 'Avata' by you, for we are many and yet one."

Slowly, the visions withdrew.

"Avata brings Panille to help you. See?"

He swung his gaze wide and saw, on his left, another hylighter descending through the blue mist, a naked Kerro Panille clutched in a loop of tentacle. Panille swam in the air like a persistent aftervision. The hylighter dropped him centimeters from the ground. He landed on his feet and strode toward Thomas. The sound of Panille's feet scuffing in sand could not be denied. The poet was real. He had not died on the plain or been killed by the hylighters.

"You are not hallucinating," Panille said. "Remember that. This is not Fraggo. It is a trading of Self."

Thomas climbed to his feet and the trailing tentacle of his hylighter moved with him, not breaking the contact against the back of his hand.

"Where are we, Kerro?"

"As you surmised—Eden."

"You read my thoughts?"

"Some of them. Who are you, Thomas? Avata expresses great curiosity about the mystery of you."

Who am I? He spoke what was in the front of his mind: "I am the bearer of evil tidings. Ship is going to end humankind forever. We have . . . less than seven diurns."

"Why would Ship do such a thing?" Panille stopped less than a pace from Thomas, head cocked to one side, a quizzical, half-amused expression on his face.

"Because we cannot learn how to WorShip."

*The forgotten language of our animal past conveys
the necessity for challenges. Not to be challenged is
to atrophy. And the ultimate challenge is to overcome
entropy, to break through those barriers which enclose
and isolate life, limiting the energy for work and ful-
fillment.*

—Kerro Panille,
I Sing to the Avata

FOR A long heartbeat, Hali stood immobile in the passage while
she stared at Murdoch and the weapon he carried—that deadly
laser scalpel. She could see Docking Bay Eight directly behind
him—the freighter and escape lay there. They had less than two
minutes now until the automatic system propelled that freighter
into space for the long dive to Pandora. A quick glance at the
unconscious Waela on the gurney beside her showed no change
there, but the target of that laser scalpel appeared obvious. Hali
interposed her own body between Murdoch and Waela. She heard
old Win Ferry gasp as she moved.

Hali kept her attention on the scalpel, cleared her throat, and
found her voice astonishingly calm. "Those things are meant to
save lives, Murdoch, not take them."

"I'll be saving a lot of lives by getting rid of this TaoLini
woman." His voice reminded her of that faraway time when Ship

had allowed her to be confronted by Foul-breath below the Hill of Skulls.

Ship? The unspoken plea filled her mind.

Ship made no response. It all depended on her then.

Ferry had stopped the gurney two paces from Murdoch and stood now at Hali's left, trembling.

Murdoch waved the scalpel at them. "This is made to excise unnatural growth from a healthy body. She . . ." He glared at the unconscious Waela. ". . . defiles us."

Again, Hali found her memory filled with the faces of the Hill of Skulls—passionate eyes and violence thinly restrained behind them. Murdoch's face was one of those.

"You have no right," she said.

"I have this." He flicked the scalpel's laser blade in a searing arc past her right cheek. "That's all the right I need."

"But Ship . . ."

"The ship be damned!" He took one step toward her, thrusting out with his free hand to sweep her aside.

In this instant, Ferry moved. He was so fast that Hali saw only the backwards jerk of Murdoch's chin, the blur of old Ferry's elbow. Murdoch went sprawling to the deck, the scalpel spinning from his hand. Hali was as shocked by the old man's speed as by his action. Desperation moved Ferry.

"Go!" Ferry yelled at her. "Get Waela out of here!"

Murdoch was scrambling to his feet as Ferry lunged for him.

Hali moved instinctively. She grabbed the gurney, jerked it past the struggling men. Its howling wheels grated on her senses.

How much time do we have?

And she asked herself as she swept the gurney through the Bay Eight hatch: *What made Ferry so desperate?*

The sealed hatch into the freighter lay directly beyond the Bay Eight opening. She wheeled the gurney across the bump of the interlock and in ten steps brought it up short against the freighter's hatch. It was then that she realized she could not escape without Ferry. He carried the freighter's transit program. She stared at the control panel beside the hatch. Without the program, the freighter would land them at Colony. Her instincts told her that something worse than Murdoch awaited them there. Without that program, they could not enter the freighter—they would be cooked alive here in the Docking Bay. Without that program, she could not switch the freighter from *automatic* to *life-support*.

The inventory in her mind stopped as she heard the panel relays click into the final stages before separation. She whirled at a grunting sound and saw Murdoch and Ferry struggling in the short passage to the freighter's hatch, Murdoch slowly pushing the old man backward toward Hali. Once more, the panel clicked. One by one, the hatches to the docking bay hissed shut. Bolts clicked into their locks, sealing the bay and the four of them from the rest of Ship.

There was a scream from Murdoch and she saw his ear skid like a fragile blossom across the red-smeared deck. It was then she realized that Ferry had recovered the scalpel. She whirled to the panel, threw it open and found a *hold program* key. In desperation, she hit the key.

I hope I haven't trapped us.

An ominous ticking issued from the control panel.

Ferry thrust her aside, slipped a small metal wafer into a slot in the panel. His trembling hand touched the *add program* key and the freighter's hatch popped open. They pushed the gurney inside and, as they moved, Waela sat up. She looked at Ferry, then at Hali, and said: "My child will sleep in the sea. Where the hylighters calm the waves to the touch of a cradle, there my child will sleep."

Her head fell forward onto her chest. They slipped her from the gurney and wrestled her gently across to a passenger couch, locked her in it. As they worked, Hali heard the freighter's hatch hiss closed. The freighter quivered. Ferry propelled her toward one of the forward control couches and they strapped in.

"You ever fly one of these?" Ferry asked.

She shook her head.

"Me neither. I had simulator experience, but that was a long time ago."

His hand hesitated over the *launch program* key and, before he could move, the red *automatics* light flashed on the board. Hali looked forward to the plaz curve nested into the bay, expecting it to separate. Nothing happened.

"What's wrong?" She felt hysteria bubbling in her throat. "Why doesn't it launch?"

"Ferry! Ekel! Shut that thing down and come back inside!"

"Murdoch," Ferry said. "Always spoiling things. He must've escaped from the bay. He's taken over the auto-pilot and we can't release the docking bolts."

"Ferry, Ekel—if we don't get TaoLini back into Sickbay, she could die. You want that on your conscience? Don't let yourselves in for trouble over a . . ."

Ferry snapped off the vocoder.

Hali took a deep breath. "What now?"

"This will either be the ride of your life or no life at all. Hang on."

Ferry cleared the console and hit the *reset* key, then *override* and *manual*. His finger hesitated several blinks over *launch program*.

"Hit it," Hali said.

He depressed the key. A powerful trembling rippled through their cabin.

Hali looked at him. She had never suspected such action and determination in old Ferry. He seemed beyond desperation, caught up in some overriding program of his own. She realized then that the old man was sober.

"If we only had a flight manual," he said.

A metallic female voice startled them, crackling from an overhead vocoder: "You have a manual."

"Who the hell are you?" Ferry demanded.

"I am Bitten. I am the system of this freighter. I am designed for conventional or conversational program in emergencies. You wish to separate from Ship, correct?"

"Yes, but . . ."

A roar shuddered through the freighter. The forward plaz displayed a blinding glimpse of Rega, then a panorama of stars as they shot free of Ship. They began a slow one-eighty turn toward Pandora, and Hali saw a gaping hole that had been Docking Bay Eight. Roboxes already were swarming over the area like insects, starting repairs on the ragged edges.

"Well," Ferry muttered, "what now?"

Hali tried to swallow in a dry throat, then: "What Waela said— the cradle of the sea. Does she know something about . . . ?"

"Life support has been activated," Bitten announced. "Does the sleeping one require additional attention?"

Hali jerked around and studied her patient. Waela lay in quiet sleep, her chest rising and falling evenly. Hali unstrapped, crept back to Waela's side and ran a test series: Everything read as normal as could be expected—blood pressure up a bit, adrenaline on the high side but dropping. No medication was indicated.

Ferry's voice intruded on Hali's thoughts then as he asked Bitten for their ETA to Pandora's atmosphere.

Hali turned and stared at the planet with a growing sense of wonder. Her shipboard life was ended. The only thing she knew for sure about her life now was that she still had it.

Bitten's metallic rasping filled the cabin: "Two hours, thirty-five minutes to atmosphere. Additional twenty-five minutes for entry and docking at Colony."

"We can't dock at Colony!" Hali said. She made her way back to her seat and strapped down. "What are our alternatives?"

"Colony is the only docking station approved for this vessel," Bitten intoned.

"What about a surface landing?"

"Certain conditions permit surface landing without damage to vessel and crew. But our departure destroyed all forward landing gear and docking valves. These are not necessary at Colony."

"But we can't land at Colony!" She stared at Ferry, who sat frozen either in fear or complete resignation.

"Survival of unprotected crew elsewhere on Pandora surface not likely," Bitten intoned.

Hali felt her mind whirling. *Survival not likely!* She had the sudden feeling that this whole thing was high drama, something staged and unreal. She looked at Ferry. He continued to stare out the forward plaz. That was it: Ferry was acting out of character—too far out.

But Murdoch's ear . . . that hole in Ship . . .

"We can't go back to Ship and we can't dock at Colony and we can't land in the open," she said.

"We're trapped," Ferry agreed, and she did not like the calm way he said it.

Behold, these are a small troop, and indeed they are enraging us; and we are a host on our guard.

—Muslim *Book of the Dead,*
Shiprecords

"WHAT YOU'RE talking about is war," Panille said, shaking his head. He sat on the warm ground, his back against a jungle tree, moon-shadowed darkness all around.

"War?" Thomas rubbed his forehead, looked at the shadowy ground. He did not like looking at Panille—a naked Pan who seemed to flow in and out of contact with native life—touching a tree here, the tentacle of a passing hylighter there. Contact, physical contact: always touching. "Shipmen have had no experience of war for many generations," Panille said. "Clones and E-clones have no experience of it at all, not even stories or traditions. I know it only from Ship's holos."

With one moon full and another raising its pale face on the jagged horizon, Panille saw Thomas haloed against night sky, a hazy outline amidst the stars. A very disturbed man.

"But we have to take over the Redoubt," Thomas said. "It's our only hope. Ship . . . Ship will . . ."

"How do you know this?"

"It's why I was brought out of hyb."

"To teach us WorShip?"

"No! To acquaint you with the need to solve that problem! Ship insists we . . ."

352

"There is no problem."

"What do you mean there's no problem?" Thomas was outraged, "Ship will . . ."

"Look around you." Panille gestured at the moon-shadowed basin, the gentle stirrings of the moist air in the leaves. "If you care for your house, you are sheltered."

Thomas forced himself to take a deep breath, to assume at least the outward appearance of calm. The jungle—yes, there did not appear to be any demons in this place . . . this *nest*, as the hylighters called it. But this place was not enough! No place was safe from Oakes or from Ship. And there was no escaping Ship's demand. Panille had to be made to understand that.

"Please believe me," Thomas said. "Unless we learn how to WorShip, we are through. No more humankind anywhere. I . . . I don't want that to happen."

"Then why should we attack the Redoubt?"

"Because you say those are the last people groundside—Colony's destroyed."

"That's true, but what would you teach those people by attacking?" Panille's tone was maddeningly reasonable, a voice which kept its disturbing pace with the sounds of breeze-stirred leaves.

Thomas tried to match that tone: "Lewis and The Boss are destroying the 'lectrokelp and the hylighters. The native life is running out of time, too. Don't they . . . ?"

"Avata understands what is happening here."

"They know they're being wiped out?"

"Yes."

"Don't they want to prevent that?"

"Yes."

"How do they expect to do that without controlling the Redoubt?"

"Avata will not attack the Redoubt."

"What *will* they do?"

"What Avata has always done: nurture. Avata will continue to rescue people when possible. Avata will carry us where we need to go."

"Didn't the kelp kill Colonists? You heard what Waela said. . . ."

"Another of Lewis' lies," Panille said, and Thomas knew that he was right.

He stared off at the jungle beyond Panille. Somewhere in there, he knew, was a large band of survivors, E-clones and normals, all scooped from Pandora's surface and *planted* here as the hylighters planted the scavenged Earthside vegetation. Thomas had not seen this collection of people, but Panille and the hylighters had described it. The hylighters could do this thing... but... Thomas shook his head in despair.

"They have so much power!"

"Who?"

"The 'lectrokelp and the hylighters!"

"Avata, you mean." Panille's voice remained patient.

"Why won't they use their power to defend themselves?"

"Avata is one creature who understands about power."

"What? What do you...?"

"To have power is to use it. That is the meaning of possession. To use it is to lose it."

Thomas closed his eyes, clenched his fists. Panille refused to understand. Refusing to understand, he doomed them all.

Such a loss! Not just humankind... but this, this Avata.

"They have so much," Thomas whispered.

"Who?"

"The Avata!"

He thought about what the hylighters already had shown him, spoke the thought aloud: "That hylighter, the one that brought me, do you know what it showed me after we were fed?"

"Yes."

Thomas went on, not hearing: "Just in a few blinks of touching it, I hallucinated the development, very nearly complete, of the entire recent geological and botanical phenomena of Pandora. Think of losing that!"

"Not hallucination," Panille corrected him.

"What is it, then?" Thomas opened his eyes, stared at the passing moons.

"Avata teaches by touch, at first. A true, but sometimes overwhelming flow of information. As the student learns to focus, the information becomes discrete, discriminated. You separate the needed bits from the babble."

"Babble, yes. Most of it's babble, but I..."

"You know about focus," Panille said. "You select which noises to hear and understand. You select which things to see and recognize. This is just a different kind of focus."

"How can we sit here and discuss... discuss this... I mean, it's going to end! Forever!"

"This is the true flow of knowledge between us, Raja Thomas. Avata moves from the mastery of touch to direct communication, mind to mind. Precise identification with another being. You have seen demons eat scraps of exploded hylighters?"

Thomas was interested in spite of his frustration. "I've seen it."

"Direct ingestion of knowledge, precise identification. Some ancient creatures of Earth did it. Planarians."

"You don't say."

"No . . . I don't limit."

Thomas jerked away as a passing hylighter trailed tentacles across his face, pausing also to touch the seated Panille. For an instant, Thomas sensed a blur of pictures, dream fragments dancing behind his eyes. And the chatter!

"Avata remains fascinated by the mystery of you, Raja Thomas," Panille said. "Who are you?"

"Ship's best friend."

Panille heard truth in those words and found himself transported in memory back to the shipside teaching cubby. A momentary flicker of jealousy burned at his awareness and was gone.

"Ship's best friend would start a war?"

"It's the only way."

"Who would fight your war?"

"It's between us and them."

"But who would be *your* soldiers?"

Thomas gestured at the jungle, hoping he pointed somewhere near the collection of remnant people brought here by the hylighters.

"And you would move against Oakes with violence?"

"Oakes is a phoney. The Chaplain/Psychiatrist is responsible for the first order of WorShip: survival. Oakes would sacrifice the entire future of humankind to satisfy his own selfish goals."

"That is true. Oakes is selfish."

Thomas remained caught up in resentment of Oakes: "Survival takes planning and sacrifice. The Ceepee should be willing to sacrifice the most. We give our children to Ship as a matter of WorShip. Oakes *engineers* more people from cloning, and on a fixed food supply. Children starve while his playthings . . ."

Thomas broke off in frustration. As he stood there, wondering how he could make this poet understand what had to be done, Alki lifted above the eastern horizon, flooding the crater's mists with milky light. The illumination picked out every leaf-dripping detail nearby but hazed away to a mysterious background of muted colors.

"We're in danger, terrible danger," he muttered.

"Life is always in danger."

"Well, we agree on something."

Thomas lowered his chin to his chest, looked down at his feet and, in that strange elasticity of time which comes with danger, he saw his boots. He remembered those booted feet dangling below him as the hylighter lifted him from the threat of a Hooded Dasher at the Redoubt.

Terrible danger!

He suddenly recalled another moment akin to this one: when he had pressed the *abort*-trigger aboard the Voidship *Earthling*, those countless millennia and *replays* past. In the century between instructing his body to push the abort-trigger and actually pushing it, he had studied the galaxies waving to him from the back of his hand and fingers. One crazy hair, only millimeters long, had poked out from the side of a knuckle on his right index finger, and he recalled the trickle of something small and wet down the side of his left cheek.

"Why did the hylighter bring me here?"

"To preserve your seed."

"But Oakes and the Lab One people will kill us. Nothing will survive. What they miss, Ship will finish."

"Yet, we are in Eden," Panille said. He moved gracefully to his feet, swept an arm wide. "There is food. It is warm. It's little over a kilometer over the cliffs to the beach, not more than ten kilometers to the Redoubt—two different worlds, and you would make them the same."

"No! You don't understand what I . . ."

Thomas broke off as a shadow passed over them. He jerked his gaze upward as a trio of hylighters swept overhead carrying a long plasteel cutter and several wriggling human shapes. Behind them, cresting the crater's crags, more hylighters appeared. The tentacles of all were burdened with people and equipment.

Panille touched a dangling tentacle as a hylighter circled over them and dumped the wind from its sail membrane. He spoke in a distant, musing voice: "Lewis has installed Lab One at the Redoubt. These people were driven out. They are terrified. We must take care of them."

A feeling of elation swept through Thomas. "You ask about troops? Here they are! And the hylighters are bringing weapons!

You said they wouldn't help us attack, but..."

"Now I know that you once really were a Ceepee," Panille said. "The keeper of the ritual and the robes—the trappings and the suits of woe."

"I tell you there's no other way! We have to take over the Redoubt and learn how to WorShip!"

Panille stared at him, eyes unfocused. "Don't you know that humans made Ship? Therefore, humans made all that proceeds from Ship. Ship tells us nothing, demands nothing which is not from and of ourselves."

Thomas no longer could contain his anger and frustration. "You ask *me* if I know that humans made Ship? I was one of those humans!"

It was an explosive revelation for Panille—Thomas, a piece of history resurrected! Ship's *hand* in this was almost visible—past, present, future woven into a lovely pattern. This thing wanted only a poem to bring it into existence. Panille smiled at his own enlightenment, and spoke in a burst of energy: "Then you *must* know why you made Ship."

Thomas heard it as a question.

"We had a Voidship, the *Earthling*, and we were commanded to turn it into a conscious being. We did it because it was succeed or die. At the moment of consciousness, Ship delivered us from one danger into another, demanding that we learn how to WorShip. It's what we were supposed to do with our new lives, us and all of our descendants after us."

Panille did not answer, but continued to stare at the arriving swarms of hylighters each with its cargo of people or equipment. The soft flutings of the hylighters and the terrified babble of the people being lowered to the ground began to fill the open area all around.

"So you talk to Ship as I do," Panille mused. "Yet you do not hear your own words. Now, I see why Ship needed a poet here."

"What we really need is an experienced military leader," Thomas said. "Lacking that, I guess I'll have to serve." He turned and strode toward the nearest batch of terrified survivors.

"Where are you going?" Panille asked.

"Recruiting."

Through the process of nostalgic filtering, Earth assumed for the Shipmen fairyland characteristics. The different strains of people, telling their different historical memories, could only make such stories mix in a paradise setting. No Shipman ever experienced every Earthly place and clime and society. Thus, over the many generations, the reinforcement of positive memories left only the faith in how things were.

—**Kerro Panille,**
History of the Avata

LEGATA SAT at a comdesk in the working space assigned to her at the Redoubt. It was a small room and showed signs of hasty construction. Directly in front of her across the desk was an oval hatch leading into her own private cubby, a space she seldom occupied now. But Oakes was busy somewhere and she had seized this opportunity.

She punched for shiprecords, keyed for her own private code, and waited. Did they still have contact with Ship?

The instrument buzzed. Glyphs danced across the screen in the desk. She punched for the Ox gate, set up a random-barrier lock and began transferring the data on Oakes into the Redoubt's own storage system.

There you are, Morgon Lon *Oakes!*

And the printout remained secreted in Oakes' old cubby ship-side should she ever need it. It was remotely possible that Oakes might stumble on this record here, might erase it and even trace back to the original to erase that. But the printout would remain, stamped with Ship's imprimatur.

When she had reviewed the data to reassure herself, and once more checked the random-barrier, she keyed the lock, then turned to the question of Lewis. It was not enough to have power over Oakes. Lewis held to his own power base like a man aware of every threat. She did not like the way he stared at her, secretive and measuring.

The Ox gate gave her its open-files response and she asked for anything available about Jesus Lewis.

Immediately the *activity* light at the command console winked out. She jiggled the switch. Nothing. She tried the *override* sequence, Oakes' private code, the vocoder. Nothing.

When I asked for material on Lewis.

It had to be a coincidence. She went through the entire contact routine once more. Ship's records could not be brought into this console. She stood up, went out and into the passage, through the tension and bustle of E-clone Processing, and borrowed one of their consoles. Same result.

We're cut off.

She thanked the pale, thin-fingered E-clone who had stepped aside at her request and returned to her own cubby. She knew that the right thing to do would be to tell Oakes. With Colony gone and no communication to Ship, they were isolated, alone in the wilderness that pressed inward all around the Redoubt.

Yes—Oakes would have to be told. She sat down at her desk, called on Voice-Only when nothing else responded, and when he snapped that he was busy, insisted that her information transcended any other business.

Oakes heard her out in silence, then: "We're trapped."

"How can we be trapped?" she asked. "There's no one to trap us."

"They've set us up," he insisted. "Wait there for me."

The 'coder *blapped* at his sudden disconnection and it was only then she realized that Oakes had not asked where she was. Did he spy on her all the time? *How much of what I did . . . how much did he see?*

In less than a minute, Oakes stepped through the hatch, his

white singlesuit drenched in sweat. He was speaking as he entered, crackling tension in his voice.

"That TaoLini woman, Panille and Thomas—they're out to destroy us!"

He stopped just inside the room, glared down at her across the comdesk.

"That's impossible! I saw the hylighter carry Thomas off. And Panille . . ."

"They're alive, I tell you! Alive and plotting against us."

"How . . .?"

"More clones have revolted! And we've had a strange message from Ferry, threatening. They're somewhere nearby, some valley, Lewis thinks. People and equipment. They're going to attack."

"How could anyone . . .?"

"Probe flights, Lewis is sending out probes. And there *is* something out there. They're able to drive our search instruments crazy—some kind of interference that Lewis can't explain—but we're still getting indications of a lot of life and metal."

"Where?"

"South." He gestured vaguely. "What were you doing when the ship broke contact?"

"Nothing," she lied. "The circuitry just went dead."

"We need that contact, the people still up there, the material and food. Get them back."

"I've tried. Here, see for yourself." She slid out of the seat and gestured for him to take it.

"No . . . no." He seemed actually afraid to sit at her comdesk. "I . . . trust your efforts. I just . . ."

She slipped back into her seat. "You just *what*?"

"Nothing. See if you can contact Lewis. Tell him to meet me at the Command Center."

Oakes turned on his heel. The hatch hissed closed behind him.

She keyed a search for Lewis and fed the message into it, then tried once more to contact Ship. No response. She sat back and stared at the comdesk. A feeling of regret swept over her, pre-remorse, a sense of sorrow over the Morgan Oakes who might have been. He was nearing the very kind of desperation she wanted.

Let someone attack the Redoubt. Whatever happened, she would be ready with the material she had stored here.

At the worst possible moment, Morgan Lon Oakes! You may

be able to appreciate my timing, although you never have before.

Would it happen in front of Thomas? Was it possible that Thomas had survived and would lead an attack? She thought it distinctly possible. Thomas—another Ceepee. The unfailing Thomas who had seen her run the P, who had helped her in that desperate hour, then said nothing of it to anyone.

Discreet. Kind and discreet. Almost a lost breed.

Doubts began to fill her mind then. Perhaps the survival of humans groundside really did depend on Oakes and Lewis. But Colony was gone and the Redoubt was clearly under siege from the planet, if not from some nebulous force headed by Thomas. She thought of the Scream Room then. Where did the Scream Room figure in any scheme of survival? The Scream Room was unjustifiable by any standards. It betrayed negative, anti-survival impulses. Everything about it, that proceeded from it, brought death or hunger or a terrifying subservience. No—not survival.

Oakes put me through the Scream Room.

Nothing would ever change that. But Thomas had guarded the perimeter hatch for her. His were survival instincts. She determined then that she would see what she could do to keep the Thomas breed from dying out.

At what cost? she wondered then, her doubts returning. *At what cost?*

A horrible feeling came over me—a terrible amusement, for I believed that humankind, through the filtering of Ship's manipulations and the great passage of time, had lost the very ability to engage in war. I thought war had been bred and conditioned out of them at the very moment when they needed this ability the most.

—The Thomas Diatribes,
Shiprecords

WHILE HALI was making another examination of Waela's condition and well before the freighter reached atmosphere, Bitten's metallic voice barked at them from the overhead 'coder.

"Do you know a Kerro Panille?"

Waela stirred and mumbled at the sound, then rubbed both hands over her mounded abdomen.

"Yes, we know Panille," Hali said. She closed and sealed her pribox. "Why?"

"You wish to land at some place other than Colony," Bitten intoned. "That now may be possible."

Ferry glared up toward the 'coder. "You said we had to land at Colony!"

"I have been in contact with Kerro Panille," Bitten said. "He asserts that Colony has been destroyed."

"Destroyed?" Hali sat stiffly in her couch, dumb with shock.

Ferry gripped the arms of his command couch, knuckles white. "But we're programmed for landing at Colony."

"I remind you that I am the emergency program," Bitten said. "Present conditions fit the definition of emergency."

"Then where can we land?" Hali asked. And she felt the stirrings of hope. *Contact with Kerro!*

"Panille asserts that I can make a sea landing near an occupied site called the Redoubt. He is prepared to guide us to that landing."

Hali checked the fastenings which held Waela in the passenger couch, returned to her own seat and strapped in. The plaz directly in front of her framed a brilliant circle of cloud-covered planet.

"They meant us to die," Ferry muttered. "Damn them!"

"Do you desire to land at the alternate site?" Bitten asked.

"Yes, land us there," Hali said.

"There is risk," Bitten said.

"Land us there!" Ferry shouted.

"A normal tone of voice suffices for conversational direction of this program," Bitten said.

Ferry stared at Hali. "They meant us to die."

"I heard you. What do you mean?"

"Murdoch said we would have to go to Colony."

Hali looked at him, weighing his words. Was the man unaware of what he had just told her?

"So it was a set-up," she said. "You staged that fight."

Ferry remained silent, blinking at her.

"But you cut off one of Murdoch's ears," Hali said, remembering.

Ferry bared his old teeth in a terrible grin. "He did something to my Rachel. I know he did."

Hali crossed her arms over her breast, hearing all the unspoken things in Ferry's words. Her gaze went to the laser scalpel clipped in a breast pocket of Ferry's singlesuit: a thin stylus with death or life in its mechanism.

He was supposed to bring the scalpel in case he needed it against me!

"I made it seem like an accident," Ferry said. "But I knew they did something to my Rachel. And Murdoch's the one they get to do the nasty stuff." He nodded at Hali. "In the Scream Room. That's where they do it."

As he said *Scream Room,* he shuddered.

"So we were supposed to go to Colony and it's destroyed," Ferry said. "Demons, yes. Very neat. They didn't like my asking about Rachel."

Hali wet her lips with her tongue. "What's . . . what's the Scream Room?"

"In Lab One where they do the nasty stuff. It was because of Rachel, I know it was. And I drink too much. Lots of us do that after the Scream Room."

Bitten's voice intruded: "Correction noted."

"What was that?" Ferry demanded.

"This is Bitten. I have acknowledged a course correction from Kerro Panille."

"You're going to land us in the sea?" Hali asked, filled with sudden concern for her unconscious patient.

"Near shore. Panille asserts there will be help where we land."

"What about the demons?" Ferry asked.

"If that is a reference to native fauna, you can protect yourselves with the weapons in this freighter's cargo."

"You carry . . . weapons?" Hali asked.

"The cargo manifest lists food concentrates, building equipment and tools, medical supplies, groundsuits and weapons."

Hali shook her head. "I knew you needed weapons to survive groundside, but I didn't know they were being made shipside."

"Do you know what a weapon is?" Ferry asked, looking directly at Hali.

She thought of her history holos, and the soldiers at the Hill of Skulls. "Oh, yes. I know about weapons."

"This laser scapel." Ferry touched the stylus shape at his breast. "Acid concentrates, plasteel cutters for construction teams, knives, axes . . ."

Hali swallowed past a lump in her throat. Every bit of her med-tech training cried out against this. "If we prepare to . . . kill," the word was barely a sigh past her lips, "then we will kill."

"Down here, it's kill or be killed," Ferry said. "That's the way The Boss wants it."

In that instant, the freighter skipped into the first thin surface of Pandora's atmosphere. Vibration hummed all through the cabin, then smoothed.

"Can't we run away?" Hali asked. Her voice was a low whisper.

"Nowhere to run," Ferry said. "You must know that. All Shipmen learn enough about groundside to know that."

Fight or *flee*, Hali thought, *and nowhere to flee*. And it occurred to her that Pandora was a place where people were made into primitives.

"Trust me," Ferry said, and the quavering in his old voice made the statement pathetic.

"Yes, of course," Hali said.

She felt the freighter's braking thrust then as it pressed her against the restraining harness, and she glanced back to reassure herself that Waela remained secure.

"We will land in the cradle of the sea," Hali said. "That's what Waela said. Remember?"

"What does *she* know?" Ferry demanded, and it was his fearful, querulous tone, the one which had made her despise him.

This the true human knows:
the strings of all the ways
make up a cable of great strength
and great purpose....

—**Kerro Panille,**
The Collected Poems

FOR A long time Panille sat in the shadows of the seaside cliff while he felt the approaching *presence* from space. The sea lay below him down a rugged path, the cliffs soared high behind. Avata had been the first to tell him about this problem and, for a few blinks, he had fallen back into Thomas' ways of thinking.

The Redoubt will know about this freighter, will send its weapons against it.

But Avata soothed him, told him that Avata would transmit false images to the Redoubt's systems, concealing the freighter's passage. Avata would continue to mask the nest's location with similar projections.

The rock was cold against Panille's back. From time to time, he opened and closed his eyes. When his eyes were open he was vaguely aware of the amber glow from Double Dusk—the sky alight from two suns dodging just below Pandora's horizon.

Ship would know he was here and what he was doing. Nothing escaped Ship. Did that omnipotent awareness work through phenomena similar to those of Avata? Was it awareness of even the

366

most minute changes in electrical impulses? Or was it some other form of energy which Ship and Avata monitored?

That *presence* from space was coming closer . . . closer. He felt it, then he saw it.

The freighter skipped up the horizon, a great stone crossing the surface of a glassy sea. The fall into atmosphere was deceptive. The freighter had entered Pandora's pull at the lowest point on the horizon. It streaked a long upward arc as Panille felt it fill his awareness. It grew larger with its approach around the planet's curvature, and he saw it now falling white-hot toward him.

The crunch of gravel told him of Thomas' approach, but Panille had only a single purpose now. The approaching freighter was himself and *he* was diving through the sky alight with amber.

"Can you do it?" Thomas asked.

"I am doing it," Panille whispered. He begrudged the distraction of answering.

Until he had seen the pinpoint of that first glow against the Pandoran dusk, Panille had not been sure he could master this thing.

"I'm thinking them in," he whispered. There was awe and wonder in his voice.

"Who is coming?" Thomas asked.

"Avata did not say."

Thomas emitted a wry, jibing chuckle. "It's a surprise package from Ship. Maybe more recruits for me."

He moved around Panille and climbed down out of sight along the narrow path, his figure a mysterious movement in the half light.

Going to the shore where the surf crashes. The surf will make this landing perilous.

As the last sound of Thomas faded from Panille's awareness, darkness fell—the Double Dark in which Pandora's greatest mysteries blossomed.

Panille thought of himself now as a beacon. He was a signal transmitter in a known position. The freighter and its unknown passengers depended on his constancy. Avata wanted this freighter to land here. He trusted Avata.

Come to the sea, he thought. *The sea . . . the sea . . .*

Hylighters began whistling along a rock ledge ahead of him and he knew it was time to join Thomas on the shore. He got up stiffly. It had been a long wait on the observation ledge. Knowing this, he had scavenged a singlesuit of white shipcloth which Avata had stored in the nest.

A hylighter positioned itself above and behind him as he began the slow climb down to the shore. Panille sensed tentacles dangling near, ready to grasp him should he fall.

Avata, Brother, he thought.

It fluted a brief reply.

The sharp rocks and the difficulty of the dark cliff path were second nature to Panille's body. He did not have to think about the climb. And he found that he could maintain the *beacon* while his thoughts wandered. His mind strayed back to Thomas' unbelieving interrogation.

Thomas demanded explanations and refused to believe almost everything he heard.

He believes Avata projects strange images into his mind. He believes I have learned from Avata, that I am a master of hallucination. He believes only what he can touch, and then he doubts that.

Panille recalled his own words: "Avata is not hallucinogenic. They are not even *they*. That's why I use the term Avata. That's why I call a hylighter Avata."

"I know that word!" Thomas was accusatory.

"The Oneness which is present in the many. It's a word from one of the old languages of my mother's people."

"Your *mother?*" Thomas was astounded.

"Didn't Ship tell you? I was womb-bred, womb-grown and nursed. I thought you said Ship told you everything."

Thomas flashed him a dark scowl which showed that Panille was striking at sensitive areas. But nothing had stopped Thomas from forming his *army*—no warnings about Avata's nature, no jibes at Thomas' limited information. Half of the army waited above them now—a mixed crew of E-clones and normals—all of them praying that the freighter from Ship was bringing weapons and other support. Some had descended earlier to wait among the rocks at the base of the cliff.

Above Panille in the darkness, his Avatan guardian shared amusement and dismay at these thoughts.

Can that army save you? Panille asked.

Avata will die in only a few diurns. Then it may be that a rebirth can occur.

Oakes hasn't beaten you yet, Panille said. *Lewis with his poi-*

sons and his virus, none of them understand about power.

Soft flutings rippled from the hylighter, the nearest Avata came to betraying doubts. Panille wondered then: Was this futility aroused by Thomas' efforts, or by the imminent end of Avata—no more of 'lectrokelp/hylighters, no more of the individual cells, the great plural-singular unity?

This thought disturbed him and he thought angrily as he worked his way down the steep trail to the shore: *If you think you're done, then you are finished!*

He emerged from a gap between high rocks onto a wide, rock-mounded sandy beach. Thomas stood far down the sand near the surf—one dark shadow among the many rocks. The surf was high, long rollers crashing onto the shingle. The air was damp with salt spray. Panille felt the surf's heavy rhythm transmitted through skin and feet simultaneously. He put a hand against one of the gateway rocks through which he had entered this sea realm. The rock was cold and wet, and it also vibrated to the surf.

Without the kelp to subdue the sea, the waves had become destructively wild—raging against the cliffs at high tide, throwing giant rocks in their surgings. Soon, very soon, all that Avata had built here would come crashing down into the wilderness of the sea.

The Avatan guardian hovered near his shoulder. One tendril touched his cheek, transmiting remembered emotions.

Yes, this is the place.

It was here, Panille recalled, that he had learned to appreciate all the centuries of poetry celebrating rock and sand and sea, and the peculiar Avata life-of-Self illuminated by the regular passage of moons and suns. Here, the occasional monotony of wave against shore had been broken by the healthy *slap* of a nightborn hylighter breaking free of its motherplant and drifting off with its long umbilicus tentacles trailing in the sea. Though all Avata was one creature, Panille had felt his own private kinship with the nightborn hylighter-Avatan. Here, he had listened for them and greeted each birth with a song. A far-off *slap* would catch his attention and fill him with all the wonder of an answered prayer. Across the gently rolling sea, the tiny creature would rise into darkness.

Never again?

Panille whispered a chant to those lost cells of Avata, feeling his whole body transmit the chant as though he were, at last, truly one with Avata.

The solitary blossom overpowers the bouquet.
Even remembering union, without embrace:
a transformation.
Oh, the golden, night-blooming truth!

As he chanted, the whole line of beach glowed with the moons-rise and the shimmering friendship of Avata. The glow illuminated the people of Thomas' ragtag army. Panille saw Thomas outlined against the dim light. Psuhing himself away from the gateway rock, Panille went down the beach to stand near this mysterious "friend of Ship."

"They're less than two minutes away," Panille said. He felt the *beacon* within him, a timed fire which linked him to that hot metal behemoth diving toward him.

"Oakes will send probes," Thomas said.

"Avata will help me jam their signals." Panille gave a smile to the dark. "Would you care to join me in this?"

"No!"

You hold back too much, Raja Thomas.

"But I need your help," Panille said. And he felt Thomas fuming, the tension mounting.

"What do I do?" Thomas forced the words out.

"It may help you to touch an Avatan tentacle. Not necessary, but it helps at first."

A black tentacle came looping down to him then from the night sky. Reluctance apparent in every movement, Thomas reached out and placed a palm against the thrusting warmth.

Immediately, he felt his awareness joined to whoever guided that freighter toward them. He could see two hylighters hovering directly ahead of him and he felt his body standing on surf-drummed sand, a *place to go*. But the pulse of flight held him in thralldom.

If anybody had told me back at Moonbase that one day I'd land a freighter with my mind and a couple of plants that sing in the dark . . .

And think!

The Avata intrusion could not be avoided. Avata would not accept that designation as plant. Thomas sensed more than the aural projection, something not quite pride, but not completely separated from pride.

Avata confuses me, he apologized.

You confuse yourself. Why do you hide your true identity?

Thomas jerked his hand away from the warm tentacle, but the Avata presence remained in his awareness.

You're prying where you don't belong! Thomas accused.

Avata does not pry. There was no denying the hurt in this response.

Panille felt like an eavesdropper on a private argument. Thomas was smouldering with anger now, aware that he could not break off the Avata contact at will, aware that Avata wanted to pierce the wall behind which this private idea of himself lay hidden.

"Let's get the freighter down," Panille said. "Probes are coming from the Redoubt."

Panille released his part of the beacon system then, telling himself that he had to concentrate on the probes. Thomas would have to make his own mistakes.

The first of the probes screamed down the beach, blazing toward them on a course which undoubtedly had been computed against a plot of the incoming freighter.

As Avata had taught him, Panille set up a terrain image all around and transmitted it to the probe. He felt the projected illusion mesh with the probe's electronic functions. The probe almost shattered from the Gs it pulled, avoiding a sudden cliff which was not there.

They're getting closer, he thought.

He knew why. Each illusion of mistaken terrain formed a pattern of error from which the computer at Redoubt could derive significant results.

Avata numbers appeared in Panille's awareness, telling him that he was being monitored constantly now.

Yes, he agreed. *The patrols have increased.*

Tenfold in twelve hours, Avata insisted. *Why does Thomas not understand his role in this?*

It is his nature, perhaps.

Have you identified your contact on the freighter?

Panille thought about this question, reviewed his own performance as a beacon, and experienced a sudden wash of insight. Knowing it was urgent, he reinsinuated himself into Thomas' performance, feeling the affirmation of contact with the freighter.

Thomas, who have you contacted on the freighter? Panille asked.

Thomas considered this. He could feel the approaching *pres-*

ence—almost palpable. If it was illusion, it was a most complete illusion.

Who? Panille insisted.

Thomas knew he could not be in contact with a Shipman up there. Shipmen would panic when alien thoughts intruded. Who could it be then?

Bitten.

The freighter's identification signal came to him clear and unmistakable: a simple intense concentration without emotion.

"Ahhhhhhh," Thomas said.

To Panille, the startling thing was Thomas' emotional response: deep amusement. Bitten was a flight-system computer, and the realization that his mind was in contact with a computer should not have amused the man. This could only be more evidence of the mystery which so attracted Avata.

They were both forced to concentrate on their mental linkage with Bitten then, but Panille could not explain why this aroused a deep fear reaction in him. He felt it, though, a fear which radiated from his own flesh and outward into every cell of Avata.

SHIP: *I have taught you about the classical Pandora and her box.*
PANILLE: *I know how this planet got its name.*
SHIP: *Where would you hide when the serpents and shadows oozed out of the box?*
PANILLE: *Under the lid, of course.*

—**Kerro Panille,**
Shiprecords

WAELA FELT that she lived only in a dream, unable to trust any reality. She held her eyes closed, a tight seal against the world beyond her flesh. This was not enough. Part of her awareness told her that she was controlling the landing approach of a freighter. *Insane!* Another part recorded the moments before the suns lifted in the shadow of Black Dragon. Panille was there, too, somewhere low in the shadow. *I'm hallucinating.*

Hali!

Waela felt anxiety coming from Hali . . . and Hali was nearby. It was an odd anxiety—tension overlain with a deliberate effort to remain calm.

Hali is terribly afraid and even more afraid that she will show it. She wants someone to take charge.

Of course—Hali has never been off Ship before.

Waela tried to move her lips, tried to form reassuring words,

373

but her mouth was too dry. Speech required enormous effort. She felt trapped, convinced that she lay strapped into a passenger couch in a freighter diving toward heavy surf.

A piece of Kerro's poem floated through Waela's awareness then, and she focused on it in both fascination and fear, having no memory of where she had heard this poem:

> *Your course will be true when you sight*
> *the blue line of sunrise, at night*
> *low in the shadow of Black Dragon.*

Hali was there, too, listening to the fragment and rejecting it. A wave of emotion rushed over Waela, made her want to reach out and hold Hali close, to cry with her. She knew this emotion— love of the same man. But she saw Pandora very close now—a raging white line of surf. Waela wanted to cringe away from it. She could feel the child in her womb, another awareness whose share of life reached out and out and out and out . . .

A cry escaped her, but the sound was lost in the abrupt roaring, metal-straining protest as the freighter made its first contact with the sea. For a few blinks, the ride smoothed; there was a gliding sensation followed by a cushioned deceleration and lifting, then a grating, grinding cacophony which ended in a thumping and stillness.

"Where are the people?" That was Hali's voice.

Waela opened her eyes, looked upward at the ceiling of the freighter's sparse cabin—metal beams, soft illumination, a winking red light. Somewhere there was a sound of surf. The freighter creaked and popped. Abruptly, it tipped a full degree.

"There's someone." That was old Ferry.

Waela turned her head, saw Ferry and Hali releasing themselves from the command couches. The plaz beyond them framed a seamed barrier of black rock only a few meters away illuminated by wavering beams of artificial light.

Ferry's hand moved to a control in front of him. There was a *hiss* near Waela's feet, then the sudden rush of cold sea wind through an open hatchway. It was night beyond those moving lights. The hatch was blocked for a moment by the entrance of two people. As though awakening from a dream, Waela recognized them—Panille and Thomas.

"Waela!" They spoke in unison, both appearing startled at the sight of her.

Hali pushed herself away from the control console, intensely aware that Panille was focused on Waela's mounded abdomen. Neither Panille nor the man with him, she realized, had expected to see Waela, and certainly not in the full bloom of pregnancy.

"Kerro," Hali said.

He faced her, equally startled. "Hali?"

Thomas threw his head back in sudden laughter. "You see? A surprise package from Ship!"

Waela fumbled with the straps holding her to the couch. Hali rushed to assist her, released the straps and helped her off the couch. The sound of the surf was loud and they could feel its pounding through their feet.

"Hello," Waela said. She took three short steps up to Thomas, hugged him.

Hali tried to identify the play of emotions across the man's face. *Fear?*

Panille touched Hali's arm. "This is Raja Thomas, leader of the army and nemesis of Morgan Oakes."

"Army?" Hali looked from Panille to Thomas.

Thomas gently released Waela's grip around his waist, steadied her while he directed a glare at Panille. "You joke about this?"

"Never." Panille shook his head.

Hali could not understand the exchange. he started to frame a question, but Thomas spoke first.

"What else is in the freighter?"

The Bitten program responded, a crackling voice from the overhead 'coder, full of *baps* and bursts of static but the listing of the cargo manifest remained understandable.

"Weapons!" Thomas said. He ran to the open hatch, shouted something to people outside, whirled back. "We have to unload this thing before the surf breaks it up or Oakes' people destroy it. Everybody out!"

Hali felt a touch on her shoulder, Ferry standing there. "I think I'm owed an explanation." Even his demands were shaded in whines.

"Later," Thomas said. "There's a guide right outside who'll take you to our camp. She'll tell you everything you need to know."

"Demons?" Ferry asked.

"Nothing like that around here," Thomas said. "Now hurry it up while..."

"You can't dismiss him just like that!" Hali protested. "If it weren't for him, Murdoch would have . . . We'd be dead!"

Panille directed a quizzical stare at Hali, then at Ferry. "Hali, this old man works for Oakes . . . and for himself. He's an expert at the game of power politics and he knows that we're a highly negotiable commodity."

"That's all past," Ferry sputtered. The veins in his nose stood out like worms.

"Your guide's waiting," Thomas said.

"Her name's Rue," Panille said. "You might remember her better as Rachel Demarest's cubbymate."

Ferry swallowed, started to speak, swallowed again, then: "Rachel?"

Panille shook his head slowly from side to side.

A single tear formed at the corner of Ferry's right eye, slid down his veined cheek. He took a deep, trembling breath, turned and shuffled toward the hatch. All the energy and urgency he had displayed earlier were drained from him.

"He really did save us," Hali said. "I know he's a spy but . . ."

"Who are you?" Thomas asked.

"This is Med-tech Hali Ekel," Panille said.

Hali looked up at Thomas—so tall! His eyes held her. He appeared to be in some ageless ring of middle age, but when she took the hand he held out to her, it felt firm and youthful. A commanding hand, confident. She grew aware then that Waela and Kerro were touching. Kerro's arm was around Waela's shoulder, guiding her toward the hatchway.

"Med-tech," Thomas said. "You'll be a great help to us, Hali Ekel. Come this way."

Hali resisted the pressure of his arm and watched Kerro reach out, inquisitive, to touch Waela's abdomen with one finger.

Thomas saw the gesture and focused on Waela. "Something's wrong with her. She should not be that big . . ."

Thomas loves her, Hali thought. The sound of concern was plain in his voice.

"My pribox says she's only a few diurns from parturition," Hali said.

"That can't be!"

"But it is. Only a few diurns. Otherwise . . ." Hali shrugged. ". . . she appears to be healthy."

"That's impossible, I say. It takes much longer for a baby to develop into . . ."

"Lewis does it. You heard what the E-clones said." That was

Kerro returned from the hatchway, not concealing a faint amusement at Thomas' confusion.

"Yes, but..." Thomas shook his head.

"Can you climb down to the beach by yourself, Hali?" Panille asked. "The rear of the freighter is already breaking up. And I think Waela..."

"Yes, of course." She moved past him—the familiar face and familiar voice, his body much thinner than she remembered, though. It struck her then: *He's not the Kerro I knew! He's changed... so different.*

Behind her, she heard Thomas muttering: "I want to examine that woman myself."

Man also knows not his time: as the fishes that are taken in an evil net and as the birds that are caught in the snare; so are the sons of men snared in an evil time, when it falls suddenly upon them.

—**Christian** *Book of the Dead,*
Shiprecords

"BLOW THAT cutter. Give me the particulars later." Lewis switched off the com-line, and turned to face Oakes across the Command Center. As though this act conveyed some deep communication, they both turned to look up at the big screen.

The bustle of activity around them went on—some fifty people guiding the Redoubt's defenses under the eyes of the armed Naturals quietly watchful at the edges of the room. But to Legata, who stood near Oakes, it seemed that the noise level went down dramatically. She, too, stared at the screen.

It was early Rega morning out there, and the light showed the massed ring of hylighters, the waiting mobs of demons at the cliffs—all strangely held in check. Something new had been added this morning, however. A naked man sat on a flat rock pinnacle to the southeast, hylighter tentacles brushing against him. Sensor amplification had showed his features in close-up—the poet, Kerro Panille.

On the floor of the plain beneath Panille stood a plasteel cutter fitted with wheels, E-clones and what appeared to be Naturals grouped around it. The cutter's deadly nozzle was pointed toward the Redoubt—too far away for that model to do any damage, but unmistakably menacing.

The most menacing thing of all was the fact that no demon moved to molest any of the people waiting beside the cutter. Pandora's terrible creatures waited with the others in mysterious docility.

"We should know in a blink or two," Lewis said. He threaded his way through the room's activities to stand near Oakes and Legata. All of them stared up at the screen.

"Can't we send some people out there?" Oakes asked. "We could take that thing with a direct attack."

"Who would we send out?" Lewis asked.

"Clones. We have clones up to *here*!" He brushed the edge of his right hand across his throat. "And we don't have enough food. They could get through if we sent enough of them."

"Why would clones do that?" Legata asked.

"What?" Oakes glared at her audacity.

"Why would clones obey an order to attack? They can see the demons out there. And there'll be Runners somewhere on that plain. Why would clones take the risk?"

"To save themselves, of course. If they stay here and do nothing . . ." Oakes' voice trailed off.

"Your fate is their fate," she said. "Maybe worse. They'll ask why you aren't out there with them."

"Because . . . I'm the Ceepee! I'm worth more than they are to our survival."

"Worth more to them than they are worth to themselves?"

"Legata, what are you . . . ?" Oakes was interrupted by a brilliant flash of light and a blast so close that the concussion popped his ears and took his breath away. Sensor images vanished from the big screen to be replaced by static flashes of light. Legata, thrown backward by the blast, steadied herself against a fixed control console. Lewis had sprawled on the floor and, as he climbed to his feet, they all heard screams and clattering feet in the passage outside the Command Center.

Oakes gestured to Legata. "Get that screen working!"

"We must've hit that cutter," Lewis said.

Legata leaped to the screen controls, keyed an emergency search for active sensors, found a high one which looked out over the Redoubt to the distant cliff with its bank of hylighters. Panille still sat on the pinnacle, the plasteel cutter and its crew remained at their cliffbase. Nothing appeared to have changed.

They could all hear the sound of pounding against the Command Center's hatch. Someone across the room opened it. Immediately, the Center filled with people, a menagerie of E-clones and Naturals, all crying and screaming: "Runners! Runners! Seal off!"

Lewis whirled to the nearest console, slapped the key for the *Seal Off* program. As hatches hissed shut, they saw on the screen the first wave of people shrieking in terror at the inner edge of the Redoubt. Legata turreted the high sensor to follow them and they all saw the smoking break in the Redoubt's perimeter, the flood of people fleeing it and being brought up short at sealed hatches. Fists beat a muffled drumming on the hatches, the sound made all the more terrible by its distance from the sensor. It gave the whole scene a marionette quality.

Lewis suddenly darted across the room, grabbed the arm of one of the newcomers and returned to Oakes with the man. Legata recognized him as a crew supervisor, a Natural named Marco.

"What the hell happened out there?" Oakes demanded.

"I don't know." The man blinked in confusion, stared up at the screen rather than at Oakes. "We took one of the new cutters, the long-range ones, and we hit within a meter of them."

"You *missed* them?" Oakes screamed it, his face red with rage.

"No! No, sir. A meter's good enough. That close will melt bedrock for ten meters all around. It's just..."

"That's all right, Marco," Lewis said. "Just describe what you saw."

"It was that man up on the rocks." Marco pointed at the screen.

"He didn't do anything," Oakes said. "We were looking at the screen the whole time and he..."

"Let Marco tell what he saw," Lewis interrupted.

"It was almost too fast for the eye to see," the supervisor said. "Our beam hit less than a meter away. I saw the ground out there begin to glow. Then the beam... bent. It bent right up toward that man on the rock. I thought I saw *him* glow, then the beam came right back at us!"

"Our cutter's gone?" Lewis asked.

"It went up so fast only a few of us escaped."

"Send out some clones," Oakes said.

An unmistakable press of bodies moved toward him as he spoke and, too late, he realized his danger. More than half the Command

Center crew was composed of clones and most of the refugees who now crowded the room were clones.

"Sure!" someone shouted from the press of people. "You stay here while we take the risk!"

Another voice, gravelly and full of gutturals, took it up from another corner of the crowd: "Yes, send out some clones. More meat for the demons. A diversion while you Naturals tiptoe home to Colony and your wine!"

Oakes glanced at the ring of faces pressing toward him. Even the Naturals among them appeared angry. This was not the time to tell them that Colony no longer existed. They would know their power then. They would know how much he needed them.

"No!" Oakes waved a hand in the air. "All survival decisions belong to the Ceepee. I am Ship's envoy and voice here!"

"Ohhh, it's *Ship* now!" someone shouted.

"We will not run home to Colony," Oakes said. "We will stand here at your side . . . to the last man, if necessary."

The guttural voice responded: "You're damn right you're not leaving!"

The room took on an odd sense of quiet into which Lewis' voice came clearly: "We will not be beaten."

Oakes picked it up: "We have almost eliminated the kelp that kept us from gardening the sea. The hylighters will go next. A few rebels will not stand in the way of the good life we can make for ourselves here."

Oakes glanced at Lewis, surprised a flitting smile there.

"Tell us what to do," Lewis said.

One of Lewis' minions in the crowd responded on cue: "Yes, tell us."

How well early conditioning pays off, Oakes thought. And he said: "First, we have to take stock of our situation."

"I've been watching the screen," Lewis said. "I don't see any Runners. Have you seen any, Legata?"

"No, not a one."

"Not one Runner has tried to enter the Redoubt," Lewis said. "They remember the chlorine."

"Have you looked at the whole perimeter?" someone demanded.

"No, but look at those people near that break in our wall." Lewis pointed. "Not a one of them's in trouble. I'm going to open the hatches."

"No!" Oakes stepped forward. "Whoever asked that question

is right. We have to be sure." He turned toward Legata. "Do you have enough sensors to scan the perimeter?"

"Not completely . . . but Jesus is right. Nothing's attacking our people out there."

"Send some volunteers out with portable sensors, then," Lewis said. "We could use a few repair crews as well. I'll go with 'em, if you like."

Oakes stared at Lewis. Could the man really be that brave? Runners remembering chlorine? Impossible. Something else was holding the demons in check. As he thought this, Oakes experienced the abrupt sensation that the entire planet was out there, waiting just for the proper moment to attack and kill him.

Taking his silence for agreement, Lewis pressed his way through the crowd, selecting people as he moved. "You . . . you . . . you . . . you . . . Come with me. Larius, you get a repair crew together, take the down-chart and get busy restoring our eyes and ears."

Lewis popped a hatch at the far side of the room, waved his *volunteers* through, and turned before joining them. "All right, Morgan, it's up to you."

What did he mean by that? Oakes watched the hatch seal behind Lewis. *I have to do something!*

"Everybody back to work," Oakes said. "Everybody but the Command Center crew outside in the passage."

They were reluctant to move.

"Nothing came in the hatch when Jesus opened it," Oakes said. "Go on. We have work to do. So do you."

"Leave the hatch open if you want," Legata said.

Oakes did not like that, but the suggestion moved them. People began leaving. Legata turned back to the control console for the big screen. Oakes moved to he side, becoming intensely aware of the musky smell which surrounded her.

"We're fighting the whole damned planet," he muttered.

He watched while portable sensors and repairs began restoring the big screen's overview of the Redoubt's operation. As service returned, it became apparent that something had destroyed some seventy degrees of perimeter sensors below the ten-meter level. Burned-out relays had put other sensors out of service. The damage was far less than he had feared. He began to breathe more easily, realizing only then how tension had tightened his chest.

Lewis returned after a time, crossed to Oakes and Legata at

the screen. "Did you want those people to stay in the passage?"

Oakes shook his head. "No." He continued to watch the screen.

"I sent them about their business," Lewis said. "Nothing seems to've changed outside. Why are they waiting?"

"War of nerves," Oakes said.

"Perhaps."

"We must devise a plan of attack," Oakes said. "The clones must be convinced that it's necessary to attack."

Lewis stared at the play of Legata's hands across the screen controls, glancing now and then up at the COA she produced. Rega was much higher in the sky now and Alki was beginning to creep above the horizon. It was brilliant out on the plain, every detail washed in light.

"How will you convince the clones?" Lewis asked.

"Get a few of them in here," Oakes said.

Lewis directed a questioning stare at Oakes, but turned and obeyed. He returned with twelve E-clones whose appearance had been held closer to the Natural standard except for the introduction of extra musculature in arms and legs. They were a type Oakes had always thought bulged in a repellant way, but he masked his dislike. Lewis stopped the group in an arc about three paces from Oakes.

Studying the faces, Oakes recognized some of the group which had fled into the Command Center earlier. There was no avoiding the distrust in their expressions. And Oakes noted that Lewis had seen fit to don a holstered lasgun and that the Naturals around the edges of the room were alert and watchful.

"I will not go back to Colony," Oakes began. "Never. We are here to . . ."

"You might run back to Ship!" It was a clone standing just to the left of Lewis.

"Ship will not respond to us," Legata said. "We are on our own."

Damn her! Oakes went pale. Didn't she know how dangerous it was to betray your dependence on others?

"We are being tested, that's all," Oakes said. He glanced at Lewis, surprised another fleeting grin on the man's face.

"Maybe we're supposed to go outside and run for it," Legata said. Her fingers danced across the screen's controls. "Maybe it's just a game like the Scream Room or running the P."

What is she doing? Oakes wondered. He shot a glance at her, but Legata continued to direct the screen's controls.

"They're doing something," she said.

Every eye turned toward the screen whose entire area she had focused on the view toward the cliffs. Panille was standing now, his right hand clutching a hylighter tentacle. More E-clones and others had massed around the cutter on the plain below him. Demons had moved out from the cliff shadows. Even the enclosing arc of hylighters appeared more agitated, moving about, changing altitude.

Legata zoomed in on a man standing beside the cutter's left wheel.

"Thomas," she said. "But the hylighters . . ."

"He's in league with 'em," Lewis said. "Has been all along!"

Legata stared out at the plain. Was that possible? She had been about to expose Oakes as a clone, but now she hesitated. What did she really know about Thomas?

As she thought this, Thomas lowered his right arm and Panille, atop the pinnacle, was picked up by one of the giant bags, carried gently down to the plain.

Thomas and his people were moving forward now, a ragged advance but spreading out on both sides of the cutter.

"There must be at least a thousand of them," Lewis muttered. "Where'd they get that many people?"

"What're the demons doing?" Legata asked.

The creatures had spread out below the cliff—Dashers, Spinnerets, Flatwings and more—even a few of the rare Grunchers. They were following the attackers but slowly and at a distance.

"If they get that cutter within range of us, we're through," Oakes said. He rounded on Lewis. "Now will you send out some attackers?"

"We have no choice," Lewis said. He glanced at the clones beside him. "You all see that, don't you?"

All of them were staring up at the screen, intently focused on the advancing cutter and the outrider demons.

"It's plain to see," Lewis said. "They cut open our perimeter and let the demons in. We're all dead then. But if we can stop them . . ."

"Everybody!" Oakes called out. "I grant full status as a Natural to every clone who volunteers. These rebels are the last real threat to our survival. When they're gone, we'll make a paradise out of this planet."

Slowly, but with growing momentum, the arc of clones moved toward the passage hatch. More joined them as they moved.

"Keep them moving, Lewis," Oakes said. "Issue weapons as they go out. We'll win by the weight of numbers alone."

Once my fancy was soothed with dreams of virtue, of fame and of enjoyment. Once I falsely hoped to meet with beings who, pardoning my outward form, would love me for the excellent qualities which I was capable of unfolding.

—**Frankenstein's Monster Speaks,**
Shiprecords

AS THOMAS gave the signal for the attack, he experienced the almost paralyzing sensation that he was not aiming a blow at the Redoubt but was striking out at Ship.

You set this up, Ship! See what You've done?

Ship gave no response.

Thomas moved forward with his army.

The air was hot on the plain below the cliffs, both suns climbing to their meridians. The light was brilliant, forcing him to squint when he looked toward the reflected glare of the suns. He smelled a flinty bitterness in the air, dust kicked up by his ragtag group.

He looked left and right at them. Had anyone ever dreamed of such a wild mixture on such a venture? The Naturals in Avata's collection were a vanishing minority—swallowed up in the press of strange shapes: bulbous heads, oddly placed eyes, ears, noses and mouths; great barrel chests and scrawny ones, thin limbs and conventional fingers, ropey tendrils, feet and stumps. They strode and rocked and stumbled along in obedience to his command. The improvised wheels they had attached to the plasteel cutter grated in sand, bumped over small rocks. Muttering, grunting, wheezing, his people moved forward. Some of the E-clones chanted "Avata! Avata! Avata!" as they shuffled along. He noted that the demons moved with him at a distance, just as Panille had said they would.

Waiting to scavenge.

What did the demons see here? Panille had said that he and the hylighters could project false images to hold the demons in check. Certain of the E-clones, too, exhibited this skill. Thomas guessed it to be a side-effect of the recombinant experiments with the kelp. It seemed a fragile defense against such potent creatures. This whole venture was based on fragility—not enough weapons, not enough people, not enough time to plan and train.

He glanced back toward the cliffs, saw the arc of trailing demons, Panille walking among them without fear. A gigantic Dasher brushed against the poet, veered away. Thomas shuddered. Panille had said he would not take active part in killing, but would protect this *army* as well as he could. The med-tech and a hand-picked crew of aides waited at the foot of the cliff. Everything now depended on whether this force could so overawe the Redoubt's defenders that Oakes would capitulate.

At the chosen moment, Thomas gave the signal for his people to spread out, dispersing wide across the plain. If Panille's powers continued to work, the defenders would see only one small tightly massed target of attackers coming straight on into range of the Redoubt's weapons. Thomas joined the crew of the cutter as they veered off to the left.

As he moved, doubts welled up in him. By his time reckoning, they had only hours until Ship carried out the threat to end humankind forever. This venture seemed hopeless. He would have to overcome the Redoubt, assemble the survivors, find the proper WorShip and prove to Ship that humankind should endure.

Not enough time.

Panille! It was Panille's fault that they had been delayed so long. To every argument for the need to attack the Redoubt, Panille had interjected a quiet remonstrance.

The nest was paradise enough, he said.

No doubt it was a paradise—a continuous growing season for Earth plants—no rot, no mold, no insect parasites . . . not even any demons to threaten the people there.

The crater nest was a blastula of Earth, a chaotic jumble of elements looking for growth and order.

A one-kilometer circle of Eden does not a habitable planet make.

And always Panille there with his senseless observations: "What you do with the dirt beneath your feet, that is a prayer."

Is that what You want, Ship! That kind of prayer?

No answer from Ship—just the rustle of sand underfoot, the movement of his army as it spread out wide across the plain and continued to advance on the Redoubt.

I'm on my own here. No help from Ship.

He remembered the Voidship *Earthling* then—the ship which had become Ship. He remembered the crew, their long training on Moonbase. Where were they now? Any of them left in hyb? He longed to see Bickel again. John Bickel would be a good one to have here now—resourceful, direct. Where was Bickel now?

Sand grated under his feet like the sands of the exercise yard at Moonbase. Sands of the Moon, not of Earth. All those years, looking up to the Earth at night—the blue and white glory of it. His desires had not been for the stars, not for some mathematical conception at Tau Ceti. He had wanted only the Earth—that one place forbidden to him in all of the universe.

Pandora is not Earth.

But the nest was a temptation—so like the Earth of his dreams.

Probably not like the real Earth at all. What do I know of the real Earth?

His kind had known only the clone sections of Moonbase, forever separated from the human originals by the vitro shields. Always the vitro shields, always only a simulated Earth—just as the clones simulated humans.

They didn't want us taking strange diseases all over the universe.

A laugh escaped him.

Look at the disease we've brought to Pandora! War. And the disease called humankind.

A shout came from off to his right, bringing him out of his reverie. He saw that a beam from the Redoubt had incinerated a large rock ahead of them on the plain. Thomas signaled for wider separation. He looked back, saw Panille with his spreading pack of demons still walking imperturbably behind the army.

A terrible resentment of Panille welled up in Thomas then. Panille was a naturally born human.

I was grown in an axlotl tank!

How odd, he thought, that it should take all of these uncount-
able eons and an ultimate crisis here for him to realize how much
he resented being a clone.

Clones from Moonbase are expressly forbidden . . .

The list of "Thou shalt nots" had stretched on for page after
page.

*It is forbidden to come into contact with Natal humans or with
Earth.*

Banished from the Garden without benefit of sin.

What is felt by one is felt by all, Avata said.

Yes, Avata, but Pandora is not Earth.

Ship had said he was original material, though, some bit of
what Earth had been. What memories of Earth tingled in the genes
sparkling at the tips of his fingers?

It was very hot out here on the plain, glaring hot. Exposed.
Could Panille's *projection* truly confuse the Redoubt's defenders?
Panille had confused the probes, that was a fact. And Thomas
recalled his own mental linkage with Bitten, the control program
for the freighter which had brought such a cornucopia of supplies.
As Panille said, the ability to communicate was also the ability
to dissemble.

What if Panille just left them out here, dropped the masking
projection? What if Panille were wounded . . . or killed? Panille
should have stayed back by the cliffs.

That's just like a clone, missing the obvious.

The old taunt rang through his ears. *Just like a clone!* All the
human efforts at instilling pride in the clones had vanished before
the taunts. Clones were supposed to be extra-human, built for
precision performance. Humans did not like that. Clones of Moonbase did not look different from humans, did not talk different . . . but
separation developed eccentricities. *Just like a clone.*

He imagined a Moonbase instructor, looking at him out of that
blasphemous screen, lecturing on the intricacies of systems monitors, reprimanding: "That's just like a clone, walking out on
paradise."

His army was almost into range of the Redoubt's smallest
weapons now, less than two hundred meters away. Thomas shook
himself out of his reverie—*hell of a way for a general to behave!*
He looked left and right. They were well fanned out. He paused
beside a tall, black rock—taller than he. The Redoubt loomed
ahead, prickly with the muzzles of its cutters. Panille could not

come any closer. Thomas turned and waved for Panille to stop, saw the poet obey. The army would have to go on alone from here. They could not risk their most valuable weapon.

The rock beside him began to glow. Thomas leaped to the right as the rock erupted in molten orange. A tiny splash of it burned his left arm. He ignored it, shouted: "Attack!"

His mob started a shambling run toward the Redoubt. As they moved, exterior hatches in the Redoubt's perimeter snapped open. Defenders swarmed onto the plain carrying 'burners and lasguns. They raced forward in a confused mass toward Panille's projected images. As they came within a few meters, their confusion increased. Targets dissolved before them. They stumbled left and right, shooting. Random shots dropped some of the army. The Redoubt's cutters began to sparkle with incandescent beams which probed the plain.

"Fire!" Thomas screamed. "Fire!"

Some of his people obeyed. But the Redoubt's defenders presented the same genetic mix as the army's. Attackers and defenders, indistinguishable without uniforms, stumbled into each other. Searing beams wavered in wild arcs, cutting friend and foe alike. Bloody bodies lay on the plain—some dismembered, some screaming. Thomas stared in horror at the arterial geyser from a headless torso directly to his left. Red spray splashed all around as the body tumbled forward.

What have I done? What have I done?

None of these people, attackers or defenders, knew how to fight a proper war. They were hysterical instruments of destruction—nothing more. Fewer than a fourth of the defenders had reached his army. What did it matter? The plain around the Redoubt was a bloody shambles.

He signaled to the cutter crew on his left. "Cut through their wall!" But his crew had been decimated, the cutter's improvised wheels disabled. It stood canted over to its right, the deadly muzzle pointed at the ground. The survivors crouched behind the cutter.

Thomas whirled and looked back at Panille. The poet stood immobile amidst the waiting pack of demons. Two Dashers crouched on his right like obedient dogs. The horrible line of Pandora's killer species reached left and right in a wide arc around the scene of carnage.

Rage coursed through Thomas. *You haven't beaten me, Ship!* He stumbled, panting across to the cutter, grasped its heavy barrel and heaved it around. Four strong clones had been needed to lift the thing back at the cliff. In his rage, he moved it by himself, tipping it against a rock until it was trained on a blank stretch of Redoubt wall. The surviving crew members cowered away from him as he leaped to the controls and activated the beam. A blinding blue line leaped out to the Redoubt, melting the wall. Upper structure sloughed away, slipping down into the molten pool.

Reason returned to Thomas. He stepped back, again, again. He was twenty paces from the humming cutter when the defense weapons found it. The cutter exploded as beam confronted beam. Thomas did not even feel the sharp chunk of metal which penetrated his chest.

Why shouldst Thou cause a man to put himself to
shame by begging aid, when it is in Thy power, O
Lord, to vouchsafe him his necessities in an honorable
fashion?

> —A Kahan, Atereth ha-Zaddikim,
> *Shiprecords*

HALI KEPT a careful watch on Waela as the E-clone assistants
prepared an obstetrics area within their temporary medical shelter.
The cliff shadow covered them, and the confusion of the army
departing filled the air with discordant noise: shouts, grunts, the
crunching of the cutter's wheels on the sand. She felt a sense of
relief as the demons moved off with Panille. He frightened her
now. Her soft-voiced poet friend had become the keeper of a
terrifying inner fire. He was keeper of the kind of terrible power
she had seen at Golgotha.

Heavy as she was with the unborn child, Waela moved with
a supple quickness. She was in her natural habitat: Pandora. This
place had changed Waela, too. Was that why Panille had mated
with her? Hali put down an anguished stab of jealousy.

I am a med-tech. I am a Natali! An unborn child needs me.
I want joy!

She tried not to think about what might happen out there on
the plain. Thomas had warned her what to expect. Where had he
learned about battle? She had been unable to suppress feelings of
outrage.

"Those people who will die, how are they different from us?"

She had hurled the question at him as they moved down from the clifftop, steadied by hylighter tendrils, the red streaks of dayside fingering a gray horizon on their right. It had been a nightmare setting: the babble of the army, the muted flutings of hylighters. The great orange bags had floated some people down to the plain, carried equipment, guarded the descent of those who stayed afoot.

Hundreds of people, tons of equipment.

Thomas had not answered her question until she repeated it.

"We have to take over the Redoubt. Ship will destroy us if we don't."

"That makes us no better than them."

"But we will survive."

"Survive as what? Does Ship say anything about that?"

"Ship says, 'When you shall hear of wars and the rumors of wars, be you not troubled: for such things must needs be; but the end shall not be yet.'"

"That's not Ship! That's the Christian *Book of the Dead*!"

"But Ship quotes it."

Thomas had looked at her then and she had seen the pain within his eyes. Christian *Book of the Dead*.

Ship had shown parts of it to her on request, displaying the words within the tiny cubby where Panille once had studied. If Thomas really were a Ceepee, he would know those words. She wondered if Oakes knew them. How strange that no one shipside had responded to her careful questions and probes about the events on the Hill of Skulls.

Thomas had frightened her then as they paused to regain their breath on a little rock platform deep in a fissure.

"Why did Ship show you the crucifixion? Have you ever asked yourself that, Hali Ekel?"

"How do you . . . how do you know about . . . ?"

"Ship tells me things."

"Did Ship tell you why I . . . ?"

"No!"

Thomas set off down the steep trail. She called after him: "Do you know why Ship showed me that?"

He stopped at a gap in the fissure, looked out at the morning light growing on the plain, the glistening brilliance of reflections off the Redoubt's plaz in the distance. She caught up with him.

"Do you know?"

Thomas rounded on her, the pain terrible in his eyes. "If I knew that, I'd know how to WorShip. Did Ship give you no clues?"

"Only that we must learn about holy violence."

He glared at her. "Tell me what you saw there at the crucifixion!"

"I saw a man tortured and killed. It was brutal and awful, but Ship would not let me interfere."

"Holy violence," Thomas muttered.

"The man they killed, he spoke to me. He . . . I thought he recognized me. He knew I had come far to see him there. He said I was not hidden from him. He said I should let them know it was done."

"He said what?"

"He said if anyone understood God's will, then I must understand it . . . but I don't!" She shook her head, tears close. "I'm just a med-tech, a Natali, and I don't know why Ship showed me that!"

Thomas spoke in a whisper: "That's all the man said?"

"No . . . he told the people in the crowd not to weep for him but for their children. And he said something about a green tree."

"If they do these things in a green tree, what will they do in a dry?" Thomas intoned.

"That's it! That's what he said! What did he mean?"

"He meant . . . he meant that the powerful grow more deadly in times of adversity—and what they do in the roots can be felt to the ends of the branches—forever."

"Then why have you created this army? Why are you going out there to . . .?"

"Because I must."

Thomas resumed his way down the trail, refusing to respond to her. Others who had chosen to climb down caught up, pressed close. She had no other opportunity to speak to him. They were at the foot of the cliffs soon and she had her own duties while Thomas set off about his war.

Ferry was one of the people Thomas assigned to medical work. She knew what Thomas and Kerro thought about the old man and this prompted her now to kindness toward him. While she worked with Ferry in the rude fabric shelter below the cliffs, she heard Thomas speaking to his army.

"Blessed by Ship, my strength, which teaches my hands to war and my fingers to fight."

Was that any way for a Ceepee to talk? She asked this of Ferry while they worked.

"That's the way Oakes talks." The old man seemed resigned to his fate but eager to help her.

The army was busy at its preparations then, Panille standing nearby like a cold observer. She did not like the nearness of the demons, but he said they would not harm the people here. He said the hylighters had filled the demons' senses with a false world which kept them in check.

Ferry shambled past her then, glancing oddly at her nose ring.

She wondered how Ferry felt about the way Thomas talked. Thomas spoke about the old man in front of him as though Ferry were not there.

"This old fool doesn't have any real power," Thomas had said. "Oakes thinks he has a corner on the real power and the symbolic power, right here on Black Dragon. He doesn't share power. He's set himself up here for easy pickings compared to what we'd have encountered at Colony."

"I told him he was moving too soon," Ferry had said.

Thomas had ignored him, addressed Panille. "Ferry's a liar, but we can use him. He must know something valuable about Oakes' plans."

"But I don't know anything." The old man's voice quavered.

One of the Naturals Thomas had named as an aide had come up then with organizational problems. Thomas had stared at the hashmarks over the man's right eye. They had gone away together, Thomas muttering: "Helluva way to slap together an army, out of somebody else's rejects."

She had seen some sense in his orders, though, the E-clones grouped according to design: runners, carriers, lifters . . . He had taken a training inventory—equipment operator, light-physics technician, welder, unskilled labor . . .

She thought about this as she prepared the medical facilities under the cliff. What difference did it make to her how Thomas organized his force? When they arrived here, they would merely be wounded.

Waela, helping with the preparations for the delivery, stopped in front of Hali. "Why do you look so worried? Is it something about my baby?"

"No, nothing like that."

And Waela heard her old inner voice, Honesty, marking time: *The baby will be born soon. Soon.*

Waela stared at Hali.

"What has you so worried?"

Hali looked at Waela's mounded abdomen. "If the hylighters hadn't brought us that supply of *burst* from Colony . . ."

"Colony didn't need it anymore. They're all dead."

"That's not what I . . ."

"You're afraid my baby would've been robbing you of your years, your life and . . ."

"I don't think your baby would take from me."

"Then what is it?"

"Waela, what are we doing here?"

"Trying to survive."

"You sound like Thomas."

"Thomas makes a great deal of sense sometimes."

Three E-clones intruded, staggering into the shelter, two of them helping a third who had lost an arm. All of them had been burned. One held the severed arm against the stump, bloody sand all around the wound.

"Who's the med-tech here?" one of them demanded. He was a dwarf with long, flexible fingers.

Ferry started to step forward, but Hali motioned him back. "Stay with Waela. Let me know when she needs me."

"I'm a doctor, you know." There was hurt in the old voice.

"I know. Stay with Waela."

Hali led the injured trio to the emergency alcove partly sheltered by the black rocks of the cliff. She worked quickly, closing up the severed stump with celltape after powdering it with septalc.

"Can't you save his arm?" the dwarf demanded.

"No. What's happening out there?"

The dwarf spat on the floor. "Hell and damn folly."

She finished with his companions, looked at the dwarf. His comment surprised her and he saw it. "Oh, we can think well enough," he said.

"Come here and let me tend to you," she said. His right arm was badly burned. She spoke to distract him from his pain. "How did you come to be with the hylighters?"

"Lewis pushed us out. Like garbage. You know what that means. There were Runners. Most of us didn't get away. I hope the Runners get in there." He gestured with his good arm at the Redoubt across the plain. "Eat every one of those shiptit bastards!"

The dwarf slid off the treatment table as she finished. He headed toward the exit.

"Where are you going?"

"Back to help where I can." He stood with the fabric flap held back and she stared out the opening at the Redoubt. Blue flashes filled the air there. She could hear distant shouts and screams.

"You're in no condition to . . ."

"I'm well enough to carry the wounded."

"There are more?"

"Lots of 'em." He lurched out the opening, the fabric falling closed behind him.

Hali closed her eyes. In her mind she could see a mill of people. It changed to a crowd and the crowd became a mob. Foul-breath and the salty stink of blood were on the wind. The tiny lips of cuts and the great smears of burn wounds filled her imagination. A pair of broken knees blurred through her memory—the men on the crosses.

"That's not the way," she muttered. She took up her pribox and an emergency medical kit, stepped to the opening, flung it back. The dwarf already was a small figure in the distance. She strode after him.

"Where are you going?" It was Ferry's voice calling after her. She did not turn. "They need me out there."

"But what about Waela?"

"You're a doctor." She shouted it without taking her gaze off the smoke billowing in the distance.

When humans act as spokesmen for the gods, mortality becomes more important than morality. Martyrdom corrects this discrepancy but only for a brief interval. The sorry thing about martyrs is that they are not around to explain what it all meant. Nor do they stay to see the terrible consequences of martyrdom.

> *—You Are Spokesmen for Martyrs,*
> *Raja Thomas,*
> *Shiprecords*

LEGATA SWITCHED the big screen from sensor to sensor, trying to make sense of what the instruments reported. Images blurred, re-formed in different perspective. Cutter beams slashed across the plain, she could see bodies, odd movements. Alarm buzzers signaled damage to a section of the Redoubt's perimeter. She heard Lewis dispatch repair and defense teams. Defense cutters beamed into action, directed by key people in the Center. She kept her attention on the mystery in the screens. In the split-screen images an occasional blur slipped past—as though some outside force were confusing the instruments.

She wiped a sleeve across her forehead. The two suns had climbed high while the confused battle went on, and the Redoubt's life-support had been reduced to minimum, shunting energy to weapons. It was hot in the Command Center and the nervous movements of Oakes at her elbow irritated her. In contrast, Lewis appeared unaccountably calm, even secretly amused.

It was carnage on the plain, no doubt of that. The clones in the Comamnd Center affected extreme diligence at their duties, obviously fearful that they might be sent outside into the battle.

Legata hit *replay*. Something blurred across the big screen.

"What was that?" Oakes demanded.

Legata hit *fix*, but the sensors failed to resolve an image. Once more, she hit *replay* and zoomed in close to the blur. Nothing sensible. She touched *replay* again and slowed the projection, asking the Redoubt's computer system for image enhancement. A slow shape writhed across the screen, vaguely humanoid. It moved between two rocks, struggled with some heavy object, then moved away.

A harsh blue beam snaked from somewhere within the blurred area, alarm signals were indicated by flashing blinkers at the corners of the screen. She ignored them—that was past, and Lewis had met the emergency. Something more important was indicated on the screen: a slow blossom of red-orange which had not revealed itself there before.

"What are you doing?" Oakes demanded. "What caused that?"

"I think they're influencing our sensor system," she said. And she heard the disbelief in her own voice.

Oakes stared at the screen for several blinks, then: "The ship! The damned ship's interfering."

Sweat droplets glistened on his upper lip and jowls. She could smell him beginning to crack.

"Why would the ship do that?" Lewis asked.

"Because of Thomas. You saw him out there." Oakes' voice was breaking.

Legata switched sensors, keyed for the broad view of the cliff-side staging area where the attack had originated. The demons were gone, not visible anywhere. The poet no longer sat his perch atop the pinnacle. The arc of watching hylighters had diminished to a thin rim atop the cliffs. The whole scene stood out in the glare of double sunlight.

"Where are the hylighters?" she asked. "I didn't see them go."

"None in close," Lewis said. "Maybe they've gone off some-where to . . ." He broke off at a commotion near the open passage hatch.

Legata turned to see a dark-haired Natural, a crew supervisor, slip into the Command Center. Sweaty and nervous, he hurried across to Lewis. There was celltape covering a gory burn on the man's bare left shoulder and his eyes showed the glazing of a pain-killer.

So there are Naturals outside, too, she thought.

"We're getting lots of wounded clones, Jesus," the man said. His voice was hoarse, tense. "What do we do with 'em?"

Lewis looked at Oakes, fielding the question.

"Set up an infirmary," Oakes said. "Clones' quarters. Let 'em treat their own."

"Not many of them understand medical care," Lewis said. "Some are pretty young, remember."

"I know," Oakes said.

Lewis nodded. "I see." He glanced at the crew supervisor. "You heard it. Get busy."

The man glared at Oakes, then at Lewis, but obeyed.

"The ship's interfering with us," Oakes said. "We can't spare medical people or any others right now. We have to devise a plan for..."

"What is going on out there?" Legata asked.

Oakes turned, saw that once more she was running through the sensors, showing several at once. He glanced up at the screen and, at first, did not see what had attracted her attention. Then he saw it—a rectangle high up on the right showed a silvery something creeping over the Redoubt's walls. It moved like a slow-motion wave, blanking out sensors, creeping up and up. Legata compensated for the obscured sensors, moving back and back through new sensors. The wave was composed of countless glittering threads bright in the glare of the double suns.

"Spinnerets," Lewis hissed.

The entire room became so quiet that the air was brittle with listening.

Legata continued, busy at the console.

Lewis turned to the Naturals guarding the Command Center. "Harcourt, you and Javo take a 'burner and see what you can do to cut through that Spinneret mesh."

The men did not respond. Legata smiled to herself at the continued quiet in the room. She could feel the tensions building to the precise moment she desired. It had been right to wait.

The men did not respond.

Legata smiled to herself at the continued quiet in the room. She could feel the tensions building to the precise moment she desired. It had been right to wait.

There was a heavy stirring in the room. She glanced back, saw more clones pressing into the center from the passage. Some of them were the more outré E-types. Most appeared to be wounded. They obviously were looking for someone. A guttural voice called out from amidst the newcomers: "We need medics!"

Lewis faced the two Naturals he had ordered to meet the Spinneret attack. "You refuse to obey my orders?"

Harcourt, his face red, repeated his protest: "Send some clones. That's what they're for."

From somewhere in the center of the room, a thin voice shouted: "We're not going out there!"

"Why should they go?" Legata asked.

"You stay out of this, Legata!" Oakes screamed.

"Just tell them why clones should go," she said.

"You *know* why!"

"No, I don't."

"Because the first out on any dangerous mission are clones. Harcourt's right. Clones first. That's the way it's always been, and that's the way it'll be."

So he's pitching for the loyalty of the Naturals.

Legata looked at Lewis, met his gaze head on. Was that amusement in his eyes? No matter. She depressed a key on the console controlling the big screen, watched the people in the room. They could not miss what was happening on the screen. She had set the program to fill it.

Yes... the room was becoming a tableau, all attention shifting to the screen, locking on it.

Puzzled, Oakes turned to look at the screen, saw his own likeness there. Below the image, a biographical printout was rolling. He stared at the heading: "Morgan *Lon* Oakes. Ref. Original File, Morgan Hempstead, cell donor..."

Oakes found it difficult to breathe. It was a trick! He glanced at Legata and the cold stare he met there iced his backbone.

"Morgan..." How sweet her voice sounded. "...I found your records, Morgan. See Ship's imprimatur on the printout? Ship vouches for the truth of this record."

A tic twitched the corner of Oakes' left eyelid. He tried to swallow.

This is not happening! Muttering drifted through the room. "Oakes a clone? Ship's eyes!"

Legata stepped away from the console, moved to within a meter of Oakes. "Your name... that's the name of the woman who bore you—for a fee."

Oakes found his voice: "This is a lie! My parents . . . our sun went nova . . . I . . ."

"Ship says not so." She waved at the screen. "See?"

The data continued to roll: Date of cell implantation, address of pseudo-parents, names . . .

Lewis came up to stand at Oakes' shoulder. "Why, Legata?" There was no denying the amusement in his voice.

She refused to take her attention from the stricken look on Oakes' face. *Why do I want to comfort him?*

"The Scream Room was a mistake," she whispered.

Someone off toward the edge of the room shouted: "Clones first! Send the clone out!" It began as a chant, grew to a pounding rage: "Send the clone out!"

Oakes screamed: "No!"

But hands grabbed him and Legata was powerless to prevent it in the crush of people without using her great strength to kill. She found herself unable to do this. Oakes' voice screaming: "No! Please, no!" grew fainter across the room, out into the passage, was lost in the shouting of the mob.

Lewis moved to the console, shut off the data, keyed a high sensor still free of the Spinneret webs. It showed the sudden gush of a 'burner opening a gap through the web where the wall had been breached by a cutter beam from outside. Presently, Oakes stumbled into view outside, running alone across Pandora's deadly plain.

This fetus cannot be brought to term. It cannot be a fruit of the human tree. No human could accelerate its own fetal development. No human could tap the exterior world for its needed energy. No human could communicate before departing the womb. We must abort it or kill both mother and child.

—Sy Murdoch,
*The Lewis Exchange,
Shiprecords*

WAELA SAT on the edge of the cot in the obstetrics alcove they had improvised. She could hear Ferry working with the wounded out in the emergency area. He had not even noticed her leave his side. Supply crates screened her area and she sat in the fabric-diffused shadows, taking shallow breaths to slow the contractions.

The prediction of Hali's pribox and her own inner voice had been correct. The baby was going to be born on its own schedule and despite anything else that might be happening.

Waela leaned back on the cot.

I'm not afraid. Why am I not afraid?

She felt that a voice spoke to her from her womb—*It will be as it will be.*

The quiet was broken by a babble of voices and another rush of footsteps into the medical shelter. How many batches of the wounded did that make? She had lost count.

A particularly hard contraction forced a gasp from her.

It's time. It's really time.

She felt that she had been put on a long slide, unable to get off, unable to change a single thing that would happen. This was inevitable, growing from that moment in the sub's gondola.

How could I have stopped that? There was no way.

"Where's that TaoLini woman? We need her help out here."

It was Ferry's familiar wheeze. Waela thrust herself upright, staggered to her feet and made her way heavily back to the emergency area of the shelter. She paused in the entrance as another contraction gripped her.

"I'm here. What do you want?"

Ferry glanced up from applying celltape to a wounded E-clone.

"Somebody has to go outside and decide which people are most in need of emergency treatment. I don't have time."

She stumbled toward the exit.

"Wait." The bleary old eyes focused on her. "What's wrong with you?"

"It's . . . I'm . . ." She clutched the edge of the treatment table, looked down at a wounded E-clone.

"You'd better go back and lie down," Ferry said.

"But you need . . ."

"I'll decide what has to be done!"

"But you said . . ."

"I changed my mind." He finished with the E-clone on the table, looked down at the bulging eyes which protruded from the corners of the clone's temples. "You. You're well enough to go outside and see that I get the worst cases first."

She shook her head. "He doesn't know anything about . . ."

"He knows when somebody's dying. Don't you?" Ferry helped the clone off the table, and Waela saw the burn splash across the man's right shoulder.

"He's wounded," Waela protested. "He can't . . ."

"We're all wounded," Ferry said. She heard hysteria in his voice. "Everybody's wounded. You go back now and lie down. Let the wounded take care of the wounded."

"What will you . . .?"

"I'll be back when I've finished with this lot. Then . . ." He leered at her, old yellow teeth. "Maybe a baby. You see? I'm a poet, too. Maybe you'll like me now."

Waela felt the old snake of fear wriggle up her spine.

Another burn victim staggered into the emergency area, a spidery young female with elongated neck and head, gigantic eyes. Ferry helped her onto the emergency table, signaled a clone from secondary treatment to come in and help. A stump-legged figure clumped in, held the wounded woman's shoulders.

Waela turned away, unable to look at the pain in the woman's eyes. How silent she was!

"I'll be in soon," Ferry called as Waela left.

She stopped at the fabric closure to the rear of the shelter. "I can tend to myself. Hali taught me to . . ."

Ferry laughed. "Hali, sweet bloom of youth, taught you nothing! You're not a young woman, TaoLini, and this *is* your first baby. Like it or not, you'll need me. You'll see."

Another contraction seized her as she stumbled into her alcove. She doubled over until it passed, then made her way through the gloom to the cot, threw herself on it. Another long, hard cramp rippled the length of her abdomen, followed immediately by an even harder one. She inhaled a deep breath, then a third constriction began. Suddenly, the cot was drenched with amniotic fluid.

Oh, Ship! The baby's coming now. She's coming . . .

Waela clenched her eyes tightly closed, her entire body taken up in the elemental force moving within her. She had no memory of calling out, but when she opened her eyes, Ferry was there with the long-fingered dwarf she had seen in the outer area of the medical shelter.

The dwarf bent over her face. "I'm Milo Kurz." His eyes were overlarge and protruding. "What do you want me to do?"

Ferry stood behind the dwarf, wringing his hands. Perspiration stood out on his forehead and all the hysterical bravado she had seen in the emergency area was gone.

"The baby's not coming now," he said.

"It's coming," she gasped.

"But the med-tech's not back. The Natali . . ."

"You said you could help me."

"But I've never . . ."

Another contraction rippled through her. "Don't just stand there! Help me! Damn you, help me!"

Kurz stroked her forehead.

Twice, Ferry reached toward her, and twice pulled back.

"Please!" Waela screamed it between gasps. "The baby must be turned! Please turn her!"

"I can't!" Ferry backed away from the cot.

Waela glared up at the dwarf. "Kurz . . . please. The baby has to be turned. Could you . . . ?" Another gasping contraction silenced her.

When it passed, she heard the dwarf's voice, low and calm. "Tell me what to do, sister."

"Try to slip your hands around the baby and turn her. She has one arm up and keeping her head from . . . ohhhhhh!"

Waela tasted blood where she had bitten her own lip, but the pain cleared her head. She opened her eyes, saw the dwarf kneeling between her legs, felt his hands—gentle, sure.

"Ahhhhhhhhhhhh," he said.

"What . . . what . . . ?" It was Ferry, standing at the exit from the alcove, ready to flee.

"The baby tells me what to do," Kurz said. His eyes closed, his breathing slowed. "This infant has a name," he said. "She is called *Vata*."

Out, out.

Waela heard the voice in her head. She saw darkness, smelled blood, felt her nose stuffed with . . . with . . .

"Am *I* being born here?" Kurz asked. He leaned back in a rapturous movement, held up a glistening infant wriggling in his hands.

"How did you do that?" Ferry demanded.

Waela threw her arms wide, felt the baby delivered to her breast. She felt the dwarf touching her, touching the infant—*Vata, Vata, Vata* . . . Visions of her own life mingled with scenes which she knew had occurred to Kurz. *What a sweet and gentle man!* She saw the battle at the Redoubt, felt Kurz being wounded. Other scenes unreeled before her closed eyes like a speeded holo. She felt Panille's presence. She heard Panille's voice in her head! Terrifying. She could not shut it out.

The touch of the infant teaches birth, and our hands are witness to the lesson. That was Panille, but he was not here in the medical shelter.

She sensed the people they had left aboard Ship then—the hydroponics workers, the crew going about their business along the myriad passages . . . even the dormant ones in hyb: All were one with her mind for an instant. She felt them pause in their shared awareness. She felt the questions in their minds. Their terror became her terror.

What is happening to me? Please, what is happening?
We live! We live!

All the other people vanished from her awareness as she heard/
felt those words. Only the speaker of those words remained with
her—a tiny voice, a chant, an enormous relief. *We live!* Waela
opened her eyes, looked up into the eyes of the dwarf.

"I have seen everything," he whispered. "The infant . . ."

"Yes," she whispered. "Vata . . . our Vata . . ."

"Something's happening," Ferry said. "What is it?" He put his
hands to his temples. "Get out of there! Get out, I say!" He
collapsed, writhing.

Waela looked at Kurz. "Help him."

Kurz stood up. "Yes, of course. The worst of the wounded
first."

In that hour when the Egyptians died in the Red Sea the ministers wished to sing the song of praise before the Holy One, but he rebuked them saying: My handiwork is drowning in the sea; would you utter a song before me in honor of that?

—*The Sanhedrin, Shiprecords*

OAKES FELT his heart pumping too fast. Perspiration drenched his green singlesuit. His feet hurt. Still, he staggered away from the Redoubt.

Legata, how could you?

When he could move no farther, he sank to the sand, venturing his first look back. They were not pursuing.

They might've killed me!

Black char fringed the distant hole in the web where the mob had burned a passage to eject him. He stared at the hole. His chest pained him with each breath. Slowly he grew conscious of sounds other than his own gasping. The ground under his hand was trembling with some distant thunder. *Waves!*

Oakes looked toward the sea. The tide was higher than he had ever seen it. A white line marked the entire sea horizon. Gigantic waves crashed against the headland where they had built the shuttle facility. Even as he watched, a great wedge of headland slid into the waves, opening a jagged gap in the shuttle hangar. He staggered to his feet, stared. Black objects moved in the white foam of the crashing sea. *Rocks!* There were rocks larger than a man in that surf. Even as he watched, the garden—his precious garden—sloughed away.

Mewling cries like near-forgotten seabirds insinuated themselves across the spume. He looked up and turned around once, completely. *Hylighters?* Gone. Not one orange bag danced in the sky or hovered above the cliffs.

The cries continued.

Oakes looked toward the cliffs where Thomas had begun the attack. *Bodies.* The battleground lay there with pieces of people twitching in the harsh glare of the suns. Figures moved among the wounded, lifting some on litters and carrying them toward the cliffs.

Once more, Oakes stared back at the Redoubt. Certain death lay there. He turned toward the battleground and for the first time, saw the demons. A shudder convulsed him. The demons were a silent mob sitting in a wide arc beyond the battleground. A single human in a white garment stood in their midst. Oakes recognized the poet, Kerro Panille.

Those cries! It was the wounded and the dying.

Oakes staggered toward Panille. What did it matter? *Send your demons against me, poet!*

Here was the fringe of the battleground . . . mutilated bodies. Oakes stepped on a dismembered hand. It cupped his boot in reflex, and he leaped away from it. He wanted to run back to the Redoubt, back to Legata. His body refused. He could only shuffle on toward Panille, who stood tall amidst the demons.

Why do they just sit there?

Oakes stopped only a few meters from Panille.

"You." Oakes was surprised by the flat sound of his own voice.

"Yes."

The poet's voice came clearly through the pellet in Oakes' neck and there was no movement of Panille's mouth. "You're finished, Oakes."

"You! You're the one who wrecked things for me! You're the reason Lewis and I couldn't . . ."

"Nothing is wrecked, Oakes. Life here has just begun."

Panille's lips did not move, yet that voice rang through the neck pellet!

"You're not speaking . . . but I can hear you."

"That is Avata's gift to us."

"Avata?"

"The hylighters and the kelp—they are one: Avata."

"So this planet's really beaten us."

"Not the planet, nor Legata."

"The ship then. It's hounded me down at last."

"Not Ship."

"Lewis! He did this. He and Legata!"

Oakes felt his tears begin. *Lewis and Legata.* He was unable to meet Panille's steady gaze. *Lewis and Legata.* A Flatwing moved away from the poet, crawled onto the toe of Oakes' boot, rested its bristling head there. Oakes stared down at it in horror, unable to command his own muscles. Frustration forced words from him.

"Tell me who did this!"

"You know who did it."

An anguished cry was wrenched from Oakes' throat: "Noooooooooooo!"

"You did it, Oakes. You and Thomas."

"I didn't!"

Panille merely stared at him.

"Tell your demons to kill me then!" Oakes hurled the words at Panille.

"They are not my demons."

"Why don't they attack?"

"Because I show them a world which some would call illusion. No creature attacks what it sees, only what it thinks it sees."

Oakes stared at Panille in horror. *Illusion. This poet could fill my mind with illusion?*

"The ship taught you how to do that!"

"Avata taught me."

A feeling of hysteria crept into Oakes. "And your Avata's done for . . . all gone!"

"Not before teaching us the universe of alternate realities. And Avata lives in us yet."

Oakes stared down at the deadly Flatwing on his boot. "What does it see?" He pointed a shaking finger at the creature.

"Something of its own life."

A crash shook the ground all around them and the Flatwing crept off his boot to squat quietly on the sand. Oakes looked toward the source of the sound, saw that another coveside section of the Redoubt had slipped away into the surf. The white line of the horizon had moved right up to the land—thunderous waves. The cove amplified the waves, condensing them and sending them high against the shore. Oakes stared in dumb horror as another section of the Redoubt ripped away and fell from view.

"I don't care what you say," Oakes muttered. "The planet's beaten us."

"If that's what you want."

"What I want!" Oakes rounded on him in rage, broke off at the approach of two E-clones carrying a wounded man on a litter. Hali Ekel, her nose ring glittering in the brilliant light, walked alongside. Her pribox was hooked to the patient. Oakes looked down at the litter and recognized the man there: Raja Thomas. The litter carriers stared questioningly at Oakes as they lowered Thomas to the sand.

"How bad?" Oakes directed the question at Hali.

Panille answered: "He is dying. A chest wound and a flash burn."

A chuckle forced its way from Oakes. He gulped it back. "So he won't survive me! At last—no Ceepee for the damned ship!"

Hali knelt beside Thomas and looked up at Panille. "He won't survive being carried to the shelter. He wanted me to bring him to you."

"I know."

Panille stared down at the dying man. Awareness of Thomas lay there in Panille's mind, linked to Vata, to Waela, to most of the E-clones whose genetic mix traced itself back to the Avata. All of it was there, the complete pattern. How profound of Ship to take the Raja Flattery of Ship's own origins and make a personal nemesis out of the man.

Thomas moved his lips, a whisper only, but even Oakes heard him: "I studied the question so long . . . I hid the problem."

"What's he talking about?" Oakes demanded.

"He's talking to Ship," Panille said, and this time his lips moved, his voice was the remembered voice of the poet, full of pouncing awareness.

A series of gasps wracked the dying man, then: "I played the game so long . . . so long. Panille knows. It's the rock . . . the child. Yes! I know! The child!"

Oakes snorted. "He just thinks he's talking to the ship."

"You still refuse to live up to the best of your own humanity," Panille said, looking at Oakes.

"What . . . what do you mean?"

"That's all Ship ever asked of us," Panille said. "That's all WorShip was meant to be: find our own humanity and live up to it."

"Words! Just words!" Oakes felt that he was being crowded into a corner. Everything here was illusion!

"Then throw out the words and ask yourself what you're doing here," Panille said.

"I'm just trying to survive. What else is there to do?"

"But you've never really been alive."

"I've . . . I've . . ." Oakes fell silent as Panille lifted an arm.

One by one, the demons moved off at an angle away from the cliffside shelter. The first of them were at the cliff and moving up toward the high plains before Panille spoke.

"I release them as Avata released them. Still they do what they do."

Oakes looked at the departing demons. "What will they do?"

"When they are hungry, they will eat."

It was too much for Oakes. "What do you want of *me*?"

"You're a doctor," Panille said. "There are wounded."

Oakes pointed at Thomas. "You'd have me save *him*?"

"Only Ship or all of us together can save him," Panille said.

"Ship!"

"Or all of us together—it's the same thing."

"Lies! You're lying!"

"The idea of saving has many meanings," Panille said. "There's comfort in the intelligence and potential immortality of our own kind."

Oakes backed one step away from Panille. "Lying words! This planet's going to kill us all."

"What are your senses for if not to be believed?" Panille asked. He gestured around him, met Hali's rapt gaze. "We survive. We repair this planet. Avata, who kept this place in balance, is gone. But Vata is their daughter as much as mine."

"Vata?" Oakes spat the word. "What's this new nonsense?"

"Waela's child has been born. She is called Vata. She carries the true seed of Avata placed there at her conception."

"Another monster." Oakes shook his head.

"Not at all. A beautiful child, as human in her form as her mother. Here, I will show you."

Images began to play in Oakes' awareness, howling through his mind on the carrier wave of the pellet in his neck. He wanted to tear the thing from his flesh. Oakes staggered backward, thrusting at Panille with one hand while the other hand clutched at the imbedded pellet.

"Nooooo . . . no . . . no!"

The images would not stop. Oakes fell backward to the sand and, as he fell, he heard the voice of Ship. He knew it was Ship. There was no escaping that presence as it expanded within him, not needing the pellet, not needing any device.

You see, Boss? You never needed a covenant of inflexible words. All you ever needed was self-respect, the self-worship which contains all of humankind and all the things that matter for your mutual immortality.

Pressing his hands to his head, Oakes rolled to his knees. He stared down at the sand, his eyes blurred by tears.

Slowly, Ship withdrew. It was a hot knife being pulled from Oakes' brain. It left an aching void. He lowered his hands and heard the crunch of many feet on sand. Turning, he saw a long line of people—E-clones and Naturals—approaching from the Redoubt. Legata and Lewis led them. Beyond the refugees, Oakes saw smoke drifting on a sea wind, billowing from the wreckage of the Redoubt. His precious sanctuary was being destroyed! Everything! All of Oakes' rage returned as he stumbled to his feet.

Damn You, Ship! You tricked me!

Oakes shook a fist at Legata. "You bitch, Legata!"

Lewis and Legata stopped about ten paces from Oakes. The refugees stopped behind them except for one tall E-clone female with fine features on a bulbous head. She stepped in front of Legata.

"You do not speak to her that way!" the E-clone shouted. "We have chosen her Ceepee. You do not speak to our Ceepee that way."

"That's crazy!" Oakes screamed it. "How can deformed monstrosities choose a Ceepee?"

The E-clone took a step toward Oakes, another. "Whom do you call monstrosity? What if we breed and breed here, and your kind becomes the freak?"

Oakes stared at her in horror.

"You ain't so pretty, you know," she said. "I look at me every day and every day I don't look so bad. But every day you get uglier and uglier. What if I don't think it's right for any more uglies to be born?"

Legata stepped forward and touched the woman's arm. "Enough."

As Legata spoke, a dark shadow flowed over them. They looked up to see Ship passing between Rega and the plain—far lower than Ship had ever been before. The odd protrusions and wing shapes of the agraria were clearly visible. The shadow moved with an awesome slowness, an eternity in the passage. When the shadow touched him, Lewis began to laugh. All who heard him turned toward Lewis and most of them were in time to see him vanish. He became a white blur which dissolved and left nothing where he had stood.

"Why, Ship?" Panille spoke it aloud, startled by the disappearance.

They all heard the answer, a joyous clamor in their heads.

You needed a real devil, Jesus Lewis, the other half of Me. The real devil always goes with Me. Thomas remained his own devil—a special kind of demon, a goad. And now he knows. Humans, you have won your reprieve. You know how to worship.

In that instant, they all saw Ship's intentions toward Thomas, the issue hanging on a fragile balance.

Thomas raised himself on one elbow, resisting Hali's attempts to prevent it. "No, Ship," he muttered. "Not back to hyb. I'm home."

Legata intruded. "Let him go, Ship."

If you can save him, he is yours.

Ship's challenge rang through them.

Panille held fast to the awareness of Thomas and sent the call to Vata back in the medical shelter at the cliffs: *Vata! Help us!*

The old presence of Avata crept into his mind—attenuated but with nothing omitted. Vata was all of what had been . . . and more. Panille felt his daughter as the repository of those long eons when Avata had lived and learned, but welded now to everything human. She reached beyond the plain into the crew remaining aboard Ship, even into the dormant ones of hyb, giving them the new worship and weaving them into a single organism. They came together an awareness at a time . . . even Oakes. And when they were united, they moved threadlike into the flesh of Thomas, closing his wounds, repairing cells.

It was done and they left Thomas asleep on the litter.

Panille took a trembling breath and stared around him at the people on the plain. In the healing of Thomas, all of the wounded had been restored. There were bodies of the dead, but not a single maimed among the living. All stood silent under the shadow presence which slid across the plain.

Legata.

It was Ship again.

Still shaken by the experience of the sharing, she spoke aloud in a trembling voice. "Yes, Ship?"

You have taken My best friend, Legata. Oakes is Mine now, a fair exchange. Where I go, I will need him more than you.

She looked up at the Rega-haloed outline. "You're leaving?"

I travel the Ox gate, Legata. The Ox gate—My childhood and My eternity.

She thought about the Ox gate, the scrambled repository in which she had found the truth about Oakes' origins, the near-mystical computer where hidden things emerged. As she thought this, she felt her own consciousness become one with Ship's records. And because they all were linked through Vata, all on the plain shared this.

Ship's words and images rode over this flooding awareness.

Infinite imagination has its infinite horrors, too. Poets turn their nightmares to words. With gods, dreams take on substance and lives of their own. Such things cannot be scratched out. The Ox gate, my morality factor. My psyche moves both ways. If it moves in symbols, it moves through the Ox. Some of my symbols walk and breathe—as it was with Jesus Lewis. Others sing in the words of poets.

Oakes fell to his knees, pleading. "Don't take me, Ship. I don't want to go."

But I need you, Morgan Oakes. I no longer have Thomas, my personal demon, and I need you.

Ship's shadow began to pass beyond the people on the plain. As light touched Oakes, he vanished—a white blur, then an empty place on the sand.

Legata stood there, looking at where Oakes had knelt, and she could not keep the tears from coursing down her cheeks.

Hali stood up beside the litter where her patient slept. She felt emptied and angry, robbed of her role. She stared up at the passing immensity of Ship.

Is this what I was supposed to let them know? she demanded. *Show them, Ekel!*

Still angry, she played the images of the crucifixion, then:

"Ship! Is that how it was with Yaisuah? Was he just another filament from one of Your dreams?"

Does it matter, Ekel? Is the lesson diminished because the history that moves you is fiction? The incident which you just shared is too important to be debated on the level of fact or fancy. Yaisuah lived. He was an ultimate essence of goodness. How could you learn such an essence without experiencing its opposite?

The shadow was gone from them, flowing away over the cliffs, carrying off the bits of humanity remaining up there—the Natali, the hyb attendants, the hydroponics workers . . .

"Ship is leaving us," Legata said. She crossed to Panille's side.

In the midst of her words, she felt the blaze of awareness which Ship had shared with them—Shiprecords, all of the pasts carried into the smallest cell on the plain.

"We've been weaned," Panille said. "We have to go it alone now."

Hali joined them. "No more shiptits."

"But alone has lost all of its old meanings," Panille said.

"Is this what the expansion of the universe is all about?" Legata asked. "The fleeing of the gods from their own handiwork?"

"Gods ask other questions," Panille said. He looked down at Hali. "You were midwife to us all when you brought us Vata and the Hill of Skulls."

"Vata brought herself," Hali said. She put a hand in Panille's. "Some things don't need a midwife."

"Or a Ceepee," Legata said. She grinned. "But it's a role we all know now." She shook her head. "I have only one question— What will Ship do with those people up there?"

She pointed upward at the vanishing ship.

They all heard it then, Ship's presence filling the people on the plain, then fading, but never to be forgotten.

Surprise Me, Holy Void!